HELL'S DITCH

SIMON BESTWICK

SNOWBOOKS

Proudly Published by Snowbooks in 2015

Copyright © 2015 Simon Bestwick

Snowbooks Ltd.
email: info@snowbooks.com
www.snowbooks.com

British Library Cataloguing in Publication Data
A catalogue record for this book is available from the British
Library.

Hardback 9781909679672
Paperback 9781909679696
Ebook 9781909679689

Printed and bound by Nørhaven, Denmark

For Pauline Marie Gardner
1945 – 2014
Who read this on the sly.

PROLOGUE

The dream never changes: a moonless, starless night without end. The road she walks is black, bordered with round, white pebbles or nubs of polished bone; she can't tell which, but they're the only white in the darkness, marking her way through the night.

She's tired. Ragged. A long black coat flaps around her; there's a gun in her hand.

That's all she has; a gun and a long coat.

Then she sees another darkness, black against the black. Up ahead. A city. *The* City. Great broken towers; tenements and ruins swept by bitter rain, lit by flickers of cold light somewhere in their depths.

She walks and walks, but the City never gets any closer. She knows that death awaits her there, but still she carries on.

Because she realises she has more than a gun and a long coat, after all: she has fury, she has vengeance, she has vision.

And, of course, she's already dead.

And with that knowledge her back grows straight: all fear leaves her, and she walks on towards the City gladly; prepared, gun in hand. Relieved. Released.

And something dark is sweeping in towards her, down the black road.

She raises her gun and –

She grunts awake, rolls out of her blankets across a bare concrete floor.

"Helen."

She spins, grabs for her gun, aims –

A man sits in the corner, a little girl on his knee. Their skin is dry and flaky, cracked like droughted earth; their eyes glisten blackish-red like clotting blood.

At first Frank doesn't speak. Not till she's lowered the gun. Which she does, because of course you can't kill the dead.

"Hello, Helen," he says. "Found you at last."

She doesn't answer.

"Cat got your tongue, Helen? Nothing to say, to Belinda or me?" He tickles the child and she giggles – a high, thin, terrible sound. "Or have you forgotten how to speak? Could be that. Do you know how long it's been?"

He wants an answer. She can't give one, not in words – isn't even sure she can remember how to any more. So she shakes her head.

"Four years, Helen," Frank says. "Four years you've been running. Haven't stopped. Lived like an animal, because that's what you wanted. No thought. Just run; find food, water, shelter. Shit, piss, then run again. Anything, so as not to think or remember. Anything, so as not to see us."

"Mummy," says Belinda, holding out a withered hand. Helen almost reaches out to her but then sees the smile on the girl's face. It's thin, unloving, and hungry; she snatches back her hand.

She can't find words. Can't look at them, can't look away. She realises she's crying; all the tears she ran from, falling on her like a great, drowning flood.

"Crying won't help," says Frank. "You lived; we died. You carry us, wherever you go."

Helen tries to form words. *What...? How...?* Her voice is like rusty machinery, grinding back into life. The tears don't oil the wheels; brine only makes iron rust.

"We'll always find you. Try not to see us, but in the end you will. And now you're ours, Helen." Frank smiles. His teeth are long and thin and sharp, like white needles. "And we're hungry."

At last, her voice returns. "My pack – there's food in my pack."

"Piss on your pack," Frank says cheerfully, reaching down to chuck Belinda's chin. "What do we say to Mummy, Chicken?"

Belinda giggles; it's a brittle, metallic echoing sound. It shows her teeth too; long white needles, the same as Frank's. "Piss on your pack."

"That's right, Chicken." Frank nods; looks up. "There's only one food we came for."

"No." Helen tries to retreat but finds the wall at her back. Belinda giggles again, and this time she doesn't stop.

"Yes." Frank advances. "You're ours now."

"No, Frank. Please."

"Please?" He stops, puts his hands on his hips. "Please? You're asking us for mercy, Helen? You *dare* ask *us* for *that?*" His teeth are clenched, a mesh of sharpened bone. "You killed us, Helen. You *killed* us."

"No." She shouts it. "No. I didn't kill you." Her voice is choked; she's crying. Belinda keeps giggling. "I did *not* kill you."

"Then who did, Helen?" Frank cups a hand to his ear. "Mm? Who was it?"

"You know."

"Tell me. Come on. Tell me, Helen. We're hungry, and we're tired of waiting. Tell me, and maybe, just maybe, we'll give you a chance."

"Winterborn."

Belinda falls silent. Frank lifts his chin, cocks his head. "Again."

"Winterborn."

Frank nods; a slow smile spreads. "Yes. Him. Winterborn. He's the only one we'd rather have than you. So – we'll offer you a deal, won't we, Chicken?" Belinda grins and nods, eyes unblinking and grin unwavering, like a decaying doll. "A bargain,

Helen," says Frank. "It's a very simple one. Give us Winterborn's soul, and we'll spare yours."

What choice does she have? None at all. "All right," she says.

"Avenge us," says Frank.

"Yes."

"Shake."

He holds out a hand like a bird's claw. She doesn't want to take it, but he doesn't lower it; won't, she knows, till she does what he wants.

She reaches out and takes his hand. It tightens around hers, gently at first, then painfully, as Frank grins, then chuckles. Belinda starts that giggling again, too. Frank's grin widens into a gaping laugh, and then he lunges at her, that mouth rushing towards her face –

She cries out, and she's alone, but for the dying echo of their laughter. She slides down the wall to the floor and huddles there, shaking.

They call it ghostlighting. Seeing the dead. Everyone does it now. Except for her. Not for a long time.

She blinks and looks around her, seeing her surroundings properly for the first time in… can it really have been four years? The room is bare concrete, dust and spiderwebs; a thin cold wind coming in through the cracks, a shattered window hung with rags.

She stands; goes to the window, looks outside.

An industrial estate, this was, nineteen years ago, before the War. Most of the roofs have fallen in. Windblown dust and rain-washed silt have clogged streets now thick with brittle scrawny grass and barbed-wire brambles. Beyond, the terraced streets that stood nearby are almost covered over and lost beneath the poisoned, but reclaiming, earth.

Cold wind keens across the desolation.

We'll always find you.

She closes her eyes, puts her forehead to the pitted concrete.

You know what you have to do.

She nods slowly to herself.

She steps away from the wall, packs her few things, checks her gun is loaded. And then, its comforting weight in her hand, she sets off, to search for the black road.

PART ONE: RESURRECTION DAY

1.

It had been a small village, clustered round two crossed streets. Stone-built houses; a pub; a chapel with an unusual design of crucifix worked into the lintel above the door; a few shops. That and a few ordinary lives. Walking in, Mordake passed a rusted but still legible sign: *Welcome to Hobsdyke.*

Liz slipped her arm through his. "Has it really been empty twenty years?"

"You always ask that." She shrugged. "The blast didn't touch it, but the wind blew the fallout here. Everyone was dead in a couple of weeks. If they were lucky."

Time and nature were Hobsdyke's only enemies now. Wooden doors and window frames gently crumbled; roots and shrubs cracked the road surface. Roofs shed their slates, and mounds of earth had built up against the walls, sprouting grass and brambles.

Liz looked up at the empty houses, away from him. "It's peaceful."

"Yes, it is." A rabbit darted from the bushes, blinked at them, bounded off.

"How's your work?"

"Coming along."

"I worry about you."

"Don't."

"Can't help it." She turned to look at him. "I think you should stop."

"I can't."

"You could. There's still time."

He shook his head. "No choice. It has to be done." He touched her cheek; her skin was smooth and soft. For a moment he was the young doctor again, a bright career ahead of him, and leant forward to kiss her. But then a steam-powered engine hissed and clanked, wheels bumped and rattled on uneven ground, and Mordake was alone, greying and unshaven, with battered, tape-mended glasses and hands that shook.

He stormed back up the High Street. Another landcruiser pulled in alongside his; a cab and a flatbed on a 4x4 chassis, the thick hump of a boiler between. Steam hissed into the cold afternoon. Two Reapers on board; one got out and ran towards him. Mordake's anger faded at the look on the man's face, and he went to meet them.

*

Reclamation And Protection Command Base Hobsdyke (Sector 12, Regional Command Zone 7, British Isles) stood on Graspen Hill, overlooking the village. A wire fence and watchtower ringed three prefab blocks – quarters for the scientists, billets for the Reapers guarding them, and the research block – arranged like a shamrock's leaves around the squat concrete bulk of the Annexe, the project's heart.

Beyond the village lay thick woodland, its pines still green amid the red and orange rust of the long, mild autumn; past that, if you lifted up your eyes, you could see all the way out to Manchester from Graspen Hill, not that Mordake wanted to. The city he'd known was a charred, broken ruin aswarm with ragged hordes who'd eat their own shit to live another day, but not so ruined that he wouldn't recognise places he'd shared with Liz. No, he didn't miss Manchester; far better to stay here and ghostlight in the gentler ruins below.

He followed the landcruiser through the gates, pulled up behind them near the Annexe. Six small, free-standing outbuildings – seclusion chambers – sourounded the drum-shaped central structure of the Adjustment Chamber, three from each side; directly in front was the Monitoring Unit, a tin-roofed shed. Put together, the Annexe and its satellites resembled the head, body and legs of a huge tick or mite. Not the pleasantest of images, but Mordake wasn't interested in aesthetics.

The Reaper Captain, Andrews, stood waiting alongside a scared-looking Reaper Mordake vaguely recognised. He glanced at the nametag on the man's black leather uniform – Kelly, that was it. "Doctor."

"Captain. What's happened?"

"Through here, sir."

Each of the seclusion chambers was accessed by a double door, much like an airlock. Both, Mordake saw, stood ajar on Chamber Three.

"Oh no. Not Subject Three."

"'Fraid so, sir."

"Bugger. Best one we had."

"I'm sorry."

Mordake peered through the open airlock. Padded concrete walls and floor – now stained red. A primitive commode in the corner, a water bowl by a pallet on the floor.

Inside, Mordake knelt by the pallet, studied the broken leather restraints, then looked across to the wall opposite, the gaping hole where the padding had been torn away, the scarred bare concrete underneath and the blood and bone and pulp congealing on it and on the floor.

Mordake didn't look up from the broken straps. "You were on duty, Kelly. Why didn't you stop her?"

"Answer him," said Andrews.

"It was too fast, sir. She was off that bed and at the wall before we knew it. Didn't realise what she was doing till …"

"All right." Mordake stood, put his hands in his pockets. Above the door, the dull impassive lens of a video camera surveyed the room. "Double the restraints on the other test subjects, right away."

"Sir."

Mordake turned to Kelly. "Anything else?" he asked. The guard's fear was like a beggar's reek; it should have evoked his pity but elicited only disgust.

Kelly bit his lip and, after a moment, spoke. "She started shouting."

"Shouting what?"

"Not sure, sir. Couldn't make it out. But she was saying it over and over."

Mordake felt his stomach tighten, his pulse increase. Couldn't be. It couldn't. He didn't dare hope. "I want to see the tape," was all he said to Andrews.

"Will do, sir. Anything else?"

He had to stay calm. Hope for nothing. Expect nothing. "Where's the body?"

"Mortuary, sir."

"Of course. Have Lyson meet me there."

*

In the research block's mortuary, under a sheet on a trestle table, Subject Three lay waiting.

"Got her file?"

"Yes, Doctor," said Lyson. He'd been with Mordake on the project from the start. Small and ratlike, hair thinning over a flaky scalp, he hardly spoke: in times like these, when you had a steady billet you learnt to keep your own counsel.

"What was she here for?"

Papers rustled. "I thought you didn't want to know about their pasts, sir."

"Not normally, no." Mordake drew the sheet back. Blood made it cling to her face and matted scalp; it pulled free with a soft, sickening rip. Mordake swallowed. Scientific detachment – had to maintain that. "Did she have any history of mental illness?"

"Be a surprise if she didn't these days, sir."

Subject Three's forehead was caved in, her face barely recognisable. He took deep breaths – in through the nose, out through the mouth – to steady himself. The room wobbled, steadied again. Scientific detachment: maintain it. He lifted her right hand; her fingertips were shredded almost to the bone, the nails were torn and split, one hanging by a shred of muscle.

"Fair point. Anything?"

"Death sentence for stealing grain from a Reaper store. Was gonna be shot, but fitted the bill for this." Lyson flicked through pages; paper rustled. "Can't see anything in particular."

"No violence? Self-harm?"

"Anything but. Docile, pliant and cooperative, it says."

"Pliant?"

Lyson shrugged. "What it says."

Mordake grimaced; he'd a good idea what *that* meant. "All right. Prep her for the post-mortem. I'll be along shortly."

"Not getting straight to work, sir?"

"I want to see that tape first," said Mordake. "Carry on, Lyson."

*

Mordake slotted the tape marked SECLUSION #3 into an ancient VCR linked up to a battered old TV set in the corner of his office. A whirr, a click and a grinding sound he flinched at, then a picture flickered into life. Static hissed from the speakers.

Mordake pulled up a chair, took a thin paper packet of Monarch cigarettes from his white coat's pocket and drew one out, careful to hold it level so nothing fell out. At least the Reapers were making cigarettes, but what tobacco was in them – fifty percent if you were lucky, mixed with god alone knew what else – was mostly dust. The room grew dimmer; the only light came from the flickering screen.

Mordake lit up, leant back in the chair. Static flickered like windblown snow, the tape grainy from years of rerecording; at last it cleared enough to show the inside of Chamber Three.

Subject Three lay on her back on the pallet, staring up; restraint straps were tight across chest, shoulders, belly, hips, thighs and lower legs. Her face was blank, eyes empty. And then she spoke.

"Mordake."

He couldn't have heard that. He rewound, boosted the volume–

"Mordake," she said again.

He went still.

"Angana sor varalakh kai torja," she said. *"Angana sor varalakh cha voran."*

Mordake's hands rose to his mouth, as if in prayer.

She began to chant the words over and over: *Angana sor varalakh kai torja. Angana sor varalakh cha voran.* Again and again. No doubt about it; no possibility of mishearing or wishful thinking on Mordake's part. She was still shouting as she bucked and heaved and wrenched against the straps, till at last one broke. She got an arm loose; after that she was free in seconds. By then she was screaming it: *Angana sor varalakh kai torja. Angana sor varalakh cha voran.* She threw herself at the wall, tore at it with her fingers, ripping padding, nails and flesh. *Angana sor varalakh kai torja, angana sor varalakh cha voran.* Smashed her head against the bare concrete again and again, till blood flowered on the wall and she sagged to her knees. And still she shouted: *Angana sor varalakh kai torja, angana sor varalakh cha voran.*

And then she stopped, swayed on her knees for a moment and toppled backwards. She hit the floor with a thud, shuddered convulsively and went limp, tangled and askew, in a posture that hurt to look at.

Mordake switched off the tape and sat there, shaking. "It's working," he whispered. "It's finally working."

*

The last sun of autumn was almost gone, a blood-red line tremoring on the sky's edge.

In his office, Mordake sat, smoked and reached for the tape recorder on his desk. The evening was quiet; he could hear the incinerator's soft, muffled roar from nearby. The last of Subject Three, the parts not now conserved in specimen jars, would be blackening and crumbling to ash and char in there, streaming up the chimney into the sky above Graspen Hill.

After a moment, he pressed PLAY and RECORD.

"Subject Three's death is unfortunate," he said. "She was by far the most responsive subject in the group, which in itself might explain the suicide. But we've still enough subjects to complete the process, and, finally, we're on the right track."

Angana sor varalakh kai torja. Angana sor varalakh cha voran.

"The post-mortem will reveal any changes in brain structure. As well as increased restraints, I've ordered a twenty-four hour suicide watch on the remaining subjects. Can't afford to lose any more of a group as promising as this."

Ash flaked and crumbled from Mordake's cigarette, scattered on the desktop. He reached out and toyed with a small cylinder of smooth, greenish stone, traced the symbols etched on them. "This time, we'll do it."

Outside, the sun sank; shadows lengthened, night fell, and the last day of November was gone.

2.

A couple of landcruisers patrolled a line of half-dead, ragged figures bent double under laden sacks in the drizzling winter rain. At the end of the line, two Reapers at a table bearing scales and a ledger. Behind them, steel storage bins: potatoes, carrots, turnips, swedes.

A woman approached, put her sack on the scales. Reaper Walters checked the weight, nodded, emptied it into the turnip bin and checked there were no rocks; Reaper Patel made notes in a ledger, gave the woman a chit. "Next!"

A man shuffled forward, his face just a pair of eyes over a thick, bristly beard. He stared at Walters, blinking.

"On the scales," Walters said.

The bearded man obeyed, shaking. Walters looked at the dial, then him. "This weight's short."

Walters drew a revolver. The bearded man screamed; it might have been a plea. Useless if it was. Walters fired; the man fell. Two potatoes rolled from his clothes; Walters picked them up, threw them in a bin. "You're paid to bring the food in from the farms," he shouted up the line. "Not eat it yourselves."

A few ragged figures unslung their bags, dropped pilfered vegetables back inside.

Two more Reapers ran up. "Get rid of that," said Walters.

They dragged the bearded man away and dumped him in a deep, open pit full of sewage, rotten food and foul water; in a few weeks they'd shovel its contents aboard a fertiliser cart. Walters replaced the spent round in his revolver, holstered it. "Next."

A fat woman waddled up. She wore a huge, splitting coat over several layers of old clothes. A yellow headscarf framed a black-grimed face; she dragged a bandage-swollen leg. She stank, too; Walters put a hand to his nose and mouth.

He weighed her sack, emptied it out. "Right," he said. "Patel, get a move on. Fucking reek on her's knocking me sick."

"And me." Patel tore off a chit. "Fuck off. Food's that way."

*

The woman shuffled down the road to the gutted and roofless shell of a large building, little more than some broken external walls around a cracked concrete floor. Inside was a mess kitchen; the woman pulled a crude earthenware bowl from under her rags and joined another queue. A few lengths of ancient, wilted tinsel hung on the walls. A sullen-faced Reaper took her chit, ladled two dollops of watery stew from a steaming metal vat, and jerked his head.

Most people ate in the hall. Speakers on the walls; a thin, cold voice piped out of them: "We are all in this together. Thanks to your hard work and the dedication of the men and women of the Reapers, not least the Genetic Renewal division, large sections of the Wastelands have been reclaimed and made productive. I am proud to command ..."

The woman sucked breath through gritted teeth; her hands shook, almost spilling the bowl. *Winterborn.* Then she rallied. Mustn't draw attention. Must blend.

We want him. Bring him to us.

She would – she'd vowed that. But such things weren't achieved in a moment. It had taken a year of planning and hard work to get her this far; that wasn't to be thrown away. And there were other considerations as well, now, considerations far beyond simple vengeance.

Bring him.

She went outside, among the bare bushes and brittle weeds. Some of the workers went out there, for whatever reason. She found a hiding place between the factory wall and a heap of brambles. There, she forced down all the stew she could, put the bowl aside and, just for a moment, closed her eyes.

*

No sound. Somehow that's the worst part of it: the silence.

She can't even hear her footsteps click on the Black Road's cobbles. Normally, when she finds herself walking of nights, when she sleeps, that sound's the one bit of company she has. Now even that's gone.

Colour begins bleeding into the night. Or at least grey does. It fills up the space on either side of the road, then covers the road itself. She feels it, soft and cushioning, underfoot.

The sky lightens. The sky, too, is ash. Somewhere beyond it there might be a sun, but it's no more than a rumour of light. In the distance, the City, or what's left of it. It's only recognisable because it breaks the horizon in the right spot.

She stops and looks about. All is ashes. Here and there, the crumbling remains of a tree, a body, or a gun sticks clear of the dead grey carpet. Then she sees motion. Things crawling. They're people, she realises. Or they were. It's hard to be sure what they are now. The ash coats them – their clothes, their skin. And many of them are incomplete, missing fingers, hands or entire limbs, sections of faces stripped away. She can't tell where their flesh ends and the dust begins, especially as they crawl in it, flounder in it, sink into it, some vanishing from sight to never rise again. Their faces – their faces are wads of ash and dust, with black gaping holes for mouths and eyes.

And the worst thing, the worst, worst thing, is the absence of sound. When those faces lift and gape wider to howl their prayers and agony to the uncaring, dying sky, she sees chests and shoulders heave as they try to scream. But there's nothing. One figure kneels and screams and screams as its hands dissolve into streams of ash, waving the diminishing stumps of its arms about as if to extinguish the invisible fires devouring it. But there's no sound. It tries to rise, trips and falls into the ash. A grey cloud billows up. When it settles, the figure has broken apart like a toppled statue, its fragments either crumbling into or being swallowed up by the soft blanket that is the end of everything. A couple of the pieces are still moving.

Darkness falling, over her and them; an end to this at last? But no, in the distance the sky is still grimily pale. And this darkness has its edge, its contours. A shape. It's the shadow of something vast and alive.

Slowly she turns and stares upwards. She doesn't want to, but, as is common in dreams, she can't stop herself. She looks up and sees something vast and hunched and black blotting out the sky, sees its huge head turn and tilt downwards, feels whatever serves it for eyes come to bear on her.

She wants to wake up. She wants to wake up. But she's still there, staring up at it from the plain of ash as the black shape leans down towards her, a scream building in her throat she knows will go unheard.

And then there's one sound. Just one. The hiss of a wind through stone; the great shape's whisper of its name:

Tindalos.

*

Helen jerked awake trying to scream, stopped herself just in time. She slumped back against the wall, breathing hard, looking left and right. Stupid. Stupid. What kind of an idiot, falling asleep at a time like this? Christ, how long had she slept? She touched the bowl: still warm, the inside moist to the touch with the stew's thin gravy.

She was probably only asleep for seconds. She'd heard once that dreams only lasted that long. Even so, incredibly stupid and careless. A few seconds is more than long enough to die.

She took a last deep breath and looked around once more to ensure she was unobserved; then, she set to work.

First, she peeled off the headscarf. Underneath, her hair was red. The reverse of the headscarf was green. She put it back on, hid her hair again.

Next, she dug an old plastic bottle, half full of water, from her coat pocket; with that and a cleanish rag, she scrubbed the grime from her face.

After that, she got rid of the coat, and the stinking layers of old rags and sweaters beneath. Underneath, she wore plain blue overalls and was trim and lean.

Last, she unwound the rags from her legs and feet. Under them were army boots; a cloth bundle was tied to her 'swollen' leg. Inside the bundle were a World War Two revolver, fully loaded, and two dozen .38 calibre bullets.

All she had to fight with. Not that she was worried. The gun might be nearly an antique, but most weapons were nowadays; the kit that had been standard issue when the War broke out was long gone, used up and broken. For the most part, even the Reapers carried guns cached back in the sixties, relics of the Second World War; only the very lucky – or the elite troops, like the Jennywrens – got the self-loading rifles, Sterling sub-machine guns and Browning automatics mothballed in the eighties.

Tindalos. The plain of ash, the screaming, silent faces, the bodies with their crumbling flesh. It was coming; she knew it was. The only choice was to fight to stop it, or die.

Helen put the bullets and gun in separate pouches of the overalls. The .38 was almost a century old, but she trusted it. Automatics were quicker to reload and held more rounds, but if one misfired, you'd be dead before you cleared the breech. With a revolver, you just pulled the trigger again.

Inside the Feeding Station, the thin, cold voice had stopped; now a crackly gramophone recording of *Hark the Herald Angels* played.

Helen got up, slipped out of the bushes and shuffled away, trying to look as lost, aimless and forlorn as everyone else.

*

Head-down against the drizzle, Danny Morwyn trudged through shit and slaughterhouse waste. It ran ankle-deep down Dantzic Street; good job he had decent boots.

Animal sounds from the old Printworks building – dogs, cattle, pigs. The pigs' squeals were almost human. Two men in stained overalls pulled a big steel vat out of the main entrance on a trolley then tipped it, pouring red and brown liquid into the sludge on the street: blood and shit from the abattoir floor. Danny trudged on, though he wanted to walk fast, even strut – *stay slow, look tired, blend in with the crowd* – but for all that, he couldn't keep a little bounce out of his walk, couldn't stop his shoulders going back and his chest out, just a bit.

A drowned rat bobbed in the water, belly bloated. A ten-year-old girl ran in, grabbed it. She glared up at Danny, bared her teeth; he stepped round her, trudged on. Places to go, work to do.

A Christmas tree – a tall shrub cropped to a point and hung with bits of coloured glass and plastic – stood outside the slaughterhouse. Further down the pavement, little candlelights flickered to his left: a road shrine. He hesitated, shuffled towards it. They'd picked him 'cause he was the best, and that pumped him up one minute, scared him the next; times like this, you needed all the help you could get.

Least he wasn't a virgin any more. Not that he really felt any different, but at least he'd done it, least he wouldn't die without knowing what it was like …

*

Training exercise, it'd been. Couple of weeks ago. Darrow'd sneaked their crew out of the city into the Agri sectors, right up near the edges of the Wastelands, clear of the Reaper patrols. Met up with Scary Mary's crew near an abandoned village. Used the houses to practice fighting techniques, raiding. Practiced with their guns. Danny remembered the Sterling kicking back against his shoulder as he fired, bullets punching holes in the target and the wall either side of it.

Scary Mary didn't like boys; her crew was nearly all girls, 'cept for the black kid, Telo. Flaps was the toughest, a wiry, blue-eyed ginger girl, tough as nails and mad as a goat. Danny liked her, when she wasn't scaring the shit out of him. But she had a nice, firm little bum and jutty little tits, and he liked her face, and he knew from how she looked at him she felt the same.

Once the training was over, they had an hour – long as they were careful and didn't stray too far. Just in case there were any Reapers – or worse still, Jennywrens – about. And that was usually a good time to breathe air that was halfway clean, see green land with hardly a building or a person in sight; but that morning Flaps'd had other plans. She'd caught his eye and jerked her head; when he'd drifted over she'd murmured, "Two minutes, then follow me."

He'd done as she said, out past the village to where the remains of an old farmhouse perched on the hillside. "In here," she'd called, and he'd gone.

There was a blanket spread out on the earth floor – fuck knew where she'd found it. Flaps sat on it naked, knees pulled up to her chest; her clothes were neatly folded up beside her with her gun on top, where she could grab it in a rush. Danny'd stood and stared. "Well?" she'd said and lain back. "Come on, then." Like she didn't give a shit, wouldn't feel owt if he'd turned and walked on out. He reckoned she *would've* though. But he didn't leave. He went inside and fumbled at his own clothes, fingers suddenly feeling thick as his legs. She'd rolled her eyes, got up and stripped him, then pulled him back down on the blanket.

It'd been good. They'd lain there for a bit, even cuddled. That'd been nice, even if you were always having to listen out, just in case someone came snooping.

"Fucking tell anyone," she said, "and I'll have you."

"Aw, come on."

"Mean it. Go braggin' 'bout doin' me, and I'll cut your fucking rogers off. Keep your gob shut an' you never know. Might do this again." She untangled herself, reached for her clothes. "Best jib back down. Giz two minutes, then you shift it, too."

Once she was gone and he was dressed again, Danny hadn't been sure if it'd been real or not. Long as she didn't get a kid off it; that'd be *too* fucking real for him.

*

Nearing the shrine now, Danny wondered if the woman he was off to meet'd been like Flaps when she was that age. Or maybe – you never knew – still was. Maybe had a thing for younger lads. Could always hope.

The shrine was nowt special. City was full of them. This one was made of old bricks and plastic sheeting, the shelves inside stacked with guttering candles and effigies of mud or twigs. Sometimes you saw a crude sketch; once he'd even seen a photograph. This was where folk remembered their dead.

Two men, filthy, ragged and matted-haired, huddled in the lee of a nearby broken wall; one, short and squat, eyed Danny while his tall, thin mate stared into the small smoky fire they'd built. Danny stared back till the squat man looked away. He wasn't here to pick a fight, but he knew their kind. Cowardly but vicious – a hint of weakness and they'd strike.

Danny lit a candle-stub, dripped wax on the shelf, pushed it into place. It was for his parents, whoever they'd been. Anyone was listening, they'd hear: *get me through this alive.*

The gun dug into Danny's side. *Get a move on. Work to do.* He fumbled at his jumper, made sure it hid the pistol. Watched the candle for a second to make sure it'd stuck fast and would keep burning, then turned and walked off. *Head down, shoulders down; don't strut or you'll be noticed.*

She was depending on him. She'd never seen him in her life, didn't know his name or who he was, but she was depending on him. And he'd be there.

He could see the Feeding Station in the distance. Below it, and between them, the reeking mess of the shantytown on the banks of the Irk. The air was thick with its stench even from here. Thick with sounds too; mutters, moans, sobs and wails. One way or another, every fucker was walking wounded now.

And on the edge of the shantytown, the market, where folk came to trade whatever they could, often with a blade or club to hand in case someone tried snatching it. He strode towards it; *she* was waiting. And he had a job to do.

*

"Samms?" hissed the squat man beside the road shrine. "See that?"

The thin one frowned. "See what?"

"The sprog. He had a gun."

"Fuck off. You talk some right shit sometimes, Quick."

"Saw it."

"One of us, d'you reck?"

"Fuck off. His age? Might be old enough for a Reaper, but plain-clothes? Never."

"What now, then?"

"Go in the bushes, like you need a shit. Then radio Central."

"'Bout you?"

"I'll tail the fucker. You get a shift on, catch us up."

"'Kay."

*

The market was a spread of tattered grass churned to mulch; traders knelt or squatted beside heaps of their wares. Some had food – cans, roots, berries – others utensils, such as plastic bottles or earthen bowls. A few had children's toys or smokeable weeds.

A crowd of bowed, tattered figures shuffled between the traders. Danny picked his way through. The stench was even worse here. Most worked in twos so as not to leave their place unattended; those forced to work alone often soiled themselves rather than move.

Don't stand out. Look down. Watch the traders. He looked up often as he dared, scanned the crowd briefly as he could.

Didn't help that a lot of people wore headscarves, 'specially in weather like this. He saw brown scarves, grey, even a pink one –

There. Green headscarf.

Danny's breath caught – what if it wasn't her? But he wove through the crowd all the same.

Green scarf. There it was again. The face below – was it her? Would he know her now? He'd seen one years-old picture of her. The red hair'd be a giveaway, but she'd be keeping that hidden.

She half-turned; pale grey eyes flicked across the crowd, found him.

Oh yes. The pale, narrow oval of her face hadn't changed at all. Yes. It was her.

*

Time stopped when Helen saw him; the traders and the shanty, for a moment, were gone. All she saw was this kid, fifteen if he was that old, coming straight at her.

I'm sending someone for you, Darrow had written. *He's a boy, but he's good.*

And here he was: all pinched pale face, spiky black hair and eyes like a big daft dog. Grinning too. *Fuck sake, Darrow.* And then she looked past him and it got worse.

Two men, tailing him: one short and stocky, the other tall and thin. Dressed like scavengers, but walking wrong – they were straight-backed and striding – not shuffling with their eyes down, looking for crumbs to live on.

Plain-clothes Reapers. He'd slipped up. They'd spotted him, followed him, and he hadn't even noticed.

But he'd seen her. And the squat one's eyes flicked towards her – now *they* had, too. She could turn and run – leave him, lose them – but then she'd never find Darrow. The Reapers might, though.

The squat Reaper reached under his rags for a gun.

The boy was two paces from her; he opened his mouth. "With me, fast," she said.

"Wh– "

"Shut up and move." She grabbed his arm, pulling him after her.

"Hey, hang on – "

"Shut up."

"What about the password?"

"For fuck sake." She snorted. The boy glanced back; his eyes went wide. "Fuck – "

"Finally spotted them? Please tell me you've got a gun."

His face burned red. "Yeah, course."

"You've used it?"

"Yeah." She glanced at him. "On targets, yeah."

Christ. "What's your name?"

"Danny Morwyn."

"Danny, you'll just have to trust me. This way – now."

She pushed through the market and beyond, into the shantytown.

*

"Fuck me," said Samms. "Have to go in fucking there, wouldn't they?"

"You're faster," Quick said. "Go round, cut them off. I'll follow 'em."

"'Kay."

*

The shantytown's huts and shacks were crammed close together in rough rows. No people in sight; in a place like this, you learned fast when there was trouble and got out of its way. Even that didn't always save you.

Between the rows were narrow paths, ankle-deep mud mixed with chunks of rubble. Easy to slip, trip or break an ankle, but she sprinted fast along them, gun in hand: Danny followed, fumbling out the revolver Darrow gave him and generally feeling a right bell-end. "What we doin'?"

"Losing those two clowns, first of all. Then we get clear of here and you take me to Darrow. Watch behind us."

Danny stumble-ran backwards in a crouch, pointing the revolver back down the row and trying to keep his balance. Don't let him tip over on this now. Just put the knobbing lid on it, that would.

A shout and a gunshot from up ahead, then the thud and splash as a body fell. He spun: the thin Reaper who'd been stalking them lay on his back, still twitching; a pistol by his outstretched hand. Helen lowered her gun.

Watch behind us. They'd been a pair; and where one was the other had to be. Danny spun back round and there he was, the short stumpy one, running in towards them, gun in one hand and a radio in the other, shouting as he went. When he saw Danny he swung the pistol up.

Everything slowed down. A hum in Danny's ears. *Feet apart,* Darrow had said, *and bend your knees.* There was no time, and yet suddenly there was. *Hold the gun in both hands, left hand cupping the right. Arms out straight, shoulders forward.* The Reaper's pistol was almost level with his face. *Aim for the stomach; the recoil knocks the barrel up, and you want the chest. The centre of mass.*

The Reaper, dead centre in the row, gun in hand, the murky grey-black sky behind him –

And fire.

Danny pulled the trigger; the hammer rose and fell. When he'd first got the gun he'd had to practice doing that, without even any bullets in it. Hard work to start with, but now he could pull it thirty times in a minute, if he had to –

And *bang.*

The gun kicked back; it stung his hand; a thin high note shrilled in his ears. Smoke and flame flashed between him and the Reaper, who rocked backwards but still had the gun pointed at him –

Fire twice, said Darrow, *always twice, and fast. A double-tap, so he can't get one off at you as he goes down.*

The trigger caved easily the second time as he aimed and –

Bang.

And the Reaper fell backwards, dropping his gun. He hit the ground, splattering mud and filthy water, writhed for a second and half-rose. One side of his body heaved up out of the mud, then a sigh rattled in his throat and he fell back. Lay still.

Smoke drifted from the holes in the Reaper's chest. *I put them there.*

The Reaper stared unblinking at the sky. And Danny Morwyn realised he'd just killed.

*

Felt like hours, but could only have been seconds before she grabbed his arm. "Let's go."

Sirens, wailing. Cries from the hovels as they ran past. Darrow'd told him the landcruiser sirens were the same kind that'd sounded when the bombs came – so all the older folk flashed back and shat themselves. Fucking Reaper bastards. Anything to put the scares on.

She was nearly twice his age but in good shape; he had his work cut out keeping up. "We need to get clear, Danny. Which way?"

"Hang on." He puffed for breath.

"Danny."

"Yeah, *all right.*" He could feel what he'd just done heavy on him, pushing down. "*That* way." He pointed. "Up Cheetham Hill. There's a tunnel."

"A *what?*"

"Tunnel." She stared at him; for a second, all the calm and togetherness were gone and he took a step back. "Look, you wanna get out or not?"

"Okay, all right." But her pale face had gone pure white. "Lead the way."

The sirens, wailing louder. Aross the bridge, over the Irk – he didn't even like to look at the things clogging up the shallow waters half the shantytowners drank from. He ran up a cracked, rubble-strewn street –

– straight into two Reapers with sub-machine guns, coming the other way. Their guns came up.

"Get down, Danny!"

He dived; she was already firing, and one of the Reapers dropped in mid-run, legs collapsing under him. The other staggered, hit in the arm, raised his weapon to shoot. Danny fired from the ground at him, three shots, and the Reaper staggered back, gun falling. Helen fired again, and he dropped.

Sirens, wailing.

She ran past Danny, flicking the .38's cylinder open, shaking out the cases, brass tinkling on the floor, like what she'd just done was nothing. "You okay? Danny! You okay?"

He was shaking. "Yeah. Yeah."

She slotted new bullets into the gun then took the second Reaper's sub-machine gun and ammunition, nodded at the first one. "Get his gun. Come on; do it!"

"Yeah, okay." He scrambled to the body, flipped it over. The siren, wailing.

"Get a shift on, Danny."

"All right, all right." He pulled the gun from around the Reaper's neck. It had a wooden butt and stock like an old rifle, plus a perforated barrel and a long magazine that stuck out at the side. The dead man had four spare clips on him.

She looked at him, nodded. "That's a Lanchester. Good gun. Watch out, it's heavy."

Was, too. He got the sling around his neck, pouched the spare clips.

"Think you can use it?"

He nodded. He'd used a Sterling a couple of times. Practice-fired a few rounds. He could remember what to do. Hoped so anyway. Didn't want to look any more of a dick than he did already.

"Move it." They ran up the street. "Shit – "

The siren, wailing: a landcruiser swung into the street ahead and barrelled towards them. A driver, a passenger, plus two more Reapers in back, all armed.

Danny fell to one knee. All of a sudden, he was calm again. You trained for this. The fear was still there, but it was like an underground river: he heard it, felt it, knew it was there, but it was in the distance now. Far away.

Danny shouldered the Lanchester. Trigger control – Darrow'd taught him that. SMGs fire fast. Keep the bursts short.

He took a deep breath and pulled the trigger.

*

The two guns spewed flame, smoke and noise. Sparks blew clear of the bodywork; the landcruiser swerved into a wall. A Reaper scrambled out of the flatbed with a pistol; the shots flew high. Danny and Helen fired together; the Reaper fell.

"Cease fire," she shouted. Danny lowered the gun, face white. "Cover me."

Helen ran to the 'cruiser. Driver and passenger were both slumped over the dashboard, both with multiple head and chest wounds. Dead, or well on the way. Another Reaper lay in the flatbed, bleeding out from a neck wound. His mouth opened and closed. "Mum," he said at last, clear and distinct. And then was still.

Helen ran back to Danny. "We need to get away, fast." Her blood sang; her heart thudded. Excitement. Adrenaline. She hadn't lost it. She could still do this.

"I can sort that," Danny said. He looked different now; focused. Might be something to him after all. "Follow me."

Helen ran after him; more sirens wailed. They'd been lucky. The Reapers had been off guard. Rusty. The bastards had forgotten what it was to be at war. But she was back to remind them, and they'd all know. And one bastard in particular; she'd make sure he knew, in the seconds before he died.

*

The dead Reapers lay in a line by the crippled landcruiser, faces covered. Two live Reapers stood guard over them; a score of others ringed the shantytown, automatic rifles held ready.

A landcruiser rolled up. A short, wiry Reaper officer sat in back. His hair was white-blond; his taut white face seemed forever on the edge of a scream. A major's insignia on his shoulder; a nametag over his left breast that read KIRKWOOD.

"Look sharp," one of the guard Reapers whispered. "Kirky's on deck."

"Shun!" a sergeant snapped.

Kirkwood marched up, looked down at the bodies. His face twitched. "Sergeant!"

"Sir."

"I want whoever did this."

"Lieutenant Colbourne's in pursuit, sir. Went that-a-way."

"I'll join him," said Kirkwood. He looked up, nodded at the CCTV camera mounted on a nearby lamppost. "That working today?"

"Don't know, sir."

"Then find out, Sergeant." Kirkwood strode back to his landcruiser. "Get through to Dowson. And find me a face."

3.

"Definitely came this way?"

"Yes, Major, that's confirmed."

"Then where *are* they, Colbourne?"

"We're still looking, sir."

Two landcruisers parked on a road, surrounded by Reapers with automatic rifles. A rusted street sign. A couple of tumbledown houses – little more than stumps of wall. All else, each side of the road, was rubble and waste.

"Then look harder. Can't have just vanished. And Colbourne?"

Colbourne turned back. "Major?"

"The shantytown. Instruct Sergeant Grover: round up twelve inhabitants. Then hang them."

"Hang them?"

"There're still some old lampposts nearby. Better deterrent than shooting. Saves bullets too."

"But why, sir?"

"Questioning my orders, Lieutenant?"

"No, Major."

"Sends a message. No middle ground. With us or against us. In their own interests to help catch these scum."

"Sir."

"Need to learn who's in charge. Any word on the CCTV?"

"Camera was running. They have footage. Checking to see if they can ID them now."

"Tell them to get a move on. Bitch's good at this. Can't be many like that. What are you waiting for, Lieutenant? You have your orders. Dismiss."

"Yes, Major."

*

Beneath the ruins, under a bramble-hidden trapdoor, in an old cellar, Helen crouched.

Trapped. A dead end. And she was underground. Oh god oh god.

Danny scrambled past her to the cellar wall, hooked his fingers into holes in the brickwork, pushed. A section of wall fell inwards: the brickwork had been carefully cut free, fixed to a wooden board; when it was propped just right on the other side, the bricks fitted flush so you couldn't see the join.

Danny hissed, fighting to keep his balance. Helen got hold of the false section, helped him lower it. Cold dank air gusted from the dark beyond.

"Through here," Danny whispered, "and stay quiet."

Helen went through on all fours, collided with something almost immediately. She fumbled in the black, found damp bricks, a curved wall. A tunnel. An old sewer, she guessed.

Danny heaved the board back upright, using two rope handles on the back to steer it back in place. Even so she could hear the Reaper officer's voice above, ringing and metallic.

"That's Kirky," Danny whispered. "Major Kirkwood. Fucking mad bastard, he is."

He sat back, hugging himself and shaking. Reaction to what'd just happened, she guessed. His first time.

"Deep breaths," she said. "In and out. Think of somewhere quiet, somewhere calm. In and out, five times."

He shut his eyes; she heard his ragged breathing slow.

She had another kind of reaction to deal with though. The earth pressing round her, and not just earth: flesh, too, cold dead flesh, the jellied kiss of open wounds. *No, you're not there. You're not there. You're not.*

"Helen – "

Muffled noises above. Frozen, shaking. The tunnel was going to collapse, trap her in the earth with the dead.

"Helen?"

And in the teeming earth they stirred, fallen eyes turning to her: bone-clawed hands reached out to claim her back.

"Helen," Frank breathed, inches away; she could feel him and Belinda close by, crouching in the dark, could smell the rankness of their breath. Their cracked, chalky faces were swimming into focus through the gloom; points of red light glimmered in their blackish, blood-clot eyes. "We're hungry," he whispered, "and there's still no Winterborn to eat. So that means... well." He chuckled; Belinda gave a high shrill giggle. "You know what that means, Helen."

Their claw-like hands, reaching through the dark; she shrank back from them, breath fast and loud in her throat like a blunt saw fighting to cut through wood –

"Easy. Easy – "

A hand caught her arm. The scream strangled in her throat. The only sound, her own ragged breath.

"It's me. Danny. You gotta keep quiet. They hear us, we're fucked."

Heavy thuds from above; dirt whispered down, pattered on her cheek. She shuddered, gasped.

"Shit," she heard him whisper. "Deep – deep breaths. In and out. Think of somewhere nice. In an' out five times."

She had to giggle, though it was a broken, near-hysterical sound. "You're a fast learner," she got out through chattering teeth.

"Sh."

She nodded. *Calm.* She breathed. Swallowed hard. Breathed again. Pictured a hillside in summer, a crystal-bright memory-shard from a time before the War. And breathed, deep and slow, till she was calm.

"You okay?"

"Yeah." At least whispering, he couldn't hear her voice shake. "Flashback, that's all."

"Eh?"

"Bit like ghostlighting."

"Right."

Danny's eyes gleamed huge and startled in the dimness. Did he ghostlight? He was younger than the War; no echoes of lost times to plague him. But everyone had their ghosts these days. What scared him, though, she realised, was her.

Helen breathed deep. Steady again. "What now?"

"Straight on. Just keep crawling."

"Okay." She fumbled along the walls. *Calm.* They were stone, not earth.

"You got it?"

Cold, sharp air. That was better. Last time it'd been hot and thick, like trying to breathe through damp cloth. "Yeah."

Sirens loud above them; that thumping sound again, further off but still nearby. "Fuck," Danny whispered: it wasn't much more than a breath. "Move it – and no sound. *Nothin'.*"

In the dark, Danny moved ahead of her. A click, and a tiny bead of yellow flame: a lighter. Last time she'd had a lighter; it'd shown her things she hadn't wanted to see. Didn't want to remember them now, either, but she didn't have a choice.

But the flame only lit crumbling brick walls. He shuffled forward on his knees, fast and sure, lighter in one hand, the Lanchester cradled in the other to keep it still. She held the Sterling steady, crawled after him.

Danny stopped. "Sh."

What? She heard nothing. And then she realised that was just it. No sound from above. A thread of dust hung between ceiling and floor for a moment, then fell and scattered. They were moving, but trying to keep silent.

"Stay still," Danny breathed. The lighter flame blinked out.

In the dark, no sound, except Danny's breath and hers. Her thumb found the Sterling's safety catch. If she rolled onto her back, aimed down between her feet at the entrance when they tried to come through …

Blow her own toes off, most like. Best she could do was save a bullet for herself. She listened for the sound of the trapdoor scraping back, the hidden section knocked aside. But there was only silence.

"Still," Danny whispered again.

Above, the landcruiser hissed and clanked. Its siren wailed; a little more powdered stone trickled down on them as it passed, and then it was gone.

The lighter flicked back on. "Let's shift."

She'd get through this. She wouldn't break.

*

"Here we are. Y'okay?"

"Fine."

"Sure?"

"I'm *fine*."

"'Kay. 'Kay."

Danny clambered out of the tunnel; Helen crawled after him. She took deep breaths: they were still underground, the air cold and dank, but it wasn't as close.

"Here," said Danny. She saw several things that looked like sticks beside the tunnel entrance. Danny touched the lighter to one of them and it flared into bright flame; dried weeds and thorns twisted together into a crude torch. Smoke stung her eyes, but a warm yellow glow spread around them to light up a wide, hexagonal chamber. She saw other tunnel entrances in the walls, some as narrow as the one they'd climbed through, some high enough to walk through. The chamber's own ceiling was twenty feet above them.

She breathed out. Better already. "Where are we, anyway?" she asked.

A footstep gritted in the shadows. Danny aimed the Lanchester at it, moving back towards the tunnel. Helen took the safety catch off the Sterling but stood her ground. If it was a trap, so be it; she'd stand her ground and fight. Crawling through that tunnel, the earth heavy above her; never again, *never* while she had breath. At one point she'd been sure her bowels must fail.

"Part of the old sewer system," said a calm, low voice. "We're lucky. There are still a lot of places in the city like this. Tunnels, basements, cellars, old foundations. A lot of them have collapsed, but not all. The Reapers largely disregard them. So we use them."

A lean, grey-haired man stepped out into the light, a Thompson sub-machine gun in his arms. "Hello, Helen."

"Darrow," she said.

How old would he be now? Over fifty – ancient, these days. Helen's mother had told her of people living to over a hundred –

Flies crawling into her mouth, crawling over glazed, open eyes.

She shook her head.

"No," he said. "It's me. Well, let's have a look at you."

"You first, you old goat."

Danny gaped; Helen tried not to smile. Unless he'd changed a hell of a lot, Helen was the only person who'd ever got away with talking to Darrow that way.

Darrow chuckled, stepped forward. He wore dogskin trousers, a battered leather jacket, an ancient sweater and army boots. There were deep lines around his eyes, and his hair was much greyer than it had been, almost white. A few liver spots on his hands, and he walked that little bit more stiffly towards her. But the blue eyes were clear, and there was little surplus or wasted flesh hanging round the jaw or throat. The wear and tear was just cosmetic; the old Darrow was very much there.

"You remember Mike Ashton?" Darrow asked. A big, bearded man, shaggy hair down to his shoulders, came out of the shadows too, holding a Sterling. Like Helen, he wore old workmen's overalls.

"Yeah. Yeah. I remember. Mike. How you doing?"

Ashton shrugged.

Helen and Darrow studied each other in silence. Helen was the first to look away.

"Good to see you," he said at last.

"And you. You're looking well."

"You too, considering."

"Meaning?"

"Considering all you've been through."

"We all have. Anyway, what've you been teaching these kids?" She nodded towards Danny. "He nearly got us both killed back there."

"Hey – " Danny began.

Darrow raised a hand. "What happened?"

"Reapers sussed him. He missed it. Led them straight to me."

"I did explain, Helen." Darrow looked weary for a moment. "We're a long way from a full-scale uprising here. We operate in crews, citywide. I command one; half a dozen other old fighters like Mike command the rest. The rank and file are kids like Danny. We find them, take them in, build our strength up slowly. None of them have seen fighting; they've been trained for it, but there's no plan, no network, not anymore."

"But you sent him to find me?"

"He's pretty much the best of my crew. He got you out, didn't he?"

"He's good with a gun," Helen said. "Kept his head, did as he was told, dropped two, three Reapers. But he couldn't infiltrate a blind man's party."

Danny blinked, not sure if he should feel slighted or complimented.

"They have to gain experience somehow," Darrow said.

"Bit hard if they're dead. Plus which we've got half the Reapers out looking for us now. You could have at least sent someone more experienced with him."

"Like Mike? Or myself? We're too well known. And we know too much. Neither of us can betray the other's crew if captured – we move around and communicate by message drops, so no crew leader knows exactly where the others are – but either of us could the fighters under our care. This is the first time Mike and I have met face to face in several years."

"And only," said Ashton, "because you wanted to see *her*."

Helen nodded. "How is she?"

"As well as can be expected. Mike's crew look after her. I visit every month or so, just before they move her elsewhere. I gave her your message."

"And?"

"She still isn't convinced it's you. And she's still very badly frightened of the Reapers."

"Who isn't?"

"You know what I'm talking about, Helen."

"Yes. Yes I do."

"She was so sure you were dead. She won't believe it's you or even consider what you're asking until she sees you for yourself."

"Then I suppose we'd better oblige her," said Helen.

"Who's *she*?" demanded Danny.

Darrow looked at the boy. "Danny, in a minute you're going to see something nobody else knows about. Just Mike, Helen and I."

"Worked *that* out."

Helen looked down to hide a smile.

"I'm trusting you to keep it secret too. Nobody else must know."

"All right."

"Nobody."

"All right."

"The rest of your people might have to know, sooner or later," Helen said.

Darrow held her gaze. "That's her choice, Helen. Not yours."
Finally, she nodded and looked down again.

At least the tunnel he and Ashton went down was high enough to walk through. Helen followed, Danny in her wake, slow anticipation knotting in her gut.

*

Only their waning torches lit the black, lightless tunnel. Danny's burned down to his fingers; he hissed and dropped it, trod it out. Up ahead, Darrow's went out too. The dark flooded in; Danny heard Helen's breath catch.

The damp, yeasty smell of the tunnel changed to a thick clogging reek: piss, shit, stale smoke. Darrow lit a new torch. Its glow spread to reveal a slightly smaller version of the chamber they'd just left.

"Alannah?" called Darrow. No answer. "Alannah, it's me. Roger. Mike's with me. And Helen. Helen's here. Remember? You said you wanted to see her. Alannah?"

In the cold, dank chamber, water dripped; shadows wavered and shifted in corners, alcoves and tunnel entrances.

"Helen?" whispered Darrow.

She nodded, stepped forward, pulled off the headscarf. Weedlight gleamed in her red hair, sparkled in her pale grey eyes.

"Alannah?" she called.

A long silence. Then the click of a gun being cocked.

4.

High above the city, Winterborn looked down from a floor-length, blast-proof window at dull grey streets washed still more colourless with rain. At least this time of year there were gleams of brightness – the green of Christmas trees and the mixed reds, blues and golds of make-do bunting.

Winterborn knew he should be happy; the reports on his desk said so. So many miles and sectors of Wasteland reclaimed: so much coal mined, so much meat or vegetables canned, so many mutants, ferals and subversives liquidated. RCZ 7 led the way, and Project Tindalos wasn't even active yet. When it was, there'd be no limits. And yet. And yet.

Perhaps after the Unification Conference. Perhaps when he led two or more Command Zones welded into one. Perhaps when he led a Britain, united once more. Like King Arthur. A pity his name was Tereus; it hadn't quite the same ring.

He returned to his desk, looked at his reports, but they didn't help. Instead he found himself reaching down to the bottom drawer of his desk.

*

When the bombs had fallen twenty years earlier, only the Tower, of all the city centre's big buildings, had survived. No one knew why, but, once decontaminated, it had served both the Regional Commissioners and, after them, the Reapers as a base of operations.

It had the best facilities available: electricity, running water, a link to the city's surviving CCTV cameras, even computers. It had a functioning lift to the Commander's office on the top floor, and that was where Dowson was going now.

Dowson – bull-shouldered, grey-haired, flash-burns down his face's right side – stopped at the lift door. He wore a Reaper's black leather uniform, a Colonel's insignia and the blue shoulder-flashes of the Commander's personal staff, plus a Browning automatic, hip-holstered. Under one arm, a plain manila file. Dowson licked his lips, took a deep breath and pushed the lift button.

The speaker above it crackled. "Identify."

"Dowson, Richard. Colonel."

"State your purpose."

"Urgent briefing for the Commander."

"Please wait."

Time ticked by; the speaker crackled again. "Approved."

"I should fucking think so," Dowson muttered through his teeth.

Gears creaked and clanked above: the lift, descending.

"You will be required to submit to a search on arrival," said the voice.

"I *do* know that."

The speaker went dead again. Dowson swallowed, tried to ignore the tightness in his stomach. Failed. Glanced down at the file; drummed his fingers on it.

A soft chime; the lift was here.

"Just get me through this in one piece," muttered Dowson, and stepped inside.

*

Winterborn took out the music box and put it on the desk. It was small, only a few inches square. Its silvery finish had been dulled and worn away, and when he popped open the lid it let out two dull chimes.

But once, of course, it had meant a soft, tinkling melody and a cool hand stroking his hair, soothing his childhood terrors away.

He sat back and stared down at it, hands resting on his desk. The old clock on the wall ticked: loud, slow and steady. Calming.

No point trying to repair the box, of course. It had meant something, yes – once. But he was far past that now. *When I became a man, I put away childish things.* And yet. And yet.

His desk intercom buzzed.

"Winterborn."

"Colonel Dowson to see you, sir."

"Very well. Send him in." It would be a welcome distraction; he'd never thought of Dowson as one of *those* before. He doubted anyone ever had. That was one little bit of history made.

*

The lift stopped at the top but the doors stayed shut. The cable creaked; Dowson clenched his teeth. Dangling twenty-five floors up in a tin can on a metal rope. Rank wouldn't save you if the cable snapped. The soles of his feet tingled. Least that'd end once the doors opened though. There were worse things waiting.

Chaos, for example. Dowson liked routine. Order, pattern. Spent his life creating it, best he could. Anything that threatened or disrupted that, he hated. Even feared. The random, the unplanned: chaos.

And there was chaos in the folder under his arm. Dead people stayed dead. Yeah, there was ghostlighting – even Dowson had had that once or twice – but that wasn't *real,* whatever some berks thought. It was in your head, nowhere else. The dead didn't really come back. Especially not with guns.

There'd be an explanation. Course there would. Clear, logical. There'd have been an error. But that didn't help. Still meant he couldn't trust what he knew.

And then, of course, there was Winterborn himself.

The doors opened. Thank fuck.

"Step out of the lift," someone called.

Dowson did. Four Reaper privates and a corporal, all with sub-machine guns, covered him from different angles.

"Step to your left. Remain still."

Two Reapers checked the lift. "Clear," one called. Another took the manila file and riffled through it.

"Your weapon, sir," the corporal said.

Dowson handed over the Browning, put his hands against the wall. A Reaper frisked him. "Clean."

Dowson took the file back. The Corporal saluted; Dowson returned it. The Reapers flanking the Commander's office doors saluted too, and opened them. Dowson swallowed hard, his gut tightening, and went through.

Floor-to-ceiling shatterproof windows provided a view stretching nearly twenty miles north, east and west. Not that there was much to see any more; ruins, ruins and then more ruins. But Winterborn seemed to like it; approaching the Commander's wide desk, all Dowson could see was the back of his swivel chair. He halted six feet from the desk, snapped to attention, and waited.

The desk was bare, except for three telephones – two black, one red – a pen, an A4 pad and that old, battered silver music-box Winterborn sometimes tinkered with when he was broody. Dowson had seen him; he'd never let Winterborn know he had.

Behind him, the double doors closed.

"Commander."

A sigh; the chair swivelled to face him.

Winterborn leant back, fingers steepled on his flat belly. He was in his mid-twenties, with long, fair hair and blue eyes so pale they were almost white. His face was smooth and pale, with a red Cupid's-bow mouth. On another man, it would've been called effeminate; on a girl, beautiful. On Winterborn it was neither. Dowson recalled a marble angel he'd once found in a ruined church; the serene, pitiless beauty of something far beyond human.

Winterborn studied Dowson, didn't blink. Dowson didn't speak. He'd learned not to. The wall clock ticked.

"Well?"

Deep breath; dive in. "There's been an incident, sir – "

"That's your job, Dowson. Dealing with incidents."

"Eight Reapers are dead, sir."

Winterborn didn't move or speak. Seconds passed; sweat trickled down Dowson's spine. Just after the nuclear attack – fresh out of officer training, half his face burned raw, the whole country rubble and fire – he'd found himself commanding a platoon; thirty-odd men and women expecting answers from him while he tried not to think of radiation sickness, or the future. Chaos playing with them all, a cat with a crippled mouse: might kill you slowly, might let you live.

Whenever he stood before Winterborn, he felt that once again; no telling what was going on, behind those blue, unblinking eyes. And today he bore bad news.

"Well." The red lips parted. "That's a little more than an incident, isn't it, Colonel? What happened?"

"Some scrote, sir. Scav kid."

"A child?"

"About fifteen, we think."

"Hardly a child, then." Still the eyes didn't blink. "Go on."

"Plain-clothes Reapers spotted him. He had a pistol. They tailed him."

"And?"

"He met somebody. A woman. New in the city, we think. He'd missed the tail. She spotted it. They shot their way out, her and the boy. Killed the plain-clothes men and six regular Reapers, stole a landcruiser, and got away."

"I see." Winterborn's eyebrows raised a fraction. "Very capable."

"Yeah. She was, anyway."

"Oh?" Winterborn smiled, cocked his head. Still he hadn't blinked.

"Yes, sir. The boy could shoot, but he's green, or he'd've spotted the tail."

"So, what's the status?"

"As I said, sir, eight Reapers dead – "

Winterborn closed his eyes. "I meant the terrorists, Dowson."

"Reaper squad in pursuit, sir."

"Who's in command?"

"Major Kirkwood, sir. Dealt with the food riots last year."

"I recall. He did well."

"He did, sir."

Winterborn smiled. "Of course, scattering an angry mob with tear gas and a few bullets isn't quite the same thing."

"Kirky did his share of street-fighting back in the Civil Emergency, sir. Best we've got in the city right now."

"Well, if that's the case ..." Winterborn's focus shifted into some far-off distance for a few seconds, then returned to Dowson. "You said she was new to the city?"

"Just a guess, sir. But she was coming from the Feeding Station. We found some discarded rags – part of a disguise, we think – near there. And like I said, the boy was green. A liability. Unless – "

"Someone needed a guide."

"Yes, sir."

"Mm." Winterborn's eyes shifted to the folder under Dowson's arm, then back to him. The smile was gone; he spoke softly. "What aren't you telling me, Dowson?"

Dowson licked his lips. "We've CCTV cameras running in the area, sir, as you know. We retrieved footage."

"So I assumed, from the detail you've already provided. Presumably it yielded results?"

Oh yes, sir, just not ones you'll like. "We got visuals of both of them, Commander. Managed to blow up a facial shot for ID purposes."

"And?" The face still blank, the eyes still unblinking.

"Nothing on the boy, but I wouldn't have expected it. The woman, though …" Dowson swallowed. "I took the liberty of running her through the computer."

"Did you, indeed?" Winterborn leant forward, voice slow and deliberate. "Colonel Dowson: you are aware, are you not, that our computer systems are only to be accessed with *my* authorisation?"

"Sir – "

"There's the small matter of parts, Colonel. Whenever we use a computer, it's just that little bit extra wear and tear on them. And, unless I missed something in one of your weekly reports, new computer parts are not part of our current output." Winterborn's smile gleamed like broken glass. Dowson's palms were clammy and damp. The blue eyes wouldn't leave his.

"No, sir."

"I don't make rules for you to break, Dowson."

"No, sir." Winterborn took breath to speak, but Dowson cut in quickly. "However, sir, as your adjutant, I *am* authorised to access the systems if the security threat merits it."

"Security?" Winterborn raised his eyebrows, smiled and settled back in his chair, fingers steepled again.

Dowson nodded. "Her face, sir. I knew I recognised it, but not where from."

"Your memory's one of your better attributes, Dowson. Heaven knows I don't keep you around for your spontaneity or personal charm. I wouldn't want to think that admirable faculty was deserting you."

"It was the hair," said Dowson.

"What?"

"It was covered. Otherwise I'd have – "

"What are you wittering about, Dowson?"

"I ran a search and match programme through the old computer files. Didn't find anything first time round, because it was only looking through active files."

Winterborn's face was expressionless. "And?"

"I ran another search, this time on all the files. Even the ones listed as dead. Just in case. Sir."

"Stop spinning it out, Dowson. Get to the point."

"We got one match, sir. Ninety-seven per cent certain." He hated saying the name; it was the kind of bad pun that had probably sounded like a clever *nom de guerre* when she was fourteen. And now he might die with it on his lips, if Winterborn shot the messenger. Dowson breathed in, closed his eyes and said it. "It's Helen Damnation."

When he finally opened his eyes almost a minute later, Winterborn hadn't moved; for a delirious second Dowson thought he'd been turned to stone. But then he spoke, very slowly, very measured, voice very soft. "Is that supposed to be a joke, Colonel?"

"No, sir."

"Well, that's a pity." He didn't move or blink; Dowson thought of a snake, trying to hypnotise its prey. "Because that means you're calling me a liar."

"Sir, no – "

Winterborn leant back in his chair, breathed deep in through his mouth and looked up at the ceiling. "I saw Helen Damnation die," he said, very slowly, very deliberately. "I saw them shoot, and I saw her fall." He looked down; Dowson flinched back from him. "I saw her body thrown in a mass grave and covered over with earth. She. Is. Dead."

Dowson's mouth was dry; the knot in his stomach was painful now. *He's afraid. The bastard's afraid, and he's lashing out.* He had to speak, had to say something or –

"The computer gave a ninety-seven per cent match, sir," Dowson heard himself say. He remembered the folder, held it out. Winterborn looked down at it, then back up at Dowson. At last he reached out and took it, so gently Dowson had to look and see if it had happened or not.

Dowson put his hands behind his back; Winterborn laid the file on his desk, looking down at it. Dowson started counting; he'd reached five by the time Winterborn opened it. The photographs were on top; two in colour, two black and white. Good quality too, considering the magnification and the equipment's age.

*

Winterborn said nothing; just sat and stared down at the pictures, face empty of all expression, utterly still. That pale oval of a face, the cool grey eyes. Yes. It was her. Could never have been anyone else.

His stomach clenched; he felt as though he were floating in space. The last five years had run smoothly. Ever since the Refuge, ever since she died. A stairway to Heaven, or at least to greater and greater power and all the security and protection it bought. Favoured of God. But now, now all of that was called into question. Nothing made sense any more.

And if he'd been wrong about this, where else might he have been mistaken? Anything else, any leap of faith where he'd trusted his instincts, might have been the wrong move. Even Project Tindalos.

The whole world trembled on its foundations. Winterborn felt a moment's terror, then overwhelming rage. He didn't look at Dowson; the urge to kill would be irresistible if he did.

"It was the hair," Dowson said again. "That's why I didn't twig straight off. She was famous for it. That's why she's got it covered. And, anyway, she was supposed to be dead. Everyone knew she was. You don't think of – "

"Be quiet, Dowson." Winterborn still hadn't looked up. He had a photograph in each hand; a black and white profile and a full-face colour shot. She was looking straight into the lens. As if she knew he'd be looking. He listened to the clock's ticking, let the rhythm soothe and steady him. Like a metronome, beating time, imposing order where there was none.

*

"Well," Dowson heard him say. "That's quite a comeback."

Slowly, calmly, Winterborn replaced the pictures, shut the folder, moved it to one side and pressed a hand down on it as if to stop it escaping. A brief silence; he looked up. "Five years," he said. "For five years she lets us all think she's dead, and now – *now* – she comes back. So where's she been, what's she been planning? Why here – and why now?"

"With respect, sir, I think we both know why she's here."

Winterborn studied him, face empty. Dowson was sure he'd gone too far now, was about to die. But at last Winterborn nodded. "Because I am?"

"It's a reasonable deduction, sir."

"I'd be very surprised if she had no interest in settling scores. But I know Helen. She very rarely lets her heart overrule her head." He half-smiled; it froze, faded. "Only once, that I recall. If she only wanted revenge, we'd have heard from her before now. And she has help. She's not acting alone." Winterborn pursed red lips. "We've always suspected there are former rebels hiding in the City."

"That's the story, sir. No more than a handful, but allegedly they take in street kids. So far, they've kept out of our way. So no idea how many there are, or how well-organised."

"I suspect we're about to find out."

Dowson shifted, foot to foot. "Could be he's just a gang member, sir; the boy, I mean. For the right price, they'd help her get in."

"You said that *they* shot their way out, Dowson. *They.*"

"Yes, sir."

"So the boy can use a gun."

"Sir."

"But not locate a tail? Guns are hard to come by outside our ranks, Dowson. Even the biggest gangs only have two or three. Why entrust one to a boy who can't even tell he's being followed?"

Dowson nodded slowly.

"If, on the other hand," said Winterborn, "you're a wanted terrorist, probably with a cache of weapons, it makes far better sense to stay hidden and send somebody unknown to us out there. Apart from anything else, the trainees have to learn somehow, don't they?"

"Good point, sir." And it was; whatever else was true about Winterborn, he hadn't survived without brains and sharp instincts.

"What gun did he use?"

"Pistol originally – an old .38 – then a Lanchester SMG. Got that off a dead Reaper."

"Did he know what he was doing with it?"

"From the CCTV footage – well, he's inexperienced – "

"We knew that."

"Sir. But – tried to control his fire, actually hit what he was aiming at. I'd say someone's at least shown him how to use one."

"The gangs have pistols, Dowson. Maybe the odd bolt-action rifle. But a sub-machine gun? No. It's the rebels. Looks like they're finally showing their hand." Winterborn looked out of the window. Dowson counted seconds. He'd reached twenty before Winterborn turned back to him. "Three things, Dowson."

"Sir."

"One: Helen Damnation is the number one priority for all Reapers. Dead or alive. It would be nice to pick her brains before I put her back in her grave, but it's not essential. We can't afford to let the rebels get hold of her; the most important thing is to deny them that asset."

"Understood, sir."

"Two: with that in mind, I want maximum vigilance on CCTV. All functioning cameras are to be activated and monitored twenty-four-seven until we have her."

"Could stretch our manpower."

"Call in additional units from outside the city if you have to. We need to nip this in the bud." Winterborn drew the red phone towards him. "Meanwhile, I'll contact Hobsdyke. If we've a potential rebellion on our hands, Project Tindalos is a priority as well."

"Sir."

"You don't sound convinced, Dowson."

"You know my views on Project Tindalos, sir."

Winterborn smiled. "Indeed I do, Colonel. Which brings me to point three."

"Sir?"

"Let's just say you're not the only one to have doubts about Project Tindalos, Dowson. We can't afford dead weight at a time like this. I think matters at Hobsdyke might run more smoothly – and quickly – if you were in overall charge."

Exile. Shooting the messenger. Dowson's stomach clenched; rage burnt his eyes. He swallowed, hid it. Better than death, at least. "Yes, sir."

"You're a good administrator, Dowson, and if Project Tindalos can be made to work, that's what we need. If not …" Winterborn's eyes hooded. "I'll leave that to you. But in the meantime, if we have a war to fight, that requires a very different skill set." Winterborn picked up the red phone and began to dial. "That will be all, Colonel. Dismiss.'"

5.

Mordake stood by the perimeter fence and lit a cigarette. The ruins called him, beckoned him down. Liz was waiting. Liz's ghost.

Silly, of course. Places weren't haunted. People were. And everyone was haunted now. But he never saw Liz anywhere except Hobsdyke village. He wanted to go. But there was too much to do here. *So I can hold you again. Because ghosts aren't enough.*

Smoke caught the back of his throat; he coughed, spat.

Eddie, you need to cut them out. They'll kill you. I'm not having kids just to tell them Daddy's gone when they're still at nursery.

She'd always nagged him about the smoking. He'd been working on it, too; by the time the War had broken out, he'd been down to one a day. And he'd have quit entirely in the end. For her, and the kids who'd never been. *More ghosts.*

Mordake trod out his cigarette, turned away.

After the War, of course, cigarettes hardly seemed a threat at all. Not once you'd seen what fallout and UV radiation from the stripped ozone layer could do. Obviously, once Tindalos succeeded he'd quit again, and any damage done could be healed.

"All shall be well," he muttered. "All shall be well; all manner of things shall be well."

Inside the Monitoring Unit, he found Lyson hunched over the control panel, staring at the feeds from the seclusion chambers. There were now two Reapers on permanent guard outside each chamber; at the first sign of danger to a test subject, Lyson would trigger an alarm. In the screens' wan light he was grey-faced and bleary-eyed.

"Have you tested the PHCs yet?"

"No." Lyson rubbed his eyes. "Not yet. Sorry, Doctor."

"Don't worry. I'll do it. Take a break. Half an hour."

"Thanks, Doctor." Lyson rose, stumbled outside.

Mordake sat and watched the screens. Something caught his eye; he glanced up. Above him, atop the monitors, was a tiny plastic Christmas tree they'd found somewhere; there was even a threadbare strand of tinsel wrapped around it.

That last Christmas before the War, it had been just him and Liz at home. There'd been a tree there, another plastic one but full-sized, hung with with glittering ropes of tinsel, baubles and coloured lights. The gas fire roaring as they lay on the hearthrug. Glasses of sloe gin, even though it always gave him a headache. A Christmas compilation CD playing on the stereo, the kind of unbridled sentimental cheese you wouldn't listen to any other time of year. *It's A Wonderful Life* on the TV with the sound off. They hadn't made love, just lain there. The softness and warmth of her was what had mattered; that and knowing she was there. That she always would be.

Mordake shut his eyes, breathed out, opened them again.

The Unit was silent; the only sound was the equipment's soft hum. The speakers were switched off.

Mordake studied the feed from Chamber Four. Strapped to his pallet, the subject stared unblinking at the ceiling. They were all like that now. That was good; inside, the changes were taking place.

And when they were done, all would be well. All manner of things. The shadows on his lungs, the rebels with their anarchy, the ghosts – this whole bereft, haunted life would be gone. A bad dream – now ended. What was lost would be restored. Liz, the children. All manner of things.

Mordake switched on the speaker and activated the microphone.

"Post Hypnotic Command Test, third of December. Command word: Candlemass."

Subject Four didn't move or speak or even blink, but his breathing deepened.

"You will hear only my voice and obey only my instructions until I repeat the command word. Lift your head."

Subject Four's head rose. Mordake sat back and lit a fresh Monarch. He smoked most of it before saying "Lower your head."

Subject Four rested it back on his pallet.

"Now turn your head to the left. Now to the right. Now recite *Mary Had A Little Lamb*. Now…"

At last he was done. Mordake ground his cigarette out. "Good," he said. "Candlemass."

Subject Four's breathing changed again. Mordake reached for the controls, to shut off the feed.

And then Subject Four turned his head, stared directly at the camera and spoke.

"*Angana sor varalakh kai torja. Angana sor varalakh cha voran. Mantakha sa niroleph chir karagh,*" the man said, voice raw, gravelly. "*Angana sor varalakh kai torja.*"

Mordake whooped, put a hand to his mouth. "Yes," he said. "Yes."

Subject Four was silent, still staring out of the screen at him. And then he spoke again.

"All shall be well," said Subject Four. "All shall be well. All manner of things shall be well."

Mordake was silent; Mordake was still. Nearly a minute passed; Subject Four spoke again. Not in his normal voice – a woman's, tinged with a Devonshire accent.

"Eddie, you need to cut them out. They'll kill you. I'm not having kids just to tell them Daddy's gone when they're still at nursery."

Subject Four kept staring, still didn't blink.

"The Night Wolves have heard your call, Doctor. And they're coming. They're coming."

Subject Four turned his head again to stare unblinkingly up at the ceiling.

Mordake lit another cigarette. His fingers shook. The speakers hissed softly, till he reached across and switched them off.

*

A pub by a harbour in the Orkneys, all those years before.

A hard-faced man in a thick, faded sweater sat in the corner, sipping a half of stout.

"Mr Duncan?" Mordake asked.

The man looked up at him, didn't answer.

"Mind if I join you?"

Duncan shrugged. Mordake sat. "I'm one of the archaelogy students working on the dig," he said. Duncan didn't answer. "At the other end of the island?" Mordake added. Nothing. What did Duncan see? A skinny, dark-haired nineteen-year-old with expensive outdoor clothes and a posh accent? Probably. And thought himself entitled to look down on him for that. Well, Mordake had handled worse than Duncan in his time. "I found something," he said. "Something that doesn't belong there."

Mordake took a small cylinder of greenish stone out of his pocket. "The symbols carved on it don't match any known culture existing in Britain at that time. Or anywhere else, for that matter. Or at any other time that I've heard of."

He was wrong: there was one, he would discover, that almost resembled an odd design of crucifix, peculiar to the churches of two or three small villages in the north-west of England. But that discovery lay many years in the future.

He put the cylinder on the table. Duncan's eyes fixed on it, and he went still.

"Now a little bird tells me," said Mordake, "that they've seen you with something like this." He leant forward conspiratorially. "I'd be very interested to know where you found it."

Duncan took a swallow of beer and finally spoke. "Things like that are best left. You don't want to know, boy."

"But I do."

Duncan studied him.

"I'll pay," said Mordake.

Duncan sighed and shrugged. "Your neck."

*

A skerry is a chunk of rock too small and bare and stark to be called an island or even an islet, but big enough that ships need to know about. At certain tides and in certain weathers, skerries can vanish under the waves completely, something Mordake was well aware of as he crouched there.

He was a good, respectable boy from a good, respectable family; joining the dig was the closest he'd ever come to rebellion. He was following his father into psychiatry as a career, but archaeology was his passion and he'd do a degree of his own in it one day. And here he was, perched on a rock in the wild North Atlantic and hoping he lived long enough to follow the trail further.

He opened the satchel at his side; inside it were four more cylinders of varying size. He smiled, and closed the satchel again.

Out of the murk ahead, a dark shape loomed; Duncan's fishing boat, hoving in towards the skerry. Mordake smiled, waved.

Duncan watched him as he clambered aboard. "Find what you wanted, then?"

"Oh yes," said Mordake, grinning. "Oh yes."

Mordake's office was a prefab hut at the back of the compound, behind the research block. All he needed was here; some days he never left. A desk with two phones – one black, one red – pens, paper, a tape recorder, a framed photograph. A hotplate, a camp-bed, a chemical toilet, a sink. The men had brought a pine tree in from the woods nearby – Gaffer's Wood, they called it – and hung what brightly-coloured things they could find off it. That had been good of them, and unexpected.

And there were windows: one overlooking the village ruins; the other, the Adjustment Chamber. He was looking at the Chamber now, had been for some time. At last he looked away. He avoided looking at the ruins, touched the photo's cracked glass instead. The picture was cracked too, and faded. Liz: smiling and round-faced, with warm, dark eyes.

Remember why you do this. He picked up the recorder's microphone, put a finger on the RECORD button. *Where to start? Thoughts in order.* He took a deep breath and –

The red phone rang.

Mordake jumped, glared. "Fuck."

The phone kept ringing.

Most calls came through on the black phone. If it'd been the black phone, he'd have ignored it; the work was more important. But only one person used the red phone. He put down the mic, took his index finger off the button.

"Mordake."

"I know that, Doctor. Well?"

"Sir?" Mordake rubbed his arms; it felt like insects were crawling over them. Winterborn's voice had that effect.

Winterborn breathed out through his nose. "Don't play games with me, Doctor. What is Project Tindalos' status?"

"Project Tindalos' status is excellent, Commander."

"Is it now, Doctor?"

"Yes. Yes, it is. We're close now. Very close."

"Close."

"Yes, sir."

Seconds passed; Mordake almost heard Winterborn counting them off for patience or effect. "You'll notice my cries of rejoicing are not ringing in your ears."

Mordake couldn't answer; there was no right thing to say. Silence probably wasn't much of a response either.

"Would you like to hazard a guess as to why? No? Well, perhaps it's because that song has a somewhat familiar refrain, Doctor Mordake. I've been hearing it, in one form or another, for almost three years."

"I understand that, but – "

"Shut up," said Winterborn quietly. "You promised me results, Mordake. Amazing results. Those were your words. Spectacular ones. And even then, there were those who questioned this project's validity, Doctor Mordake. Actually, 'questioned' might be too kind a word: 'pissing time and resources up the fucking wall,' was how I believe Colonel Dowson put it in an unguarded moment. But... I had faith."

A bead of sweat stung the corner of Mordake's eye.

"After all, you didn't require *much*. A research facility at a specified site. A few condemned prisoners to use as test subjects. Oh – and a detachment of Reapers. To keep you safe at the rather far-flung and isolated site you specified. An electrical generator; fuel to run it on. And, of course, computer equipment. I think you'll agree that's something of a luxury in these times."

Winterborn sounded amused, even flirty. He was, Mordake knew, never more dangerous. "Yes, Commander."

"For three years, I have maintained the Hobsdyke facility. And for three years, you've been close. Making progress. On the verge of a breakthrough. You'd agree?"

"Commander, please: we're now actually at the point where – "

"You would," Winterborn slowly repeated, "agree?"

"Yes."

"Yes. And yet, here we are, and all I seem to have to show for it are a large number of prisoners who've died unusually prolonged and expensive deaths. So do you understand, Mordake, why I'm not particularly interested in hearing how, once again, you are *close?*"

"But we *are,* sir." Couldn't the bastard have called half an hour later? Mordake would have completed the report; it'd be easier to explain then. He'd never been a good improviser; method and preparation had always been his way.

"I think I've wasted more than enough time and resources on this little pipedream of yours, Doctor."

Mordake's stomach cramped and clenched. *He's going to shut us down. He can't. He can. He will. He's going to. But so close. Liz almost alive again. No. Can't, mustn't, won't let it happen. But there's nothing. Nothing I can do to –*

"Especially," Winterborn continued, "as I now have other demands on them. Does the name Helen Damnation ring any bells?"

"She's dead, isn't she?"

"It seems death isn't what it used to be. But I rather need it to be, in her case. It's very important. Far more important than maintaining a project that promises results but never delivers them. Do you see?"

"Commander." Mordake's legs were trembling where he sat. Now, quickly. "The latest batch will be ready in twenty-four, forty-eight hours. But we had a result earlier this week."

A beat. "A result?"

"One of the pr– test subjects. She went mad, killed herself – "

"Well, that's nothing new, Mordake. Par for the course at Hobsdyke these days, isn't it?"

"But *before* she died." Mordake clenched his fingers to stop them shaking. "She spoke to us."

"And?"

"The Gaffscote language."

"What?"

"She used the Gaffscote language. The broken language. You recall. It basically seems to be the language of the glyphs, but – "

"Yes yes yes, I remember. And?"

"Sir, the subjects only ever see the glyphs themselves. *None* of them hear the spoken language. They shouldn't be able to speak a single word of it."

A silence. "Which means?"

"That it's finally happening. The process is starting to activate the subjects' dormant faculties, for us to use. It's just keeping the remaining subjects alive. We lost another today."

"How much longer?"

"Two days."

"I need results now, Mordake."

"Commander Winterborn, if there's one thing we've learned it's that this has to be absolutely precise. It can only work with *exactly* the right combination of drugs, surgery, sleep deprivation and exposure to the glyphs."

"You knew *that* three years ago."

"Yes, we did. But what we *didn't* know was what that combination was. Imagine…" Mordake bit his lip. "Imagine you've never cooked before and you want to bake a cake. You're told you need eggs, fat, flour and sugar, but no one tells how much of each. You know you need heat, but not how much, how long for, or even whether you bake or grill or fry the damned thing. That's the position we've been in here."

"I see." Winterborn's voice was toneless, giving nothing away.

"We've progressed the only way we could, by trial and error. Yes, we've failed. Many times. But from each failure we've learned something. And now – "

"Yes?"

"Now I think we're finally there."

"You think."

Mordake took a deep breath. "We won't know for certain until the day after tomorrow."

Winterborn sighed. "So in reality we're still no closer."

"If this isn't the right one, the next one will be, or the one after that …"

"And so we're back where we started. Aren't we?"

"Sir – "

"*Aren't* we, Mordake?"

Do I have to beg? Is that it? I will if I have to. But then Winterborn sighed, as if bored. "I don't want excuses, Mordake. I want results."

"Sir, I've already explained – "

"You always have an explanation, Mordake. I'm not listening to them any more. Colonel Dowson will be with you tomorrow."

"Dowson? But he's – "

"One of the best project managers I know. Whereas I, now, need an adjutant with rather different skills."

Mordake licked his lips. He knew what was at the back of this, even though Winterborn was doing all he could to hide it. *The bastard's afraid.*

"If you can convince Colonel Dowson this project can be made to work, Doctor, then he will *make* it work. And if you can't – " Winterborn's voice grew soft, each word precisely enunciated " – if I learn I have been misled into squandering our resources on pseudoscience and fantasies for the past three years, then I shall be most displeased. Do we understand each other?"

"Yes, Commander." Mordake's voice was so weak he barely heard it himself. "I understand."

"Good. You have work to do, I'm sure. Get on with it."

The line went dead.

Mordake sat there, phone in hand. Numb, he watched the light dim, the hands on the wall clock creep round. Then came the fear; he replaced the receiver, his breathing ragged, his palms sweaty, hands shaking. Last came the anger, and that felt better; he could move again. Winterborn was threatening not just him, but Tindalos. *Liz.* Yes, anger was better.

Then he breathed out. "Convince him," he muttered. He went to the filing cabinet, pulled out the first files, and went back to his desk. Then stopped, reached down and opened the desk drawer.

The Night Wolves have heard your call, Doctor. And they're coming. They're coming.

The drawer had never been opened since he'd first shipped out to Hobsdyke and seen what lay in it; there was barely a speck of dust on the dull grey pistol inside.

I won't let him destroy this. All I've built. Not when I'm so close.
Mordake took the gun out, laid it on the desk.
One way or the other, I'll finish this.

*

Winterborn leant back and chuckled to himself. "Well, that was quite fun."

Silence in the empty office, but for the clock's tick. His smile faded. He toyed with the lid of the music box, lifted and lowered it, lifted again. It made a single, desultory chime. He snorted, shook his head, then opened the desk drawer and replaced it.

There were files on his desktop. Three had been closed again and placed to one side. The other was open before him. He traced his fingers across the top page. Instinct, intuition: sometimes it was all you had to trust. His hadn't betrayed him yet. He pushed the intercom button.

"Yes, Commander?"

"I need to contact GenRen Unit Seventeen."

"They're out in the Wastelands, sir."

"I don't need you to tell me that."

"Sorry, sir."

Fear in the young Reaper's voice. Winterborn smiled. "Can they be contacted?"

"Yes, sir. Think so."

"Can they or can't they?"

"I-I'll contact them now, sir."

"Good. Good."

*

Jarrett went still as the red-haired, grey-eyed woman aimed the gun at her.

It was a sub-machine gun, and she had nowhere to run. No chance of getting her own weapon into play. She wanted to beg; refused to. It'd do no good anyway.

The red-haired woman's lips tightened, and she pulled the trigger. The gun flashed. Smoke. Shots.

The bullets hit her like punches; she staggered, fell back. Then the pain shocked through her. She couldn't move.

Lying there, waiting for the final shot –

Jarrett woke with a muffled cry, sat up shaking. Her eyes darted round the inside of the tent.

It was empty. Silent too, apart from her fast, ragged breathing and the brittle hiss of windblown dust on the tent's exterior.

She clenched her jaw and fists and breathed. In, then hold, then out. In, then hold, then out. Even when her breathing slowed, her heart still thudded. She bowed her head, put her face in her hands, sweating. She breathed out. Hadn't had that dream in a long time – years.

Movement; she looked up. A shadow moved on the tent door. She snatched up the pistol beside her, aimed at it.

"Major?" called a voice.

"Yes?" Her thumb rested on the hammer, ready to cock it.

"Comm for you." She recognised the voice now: Sergeant Harper. "From Central Command."

She released a breath. "I'll be right out."

When Harper had gone, she reached for her clothes. She paused only to clench her fists. Over and over again, till the shaking stopped.

*

The pyre smouldered. The bodies were mostly ash, but there were a few pieces she recognised; a six-fingered hand, a skull with three eye sockets. One corpse – female – badly charred but almost complete. When it rolled over as some part of it gave way, for a second it had a face: round, bespectacled, a wart on its chin, a frame of wavy grey hair about it.

Mum —

Jarrett blinked, and the corpse was faceless, just so much featureless, smouldering black.

Just ghostlighting. Nothing more.

"Harper?"

"Ma'am?"

"Break those pieces up, get the fire going again. I don't want anything left."

"Yes, ma'am."

She breathed out, walked on fast. First the dream, now this. She hadn't seen anything like that for years, either. Stay calm. Breathe in. Breathe out.

Three landcruisers rolled into the camp. An officer dismounted, saluted her. "Ma'am."

"Majid. Any joy?"

"Found another encampment, 'bout a mile to the northwest." He nodded to the pyre. "Mutants again. Half-feral, too. We cleaned house."

"Good work. You and your men rest up for a couple of hours. Then you're on perimeter duty so Walton's squad can sweep south."

"Yes ma'am."

Majid saluted, headed off. Jarrett strode to another, parked landcruiser. The radio set was on its flatbed; she picked up the mic, her hand almost completely steady. "This is Major Jarrett. Over."

"Major. This is Commander Winterborn."

Jarrett snapped immediately to attention. "Sir."

"At ease, Major." A hint of amusement. "Major Jarrett, who's your second in command?"

"Captain Majid, sir."

"Capable?"

"He's GenRen, sir."

"How capable?"

"He's my 2IC, sir."

"Good. Give him command of your unit."

"Commander?"

Winterborn chuckled. "You're promoted, *Colonel* Jarrett. As of this moment, you are my adjutant and relieved of your duties in that sector."

"Adjutant?" she finally managed.

"According to your file, you distinguished yourself in counter-insurgency operations during the Civil Emergency. Correct?"

"Yes."

"You did, I'm told, a very good job. 'Brutally effective' was the term your former CO used, in fact. A counter-insurgency specialist is what I need here in Manchester, now; and in terms of your record, I can find no officer better qualified for the task. So get in your landcruiser and report to Central Command forthwith."

"Yes, sir."

"Winterborn out."

6.

"Alannah?" Helen called.

"Careful," whispered Darrow.

"Yeah." She stepped forward. "Alannah? It's me." She held her arms out, hands empty. "It's Helen."

A long silence. Danny thought of the cocked gun, somewhere in the shadows.

"Helen?" a voice whispered.

"Yes."

"Helen?" The voice shook. "Jesus."

"Make your mind up."

A moment's pause, then a laugh from the shadows. Or it might have been sobbing. Then: "It *is* you."

"Yeah."

"I didn't believe it. Thought you were dead."

"I was."

Footsteps shuffled in the dark. The shadows stirred, and a tall, thin woman crept out into the light, a Mark Five Sten gun at her shoulder.

She was hollow-cheeked, with dark, bloodshot eyes and silver-grey hair swept back over her shoulders. Old. Ancient, Danny thought, with hair like that. Had to be. But when she lowered the gun, her face was smooth, like a girl's, except for the crow's feet at her eyes.. Sharp chin, beaky nose. Shouldn't have been pretty. But it was, somehow. Even with the hair. Even if she was old. She licked pale lips.

"You'll have to take as you find me, I'm afraid." Her voice shook. "I'm not… used to people. Haven't seen anyone but Darrow and Ashton in five years."

Jesus. She looked like she'd been wrapped up somewhere, in storage, like an old gun. Her face and hands were white and clean; even the overalls she wore looked fresh.

"They've been preparing me," she said. "Told me something was coming. A change. They mentioned you, Helen. But – didn't really believe them. Not till now."

Helen smiled, or tried to. After a moment, she moved forward. They stood looking at each other for a moment, then embraced.

Alannah's eyes were squeezed shut. Then they opened and found Danny's. "Who's that?"

Helen looked back. "Let her see you, Danny."

Danny shuffled forward; a silence gathered and fell. Alannah kept staring.

"Stephen?" she whispered.

"What?" Helen blinked, stared, but Alannah had already pushed past her.

"Stephen?" Alannah said again. Her voice cracked. The look on her face – the fuck was that look supposed to be? Danny looked at Darrow and Ashton; neither of them looked like they knew what to do either.

She reached out, touched his face; Danny stayed still, tried not to flinch. She started crying, stroked his cheek; her hand was rough. He wanted to run away. *Mad. She's fucking mental.* But she still had the Sten gun in her other hand.

"Stephen," she whispered again. She leant in. Fuck. She was gonna kiss him.

Danny flinched; Alannah went still. She blinked fast, shaking her head. "No. You're not Stephen. Stephen's dead."

She stepped back, staring at him. The Sten came up. "What are you? What the fuck are you?"

"Alannah – " said Helen, but the Sten swung to cover her too.

"Shut up. You're dead. Helen's dead. Stephen's dead. Everybody's dead."

"Alannah," Ashton spoke now, a hand raised. Like a man quieting a dog. "Alannah, it's me. Mike. And this is Roger. You know us. Don't you?"

Alannah stared at him, nodded slowly. "Yeah."

Darrow pointed. "This *is* Helen. You know her. You've fought with her. Yes, we thought she was dead. We all did. But we were wrong. That's all. She survived. And now she's back."

Darrow reached out, put a hand on Danny's shoulder. Danny jumped. "And this is Danny. He's one of my best men."

"He looks like Stephen."

"Like Stephen did. Alannah, you know Stephen's been dead for ten years."

"He looks like Stephen," she said again.

"He can't help that."

"No, but you could help bringing him here."

Darrow glanced at Helen. "I never saw a resemblance myself."

"Could be he's just got one of those faces."

"'Scuse me," said Danny, "I am fuckin' *here*, you know."

Alannah started laughing. It trailed off, became sobs. She stood, shaking, eyes wet, then looked at Danny again. No anger now, just sadness and hurt. Danny understood them, and he wasn't scared any more. He felt something else instead, but he was fucked if he knew what to call it.

"I'm sorry," she said at last.

Danny realised she meant him. "S'all right," he mumbled.

Alannah's face crumpled; she sobbed. Helen, Darrow and Ashton stood, staring at each other. *One of you do something, for fuck sake.* But none of them did.

So Danny ventured forward instead. No one had ever looked

at him the way she had, even if she'd thought he was someone else. She'd given him something, even if she hadn't meant to. He felt something – new, sudden, unfamiliar. He didn't know what it was. Had he felt something like it, that time with Flaps? Maybe.

Whatever it was, it made him want her not to be frightened, or cry. He reached out, touched her arm. Her head snapped up. He nearly flinched but stood his ground. She stared at him. He squeezed her arm gently. "It's all right," he said. "It's all right."

*

Alannah lit a fire; it thickened the air with smoke but eased its dank chill. They huddled round it; Alannah put a pot full with leaves and water over it and let it boil.

Danny couldn't *not* look at her, somehow, as she laid four mismatched china cups out alongside her. She was old, forty at least, with the grey hair and the sharp lines round her eyes, but in a weird way still there was something about her. There was when you looked for it, anyway, and something about her made him want to.

She glanced sideways, met his eyes. He went still, but she smiled. Nice smile, too. Shy. Warm. "I know," she said. "I'm a sight. Should've seen me before the War. Used to be quite the looker."

"Yeah?" Danny never knew what to say when folk said that.

"Oh yes." Smiling and firelight softened her face, made her look younger; for a second Danny saw the girl she'd been. "Old history now. But yes, I had a husband, and he looked a bit like you."

"Did he die in the War?"

"Danny!"

"It's all right, Helen. No. Not that. It was cholera. Contaminated water." The smile tremored on Alannah's face. "He survived the War, years of fighting the Reapers, and a bloody *germ* killed him. I

74

fell apart, a bit, when that happened." She looked at Helen again. "You helped get me back."

"I had help." Helen glanced at Darrow.

"Both of you." Alannah smiled at Danny. "They reminded me I had a job to do. Kept me going. I'm glad they did. Think Stephen would've liked me to live."

"You know he would," said Darrow.

"Hm." Alannah's smile faded, and Danny found himself wishing it'd come back. Didn't know why. Everyone'd lost *somebody*. 'Specially if they'd been around before the War. Every fucker grieved about something; one more shouldn't bother him. 'Cept … somehow she did.

The pot bubbled; Alannah lifted it off the fire. "Shall I be mother?"

"Eh?"

"Sorry. Never mind." She filled their cups, passed them out. Alannah looked at Helen, raised her cup. "Absent friends."

"Absent friends," Helen said.

Danny cradled the cup in his hands. Anything hot had to be good right now. He took a sip; it was all he could do not to puke then and there. "Jesus!"

Alannah laughed. "It's an acquired taste."

"Yeah." Danny spat to get it out of his mouth. Helen took a large swallow of the drink, sighed and patted her stomach.

A hissing, pattering noise sounded; Alannah grabbed for her Sten.

"Alannah – " Darrow began.

"Easy," said Helen. She had a hand on her gun too.

Ashton crouched, gun aimed up. He lowered it, breathed out. "It's all right," he said. "Just started raining."

"Again," said Helen.

"Supposedly we're due a mild winter," Darrow said. "Looks they could actually be right for a change."

Alannah let out a breath. "Damn it." She sat up, let out a high, cracked chuckle. "Sorry about that." She put the Sten down. "Old habit. Not used to people anymore. But apparently I better had do." She'd stopped smiling. "That's what Darrow's telling me anyway. Except I won't. Not without a *fucking* good reason."

Helen put her cup down. "All right," she said. "What's Darrow told you?"

Alannah shrugged. "You were back. Still wanting to change the world."

"Something like that."

"It's been tried, Helen. Look how we ended up."

"You've given up then?"

"Who hasn't?"

"Darrow, for a start."

"Darrow – Roger – does his best to pull kids like Danny out from under. Save a few of them. Fuck knows what *for,* but hey. Oh, yeah – and he keeps me alive."

"And you're happy with that? Living in a hole in the ground?"

"Happy? Who's happy? No one's happy, not now. We take what we can get, where we can get it. 'Cause that's all there is. But we both know what this is *really* about, don't we?"

"Do we?" said Helen. Dead quiet. Not blinking.

"You're not a kid any more, Helen. You're thirty. That's old bones now."

"Look who's talking."

Alannah nodded. "Yeah. I'm old. Old enough to know better. And so are you. But you get more followers with a cause than you do with revenge. Don't you?"

Danny looked from her to Helen, lost.

"That's unfair, Alannah."

"Nothing's fair, Helen. Haven't you got your head round that yet? Stop pretending that's what you've come back for."

"And what have I come back for?"

"You know exactly what you've come back for. Or rather who."

"That's enough."

"You'll put us all at risk, sacrifice us all; get kids like Danny to throw their lives away, just to get revenge on Tez – "

"Who?" said Danny.

"Alannah, that's enough."

They glared at one another; Alannah looked down, sipped from her cup again. "Don't you think I want to kill him too? I lost people as well."

"Who?" demanded Danny. "Who's Tez?"

It was Ashton who spoke. "He calls himself Tereus now."

Darrow nodded, looked up from the fire. "Tereus Winterborn. But he used to be one of us."

"Winterborn?" Danny stared.

"Yes."

Helen folded her arms. "A long time ago I promised to kill him. And yes, a successful uprising would probably do that. But if it doesn't, that's between me and Winterborn. I will *not* put anyone else's life at risk." She held her cup out. "Refill?"

Alannah actually laughed. "Now I *am* impressed. No one else drinks it except out of politeness."

"I've drunk worse."

"I remember." Alannah refilled Helen's cup. The fire crackled; she turned to Danny. "That's why I'm valuable, Danny."

"What, because you can drink this stuff?"

Alannah laughed. It made her eyes crinkle up, which made Danny want to make her laugh again.

"Photographic memory, Danny." said Helen. "Ever heard of it?"

"I know what a photograph is." Danny looked down. They all knew stuff he didn't. Made him feel proper thick.

"I don't forget things, Danny," Alannah said. "Ever. Can be very handy. Or it can be hell."

"Alannah was an intelligence officer," Helen said. "Best we had."

"I had my moments."

"Especially with computers. No one could touch you when it came to them."

Alannah's smile faded. "So that's why."

"Yeah."

"They think I'm dead, Helen. The one thing that would tell them I'm still alive, and you want me to do it." Her breathing quickened, then steadied. "Do you have even the slightest idea what you're asking?"

"Alannah, I know – "

"No. No. You don't. You can't." Alannah glanced over at Danny and forced a crooked smile. "The Reapers caught me," she explained. "They wanted me to talk. I wouldn't. So, they tortured me." She put her cup down; her hands were shaking. "Quite badly, as it goes."

"Alannah," began Darrow.

Alannah tapped her forehead. "Once something goes in here, Danny, it stays. Never comes out. Feels like it was yesterday." Her lips trembled. "If I'm lucky."

Danny felt angry and sad all at once. The fuck was this? He didn't even know her. He'd reminded her of someone. Nowt else. Meant fuck-all. But all the same, he reached out and took her hand.

"Danny – " began Darrow.

Rough, warm skin; he stroked the back of her hand with his thumb, squeezed. She squeezed back, hard, and kept hold of him. And that, he found, was fine.

"You're very sweet," she said. "Helen got me out. Of course. That's the kind of person she is."

"You would have done the same for me."

"Would have. Now, I'm not quite sure what I'm capable of any longer." Alannah gave Danny's hand a last squeeze, let go. "Anyway. You were saying."

"Oh, yes." Helen blew on her brew, took a sip.

Alannah rolled her eyes. "You always could spin a tale out. Come on."

*

"I spent most of the last five years in the Wastelands," said Helen. After…" she trailed off and gestured.

"After what happened at the Refuge."

"Yeah. I…" Helen faltered. "I dug myself out. I was in a bad way. Practically insane. I ran off. Lived like an animal. After a while, I started getting some sense back. Had to really, or I'd be dead. Still a lot of hot spots out there. Anyway, I kept on the move, watched out for radiation, lived off whatever I could find. The important bit was to keep moving. Stopped me thinking." Helen picked up her cup and drank from it again. "Nights were the worst. It all comes to get you when you're asleep."

Alannah nodded, silently.

"Kept having this dream, about… doesn't matter. But one day, I woke up and it'd been four years. I decided to find my way back. But I knew if I did – "

"What?"

"I had to finish what I'd started."

"Revenge."

"A cause. Bring down the Reapers. Things are bad, I know that. They can't ever be what they were." Helen took a deep breath, drank again. "But there's got to be something better than this, Alannah. There's just got to be, otherwise we might as well all be bloody dead."

"Liar," a new voice whispered, but no one reacted; only Helen heard it. It was Frank, of course; Frank standing hand in hand with Belinda behind Alannah and Danny, at the edge of the firelight. "You know why you're still here. Why we didn't take you. You're here to give us Winterborn. Bring us his soul or – "

– or you'll take mine. Yeah, I know. Change the bloody record.

Alannah looked down and no one spoke. The flames crackled. Helen drained her cup. When she looked again, Frank and Belinda were gone. "Anyway," she said, "that was best part of a year ago."

"Jesus. That's what I call a long journey back."

Helen shrugged. "It wasn't just that."

"What do you mean?"

Helen chuckled. "Alannah, in all the time you've known me, when have I ever gone charging into something half-cocked?"

"I see. Preparation."

Helen nodded. "It's strange out there in the Wastelands. There're little groups of survivors. Some ex-rebels. Ex-brigands. Ferals. And then there're the tribes. "

"You've met them?" asked Darrow.

"Oh yes."

"What are they like? You only hear rumours and wild stories out here."

Helen shook her head. "They're scary. Not in themselves so much, as ..."

"What do you mean?"

Helen sighed. "They worship idols and totems, animal and nature spirits, dress in animal hides, and... even how they talk has regressed. They're not stupid, but they're like cave people. In less than a generation, they've slipped back to that level. Maybe that's why the Jennywrens want to wipe them out. They're proof of what we've done. How far we've fallen, or can."

There was silence for a moment or two; Helen gazed into the fire. She shook herself, looked up again. "The Jennywrens have been stepping things up, trying to reclaim more of the wild sectors. It's forcing the tribes and the others further and further back. Some of them have a chance of survival as slaves if they obey. But most of the tribes are heavily mutated, so the Jennywrens slaughter them out of hand."

"How many are there?" Ashton asked.

"If they were united? Enough to be a serious threat to the Reapers."

"But?" asked Darrow.

"They spend half their time fighting each other for territory. But they *all* hate the Reapers. They could unite – *if* we can show they stand a chance. So, there are people who'll fight with us. There are also arms caches out there. I've found a good half-dozen already. There'll be more."

"That why I'm supposed to risk my life?" asked Alannah. "For a few old guns?"

"No. Wish that's all it was."

"Well? Go on."

"There's another Unification Conference planned for the New Year. You know that. The Commanders will talk about merging some or all of the Regional Commands back into a unified authority. One nation, the way it was before the War."

"So?"

"So, there'd have to be a Supreme Commander, controlling the whole thing. And Winterborn wants that to be him."

"I've been in a hole in the ground for the last five years, and even *I* know that."

"What if I told you that Winterborn's trying to perfect a new weapons system? That he's messing with something worse than any bomb? Something that might leave nothing at all, for anybody, anywhere? Not even a hole in the ground?"

"Like what?"

Like miles of grey ash stretching out into eternity. Like that total silence. Like that great shadow, falling across the plain. "Does 'Tindalos' mean anything to any of you? Roger? Mike? Alannah?"

Alannah shook her head. "What is it?"

"That's what I need your help to find out."

7.

The village was a huddle of tents, animal hide stretched on frames of wood and bone. Daubed on the side of each, the image of a fox; above the biggest of the tents hung a real one's head, skin and brush. The pelt was thinning, the hide tattered, the head eyeless and the tail limp and faded. For all that, Helen had knelt to it when she'd arrived earlier; she'd seen enough like it to know what it meant.

The tribes' genesis lay in the exodus from the devastated cities following the War. Among the scattered bands of survivors had been groups of children, many of them from the inner cities and sink estates. These groups were often aggressive, near-feral and operating without adult leadership.

Stranded in the Wastelands and cut off from the rest of the country when the contamination belts settled, some, at least, had survived. With no adults, no one to teach them, the children forgot nearly everything they knew, because all that mattered was survival. Some turned wholly feral; others learned to hunt and gather, retained what rudiments of language they needed to live by, and had children of their own. Their world was the Wastelands, their gods the capricious agencies that offered food, water, shelter and safety from that world's many dangers.

Helen sat back against a rock and waited. Many of the tribe were staying inside, away from trouble; others, braver or more foolish, watched her as she sat. One – a thin, wiry, bird-faced woman in her mid-teens – padded over and stopped a few feet away, looking down at her. She wore hide boots, a loincloth, a belt with a knife in it, bindings across her thin chest, and a headband with a fox's brush hanging down. A warrior. She dug the butt of her spear into the ground and scowled at Helen. Helen leant back, drummed her fingers on the Sterling's barrel and scowled back.

The tribeswoman's mouth pursed. She bared her teeth, lifted her spear to throw. Helen had the Sterling aimed at her before she'd completed the move. The tribeswoman smirked, lowered the spear. After a moment, Helen lowered her gun.

They studied each other in silence, then the warrior grinned; suddenly she looked like the girl she was or should have been. "Wakefield," she said, jerking a thumb at her chest.

Helen smiled back. "Helen."

Wakefield leant on her spear. "Why you come?"

"We both have enemies," she said. "The same enemies."

Wakefield frowned. "Crow Tribe? Hawks?"

Helen shook her head. "Reapers. Jennywrens."

"Jennywrens!" Wakefield turned her head and spat in the dirt.

"Pretty much," Helen agreed.

"But none fight Jennywrens. Too strong."

"Maybe not. If we join together."

"You and us?" Wakefield's eyes went to Helen's gun.

"You. Me. The other tribes. Others."

Wakefield laughed. "Crazy. Other tribes not fight. Jennywrens. Fight us Foxes, yes. Not them."

"The Hawks have said they will." Wakefield stopped laughing. "The Pigs and Cats too. They'll stop fighting you and fight the

Jennywrens if you'll do the same. Tomorrow I go looking for the Crows."

"Crazy," said Wakefield. She turned and looked at the tent with the fox above it. "You tell the Chief this?"

"Yes. I'm waiting to hear."

"Crazy," said Wakefield and shook her head again.

The big tent opened, and a man came out. Helen stood, took two paces forward and held out her open right hand, her left pointing back and to the side. Weapon hand empty, shield hand pointed away. That was how you showed respect.

The man was little taller than Wakefield, and wiry. He wore a belt, loincloth and a foxfur cape whose cowl was crowned by another eyeless fox-head. He was about Helen's age, she guessed, but looked twenty years older, with grey hair and a seamed face. White ridged scars criss-crossed his body, but he moved well for his age.

"Chief Loncraine," said Helen and bowed her head.

"Up," he said.

She stood straight.

Loncraine pursed his mouth and jabbed a finger at her. "You," he said. "Crazy. Crazy ginger." He pronounced both g's hard. "But – life too short for fear. Tell others. We fight Jennywrens, not them. If they do same."

"I'll tell them."

"Good. Now peace between Hawk, Pig, Cat and Fox. Soon peace with Crow too?"

"Yes."

"And war with Jennywrens?"

"Yes."

Loncraine nodded, looked at Wakefield, who stared. He smiled at her, looked back to Helen. "So be it," he said, and walked back to his tent.

Wakefield turned and stared at Helen, then laughed. "Crazy ginger," she said. "Crazy ginger."

*

"Go now?" asked Wakefield.

"Yes."

"Could stay. Feast tonight."

Helen smiled, shook her head. "I'd love to, Wakefield. But I've got to crack on. Need to find the Crow tribe next."

"Crow tribe," Wakefield snorted. "No need Crows now! Have us as friends. Fox tribe, brave."

"I know. But we need all the help we can get."

Wakefield snorted, shook her head, then pointed towards the hills a few miles off. "Go sunset-wards. Past Tooth Hills."

"Okay."

"Across plains, to Red Hills. Find Crows there. Go round – "

"The Black Woods. Yes. Not through them."

"Yes."

Helen nodded. The Black Woods spread all across the Tooth Hills; skirting them would put over an hour on her journey, but the Foxes didn't avoid places without cause.

"Empty village on the plain. Grainford. Empty houses. Clean. Dry, some of them. Good sleeping place."

"Thanks."

Wakefield nodded. "Go safe. See again?"

"See again. Go safe, Wakefield."

The tribeswoman pulled a coarse head-cloth over her brown, bird's nest hair to shield it from the drizzling rain, then darted lizard-quick up over rocks, grass and bare shrubs. Helen blinked once, and she'd lost her. *Fox tribe land* – Wakefield's folk knew its every inch.

"Go safe," she whispered again. Rain stung her eyes. Blinking it away, she thought she saw a man and a small child stood by a nearby tree, watching.

Winterborn, she thought she heard, like a whisper on the wind. *Winterborn's soul or yours.*

Helen wiped the water from her eyes and looked again; the tree stood alone, shivering in the rain.

Ghosts.

Helen slung her backpack on, picked up her gun, and started westward.

*

By the time she reached the village the sun hung low and red in the sky, and she had maybe an hour till dusk.

Grainford wasn't much, probably never had been: a church, a couple of shops, two rows of huddled, windowless terraced cottages with the occasional ginnel between them. But it was safe enough – the nearest she found to a sign of life were a few dead fires – and the interiors of the houses were in good condition, considering. Clean and dry, as Wakefield had said. Helen found a dry room in one of the least damaged houses. She'd unslung her pack and was considering a fire of her own when footsteps slapped on stone outside.

Helen scooped up her Sterling and crept, crouching, towards the window. Before she got there, there was another noise, further off: a landcruiser's hiss and clank.

From the street, a weak cry. The footsteps pattered closer to her position. The landcruiser was further off, but getting close.

Reapers, gaining on some poor bastard. Helen slowed her breathing, flexed her fingers on the sub-machine gun. No knowing how many there were, or what their prey had done. He or she might deserve all that was coming. Besides, she couldn't take unnecessary risks; she'd started things she had to see through.

The footsteps got louder, slowed to a stumble. Helen glanced round the edge of the window.

God knew why the Reapers were bothering; poor bastard didn't have long left. He wore only casual clothes and a scientist's white coat, stained with dirt and blood. Nearly all his hair was gone, and red sores dotted his pale face. He doubled over, vomited. Blood splattered the ground. No protective gear, no Geiger counter to warn of a hotspot; she'd seen a hundred creeping doses, and the story was always the same.

The landcruiser stopped clanking. A hiss. Silence.

"Carter!"

The man in the white coat moaned, showing a mouthful of raw sockets where his teeth had been, and slumped back against a wall. Boots clattered down the street.

Three Reapers, maybe four, black uniforms bearing the white shoulder-flashes of the Reapers' Genetic Renewal division. GenRen: the Jennywrens. They never missed a chance to kill.

The Jennywrens had begun as the Reapers' extermination squads, to murder deformed children in the cities. Dirty work, fit for men under punishment, an alternative to execution. But later the wastelands outside the cities needed 'cleaning up' – by eradicating mutants, ferals and anyone else the Commanders didn't like. And the Jennywrens were good at that kind of work. So they were given advanced military training and sent out, working in small, well-armed, highly mobile units.

By the time of the Civil Emergency, they were a highly efficient fighting force. So the Reapers turned them loose on the rebels. Told them to stamp any resistance out, by any means necessary. Whether they were fighting partisans behind Reaper lines, securing captured territory, invading sectors of Wasteland and slaughtering the occupants or serving as frontline shock troops, they were ruthlessly efficient and capable of anything. In fact, they prided themselves on it.

Helen crouched, peered over the sill. The landcruiser had stopped almost directly opposite, one Reaper in the back, behind a tripod-mounted machine gun. Helen ducked as the barrel swung towards her, breath held, praying he hadn't seen her. When she looked up, the machine-gunner was scanning the houses opposite. The other three carried automatic rifles, all with much more range and power than her sub-machine gun, as well as Sterlings of their own, hip-holstered pistols and bootknives. Jennywren One – the only female – advanced on Carter, who slid to the ground, moaning; Jennywren Two aimed down the street while Number Three, walking backwards, aimed up it, the way they'd come.

"Fucking pathetic," said Jennywren One. "Fucking moron. Calls himself a boffin and he doesn't even think." She paced back and forth around Carter, jabbed him with her rifle. Carter groaned, coughed up more blood; she snorted, tapped her head. "Should've fucking used this, shouldn't you pal?"

One burst would drop her from here. *No, Helen. You're outnumbered and outgunned. Besides, the poor sod's dying; be a mercy when they shoot him.*

"State's he in?" asked Jennywren Three, now kneeling, rifle shouldered.

"Fucked, I'd say," called Two.

"Cut the chatter," said One. Obviously in charge. "But yeah. It's a creeping dose. We might as well've stayed at base."

Helen couldn't save Carter, whoever he was; would only expose herself to risk.

One feinted a kick at Carter, who flinched back, moaning. "Might as well have a bit of fun before we go back, though, eh?" She lowered the rifle, drew her bootknife and grinned; the dying man raised feeble hands to shield himself and mumbled a plea. Jennywren One laughed. "Stupid cunt," she said. "Let's start with – "

Helen triggered a four-round burst, knocking the machine-gunner back and down, spun to aim at Jennywren Three. A buzz in her ear as a bullet flew past. She fired again. Jennywren Three dropped his weapon, pitched sideways.

Jennywren One dropped her knife, grabbed her rifle. Helen fired high to avoid hitting Carter: One fell back across him, but by then Jennywren Two was firing. Helen ducked. Bullets smashed the window frame and whizzed through to hit the walls.

Two kept firing as he ran in. More bullets hit the window, the doorway too. Pinning her down. Then a clink of metal; something flew in through the window, trailing smoke.

Grenade. She picked it up and threw it back, then dived to the ground, hands over her ears.

A percussive thud; the house shuddered. Dust and broken plaster fell from the ceiling; for a moment she thought it was coming down on her, but it didn't.

Up. Up. She got into a crouch. A high-pitched noise in her ears: *eeeeeeeeeeeeeeee*. Over it she heard screaming.

" – fucking fucking fucker bastard – "

She ducked down as a bullet hit the window frame. A couple more flew in through the door.

"Fucking fucking fucker – "

She crawled through the house and out through the back door into a wilted garden. Scattered bones and rags of faded cloth lay in the tangled grass. Through the garden and out into the narrow cobbled alleyway between the house and its neighbour. The noise in her ears faded. Jennywren Two screamed curses, in between rifle shots.

"Fucking fucking bastard – "

Helen risked a glance round the corner when the rifle clicked empty. Jennywren Two lay in the road, the tarmac around him wet with blood from a bad leg wound; looked like an artery had been hit. The shrapnel that had hit him had scored the front of the cottage and smashed the landcruiser's boiler; it bled steam into the autumn air. He was slowing already, struggling to reload. He threw the rifle aside, grabbed his Sterling. Helen aimed and fired another burst.

Helen waited. Two twitched, lay still. A few last wisps of steam rose from the landcruiser's boiler. She crouched and squinted under the landcruiser. The driver lay still. One and Three lay unmoving as well. She kept the gun on them, ran sidewise across the street to the landcruiser, keeping low.

Once she'd checked the driver was dead, she closed in on the other two. Carter moaned "Please," and stretched out a hand; she ignored him.

Three was dead; he'd been hit in the neck and bled out. Jennywren One was alive, barely; when she saw Helen, she fumbled for a weapon. Helen drew the .38 and shot her in the head.

"Please," said Carter.

"Quiet," she said. Stupid. Stupid. Shouldn't have taken the risk. Should have stayed hidden. There could be more.

She listened. Jennywrens usually worked in small, heavily armed groups like this. But you didn't take chances with them. She'd learnt that the hard way.

But she listened, and there was only the wind. They were alone. She only went over to Carter when she was sure of that.

*

When she knelt beside him, he croaked: "Water."

They both knew it wouldn't do him any good. Radiation poisoning stopped the intestines renewing their lining; he'd just vomit it up. She gave him a swig from her flask anyway, looking away as he retched.

"What are you?" he said.

She frowned at him. "What?"

"Killed four Jennywrens on your own. Not many could do that."

"Don't try to talk. You're ill."

"I'm fucked. We both know that."

She didn't answer.

"You're not tribal. Not a brigand, either." He stared at her, breathing, bloody mucus on his mouth and chin. She waited. "You're a rebel," he said at last. "Thought you were all gone."

Her hand went to the .38 then released it. He was no threat, state he was in. "So?"

"Need your help."

"Only one thing I can do for you now," she said, and put her hand to the gun again.

"Not about me," he said.

"I'm listening." Did he have a lover, a child? Was that it? She wasn't making promises yet; couldn't.

"Was trying to find you. Or someone like you."

"That why they were chasing you?"

"What's your name?"

"Helen."

"Carter."

"Yes."

"Mike. Mike Carter. Doctor …" He coughed up more blood. He hadn't long left. "Doctor … Mike Carter. You have to …" His head lolled back for a moment, his wheezing breaths like a blunt saw caught in wood.

"Mike?"

His head rocked forward; his hand fastened on her sleeve. "Tindalos," he said.

She stopped herself knocking the hand away. "What?"

"Project Tindalos," he said. "I was working on that."

"What's Tindalos?"

He turned his head, spat blood. "Weapons system. Special project. Winterborn commissioned it."

"Winterborn?" Helen's lips were dry. "What is it? A chemical weapon? Germs?"

"Nothing like that. Worse."

"Nuclear? Radiological?"

"Worse than that."

Worse? What could be worse? "What does it do?"

"Destroy … all resistance."

"Clear the Wastelands?"

Carter was shaking his head. "Not just the Wastelands. The City, too. Everywhere."

"How? How does it work?"

"It'll destroy everything." Carter's fingers dug into her wrist. "Understand? *Everything*. Every*one*. There'll be *nothing* left. Nothing at all. No one. Make the War, the Bomb – look like nothing."

"But what is it, Mike?" A better question occurred. "*Where* is it? Carter?"

91

A violent coughing fit racked him; he brought up tissue as well as blood. "He won't listen. I've told him he's mad. But he thinks... he thinks he can..."

"Thinks he can what?"

"You have to destroy it," he whispered. "Or we're all fucked. Everyone. Everywhere."

"Where is it, Mike? Where? Where is Tindalos?"

"Tindalos," Carter whispered. "Destroy Tindalos. Dest– "

Another coughing fit; more blood. He wasn't seeing her any more. "Holy Mary, Mother of God... pray for us poor sinners... now and at the..."

And then he just – stopped. His eyes didn't blink; his last breath escaped in a soft sigh.

Helen felt for a throat pulse anyway; finding none, she scraped up a handful of loose earth and used it to cover his eyes.

*

In the morning, she took Jennywren One's rifle and shot Carter in the head with it. He was already dead; it wouldn't matter. She brushed the earth from his face too. She didn't like doing it, but there were still a few brigands in the Wastelands and she hoped the Reapers would think they'd killed the Jennywrens as they completed their mission. Brigands tended not to bother overmuch with respect for the dead.

She kept the Jennywrens' provisions; the weapons and ammunition she greased with mutton-fat, wrapped in sacking and buried in a nearby field. She marked its location on an old map she kept updated as best she could.

Tindalos.

The reckoning was almost due anyway; this latest information only brought it forward a little.

Winterborn.

She marched west, towards the Red Hills.

8.

"Jesus." Danny retrieved his cup. The 'tea' *still* fucking minged, but it was warm; he needed it after that. He shifted on the gritty floor. The damp cold of it seeped up through his thighs and arse.

"So?" said Alannah. "Poor bastard's dying in agony from a creeping dose. Probably half out of his mind with pain. He said Winterborn's name and – "

"We've been over that, Alannah. Yes, I owe Winterborn." Helen's voice was level again. "But I'll see to that another day. This is me you're talking to. When did I ever let my feelings overrule my judgement?"

"Just once. But it was enough."

"Fuck off." Helen glared down at the flames. White breath spilled from her mouth, coiled upwards and vanished. The rain drummed on the ground above; nearby there was a loud spattering noise as some found its way through a crack in the ceiling and poured to the concrete floor, irrigating a mass of spongy weed cultivated by earlier storms.

Alannah breathed out. "I'm sorry. That was harsh."

"Yeah." Helen sighed, looked up. "But true."

"It was five years ago. None of us are quite the same people we were then."

"No." The fire crackled. "Alannah, the Jennywrens didn't go after Carter for no reason."

"Come on, Helen. They're Jennywrens. They'd go after anything that moved."

"They knew who he was. It wasn't random. They'd been tracking him. Alannah, stop trying to dismiss it. Look, I know you don't want to do this, but – "

"Do *what*, Helen?"

Helen didn't look away. "You know what I've come to ask you."

Firelight played across Alannah's face; suddenly she *did* look old. "Yeah."

"What?" Danny didn't bloody get it. "*What?*"

Alannah's mouth twitched. "Computers, Danny. Heard of them?"

"'Course I have." Pissed off at her now. "Not thick."

"Do you know what hacking is? Danny?"

"No." He knew he sounded sulky. Pissed him off even more.

"It's all right," Alannah said. "Doesn't happen much these days. Not many computers left. Basically, a hacker gets information off a computer – whether the people it belongs to like it or not. Sometimes even without them knowing."

"O… kay."

"I was a hacker," Alannah said. "Before the War. And I was good. I was very good. Then I started working for the police as an IT technician… Sorry. That won't mean much. Point is, I should still be able to do what Helen wants. 'Cause that *is* what you're after, isn't it, Helen? You want me to walk out of here, into a Reaper base, get on one of their computers – "

"Not just walk in, obviously. We'd need to get you in and out safely."

"Oh, that's nice of you."

"There's nowhere else to look, Alannah. I've looked everywhere and I've found nothing."

"Maybe 'causethere's nothing to find. Maybe Project bloody Tindalos didn't even *exist* outside Carter's head. That ever occur to you?"

"Alannah, you know Winterborn. Special projects? Secret weapons? You don't think that sounds like him?"

Alannah snorted. "Oh no. That's him all right."

"Alannah, I know what I'm asking."

"Stop saying that!" Alannah's hands shook; she clasped them together. "I told you. You *can't* know. So stop pretending."

Darrow sighed. "I hate to say it, Alannah, but ..."

"Darrow?" She stared at him. "Darrow, please. Don't. Don't ask me to do this."

"I'm sorry, Alannah. We have to know."

"You bastard." She bit her lips, eyes glistening.

Helen looked down; Ashton was studying the entrances. Keeping watch. That's what he'd say, anyroad. And Darrow; fuck knew what went on in his head.

And Alannah – Alannah was shaking. Fuckers, putting her through this. Danny reached out, took her hand again. "If it'll help," he said, "I'll go wi' you. Keep you safe."

Alannah looked at him. For a second or two, there was no one else – just him and her. Then she looked over at Darrow and said, "Where did you find this boy?"

"Under a cabbage leaf," said Danny. He'd no idea where he'd heard that, never mind what it was supposed to mean, but Alannah laughed. For a mo. Then it faded again. She blinked fast to clear the moisture from her eyes. And again, the others faded away; there was no one there but Danny and her. He put his other hand over hers; her free hand covered his.

"You mustn't let them take me, Danny," she whispered at last.

"I won't."

"You have to promise."

"I promise."

Her grip tightened. "Do *you* know what *I'm* asking?"

"Yeah." His throat felt tight. "I know."

"I can't go back there," she said, head bowed. "No matter what, I can't."

"You won't have to. Swear on me life."

She nodded, looked up. "All right." She sucked a deep breath, released Danny's hands and straightened up. "I'll do it," she said, and dragged a sleeve across her eyes. And then she shook her head, sat up straight, and suddenly she was someone else. "Darrow, you'll need to find us a Reaper station, obviously. It'll need to be a good-sized one. A section house at least."

Helen frowned. "Wouldn't any Reaper station would have computer access?"

Alannah sighed. "Helen, *if* Tindalos exists – "

"It does."

"*If* Tindalos exists, it's going to be under maximum security. Yes? So what do you think will happen if we get close to it? Hm?"

Helen pinched the bridge of her nose. "An alert."

"Correct. Somewhere in the Tower, an instrument panel's going to light up like a Christmas tree."

"Eh?" Danny'd seen Christmas trees – overgrown shrubs stuck with bits of old glass and plastic with any colour left in them. They didn't light up.

Alannah, Ashton, Helen and Darrow exchanged glances and smiled; for a second, Danny hated them. Everyone who hadn't lived before the War hated ones who had. From time to time, at least. "Tell you later," Alannah said. "Point is, when that happens, Winterborn will throw everything he's got at us, wherever we are."

"So why a section house?"

"We need to minimise the time taken to have a chance of this working. If we can take the officer in charge alive, we can make him give us the passcodes to get into the system. The more senior the officer, the higher level of access. At a smaller station, we'll be lucky if there's a captain on duty. A section house will have a major, maybe even a colonel. And even then, I'll need time to get to the files you want."

"How long?" asked Darrow.

Alannah pursed her lips. "Back in the day, I could have done it in fifteen minutes. Maybe. Now? We're talking thirty, minimum. Maybe an hour."

"An *hour?* Alannah – "

"You'll have to hold that station for up to an hour, probably against a Reaper attack in force. No, it won't be easy. Probably get everyone killed. But yes, it's the only way." She looked straight at Darrow. "You're the one who wants this. That's what it will cost. Still think it's worth it?"

Darrow looked at Helen, then back to Alannah. At last he nodded.

"Good," said Helen. "I can leave that in your capable hands then."

Alannah stared at her. "What about you?"

"Something else I've got to do. And I might not make it back."

"Oh?" asked Darrow. "And what's that?"

"Do you know of a place called Deadsbury?" Silence. "Well?"

"We know of it, all right," said Darrow.

"Well, I need to go there."

"Are you mad?" Danny said it before he could stop himself, but not even Darrow ticked him off for it.

Helen raised an eyebrow. "Not popular, then?"

"You could say that," said Darrow.

"Everyone knows about it," said Danny. "No one knows what the fuck's in it, but the Reapers send a landcruiser in once a month. Three Reapers, all in monkeysuits. It's the only thing goes in and out of Deadsbury. Nowt else that goes in ever comes out again."

Helen looked at Darrow. "That your understanding of it too?"

"Close. Of course, there are some stories about what's in there."

"Surprised you don't know. One piece of information I did manage to pick up out there. I ran into a Reaper officer out in the Wastelands who'd done a couple of the runs into Deadsbury. Before he died, he told me what they carried."

"Which was?"

"Goliath serum."

Alannah drew in a breath.

"It can't be that," said Darrow. "There are none left. The ones that weren't killed at Sheffield …"

"Even so, that's what he said it was."

"You sure he was telling the truth?" Alannah asked.

"Oh yes." Helen's voice was flat and calm; Danny shivered. "Besides, what else could live in Deadsbury that long? It's still radioactive."

"Which is why you're going in there?"

"It's low-level. Only dangerous if you plan on living there. Like something has for the last four years."

"Point."

Danny was staring from one of them to the other, expecting an explanation but not getting one.

"So what's this Grendelwolf doing there?" said Darrow. "They were fighters."

"Monsters," said Alannah.

"Not all of them. Not in the end."

Alannah flinched, shook her head hard, like she was trying to shake something off. Another of those memories that lodged in her skull and wouldn't come back out.

Helen turned back to Darrow. "Winterborn and his secret weapons again. Having the last Grendelwolf on his side certainly wouldn't hurt his standing. No luck so far, I'm guessing, but he offers a home and a supply of serum and hopes for the best."

Darrow nodded. "Sounds like Winterborn all right. So what's your plan?"

"Get into Deadsbury and find the Grendelwolf."

Darrow raised an eyebrow. "And then? Assuming he doesn't dismember you out of hand?"

"It's not just weapons I've found out there."

"A supply of the serum?"

"Several."

"And if you can't persuade him to switch sides?"

Helen slipped a folded wad of grimy yellow paper from a pouch on her overalls, handed it over. "These are the contacts I've made in the Wasteland. Plus the locations of the arms caches, plus anything I've found out there that could help. If I don't make it out again, I've told the Wastelanders about you, Darrow. I've told them they can trust you."

Darrow gave a crooked smile. "Thanks for the compliment."

"Pretty big chance," said Alannah. "Do you want to die, Helen? Is that it?"

"It's a calculated risk," said Helen. "Besides, the Grendelwolf hasn't just jumped straight in to kill for Winterborn. Could be one of the ones who rebelled at Sheffield."

"Or maybe he likes living the life of Riley in Deadsbury better than fighting for Winterborn."

"I think it's the first category. I got a name for him."

"What?"

"Shoal."

Meant nowt to Danny, but everyone else gawped. "Jesus," said Ashton at last. "Him?"

"Hard to imagine two Grendelwolves with that name."

"Even if it is," said Darrow, "people change."

"Question is," Alannah said, "do Grendelwolves?"

"Only one way to find out," said Helen. "Besides, he's neutral at the moment, but if an uprising kicks off he might end up fighting for Winterborn to protect his serum supply. Better to take a calculated risk now."

The fire popped and crackled.

"Fair point," Alannah said. "All the same, Helen, considering you just come back from the dead, you seem in a big hurry to get killed again."

Helen snorted. "Thanks for the vote of confidence. Darrow, can someone guide me over to Deadsbury? My geography's a bit rusty."

"I'll go," said Danny. Alannah went wide-eyed; he touched her hand again. "I can do that, can't I? We got time." Fuck was he saying? Him and his bucket gob. But it was 'cause of *her*.

Helen. Wanting another chance to show her. But now here was Alannah. Old enough to be his mum. But she needed him. Him and his bucket fucking gob.

"He's right," Darrow said quietly. "We'll need time to pick a target and get our people together."

Alannah's face fought with itself; Danny could tell she hated the idea. "You can always get them to die for you, can't you, Helen? They'll do it for you at the drop of a hat."

Helen didn't answer.

"I got a mind of me own," said Danny. "No one's making me."

Alannah opened her mouth, closed it again. Finally she nodded. "Just be careful, then, for God's sake."

"When do you want to set off?" asked Darrow.

"No time like the present."

"Well, that's true."

"And time's in short supply. Faster we move, better our chances."

"All right." Darrow stood, wincing. First time Danny ever remembered seeing him show any discomfort. "I've got an operation to plan. Alannah, are you sure you can do this?"

"How sure are you about the kids you'll be sending on this job?"

"I've taught them all I can. Now I just have to hope my skills and planning are still what they were."

"Yeah. Same here." Alannah started getting to her feet; Danny held her arm, helped her stand. "Merry Christmas, Helen. You got just what you wanted. Your own way. Again."

*

Darrow handed out two crude, hooded ponchos. "These will keep the rain off. More to the point, they'll hide the guns."

"Thanks." Helen adjusted her hood. The scarf already hid her hair; now her face would be in shadow too. On the downside, it narrowed her field of vision, made it harder to see an oncoming threat. But everything came at a price. Everything.

Darrow turned to Danny. "You know the way?"

"Course." For a second Helen thought his black spiky hair would bristle up, like a hedgehog's. She'd seen one out in the Wastelands; she'd been sat against a dead tree, tearing at a piece of dried meat with her teeth, and a young one scampered by, paying her no heed at first. When she'd approached, it curled into a ball. They were said to make good eating, but she'd left it alone till it uncurled and scampered off again.

"Remind me," Darrow said.

Danny pointed. "Down that tunnel, then get up top. Then down the manhole on Shirley Road." He turned to Helen. "Take us right under the city centre. We'll come up in Northenden. Right next door to Deadsbury. And yeah, I know; keep me head down, don't draw attention, stick to the backstreets."

Darrow half-smiled. "Be careful," he said at last. "Both of you. It's good to have you back, Helen. I want that to last."

"Me too." Did she, though? "Take care of Alannah."

"I always have," he said gravely. "Once you're gone, we'll move her out. Just hope she copes all right."

Helen nodded. To forget five years hidden away underground and just walk out into the daylight was asking a lot. Alannah had always been tough, though. But still. "She'll manage," she said at last, although it sounded almost like a prayer.

"Let's hope so." Darrow nodded slowly. "We'd best get moving, anyway," he said, and went back down the tunnel.

"Come on," said Danny. She followed him down the tunnel to a set of iron rungs leading upwards. They climbed. Danny slid the manhole cover aside; rain fell into her face, and a dazzle of light.

Danny climbed through, helped her out, slid the cover back into place. A thick reek of sewage, decay and smoke washed over her. She squinted round, eyes adjusting; they were in another shantytown, almost exactly like the one by the Irk.

"We goin' then, or what?" Danny asked. Rain drummed on the puddles between the houses. Someone was crying. From elsewhere came a hacking cough; from elsewhere still, a low moaning Helen knew of old, from the mortally injured with no drugs to treat them, too weak now to scream, waiting dully for the end.

To live like this. She shuddered, but took breath and strength from it all the same. This was why she fought – part of it at least.

"Helen?"

"Yes." She managed a smile. "Lead on."

He stepped round the puddles. A leaky boot, maybe. Hers were whole, but she stepped round the puddles too. Just in case he knew something she didn't.

The Sterling bounced against her thigh. Useful if they encountered any Reapers; against the Grendelwolf, of course, it wouldn't do much good. But that was for her to worry about, not Danny. He could take his chances with the rest of them if it came to a battle, but this was practically a suicide run. Besides, he'd reached Alannah; that had surprised even Darrow.

"Here we go." Brambles grew over the tunnel entrance; Danny pulled the trap aside. "Down you go."

The cold damp dark reached up for her. Danny looked the other way. She climbed down fast and crouched in the shadows, clutching her gun, till the light above vanished. Danny dropped down beside her, lit a torch. "This way."

The walls were brick, but in places they'd fallen away. Raw earth pressing down on her. The bodies of the dead. Deep breath. Move on. She picked her way over the uneven floor. The roof was high enough for her to walk upright. There was that, at least.

"So tell us about the Grendelwolves," Danny said.

"What do you know?"

"Monsters, aren't they?"

"Not exactly."

"What, then?"

The earth pressing close around her, the embrace of the dead, naked under the earth, naked in the grave…

You're not naked, you're fully clothed. You're alive. You're here and not there.

She'd vowed not to go into a place like this again. But needs must.

"Can we talk as we go?"

"'Kay." He was taking her mind off it, or trying to.

"All right." They walked on. "Supposedly they developed the project before the War. God knows they wouldn't have had the resources to do afterwards. The idea was to turn ordinary people into – well – super-soldiers, basically."

"How'd they do that?"

"You're asking the wrong person. All I know is that they cracked it before the War broke out. The conversion process – how they changed you – and the serum."

"You were talkin' 'bout that before. What is it?"

A magic potion, Helen almost said. And in truth, it might as well be. "The Grendelwolves needed it to survive. With it, they're stronger, faster, more powerful – could see and hear about a hundred times better – than you or me. And they could heal from almost anything. Something that would kill us, they'd just shake off."

And they had claws. And they had fangs.

"The Reapers started the programme back up again in the Civil Emergency." Stale air. Cold raw earth bearing down on the walls, ready to cave them in. "They took condemned prisoners, or people from the clearance crews, which was pretty much the same thing. The clearance crews removed the topsoil in contaminated areas, without any protective gear – "

"Yeah, I do know *that*."

"Sorry."

The worst part had been the moaning. She hadn't been the only one under the earth. There'd been others, buried deeper. But she couldn't save them. Just herself. Sometimes that was all you could do. Sometimes you couldn't even do that.

She dreamt sometimes that they crawled through the earth and the corpses, the ones she'd left behind, bird-claw hands reaching for her as she broke her nails, shredded her fingertips on the earth above, her lungs full of stale heat and the reek of death, trying to claw her way through. But death was all around her, not to be denied; the hungry dead, the abandoned and the betrayed, reaching up to drag her down.

"So?" Danny's voice snapped her out of it. "They changed those poor fuckers into Grendelwolves, then?"

"Some of them. Most of them died anyway. Only worked on certain blood groups."

"Certain what?"

"You know when someone's badly hurt, you can give them blood from someone else – "

"Oh, aye. Heard of that. Darrow tried it with one of ours a couple years back. Poor bastard died anyway."

"Right. Anyway, there are different blood groups. Different kinds of blood. And the process they used only worked on one of them. Quite a rare one, too. And even if you had that blood group, only one in nine people actually survived the change. But by the end of it, they had an army."

"You fought them?"

"Yeah. We were pushing the Reapers back, taking sector after sector. And then they set the Grendelwolves on us. You'd shoot them and the bastards wouldn't go down. You'd just – annoy them." She shook her heard. "Most of them fought bare-handed. It was all they needed. They tore people apart. Literally." She'd shot one in the face with a Thompson gun; it'd fallen, only to rear up again and come for her.

"Why'd they fight for the Reapers in the first place, then? I'd've just ripped the cunts' arms off and told 'em to sling it."

Helen had to laugh, then put a hand to her mouth. "Without the serum, they died. Simple as that. Once they'd changed, there was something their bodies needed that they couldn't make on their own. Maybe that was deliberate. Keep them under control. Without a regular dose… we found one once, they'd deliberately withheld its serum. To make an example. It had died in agony."

"So what happened?"

"Well, most of the Grendelwolves had been prisoners facing a death sentence. Some of them were rapists, murderers, whatever. But others were politicals. And they were the ones who made it happen."

"Made *what* happen?"

Helen sighed. "It was Sheffield. One of the last big fights in the Civil Emergency. We were pushing the Reapers back and they turned the Grendelwolves loose. But instead of attacking us, the Grendelwolves turned on the Reapers. Ripped them apart. Reapers ended up fighting us *and* them."

They walked on in silence. "So what happened then?"

"The Reapers scrapped the whole programme after Sheffield. Most of the Grendelwolves died in the fighting anyway. The rest of them died without their serum."

"Except this one."

"Yup. He must have had his own supply, then come here when it ran out."

"So you're gonna walk into a death-zone looking for a chinwag wi' something gets its jollies ripping people's arms off?"

"Wouldn't put it quite like that."

"Near enough."

"Besides, I think I know who he is."

"Yeah, you said. Shoal. Who's he?"

"Gevaudan Shoal led the Grendelwolf revolt at Sheffield. He made them turn on the Reapers and kill them, despite everything they'd been trained to do."

"But now he's Winterborn's pet Grendelwolf?"

"Might be doing it because it's that or die."

"Might."

"He's not fighting for Winterborn either, is he? How much further?"

"We're there." Danny climbed up another set of rungs, pushed the cover back. Weak sunlight streamed through. "Least it's stopped raining. Here we go."

Up top, Danny pulled the hatch back into place. He led her out from behind the stub of wall that was all that remained of a house – of the whole street, in fact. The pavement and the road surface were still there – most of the tarmac had cracked and broken off, leaving only bare cobbles – and an old, rusted lamppost. Something clung to it –

"Shit!"

"'Sall right." Danny put a hand on her arm. "It dun't work."

Helen breathed out, nodded. She gave the CCTV camera's dull black lens a last glance, then followed Danny down the ruined street.

*

In a room in the Tower, Reaper Twemlow rubbed bleary eyes, pushed thin fingers through his buzz-cut sandy hair and watched a grainy screen. Hundreds of CCTV cameras all over the city, even after the bombs; you didn't waste electricity to run them all, but usually there'd only be a few switched on at any time – now and then and at random. You couldn't tell if they were on or off by looking, so most folk didn't want to chance it. But there were always some who'd call the bluff, and often it'd work.

Today, though, they were *all* switched on. Commander's orders. Extra Reapers were jammed into the room to keep watch. Twemlow – fifteen years old and a fortnight out of Basic Training – had been on shift here for two hours and it felt like six.

But here was something interesting. A lad about his own age came popping up out of nowhere from behind a wall. That couldn't be right. He must have missed the boy walking up, must have zoned out. But then a woman popped up after him. They came out into the street, and suddenly she looked right into the lens. Her mouth moved; she grabbed the boy's arm.

Twemlow hit the zoom button and her face filled the screen. As she turned and headed off, he rewound the tape, freeze-framed it on her face, held one of the photographs they'd all been issued up alongside it and shouted for an officer.

*

"Here we are."

Wooden sawhorses, topped with coils of rusty razor-wire; the middle one had a wooden sign on it: a crudely-lettered 'DEADSBURY – KEEP OUT' above an equally crudely-drawn skull and crossbones. Beyond them, a heap of broken concrete where a motorway bridge had collapsed years before, now half-buried in dirt and overgrown with grass and weeds. Past that, a bridge over a slow, murky river; beyond that, stunted trees and lines of houses. Deadsbury itself.

Most of the houses were missing a few slates, but they still had roofs. And the road ahead was empty; a bird cawed and flapped across the road, but nothing else. Anywhere else there'd be sewage running down the street, ragged scavengers shuffling up and down it. But not here.

"You sure about this?" asked Danny.

Helen couldn't remember feeling less sure of anything. "Got to try."

"You might not even get a chance to talk."

She blinked, and Frank was standing beyond the barrier, in the middle of the road, holding Belinda's hand. "This place belongs to the dead," he called. "Will you come to us? Or shall we come to you?"

"Yeah," she told Danny, "I know."

"Well, what if – "

"If you're going to be a soldier, Danny, you need to learn one thing."

"What?"

"Don't think too far ahead, or you'll never get anything done. You'll paralyse yourself." She glanced at him. Might be the last she'd see of any of them. He looked so solemn and so young. "Just remember to watch your back. I won't be there to save your arse next time you've got Reapers trailing you."

She nodded back down the road to Northenden. The last fifty yards were empty too; no one wanted to live that close to Deadsbury. "You'd better get back …"

And then the sirens sounded, over the rattling hiss and clank of landcruisers.

They spun. Down the road, the scavengers in the streets scattered out of the Reapers' way.

Danny looked from side to side. But it was all open here. Exposed. Nowhere to run.

The first landcruiser cleared the crowds, surged towards them. Someone shouted, pointed.

"Aw, shit," Danny moaned.

"Want to live?" asked Helen.

"What?"

"With me!" Helen flipped up the poncho, fired a burst at the landcruisers and dragged Danny past the sawhorse, shoving him up the piled concrete. "Move your arse." She turned, fired again. In the lead 'cruiser, a Reaper shouldered his rifle.

"Down!" She leapt up, pulled Danny down in sight of the top. Dust and stone chips spewed from the ground a foot above his head.

"Go!" She shoved him up ahead of her and fired out the Sterling in rapid bursts. The landcruisers halted. A Reaper fell out of one into the road, lay still.

Danny reached the top of the heap; she shoved him headlong over, dived after him herself. Bullets whipped through the air above them. Jesus. She threw off her poncho and ran for the bridge, Danny alongside, gasping "Aw fuck, fuck, fuck …"

Hard not to agree with him there.

*

Kirkwood fired twice over the landcruiser's hood, but the woman and her friend were gone; the bullets only threw up more dust and stone chips. "Bitch," he said.

"Sir," said Colbourne. "Terris is dead. Martinson too. Williams is wounded."

The Reaper she'd hit as they rode in lay where he'd fallen; one of the drivers had slumped over his cruiser's wheel, and a third sat pale and shivering, clutching his shoulder.

"Bitch," Kirkwood said again. "Can shoot though. Not bad going at all with an SMG." He was shaking. Adrenaline. Enough of that. There'd be more of that soon enough. He wiped his mouth. "All right. No way of getting the cruisers past that bloody rubble. No time to try. Be moving like the clappers. Have to pursue on foot."

"Sir?"

"Catch them if we're quick, but need to stay alert. Tell the men to 'ware ambushes." Colbourne was staring at him. What was wrong with the man? "Come *on,* Colbourne!"

"But sir, that's Deadsbury – "

"Don't care if they're the gates of hell, Colbourne. We're going." All to play for here; get her and he'd make Colonel. Adjutant even, maybe; anything was possible, if he brought Helen Damnation to Winterborn. "Or are you a coward?"

"Sir." Colbourne, at attention. "Standing orders state – "

"Interpreting the regulations for a senior officer, Colbourne? Could be construed as insubordination."

"Sir – "

Kirkwood raised his rifle. "Are you refusing my orders, Colbourne?"

"No, sir."

"Good. Because that's mutiny. And I shoot mutineers. Understood?"

"Yes, sir."

Kirkwood lowered the rifle. "Then move the men out. Fast. Wasted enough time already. Leave Williams. Have him inform the Tower we're in pursuit. Request additional units to join us."

Kirkwood made towards the barrier; behind him, Colbourne barked orders.

How far would she have got now? How much would she have gained in the time they'd lost? His trigger-finger twitched. He'd shoot Colbourne himself if they lost her. Deep breath. Calm. How many men did he have left? Colbourne and six Reapers. Against two rebels, one an inexperienced boy, that would be enough.

Kirkwood scrambled up the rubble heap. His men followed, scrambling after him down the slope beyond and across the bridge, into Deadsbury.

*

The world was full of heavy breathing. Inside the NBC suit, it was nearly all Jarrett could hear, and it threatened to fog up the lenses of the protective mask. She made herself go slower. If it steamed up, she couldn't take the mask off. Well, she could, but it would kill her.

Would that be so bad, though? Why else was she here if it wasn't to die with Mum and Dad, her sister, her boyfriend? It was too late to help. As if to prove it, she saw the bodies littered on the ground as she walked.

Tom, her lovely Tom. Tom with his Welsh family and the home that had been his Mum's that he still hadn't sold. Tom who she'd begged and badgered: "Go there. You too, Mum, Dad. Take Amanda with you. You'll be safe there."

Safe, when the bombs fall.

Except, come the day, what did she learn, at her post in the bunker, watching the Met Officer plotting the course of winds, sketching the sweep of fallout across the country? "That part of Wales? Blanketed. Lethal. God help any poor bastard caught in that."

The bodies in the street — thin and wasted, clothes spattered with bloody vomit, most of them hairless, many without teeth. A horrible death, slow and painful and without dignity. Mad, wild laughter welling up in her. Yes, I saved you; saved you from quick clean fire for a death like this.

Don't cry. Don't cry inside the mask. The lenses will fog up, and you can't take it off…

But she was doing. Her hands were moving even though she didn't want them to, unfastening the suit, opening her up to the death around her—

"Ma'am?"

"Uh?" Jarrett blinked herself awake.

"We're here, Ma'am," said Sergeant Harper.

Harper. Yes. Of course. She looked about them. Harper was behind the wheel of the landcruiser; she was slumped in the passenger seat, and all about them lay the noise and hustle of the city. And up ahead of them, rearing twenty-five storeys up into the air, was the Tower.

"Yes," she said. "Yes. We're here."

Of course. Where else? Certainly not the little Welsh town where Tom's mother had lived; she'd never been there. Except in her dreams.

Jarrett got out, grabbed her backpack. "Get something to eat in the mess, Harper, and some rest. Then head back and rejoin your unit."

"Yes, ma'am. Best of luck."

"You too," said Jarrett, striding toward the Tower.

9.

"Sh."

Stood by the window, Helen held a hand out. Danny crouched low, knuckles white on the Lanchester's grip. He kept his finger off the trigger. State he was in, he'd fire half a clip if a rat squeaked.

The upstairs room of a big, grey, fancy house. It *had* been fancy, anyway. Once. Now the carpet had rotted, and crumbling plaster and flaking laths showed beneath the peeled-back wallpaper. Holes in the ceiling. In one corner, a chalky huddle of bones. Danny peeped over the sill.

Below, in a street covered in rotten leaves, the Reapers passed in two groups of four. Each man's rifle covered a different point of the compass; the second group's guns aimed up, at broken windows like theirs.

"What do you rec?"

"Sh." Helen pointed through the window. "Watch."

Danny did and started to understand. A dozen yards down from them, the straight road split four ways. A crossroads.

Wait and see which way the Reapers go.

Danny flexed his fingers; damp with sweat, they left traces on the Lanchester's wooden grip and steel barrel. He glanced at Helen. *She* looked calm. Hands dry and steady on her gun; grey eyes like pools of clear still water.

He was fighting beside her. At last. That's what he'd wanted. But now there was Alannah. Had to get back to her. He'd promised. And then he remembered summat else.

"Shit."

"What?"

"What about the radiation?" Panic – he mustn't, it'd kill him, but the knowledge was there. "How long before we –"

"I told you, it's low level. We'll be okay as long as we're not spending all week here." She glanced at him, gave a crooked grin. "Besides, it's not the radiation we've got to worry about."

"Oh. Yeah. Course." They were going *looking* for the most dangerous thing round here. Kicking himself now for volunteering. *Yeah, I'll take you to Deadsbury.* Fuck fuck fucking fuckarse shitlock bollocks.

The Reapers had taken up positions at the junction, aiming rifles ahead and behind and down both side roads. One made a gesture; a man ran across to the opposite corner.

"We could get 'em from here," Danny whispered.

"If we had rifles and they had sub-machine guns instead of the other way round, I'd give it a try," Helen whispered back. "As it is, they'd cut us to pieces. Now be quiet and watch."

Danny's cheeks felt hot. *You got told.*

Eight Reapers. There were two, now, on each corner. One watched the road behind, the other the road ahead.

"Come on, you fuckers," Helen breathed nearby. "Make your choice."

Danny put the Lanchester down, wiped his hands on his trousers, picked the gun up again.

"There," Helen said. One of the Reapers was pointing. "That's their officer," she murmured.

The Reapers jogged over the crossroads as Danny watched. "Which one?"

"The one giving the orders."

"Oh. Right. Dun't look any different from the others."

"Well, he wouldn't, would he? Otherwise you might as well hold up a big sign saying *'Snipers, come and kill me!'*"

"Oh. Yeah. Course." Danny's face burned again.

Helen smiled. "Hey. This is how you learn. Better make that mistake now rather than when you're in charge."

"Okay. And we're not shooting at him even now we've spotted him, 'cause – "

" – his men don't need anyone to tell them what to do if someone starts shooting." The last of the Reapers had disappeared from sight. "Let's go."

"Where to?"

"Away from them."

"What about the Grendelwolf?"

"Effectively, we're in his house, Danny. I expect he'll find us."

*

The lift doors opened; muffled voices sounded outside. Winterborn tried to block them out and focus on the greying sky outside. On his desk, the intercom hissed and crackled. "Major Kirkwood?" he said through his teeth. "Major. Kirkwood. This is Commander Winterborn. Come in. *Now.*"

No answer; he raised a hand to smash it down, then breathed out and lowered it. "Bloody fool," he said finally and took a deep breath. Remain calm. The rage threatened to overwhelm him; as if Helen's return wasn't enough, now he had enemies within, in the form of idiots like Kirkwood. If Kirkwood angered the Grendelwolf – and he would, breaching the terms of their agreement like that – he'd put everything Winterborn had worked for at risk.

Probably how God felt, Winterborn reflected; he had a special plan for the world – and he saw it in his head, clean, shining and perfect – but needed stumbling, myopic creatures like Kirkwood, with their stupid little lusts and obsessions, to carry it out. God struck humanity with plagues and tribulations out of sheer exasperation: *This time, learn to do as you're told.*

If Kirkwood ever left Deadsbury alive, Winterborn would personally devise the most painful and protracted death possible for him. But that was for later, and to be carried out as a matter of policy. An object lesson: *my orders are to be obeyed.* But to command others, he had to command himself. Another deep breath, then he pushed another switch on the intercom. "Winterborn here. Keep trying to raise Kirkwood."

"Yes, sir."

Winterborn toyed with the lid of the music box, was rewarded with a couple of desultory, off-key *tings*. He sighed. "And send in Colonel Jarrett."

The doors opened; Jarrett entered. "Colonel."

"Sir."

"You're here already. Come in."

Jarrett marched up to his desk. The doors closed behind her.

"At ease." Winterborn studied her; her uniform was still dusty from the Wastelands, her face pale, emotionless. "You heard the latest?" he asked finally.

"Sir?"

Of course. He'd told her nothing earlier. Careful – such small details could topple empires, and Winterborn was in the business of building one. "My apologies, Colonel. Please be seated."

"Sir." Jarrett pulled up a chair.

"Drink?"

"Thank you, sir."

"I have whisky, brandy and water ..."

"Just water, please, sir."

He filled two glasses, passed one to her. "Helen Damnation," he said.

"Commander?"

"You don't know the name?"

Jarrett's face, blank till now, showed a flicker of feeling. *Hatred.* Winterborn suppressed a smile. Oh, yes. This was what Dowson lacked: fire and steel. "Oh, no, Commander. I'm very familiar with her."

"Continue."

"Former rebel leader, sir. Caused us all a great deal of trouble and inconvenience for several years."

"That's one way of putting it."

A smile – a very tiny smile – tugged at the corner of Jarrett's mouth. "Yes, sir. She was killed during the Refuge operation, and – "

"Update, Colonel." Winterborn hadn't enjoyed being on the receiving end of this particular surprise, but there was, he had to admit, a certain pleasure in passing it on. "Helen Damnation is still very much alive."

Jarrett's smile froze and faded slowly; already pale, she grew paler still. She seemed to shrink, as if some vital internal support had been torn out of her.

"Quite," sighed Winterborn. "Reports of her death were greatly exaggerated."

Jarrett's mouth twitched; an attempted smile. "Mark Twain, sir?"

Winterborn raised an eyebrow. "Very good, Colonel." Dowson wouldn't have recognised an allusion if you'd tied it to a half-brick and thrown it at his head with some force, although Winterborn had occasionally been tempted to try. "She's alive, she's in Manchester and she's doubtless planning something. Hence your presence."

Jarrett straightened in her chair, seemed to grow again in front of him, rallying, mouth a pressed white line like an old but painful scar. Hatred. Fire and steel. Determination. *Will.* Oh yes. He'd chosen well. She sipped her water, hand steady. "I see, sir."

So did Winterborn; he watched closely, and what he saw he liked. Rage, hatred and, yes, fear. That was good. The one would balance the other. And above all, he saw control. Winterborn was a student of others, found auguries in the tiniest tics and gestures. Without it, he'd have missed a dozen signs of danger and would have been lying in a shallow grave long ago. All he needed was here.

"As I may have said, I need a counter-insurgency expert. I was told you're the best we have. To say I'm dissatisfied with the officer currently dealing with the situation is an understatement."

"Which officer, sir?"

"Major Kirkwood. Ah, I see you know of him."

"I had the pleasure."

"And?"

"Competent, but he isn't much for subtlety. Any Reapers killed?"

"Eight."

Jarrett nodded. "So he hanged some civilians in reprisal. Am I right?"

"Yes. You are."

"Kirkwood's approach in a nutshell. Bit limited."

"Seems so."

*

Winterborn leant back. Jarrett had met him two, three times before today. Brief, official meetings, but her opinion hadn't changed. He didn't look like much, but she hadn't lived this long without knowing danger when she saw it.

Inside, she was still reeling. Helen, alive; the bitch just wouldn't die. And yet the old dreams had come back to her before this, as if some part of her had already known.

Jarrett had done a hundred things she'd once have blenched at, but the world's Helens never understood that they were *necessary*. You became a weapon, an instrument, forged to the task. Did whatever had to be done. No questions, no doubts; it worked because it was the only way. The proof was in the Reapers' survival, their slow but steady progress, while Helen and those like her were nought but dust.

Except she wasn't dust, not any more. And that knowledge made Jarrett's world shake.

But there were other dangers, and she mustn't overlook them. The biggest, right now, was sat across the desk from her. Helen would love her to make a wrong step here, get herself killed before she could even start on the bitch's trail. That wasn't going to happen.

"So," she asked, "what's Kirkwood done?"

Winterborn sighed. "He found her – effective enough, I admit – but then followed her. Into Deadsbury."

"Oh."

"As you say. At least it's only him and seven others. He requested reinforcements, but luckily *that* didn't happen." Winterborn gestured to the intercom. "I've tried ordering him to withdraw, but all I'm getting is static."

"Bad atmospherics in Deadsbury in general, if I recall, sir."

"Mm. I'd say the chances of our seeing Kirkwood again are fairly slim. If Damnation doesn't get him…"

"…then Shoal will?"

"Exactly. Which is my main concern. I don't particularly care if Kirkwood reaps the reward of his own stupidity, but I still have hopes that our arrangement with the Grendelwolf will bear fruit in due course. The last thing I need is Shoal thinking we're not keeping our end of the deal."

"What about Damnation, sir?"

"I'd like to think she's solved the problem of her continued existence for us."

"With her track record, sir, I'll believe it when I see the body."

"Ah. Yes. There is that."

"And still the question remains: why'd she want to get into Deadsbury in the first place?"

"True." Winterborn leant back. "There's only one thing there, after all."

"My thoughts exactly, sir."

"Well, we can't send anyone else in. The Ops Room is still trying to raise Kirkwood out of there. In the meantime," he picked up the red phone "I'll try again to contact Shoal himself."

He dialled, listened. Jarrett waited. Winterborn replaced the handset. "No answer. Knowing Shoal, that could mean anything."

"So what now, sir?"

"I'll keep trying, as will the Ops Room. In the meantime, there's plenty for you to do. If she's come back to the city, there'll be more like her crawling around. We're working on something to deal with our rebel problem once and for all, but I'll brief you on that later. We can't be sure if or when that project will yield results. Hence Colonel Dowson's absence. He'll either produce some or prove beyond doubt I've been wasting my time. In which case I won't be happy. Either way, Colonel Jarrett, you should be busy for a while. And if we *do* hear from Helen Damnation again, I'm sure I can rely on you to deal with the problem."

"It would be my pleasure, sir." More than that. A necessity, if Jarrett were to know a good night's sleep again.

Winterborn smiled. "I know. More water?"

*

The house's back garden was overgrown, with brown, brittle, waist-high grass. Only two concrete fence-posts remained of the fence dividing it from its neighbour; the others had collapsed, and the wooden fence panels were long rotted away.

In the neighbouring garden, a child's faded, discoloured plastic swing-seat hung from one surviving chain. Most of the paint on the frame had flaked away, the metal badly rusted. A birdbath below the kitchen window, topped with crusted ice. A crow perched on it, studied them, then flapped off with a lonely, echoing caw.

"Shit," Danny whispered. Helen held a hand up for silence, listened. A couple more crows cawed in answer. Their wings clattered. Then silence again.

Danny stared at the swing-seat, the house, head cocked. Helen touched his arm; he blinked at her, dazed. "You okay?" she whispered.

He nodded. "Just… almost got it. What it used to be like here. Before. Could nearly see it for a second."

And she'd broken the spell. "We've got to keep moving, Danny. We're not here to sightsee."

"All right." His voice was sharp. He raised a hand, bowed his head. "I know. I know. Let's go, then."

They crossed the garden, then the house's driveway, hiding for a moment behind the rusted shell of a motorcar, its tyres and windows long gone. Danny stared at it, touched the bonnet, then walked on.

In this way they moved along the row of houses. They were what had been called semi-detacheds, joined together in pairs, divided by the long-decayed fences. Easy enough to pass through.

"Stop here," she whispered, under a weeping willow. "Two minutes. Catch your breath and listen."

They waited.

"Soz," Danny whispered after a moment.

"What for?"

"Snappin' at you. You're right. Got a job to do. Just… this is freaky. This whole place."

Helen shrugged. "Seen places like this in the Wastelands. Didn't get damaged in the War, just abandoned. Fallout, starvation, disease. Take your pick. Lot of it rots, but you're surprised sometimes what's still there."

Mum's old photograph album when she'd been little: *This is your grandfather, Helen. Your great-grandfather, your great-great-grandfather.* It'd bored her then; later she'd grown interested. Too late. If she could've just kept one of those pictures. Just one of Mum.

Mum. Best not to think of her just now.

"But yes," said Helen. "You're right. It's weird."

The rain had stopped; the wind hadn't. She clenched her teeth so they wouldn't chatter. Winters weren't as bad as they'd been just after the attack, but they were still bitter and cruel. Soon the snows would come, honing the wind to a cutting edge; they'd pile up in the streets, bury the unwary and helpless, leave the thaw to uncover them in spring.

"Let's go," she said.

Funny; every corner they went round, every time she turned her head, she expected to see Frank and Belinda, but she'd seen neither of them since entering Deadsbury. Maybe there were too many ghosts for their liking here.

Danny trailed after her, cradling the Lanchester, but she could see him stealing glances at what lay around. *'Tis new to thee.* His breath caught; he aimed up.

Helen looked. A face stared down from a shattered upstairs window. Then she saw it was eyeless and lowered her gun. Some flesh – dried by the icy wind, she guessed – still clung to it; swatches of faded hair flapped around it in the breeze.

Danny swallowed hard. She touched his arm lightly, breathed: "Come on."

They made it through two more front gardens, then reached the one with a brick wall.

"Shit. What do you reckon?" Danny asked.

Helen peered round the side of the house. The drive was empty; she padded over to the wall, which stood about eight feet high, topped with broken glass in a layer of cement. Some of the cement had crumbled; thin white stalactites hung from the sill, many-coloured pieces of glass lay at its foot, but the top was still jagged. Helen glanced down the drive again. "We go round."

"'Kay."

A quick glance back down the road – nothing. She looked up the road. Beyond this house was a butcher's shop, then a fishmonger's, which was on one corner of another crossroads. Beyond that: more shops, their awnings faded, everything frozen in time. Another picture in a book of Mum's: a fly trapped in amber, held there for millions of years. She stepped out and –

"Helen!"

She spun, ducked; Danny had already dived back into the drive. Down the road where she'd already looked but she'd missed it, Danny hadn't – at the corner, at that last junction, there was a Reaper, rifle at his shoulder. He shouted; she dived as the muzzle flashed. The bullet whined overhead; brickwork shattered behind her.

She fired as she hit the ground, bullet cases jumping out of the gun's breech – not that she'd much chance of hitting the bastard with a Sterling, not at this range. Danny, knelt behind the driveway's heavy stone gatepost, fired two short bursts at the Reaper, yelled without looking at her: "Go! Go! Go!"

He trusted her to know what to do, not to let him down – but, Christ, did she, anymore? She'd almost walked into that bullet. No time for questions now – she ran up the street, zigzagging. Another bullet whined past. The crack of rifles. The Lanchester's clipped stutter.

Two empty shops between her and the corner. A bullet whined past; stone chips spat past her. She threw up an arm to shield her face, her eyes –

– then she was at the corner and round it, back pressed flat to the tiled wall. A moment's relief, and then remembering; *Danny*.

Looking round the corner: he was still in the driveway, firing at the Reapers. There were three of them now; one took cover behind the rusted shell of an old postbox, the others scurrying across the junction to the far corner. Triangulating their fire.

They'd been waiting. Must have known where she and Danny had gone. How? She must have fucked up somewhere...

Didn't matter now. Danny did. She knelt, shouldered the Sterling. "Danny!" He glanced up the road at her. Fuck. He was a boy. *What was I doing, bringing him out here?* "Run to me! And fucking *weave!*"

He fired two more bursts at the Reapers then did a fast tuck and roll, out of her line of fire, into the road – then up on his feet and running, zigzagging as she had. She started firing, burst after short, neat burst. One spare clip for the Sterling; after that, she was down to the revolver. Don't think about that. Time had almost stopped; only Danny moved. He ran towards her, but so slowly. Didn't seem possible they could miss him.

Muzzle flashes down the road. Danny weaving. Her shooting and shooting, despairing of a round even coming close. He was nearly there, but time seemed slower still; he *had* to take a bullet, now, it was inevitable – so near and yet so far. She'd promised Alannah. If he were hit –

He dived, hit the pavement, rolled again, came up beside her. He actually grinned, face flushed. Adrenaline. "Where now?"

Bullets chipped at the corner of the wall, zipped across the junction. The bastards were making sure she and Danny only went one way. She peeped round the corner. The three Reapers down the road gave the covering fire; two more now ran along the pavement, with another pair behind them. "Don't get cocky. Just follow me."

They ran fast up the road they were driven onto – Wilmslow Road, a sign told her. It was a straight line. No side-roads, just dead-end alleys.

The rusted hulks of parked cars. Shopfronts. A bistro – whatever that was, or had been – a pub, a bank, a newsagent's, a Chinese takeaway. All empty, faded, dead. Ghosts. Naked trees looming each side of the road, their roots swelling underneath the surface, cracking the tarmac.

The street was open and exposed; they'd be cut down in seconds. Hide behind one of the rusted cars at the roadside? Stupid – rifle bullets would punch through them like cardboard. The buildings, the shop fronts – *pick one, any one.* Hide. The only chance. Hide and hope the Reapers passed.

She pointed. "Here!"

In through the door. A reception counter; behind that, desks with stacked plastic trays and computers filmed with grime. And a flight of stairs. "Up here." Danny scrambled after her.

Dirt everywhere, but the damp air made it soggy. They didn't disturb it. Something scratched at the corner of her mind. *Something important, Helen. You need to know.* No. No time now; she swatted it aside.

The top floor. A landing; three rooms. Straight ahead, a toilet. Danny stared at the bowl, fascinated. The second, to the side, was little larger, packed with filing cabinets; a tiny barred window overlooked the back yard.

The front room – it gave a good view of the stairs. They'd either have their backs to her and Danny or have to walk up backwards. It wasn't much but it was an edge. Any edge was good, however tiny. Could make the difference between life and death.

She waved Danny into the front room. Laminate-topped desks, plastic chairs, filing cabinets. A blackened mound of rotted paper on the floor. She dived to the floor beside the window. Flaking paint on the windowsill, the wood below crumbling. She peeped over it; the window itself was cracked, but, amazingly, whole. Good view of the street. No Reapers yet. It'd take time for them to search every building.

She checked the Sterling's clip. Six rounds left. "How are you for ammo?"

"Half a clip here. One spare."

She inserted her last full magazine; he put the half-clip back into place. "Still got your pistol?" she whispered.

"Yeah. No spare rounds, though."

Her .38 was fully loaded, too, with eighteen loose rounds she could split with Danny. Not that it would change the big picture.

"What d'you wanna do?"

"Wait. Hope they go past."

"An' if they don't?" Danny breathed out through his teeth. "Should've gone out the back, kept running."

"Sounds carry out here. It would've drawn them. We need one of those rifles. Even things up a bit. They've got more range than these things."

"You're bleeding."

"I – " A warm trickle at her neck; her fingers traced it back to a small nick above the right eyebrow. "I'll live," she said.

Danny looked round, raised his eyebrows. "You reckon?"

Helen bit back a laugh. Danny grinned. She put a finger to her lips, peeped over the sill again. The Reapers were moving up the leaf-littered street.

That funny scratching feeling again. Something she'd missed.

They moved in pairs, the others covering their approach. Like a machine, well-oiled... and observant.

A Reaper stopped outside their building, pointed at the road. At the leaf-littered road. *Leaf-littered*. The scratching intensified. And then she saw.

"Oh, fuck," she said.

"What?" said Danny.

"The leaves," she said. "That's why they doubled back before."

"Eh?"

"The road into Deadsbury; there were dead leaves all over it. We left a trail in them. They couldn't see exactly where we'd gone, before, but they knew we'd turned off the road. So they pretended not to notice, went on ahead and then doubled back."

"Oh shit."

Idiot, fucking idiot. A stupid error, the stupidest. That's how they found you before; that's how they've found you now. Who wouldn't spot a trail you'd left in twenty autumns worth of dead, fallen leaves? How hard could it be?

The Reapers were outside. One of them looked up at their window, pointed.

"Danny, move, *now –* "

The window exploded above them, glass splinters raining down.

*

He stroked the guitar's smooth wooden neck, started to play.

Each instrument raised a different ghost. With the mandolin it was Michaela; pillowed on Jo's breast after birth, graduating from University, marrying Keith. The fiddle brought back David; the accordion, Gloria. The piano, Mum and Dad. And the harp, Gideon. The dead. The lost.

But the guitar – the guitar brought back Jo. Always Jo.

Before Michaela, when it was just the two of them. Midnight in December; doors and windows shut tight, a gas fire glowing in the grate. Music in the CD player. Sips of smoky single malt. Then he switched off the CD, lay on the couch with his guitar and played for Jo, while she stretched out on the hearthrug like a cat, smiling. Crawling over to him like a cat as the tune died;

holding up a sprig of mistletoe. *Under the mistletoe. You've got to kiss me now.* And he'd laid the guitar aside.

Afterwards they'd huddled together beneath a blanket and didn't speak. Nothing needed. Jo had drifted off; he'd lain stroking her hair as sleep came for him too, thinking *this is perfect–*

There were gunshots, and a scream.

And he lay in an empty bed, in cold, still darkness. The church was silent. He blinked. Another burst of shots rang out.

How far away? Not far enough. *My territory. My home.*

Jo was gone. She'd never been here. He'd known that but hadn't wanted to remember it. And now he had, there was anger. Anger at the illusion's breaking; at the reminder it *was* an illusion, at his own reliance on it. He had one dependency as it was; that was more than enough.

More shots rang out. His jaw clenched. He breathed deep.

Admit it. The excitement makes a nice change.

He got up, replaced the guitar carefully in its spot, then strode to the door and out into the ruins beyond.

*

Kirkwood crouched inside a shopfront, rifle at his shoulder. A muzzle flash in the shattered window above; he fired twice, ducked as another burst came back in return.

Out in the street, Colbourne and three Reapers fired too, raking the shop front. Kirkwood aimed again. Let the bitch show her face. Then he'd blow it off. Now *there* was a thought. Not just the commander of the squad that killed her, but the one who fired the actual shot – what reward couldn't be his if he managed that?

Bring the corpse back with him, of course. Proof positive this time. No possibility of a mistake.

"Go!" shouted Colbourne; three more Reapers ran for the shopfront, kicked in the door.

A crash from downstairs, the thunder of boots on the floor. Danny scrambled to the doorway, keeping low, aiming the Lanchester at the staircase. Any minute. Any minute.

Bullets flew up the staircase, punching into the frame of the toilet door at the top. Running footsteps; the back of a Reaper's head came into view. *Wait, Danny. Wait.*

The Reaper came up the stairs, hugging the wall. He turned, his gun sweeping the landing, towards Danny.

Now.

The Lanchester kicked back with a dull chatter and spat out a flurry of spent brass: the Reaper threw his arms up, dropping his rifle, and collapsed on the stairs. Shouts from below and fresh gunfire, punching holes up through the floor. Danny threw himself back, rolled away. Holes erupted in the withered, faded carpeting he'd laid on a second before, spewing dust and splintered wood into the air.

Coughing in the dust, eyes streaming, Danny scuttled back to the door. Another Reaper ran up the stairs, arm drawn back. He threw as Danny fired; something round and black arced over the banister rail, landed in the doorway as the Reaper fell –

"Grenade!" Danny remembered what Helen had done with the Jennywren's grenade, back in the ruins of Grainford, and he got up, heading for it –

Helen moved from window to window. They were shooting at her muzzle flashes, so if she was never in the same place it was better. Fire, duck, move, fire again. The magazine must be nearly empty now; after this, there were the scant half-dozen rounds in the other one, and then her revolver. But you didn't think about that; you just went moment to moment.

"Grenade!"

Turning at Danny's shout, seeing him run towards the hissing thing in the doorway.

"Danny, no!"

Slow time again. She got up, ran forward, but it was like running through mud. He'd heard her story and he was going to try to do what she'd done. And she'd have to tell Alannah why he was dead.

He kicked at the grenade and it went through the door. A moment later she'd hit him with a tackle, knocking him sideways, away from the doorway, rolling –

*

A dull thud, and Kirkwood saw the upper windows blow out in a cloud of splintered glass, dust and smoke.

"Move in!" he shouted. "Move in!"

Someone was calling his name. At his belt, his personal communicator was crackling. Not now. Not now. This was important. History was being made here, and he was making it.

"Move in!"

*

A humming in Danny's ears. He could hear someone shouting. Bullets punched into the walls overhead; dust and smoke everywhere. A thumping sound; more footsteps on the stairs.

He coughed, spat, reached for the Lanchester, but everything felt so fucking *slow*, like he was buried up to his neck. Footsteps on the landing. Shots flew through the door, smashed into the far wall; a Reaper came through, rifle sweeping round towards Danny. Two shots rang out, knocking the Reaper backwards. Helen stepped past Danny, fired again; the Reaper's visor shattered, blood flowering across the peeled wallpaper and crumbling plasterboard.

The body slid down. Helen ran to the doorway and crouched, aiming the revolver at the stairs. Danny moved to her side with the Lanchester, but no one came up. Helen picked up the dead man's rifle.

"Move in!" a voice shouted outside.

Someone screamed. Someone else let out a short, choked cry. Then nothing; just the wind, blowing down Wilmslow Road.

"The fuck?" Danny whispered. His palms were sweating; he dried them on his trousers.

There was no more shooting. A piece of splintered glass dangled from the window frame, fell and smashed with a tinkle on the floor.

Helen inched towards the window. Danny followed.

Outside, someone called: "Colbourne?"

*

"Colbourne?" Kirkwood moved back from the window. There was a tremor in his arms. A shake in his hands. No. He wasn't *shaking*. That implied fear. He wasn't afraid. He was on edge. In the zone. "Colbourne!"

No answer. Only silence, and the keening winter wind.

A noise outside. Something gritting underfoot.

Kirkwood rose; shouldered his rifle. He was a Reaper officer, by God. Fought worse enemies than that damned woman. Faced worse odds. What was there to fear? He couldn't see anything, or hear anything. Was he afraid of silence?

Except there shouldn't have been silence. There should've been shots and running feet. His men should be obeying his bloody orders.

Kirkwood started forwards. There's nothing out there. And if there *was,* he'd face it. By God he'd face it. Whether it was Helen Damnation or –

No, he wouldn't say it. Not even to himself.

He feared nothing. He was a Reaper officer.

"Colbourne!" He was almost at the shop's doorway now.

Something huge and dark filled the shattered door-frame; before he could react, it had seized the barrel of his rifle and plucked it from his grasp.

"*Oh, Spartan dog,*" it said in a rumble of thunder, the growl of a hungry beast, the grating of stone, "*more fell than anguish, hunger or the sea…*"

"Colbourne!" Kirkwood backed away, fumbling for the Browning at his belt. "Where the hell are you?"

"Dead," said the dark thing, tossing the rifle with a clatter to the cracked pavement outside.

Kirkwood stumbled backward. Someone whimpering. No. Wasn't him. Couldn't be him. No. No. His legs were wet. Oh god, no. Not that. Not in the face of the enemy.

The PC at his belt crackled. "Kirkwood?" it said. "Major Kirkwood, report!"

The dark thing stepped through the doorway, feet crunching in broken glass. Kirkwood backed away.

"And so," said the dark thing, "are you."

*

More screams from outside. They couldn't have lasted more than a few seconds, but it felt like longer.

"The *fuck* was that?" Danny whispered.

Helen swallowed. "Someone dying."

"I know *that!*" He was white. "What the fuck *of?*"

"I'm guessing it wasn't old age."

"Aw, *fuck.*"

Helen went to the window, keeping low. Just in case. She had a fairly good idea what she'd see, but she wasn't taking chances. She'd fucked up twice today already; stupid elementary errors that could have killed them both. It shook her to think she could have made them. And she was planning to lead a new rebellion? Christ, she'd be kinder shooting her own people. It'd be quicker; no torture at least.

No one shot at her. She surveyed the street. Four bodies lay in it, all in black Reaper uniforms. A Reaper helmet lay in the gutter. Her stomach rolled; the helmet wasn't empty.

The wind whistled, keened and moaned.

Danny moved to her side. "Fuck me," he whispered.

"Yeah."

"What now?"

"Two choices."

"What are they?"

"We stay here and wait for him to come to us."

"What's the other?"

"We go out there and look for him."

"Are you mad?"

"It's why we're here, Danny."

"Why *you're* here."

"I know."

Danny rubbed his mouth. "Well, not like you twisted me arm or owt. I volunteered. Don't suppose we could just try tiptoeing out?"

"He knows we're here, Danny. And this is his territory. How far do you think we'd get?"

The stairs creaked. They stared at them, but nothing happened. Danny released a long sigh. "Fuck it. Let's get it over with, then."

"Okay." At least she wouldn't have to face Alannah if they both died. Christ. What'd she been thinking? "Let's go."

They walked out onto the shattered landing. Half the ceiling had come down, broken plaster scattered on the carpet. It crunched underfoot.

One dead Reaper on the stairs, another at the bottom. They stepped over them both, went to the shattered front door.

"Danny?"

"Yeah."

"You did a good job. I'm sorry."

Despite it all, he flushed; more pride than embarrassment, she hoped. They walked through the devastated shopfront and out into the street.

There was blood on the road; it clung to her boots. A rifle lay on the pavement outside the shopfront opposite. A thin, cold, tinny voice echoed from inside. "Kirkwood? Major Kirkwood! Report!"

That voice; she knew it.

"Helen?"

"Mm?"

"What's a Grendelwolf look like?"

"Tall. Built like a brick shithouse. Very pale. They had weird eyes. Yellow." She peered inside. An arm lay severed on the floor. Further back, something else that glistened; there were glints of white bone. "They could see in the dark. Another thing that made them so dangerous."

"Long black hair? Long black coat?"

"No. Tended to wear military uniform." She could see what'd been done to the last of the Reapers now; it was hard to look away, even though she wanted to. "Why?"

"'Cause that's what this bloke here looks like."

"That's not fu– "

"Good afternoon."

Helen yelped, spun round, raised the Sterling. The voice wasn't Danny's: it was deep and rich, low and sepulchral; it rumbled like thunder.

He stood outside the shop they'd just emerged from. He must have stood six feet six in height, with shoulders to match. Yes, he had those yellow eyes. She thought of a wolf she'd once seen in an old film. Grace and beauty mixed with something pitiless and terrible.

"I have that effect on women," he said, smiling.

Black trousers, black boots, black sweater. A long, black coat. Black hair, too, very long and very fine, blown easily about his face in the wind.

Her mouth was dry, her stomach clenched. The gun was at her shoulder. "We don't mean you any harm," she said at last.

He chuckled; his teeth were very white. "I'm sorry. That's the funniest thing I've heard in some time." The smile faded. "By the way – if you want to live, point that gun somewhere else."

Danny had already put down the Lanchester. Helen laid down the rifle.

"Oh no, you can hold onto it if you want. It's about as dangerous to me as a dead cat. I just don't like them being pointed at me. It's impolite." He stepped off the pavement and took a few steps towards her. Muscled but lean, like a black river flowing. Danny backed away, drew close to her.

The pale eyes held her and seemed to grow, till they were all she could see. "My name is Gevaudan Shoal. You've been looking for me, and now you've found me. Perhaps you'd like to tell me why, before I eat your hearts."

10.

The Grendelwolf studied her. The pale eyes didn't blink: there was a wild look in them, a cold and distant stare. She knew it too well from battle, had seen it in her own reflected eyes; when the adrenaline had kicked in, you didn't want the fight to stop.

His chin lifted. What did he see, and what did it mean to him? A cat, toying with a mouse? She hadn't felt this helpless since – not for five years, anyway. If he came for her, or Danny, there'd be nothing she could do.

When she'd been a little girl, there'd been a picture book. Red Riding Hood. The Big Bad Wolf. The angry, snarling face. Frightening, but she'd never been able to look away from it. When she was a bit older, they'd gone to Chester Zoo for the day, and she'd kept going back to stare at the wolves. She'd been scared of them to start with, but that had faded as she'd watched them pacing their enclosure. Their faces had been sombre rather than cruel; their sleek grey bodies had suggested fierce strength rather than savagery. Gevaudan Shoal brought them very sharply to mind, and not just because his eyes were yellow like theirs.

But now he smiled again. Did that mean good or bad, life or death? She couldn't tell. But he blinked; the wild stare started fading. Whether she was any safer with what it left behind remained to be seen.

"Kirkwood? Kirkwood!"

Who was that? Oh yes: the cold, tinny voice from the communicator. She knew the voice, but couldn't remember where from. Didn't really matter now.

"Excuse me for a moment," Gevaudan said.

Helen blinked; he strolled past her and Danny and in through the shop front. He emerged holding the communicator. "Major Kirkwood!" it said.

None of this felt real. She'd only ever met Grendelwolves in battle before; all she'd seen had been teeth and claws. She'd never spoken to one. Too busy trying to kill them – usually with high explosives or artillery – before they killed her. Never really gave you a chance to notice their looks. This one wasn't handsome, not exactly, but there was something about him that, despite everything, made her notice him in a way she hadn't noticed a man in years.

Gevaudan raised the communicator to his lips. "Good afternoon, Winterborn," he said.

Winterborn. Of course. Christ, in that long, frozen moment she'd forgotten even that.

A pause. "Shoal?"

"The same."

"Where's Major Kirkwood?"

"Somewhat indisposed."

"Indisposed?"

Gevaudan glanced back at the shopfront. "Well, he's dead."

*

Winterborn nodded slowly, licked his lips. They looked dry, thought Jarrett. The hand not holding the mic twitched and flexed on the desktop. "That's very indisposed," he said at last.

"Indeed."

Winterborn settled back in his chair, lips pressed white. "Shoal." He sounded almost wheedling. "Shoal, I want you to know that Major Kirkwood had no authority from me to enter your territory. He did so in direct violation of standing orders."

"That was obvious. You're many things, Winterborn, but you're not stupid."

Winterborn raised an eyebrow at Jarrett, tried to smile. It wasn't convincing. "Do you think that was an insult?" he asked her.

"Couldn't possibly say, sir."

Winterborn spoke into the mic again. "If he had got out of there alive – "

"He'd be just as dead when you got through with him?"

"Most probably."

"Most probably?"

"Yes." Winterborn licked his lips again. "Yes, he would. Shoal – "

"Winterborn?"

"He was in pursuit of somebody."

"So I gathered."

"Have you seen – "

"I'm sorry, Winterborn, you appear to be breaking up."

"Shoal – "

"I have better things to do with my time right now, Winterborn. I'll get back to you."

"Shoal?" There was only a hiss of static in reply. "Shoal!" Winterborn was on his feet, shaking, face white. A tic started below his eye; he reached up and rubbed at it, breathing hard, then closed his eyes for a moment. He breathed out and tossed the mic onto his desktop. His hands clenched, then slowly opened. His head swivelled, like a machine's, towards Jarrett; his eyes opened, not blinking. "I think," he said, "I'm finally starting to lose patience with him."

"Sir," said Jarrett.

Winterborn didn't answer, just kept staring at her. There was a rumour Jarrett kept hearing; that from time to time Winterborn had a woman brought to his quarters. Some said he tortured them, others that he put his head on their breasts all night, crying for his mammy. But all agreed that those women never lived to see morning.

Jarrett found the second version easier to believe, always had. Torture was everyday; no one would care. But weakness – weakness had to be hidden, the witnesses silenced. And now she was a witness. Winterborn liked others to think he negotiated with Shoal on more or less equal terms; she'd seen the Grendelwolf's open contempt for him. The kind of thing no one could be allowed to know.

In the silence, the clock ticked.

Not like this. She wouldn't die so stupidly, not with Helen still alive. Be easy to beat her this time, if she could get past this; Winterborn had colder blood by far. The rebels liked to see themselves as the good guys; sentiment, crippling them –

Weakness.

There it was, the chink in the armour. And an instant later Jarrett saw it all, saw how she'd win, and smiled.

*

Gevaudan tossed the communicator aside; it clattered on the broken road. "Now. Where was I?"

"Something about eating our hearts," said the woman.

"Don't remind him!"

"And you are?" The Fury hadn't quite left Gevaudan; the urge to slash, tear, destroy made his fingers twitch. The boy blanched, stepping back, under his gaze.

The woman stepped between him and the boy. "Leave him alone."

Was it the set of her jaw, her clear, direct stare, the lack of visible fear she faced him with? Something, anyway, reminded him of Jo. But Jo had never looked at him like this, with the anger and contempt you owed those who preyed on creatures weaker than themselves. The last of the Fury drained away, leaving only resentment and self-disgust. The second, for now at least, was stronger. Gevaudan took a deep breath.

"You're right, of course." He inclined his head. "I apologise."

The woman blinked.

"I've been alone here for many years. I treasure my privacy. I resent those who invade it. However, I am not a sadist. Nor do I like such people."

"So, why aren't we dead yet?"

"I'm here because I have to be," Gevaudan said. "That doesn't mean I don't despise the Reapers. This little business at least gave me an excuse to rid the world of few of them. They must have wanted you badly to follow you in here. But then, there must have been something you wanted too."

"To speak with you."

"I see. Well, you have me at a disadvantage. You know me, but I don't know you."

She nodded to the boy beside her. "This is Danny Morwyn."

Gevaudan smiled at him; Danny looked as though he'd faint on the spot. *You've been alone too long,* Jo would have said. *This is what happens when you cut yourself off. You forget how to be with people.*

"And you?" Gevaudan asked.

She loosened her headscarf; red hair caught the failing winter light. "I'm Helen Damnation," she said, chin up; not giving an inch, yielding nothing, no matter how hopeless the odds. So like, but unlike, Jo, and so rare, foolish or wonderful; all he could do was smile.

*

"What's so funny?" Helen demanded, then wished she hadn't. Menacing first, apologetic next, mocking now; couldn't get a handle on the bastard. Maybe he was crazy. Christ knew what being a Grendelwolf did to your head. And if he hadn't been mad before, he'd been living here alone for the last five years.

Gevaudan's smile faded. "Nothing. Explains why the late Major Kirkwood followed you in, that's all. I assume he was an ambitious man. As corpses go, I have to say you look rather healthy. Not to mention active."

"Eh?" muttered Danny.

"Death isn't what is used to be," Helen said.

The smile hovered on the Grendelwolf's lips again. He could attack at any second. For all that, her fear was ebbing – not gone, but fading. There was something about that smile she rather liked; that and the sleek build and high-cheekboned, saturnine face.

God, not this, not now. Behind Gevaudan she saw movement; Frank's face, white above the Grendelwolf's shoulder, lips tight and nostrils flared. She managed not to laugh at Frank's comic wrath, or at the absurdity of desire's stirring, in this time and place and with this man – if that's what he still was – after so many years dead to it. No time for it now; push it down, lock it away, all thought of how it might feel to kiss that thin mouth, or to test the strength of a body that might never tire...

"All right," he said, "you've impressed me. A little. I've heard of you."

"Likewise." Frank had disappeared. Good; perhaps he'd realised she didn't need distractions just now, not if she was to give him what he craved.

"That's what I thought. The answer's no."

She blinked. "I haven't asked – "

"You don't have to. You were a ringleader in the Resistance. I fought against the Reapers at Sheffield. In all modesty, I'd be an asset to any military campaign. It doesn't take a genius to guess why you're here. But I don't fight other people's wars for them anymore."

"I see."

"On the other hand, we still have things to discuss, don't we?"

*

Gevaudan saw the puzzlement on her face, watched her eyebrows lift. "Do we?"

Again, so unlike Jo, yet so like. So utterly herself, somehow. A long time since another's opinion had mattered to him. And perhaps the time was ripe for someone to break the monotony of this life of his. A little excitement.

"Oh yes. For instance, there's the question of what's to become of you both."

Winterborn would want her, and he needed Winterborn. Or what Winterborn had. And that would mean choosing a side, losing security or whatever he still had in the way of a soul. Not a choice he wanted; one, indeed, he had sought to avoid.

"You're still here uninvited," he said, "after all."

You find a middle ground, and it all starts washing away. A moment of white rage, at her bringing him to this, that could so easily become the Fury; so easy to kill her, unravel them both, and the dilemma would be gone.

They studied each other. She didn't have the decency even to look afraid. Did she see, perhaps, what he already knew; that it wasn't him, that kind of cowardice or savagery? That he was still himself, that there were still depths he wouldn't lower himself to in the name of bare survival? Even though it felt at times that precious few remained?

Gevaudan exhaled. "Follow me," he said, at last.

"What...?"

"For the time being, you're my guests. And that is more than I have offered any man or woman in five years. This way, and walk only where I walk."

*

Breathe in. Breathe out. Remain calm. The urge to kill filled Winterborn again. Jarrett. Jarrett had seen. No witnesses. She had to die. But she was valuable. He needed her. His huntress, to find Helen. Channel your rage. Use it. Don't allow it to use *you*.

And then she spoke. Said something. Winterborn finally blinked. "What?" he said. "What did you say?"

"I said we've got her, sir."

"Got her?" Winterborn exhaled, leant back. "How, exactly, have we 'got her', Colonel Jarrett? If you mean that Shoal will do the job for us – "

"Not at all, sir." Jarrett was white – the present danger, or knowing that Helen was back? – but straight-backed and composed. "I don't trust the combination of those two any more than you do. He's fought against us in the past, after all."

Winterborn felt the tic begin again beneath his eye. Jarrett saw it too; he could read the signs in her face: *Dangerous ground. Move on.* "I'm only saying, we know where she is. It isn't safe to leave her there, so the question is how we get her out. Luckily, I have some ideas about that."

"I'm glad to hear it." Winterborn steepled his fingers. "It's why you're here, after all."

"We *could* launch a frontal assault on Deadsbury, but we could sustain very high casualties in the process if Shoal, er, objected."

"Ha."

"And of course we'd lose any future prospect of alliance with the Grendelwolf."

"Not necessarily. Remember, I control the serum he'll die without."

"With respect, sir, that didn't stop him at Sheffield."

Winterborn gnawed a thumbnail, then glanced at her and stopped. Jarrett swallowed hard. He let her stew for a moment, let her think she'd gone too far – a little fear was always good for your subordinates, the sense that danger might always be close – then nodded. "There is that. So what do you propose?"

"I take it you've no objection to a few civilian casualties, sir?"

"What do you think, Jarrett?"

Jarrett smiled. No longer pale; still, calm.

"So how do we get her?"

"We don't, sir."

"What?"

"That's the beauty of it, Commander. She'll come to us."

The clock ticked. Winterborn stared at her for nearly a full minute, then chuckled. "Now that," he said, "I'd pay to see."

*

"So tell me again," said Liz, huddling up against Mordake in the bed.

"All right," he said at last. "The evidence comes from scattered outlying islands in the Orkneys and the Shetlands, and a few skerries in the North Sea. Hence – ta-da! – the North Sea Culture."

"No one can say you're not imaginative with names."

"You want to hear this or not?"

"Yes, O Lord and Master."

"Whoever they were, they had a written language, but it doesn't bear any resemblance to any known one. Something happened, some sort of cataclysm; probably flooding or a storm surge that effectively destroyed that entire civilisation."

"Which no one knew about until you stumbled on it on your summer vac."

"Just one little item that shouldn't have been there. Sometimes that's all it takes. Some cultures leave more behind than others; some leave next to nothing."

"Just teasing you." Liz propped her chin on his chest and grinned at him. "Go on."

"Well, what seems to have happened is that the survivors ended up in Scotland to start with, then migrated slowly south through Northumbria and possibly into northwest England. As they went, they gradually assimilated, to fit in with the natives. So, with a bit of luck, I might eventually find

something left of their culture that's in a language I can understand. Which would be quite a find. What?"

"Nothing." Liz smiled, doodled on his chest with a fingertip. "Just nice to hear a bit of passion from you. Never heard you get that excited about psychiatry."

"Meh."

"So, are you finally going to stand up to your dad and go back to college, then?" Mordake didn't answer. "Eddie – "

"I want to. I do. It's just, you know, the bills won't pay themselves."

"I told you. I've got a good job lined up for when I graduate. Never underestimate us mature students. I can keep us tided over for the duration."

"But – "

"We'll put off starting a family for a few years. I'm not that old. And neither are you. So? No excuses now, Eddie."

"I love you, Mrs Mordake."

"Bleuchh." She grinned. "Stick with me, kid, and you'll wear rags."

"Probably right," he said. "But what the hell."

*

Mordake fumbled for the cigarette packet. It was his last. His fingers shook. He looked inside: only four left. Christ. He hesitated, then lit one up.

His desktop was covered with opened files, scribbled notes and scattered fag-ash. It speckled his white coat too. His ashtray was brimming. He'd been smoking non-stop; his mouth and throat were raw.

No time to go to the village. If only. He needed Liz, even if it was just ghostlighting; her hand stroking his hair, her voice soft in his ear. But it was all to play for now; convince Dowson and she'd be his again, not a ghost but real. But fail to convince Dowson and she'd be lost forever.

He drew on the cigarette; the tip crumbled, scattering more ash on the table top. His eyes drifted from the files to the pistol beside them.

A rap on the door. Mordake started; the Monarch crumpled in his fingers, strewed hot embers on the desk and floor. He slapped and stamped them out, grabbed a loose file, pulled it over the pistol, stood and brushed ash from his coat. "Come."

"Doctor?"

"Lyson." Mordake breathed out, glowered. "What?"

"Colonel Dowson and his escort, Doctor. They're almost here."

"How long?"

"Few minutes."

"All right. All right. I'll be out in a moment."

Lyson opened his mouth, then closed it again. The door clicked shut.

Mordake swept the cigarette's remains together, tipped them into the packet; if he found papers, he could roll a new one later. He gathered up the files and stacked them finally atop a filing cabinet, tidied the notes on his desk. They'd wait.

And when the files and notes were gone the dull-grey pistol lay on his desk; it waited, as guns do. Mordake touched it, then withdrew his hand. It was a surrender to brute force over reason; a step into territory he'd never know or understand. Never fired one anyway; either miss by a mile or put a hole in his foot if he tried. Best thing he could do was stick it back in its drawer.

Mordake hefted the pistol for a moment, then slipped it in his pocket. *If the dream dies, so do I; whatever it takes, I'll stop that.* A last brushdown of his clothes, one more deep breath, then he opened the door and crossed the compound; past the Adjustment Chamber and the other blocks to join the others on the parade ground.

Andrews' men were lined up, waiting; Lyson and the other technicians huddled outside the staff quarters. Beyond the wire fence, three landcruisers rolled up to the gates. Two had .50 calibre machine guns mounted on their flatbeds; the third, a grenade launcher. The Reapers crewing them all wore white shoulderflashes. Jennywrens; escort duty in the Wastelands was their business. Among other things Mordake didn't like to think on.

Lyson tried to smile; his lips quivered.

"Just stay calm," said Mordake, both to Lyson and his own thumping, traitorous heart. He wanted to be in the village more than ever now, Liz's hand warm in his. Well, that wasn't to be. Not today. But today didn't matter; he was playing for tomorrow. And one way or the other, he'd win.

The gun's weight, heavy in his pocket.

The gates swung open; Mordake took out one of his remaining cigarettes, lit up and drew the smoke into his lungs.

PART TWO: GHOSTS

1.

The Grendelwolf led them up the road, muscles rolling under the long black coat, long, fine hair billowing out behind. Danny'd never seen anyone move like it before; smooth, flowing, like water over rock.

He still had the Lanchester, and the revolver in his waistband; still time to turn one on himself, finish it quick. But then the Grendelwolf had promised them quick deaths, if nowt else. Fuck. Was that the best he'd got to look forward to?

Helen touched his arm. "You okay?"

He nodded mutely, eyes still on Gevaudan's back.

"I'll do my best to get you out alive, at least, Danny. My fault you're here."

"Thanks."

"Can't promise anything."

"Well, no. All up to old creeping death over there, innit?"

"You know," said Gevaudan, "my hearing really *is* rather good."

148

"Oh shit."

Gevaudan glanced back at them. "Enhanced night vision and extremely sensitive hearing come as part of the package." He smiled. "Among other things."

Get a grip. If he's gonna kill you, he's gonna kill you and that's that. Helen's still got it together. You wanted to be like her. Now's your chance.

Danny nodded. "I'll bear it in mind."

Gevaudan walked on. Danny took a deep breath and followed.

*

Helen looked away from the Grendelwolf's long black hair, the broad shoulders, the fluid, loping walk. The trees flanking the road got bigger, branches meshing overhead. They passed a faded, rotten sign: CHER MOSS PARK. On each side of the cracked asphalt path beyond, the trees' and bushes' branches had been snapped off to leave it clear.

Gevaudan stopped. "We're here."

Beyond the park, a large grey church loomed out of the gathering mist. Gargoyles scowled from the roof, mouths dripping the last of the rain. Moss clung to rusted, tottering gutters.

"Be it ever so humble," said Gevaudan, "there's no place like home."

They followed him up the overgrown path to a heavy wooden door; he pushed it open, clicked a switch.

Lights came on – in the ceiling, above the altar, in sconces on the walls – and revealed the inside of the church. The pews were gone. Below a stained glass window, a huge, dust-coated television screen, flanked by speakers; in one corner a four-poster bed with moth-eaten drapes. A stack of tins, a camping stove. Guns and ammunition stacked on the altar, beside a radio-telephone; an array of musical instruments – guitars, violins, a cello, a harp – on one wall.

"Fuck me," said Danny.

"Electric light?" said Helen. "Winterborn doesn't spare any expense."

"Some old solar panels on the roof," said Gevaudan. "And a few old car batteries that are recharged from it. As far as he's concerned, it's a small investment compared to what he hopes to get."

Cardboard boxes beside the bed; inside one, something glimmered in the candlelight. Helen looked; saw gold lettering along a book's spine. All the boxes were filled with books.

"Help yourself," said Gevaudan. "Can either of you read?"

"I can. Danny?"

"Yeah! Course. Darrow taught us."

"Well, that's good to know. Gives me some hope for the rising generation. There's more to life than just survival."

"I feel the same way," Helen said.

His yellow eyes glittered almost golden in the light; she couldn't look away. "Never talk politics or religion among friends, Helen."

"Friends?"

He smiled; white teeth glinted. Those eyes. Bloody hell. "Well, you're not dead yet. Are you?"

"Fair enough."

"We'll get to that in due course. But till then, there's no reason not to be civilised." He held up a tin. "Coffee? It's real, I can assure you. No idea where Winterborn obtains these little surprises, but they pop up in my food parcels from time to time."

"Food parcels?"

"Grendelwolves do not live by serum alone, Danny."

"Eh?" Danny blinked then nodded at the tin. "What's coffee, anyway?"

Gevaudan turned and studied him. Danny flinched, then relaxed; the Grendelwolf looked sad, rather than anything else. A low sigh escaped him. "Something every man should try at least once. I have sugar, too. Even dried milk." He filled a pan with water, put it on the camping stove.

"Gevaudan – " Helen began.

"Sh." Gevaudan lit the stove. "This is a special occasion. Even I don't drink this often. When did you last have coffee, Helen?"

"Years ago."

"And Danny's never had the pleasure. Let's make this moment last."

Helen watched Gevaudan spoon coffee into a cafetiere, pour boiling water from the pan. He let the cafetiere stand; a rich, roasted smell filled the air. He sat, elbows on knees, chin on steepled fingers. He might have been carved from stone; solid, unyielding, he'd endure, she thought. That was rare. Was it that simple? A man who wouldn't let her down? He pushed down the plunger, poured coffee into clean white mugs.

"Here," he said.

"Thank you," Helen said, and she didn't just mean the drink. She was glad he'd made her wait and be silent; it was was the stillest, calmest time she'd known since entering the city. Of course it couldn't last; too many memories, circling like carrion birds, waiting their chance to strike.

Like this one, here: she'd last drunk coffee at the Refuge, after they'd captured a supply convoy. There'd been luxury rations for the Reaper brass. To the victor the spoils; hers had included a few ounces of coffee, which she and Frank brewed and drank. They'd even let Belinda try a little, with plenty of sugar. Not much, just some.

Helen blew on the surface of the drink, swirled the coffee in the cup.

"You can never forget." She looked up; Frank stood on the altar, behind Gevaudan, Belinda at his side. "We're always with you."

"This is good," whispered Danny. Helen blinked, and the ghosts were gone.

Gevaudan smiled a little sadly. Was that pity she saw? If so, she might have something to work with. "Yes," he said. "It is."

"Yes," Helen said.

They drank in silence. Danny tried to go slowly, but his cup was soon empty; a moment later, he put a hand to his stomach, eyes going wide. Gevaudan pointed to the vestry. "The latrine is over there."

Danny bolted. A door banged. Gevaudan chuckled.

"That was cruel," said Helen.

"A common reaction to good coffee, unfortunately. But worth the discomfort, I think. As I said, everyone should try it at least once."

"Think you said every *man* should."

"I stand corrected."

"Are you going to kill us?" she asked finally.

His smile faded; he put the cup down. "I still haven't decided."

"He didn't want to come here. He was never supposed to. He just guided me to the outskirts and – "

"All right, spare me the violins."

"Violins?" Her eyes flicked to the instruments on the walls.

The sound he let out was half-laughter and half-exasperated sigh. "Never mind. You can both live. There. Happy now?"

"Definitely relieved."

Gevaudan shrugged. "Nice to meet someone who can sustain a conversation. They're thin on the ground."

"*People* are thin on the ground round here."

"True. My only human contact is the occasional call from Winterborn. If that counts."

"Call?"

Gevaudan nodded at the altar. "Another of the little strings he likes to attach. The 'hotline', he calls it. So he can call me whenever he likes. Of course, whether or not I answer is a different matter."

"Hear from him often?"

"From time to time. Usually to ask if I've changed my mind. So far I haven't. And once a month, two Reapers deposit a landcruiser-load of supplies at a prearranged location. Serum, food – "

" – and life's little luxuries, like coffee?"

He smiled; the corners of his eyes crinkled. "They're the only people I see. Sometimes I can't resist frightening them a little."

"Sounds lonely."

"There are compensations. Look around you. I have books. Music. A measure of peace. It's far more than most can say."

"Yes, it is."

"Was that disapproval?" The smile faded. Careful, Helen; focus on why you're here, and remember what he is. If he tried to kill you, a part of you would welcome it. "Have you ever seen what happens to a Grendelwolf deprived of its serum?"

"A body, once."

"No, not a pleasant sight. But I take it you never actually saw the *process* of a Grendelwolf dying that way. During our – training – they made an example of one troublesome case. And made us all watch. I've seen many kinds of death, Helen, but that was the worst."

"I'm sorry."

"I don't want you to be sorry." Gevaudan leant back. The big shoulders flexed; the black sweater pulled tight across his chest. He'd be like a tree, falling on you. *Enough.* "I want you to understand. The Regional Commanders are all – allegedly – working towards the goal of reunifying Britain under a single centralised Command. If and when that happens, Winterborn intends to lead that united Britain. Control's very important to him."

"I know that."

"Do you now?"

"I know Tereus Winterborn very well."

"Good. You should always know your enemy. I knew, when I came here, he'd grasp at anything that might give him an edge. An advantage. That gave *me* an advantage, in turn."

"Oh?"

"I came here when my supply of serum was almost exhausted. Without it, I'd be just another corpse. With it, I'm the last Grendelwolf. There aren't any others – believe me, I've looked – and even Winterborn wouldn't risk starting up a new programme. Too unstable. But I'm a known quantity, one that could be very useful to him; if not now, then one day."

"You bluffed him?"

"I will never fight for Tereus Winterborn, but I've kept the possibility dangling in front of him for the past few years. It's a small victory, but I've learnt to savour them."

"And in return, you get this?"

"Grendelwolves don't age. The serum returns us to, and sustains us at, peak physical condition." Gevaudan smiled. "If I was to tell you my true age, you wouldn't believe me. Let's just say I wasn't young, even by the standards of the time, when the War came. I had a family, and only I survived. So, this is a piece of an old world I remember very well. It rather suits me, and it's distinctly preferable to the new." Gevaudan's tone had turned sad; for a moment she felt the twinge of pity she'd felt for the wolves in their zoo enclosure, all those years ago. He nodded towards the vestry. "Maybe he's the lucky one. You don't miss what you never had."

"So I'm told."

Danny emerged from the vestry. "Did I miss owt?"

"Only my life story. It wasn't the most fascinating event of the year."

Danny sat gingerly. "Not bad stuff, that. Goes right through you, though. Burns and all."

"Gevaudan?"

"Mm?"

"Don't you even want to hear what I have to offer?"

"Not particularly. But, if you must, feel free."

"Thank you."

"More coffee?"

She smiled. "Thank you again."

Danny blinked and stared at them, but held out his cup for a refill.

"I haven't been idle this last year," said Helen. "I've been making connections. People – rebel crews that survived the massacre, the tribespeople out in the Wastelands and supplies. Guns, ammunition, explosives – "

"And the Goliath serum."

"Yes."

"You'd have nothing to bargain with otherwise. And, of course, it's mine if I fight for you."

"No."

Gevaudan raised an eyebrow. "All right." He tilted his head to one side, the light sketching shadows beneath his high cheekbones. "Go on."

"Whatever you decide, it's yours. And I've found enough to last you years."

"No strings?"

"None. I'll bring it to the City, or you can come out and collect it. Stay here or leave. Join a side, stay neutral. It's up to you."

Gevaudan smiled. "Very good. Clever, too."

"What?"

"Reverse psychology, I believe it's called. I have a choice. Because to you, I'm not a military asset, but a human being. Because you're so much better than Tereus Winterborn. And so, of course, I'll fight for you, because you've shown yourself to be better than him." The smile faded. "Was that the idea?"

Danny looked utterly lost.

"I'm offering you your own supply."

"But sooner or later it will run out."

"And Winterborn's?"

"He has the formula."

"Which I can steal."

"If I make it worth your while."

"I mean what I say, Gevaudan. You can have the serum, no strings. Are you telling me that means nothing?"

"I don't like people trying to play me, Helen."

"I'm not."

"Hm. Well, your gesture is appreciated for what it is."

He looked so smug; Helen's anger tipped over. "You're really happy just sitting here? All on your own, while the whole world goes to hell around you?"

"The world, in case you hadn't realized, went to hell twenty years ago."

"And you're just sitting pretty."

"It's all that's left."

"Do you know what it's like out there? No, because maybe then you'd have to give a damn about something. You've got people starving to death. Eating each other. You've got the Jennywrens butchering men, women and kids in the Wastelands. And how about the clearance crews? Ever seen one of those?"

"I am familiar – "

"They make them clear the contaminated topsoil away. No protective clothing, nothing. And they pick up creeping doses and they die slowly. If they're lucky, they get a bullet – "

"I am *very* familiar," Gevaudan said through his teeth, "with the clearance crews. Do not, *ever*, make the mistake of patronising me."

"Do you want to be Winterborn's pet Grendelwolf forever?"

Danny made a strangled noise. The moment stretched out; finally Gevaudan spoke, something close to a tremor in his voice: "I am nobody's *pet*."

They glared at one another. Silence. Gevaudan finally looked away.

Hit a nerve there. Helen put down her half-empty cup. "Don't you dare sit there, safe and secure, and pick my motives apart. It's what I'm *doing* that counts."

"And what *is* that, exactly? Another campaign? Another war? Hardly an original achievement."

"I'm trying to get rid of bastards like Winterborn."

"To be replaced with what? Total chaos? Bastards of your own choosing? Or... what?" Gevaudan looked up. "Elections, democracy? People who struggle to survive from day to day, casting votes on issues they're too damaged and uneducated to understand? Or have you a comprehensive education programme planned out as well? Please, tell me your vision."

"When I was thirteen years old," said Helen as calmly as she could, "the Reapers put a bullet in my mother's head. Why? Because she was in the way. And all I remember – not even very well – is that once upon a time, things were better than that."

"You were a child, Helen. Things always look better from that perspective."

"You're saying it's better now?" He didn't answer. "I remember we had food, light, heat. I remember we were free. We weren't afraid. I remember a different world, Gevaudan. Do you?"

Gevaudan nodded. "Yes. But I try not to, because it's gone. And it won't come back. If anything does replace the Reapers, it'll be different from anything you or I are unlucky enough to recall."

"But still – "

"Before the War, Helen, I spent a good part of my life banging my head against the wall, trying to change things, or to save them. And it amounted to the same thing; even before the bombs fell, I saw near enough everything I valued destroyed by cockroaches like Winterborn. Same disease, different strain. Viruses mutate."

"What?"

"It doesn't matter. They cared for nothing but their own enrichment and power, which became an end in itself. They tore down anything that stood in their way and preyed on the defenceless. They are the vermin of the earth, but they never die out. I, and others, fought against them, but without success." Gevaudan sighed, leant back again; when he spoke again, he was quiet. "Some fights you can only carry on so long; you run out of strength."

Helen picked up her cup and swirled it.

"Was there anything else?" asked Gevaudan, almost gently.

"No," she said, almost in a whisper.

And then the phone rang.

2.

Mordake fished another crumpled stub from the ashtray, straightened it with ash-grimed fingers and lit up.

"I'm grateful for this opportunity to defend my work," he muttered. "I have here a summation of the results… the experimental results of… no. No. Start again."

He ground out the cigarette, cleaned his hands on his lab-coat as best he could, got up and paced. He glanced through the window. No sign of Dowson.

"This is bloody intolerable." He strode to his cabin door. "Look – "

The two Jennywrens Dowson had posted outside his door were aiming sub-machine guns at his face before he'd finished the word.

"Get back inside," one said.

"I just wanted to know – "

"Did you hear what I said?" the Jennywren answered.

" – how much longer – "

"I won't tell you again."

Mordake shut the door. His legs shook; his face burned. Jennywren bastards. The pistol bumped against his thigh. Useless against them; he'd only the vaguest idea of how to use the damn thing, and a Jennywren knew every bloody way there was to kill. They probably hardly knew anything else, but they knew that.

He went back into his office, fished another stub from the ashtray, lit it and paced again.

"I'm grateful for this opportunity to defend my work… I've reviewed our files from the inception of the project, so that you can see the progress we've made, the stage of development we've now reached…"

But what if he didn't see it? Dowson wasn't a scientist. And even if he had been, this was new territory, far beyond the known. Most scientists would call this project unethical quackery, pseudoscience, madness. Mordake would have himself, before the War.

But that was then. He'd travelled a long way. His biggest fear was *how* far; of what Liz might see, if – *when* – he got her back. If there'd be anything left of the man she'd loved in the one he had become. And what she might say if, faced with the price he'd paid in suffering and corpses, he told her that all of it had been for her.

He could handle that. He could control it. He could even, quite literally, *make* her understand. But then would it still be Liz?

But that what was made Project Tindalos so seductive and so terrifying; the potential for control was limitless. And that was why he, and only he, would ever use it, to achieve a set, specific goal. Let Winterborn believe this was a weapon to sweep his enemies aside; Mordake wasn't fool enough to grant him that kind of power. Winterborn was a child, and Dowson – no, Dowson would never be able to look beyond Tindalos as a weapons system either. Too dull, too prosaic a mind. They couldn't think beyond reordering things as they were, couldn't grasp the idea of changing *everything,* wiping away the blighted present, restoring what had been.

But that was where the fear began. It would be so easy, so seductive, to change just one more thing when all creation was putty in your hands. And another, and another, till all reference points were lost. Easy to lose all proportion and perspective; frighteningly easy to become a mad god.

That must not happen; he mustn't lose sight of his goals. Tindalos was fated to be used once and once alone. The specifications were precise. He would restore the old world, with all its flaws except for a few; nuclear weapons, for instance, would play no part in it. And when his work was done, when he'd ensured he and Liz would live out their natural spans, happy and contented …

"*I'll break my staff*," he murmured. Liz had always loved her Shakespeare. "*Bury it certain fathoms in the earth; and deeper than e'er did plummet sound, I'll drown my book.*"

And all manner of things shall be well.

"Talking to yourself, Doctor?"

Mordake clutched his chest; for a second he thought his heart would stop. The door banged shut; Dowson strode past him, dropped into the chair behind his desk. "First sign of madness. Pity we didn't catch it in time. Save us a lot of wasted time and expense."

Mordake's guts clenched. The pistol, heavy in his pocket. Shoot the bastard. *No. Don't be stupid. You're a scientist.* He's a threat. He has to die. *Killing him won't work. You have to convince him.*

"Nothing to say, Doctor?"

Deep breath. *Convince him.* "I'm grateful for this opportunity to defend – "

Dowson rolled his eyes, nodded. Not to Mordake; to someone behind him. Mordake half-turned, but too slow. Something slammed into his kidneys; a booted foot hooked his legs out from under, kicked him in the ribs when he hit the floor.

"Bring him," Dowson said.

Hands grabbed his arms. The two Jennywrens from outside. He tried to stand, but they shoved him down, cuffed him round the back of the head and dragged him. They cuffed him again whenever he moved, even when he tried to lift his knees to stop them hitting the edge of the doorframe, the wooden steps, or the rocky ground.

*

Their living room. Clean and cosy; a sofa, thick pile carpet, a plasma screen TV. And on the television, talk of war. International situation; ultimatum; conflict seems inevitable. *Liz huddled on the sofa.*

"Talk to me," she said.

"About what?"

"What do you think? That last dig. The one you were so excited about."

"You don't want to hear about that. Been boring you to death with it lately."

Liz picked up the remote, switched off the television. "Please. I'd rather think about anything else."

"All right." He sat beside her, slipped an arm around her.

"You found something important, then?"

"Important? Only the Rosetta Stone."

"Come again?" she said.

"That last dig," he said. "In the Trough of Bowland." His fingers twitched; he badly wanted a cigarette but Liz, of course, didn't approve. "It was a DMV site."

"Deserted mediaeval village, right?"

"Clever girl."

"Piss off."

"The clue was something in a nearby village called Hobsdyke. There's a funny design of crucifix in the church there; in the stonework, and in the church itself. The Hobsdyke Cross. Thing is, it looks like a crucifix, but it isn't one, not quite. If you look closely, the configuration's subtly different. It's actually a symbol from the North Sea Culture. That helped me trace the location of the settlement."

"Well, come on, then. Tell me."

"They called themselves the Beloved. The survivors of the North Sea Culture. In their own language. As they moved south, they assimilated. What that ultimately meant was trying to behave like the rest of the locals – Celts, Saxons, whoever – while secretly preserving their own language and religion to teach their children when they came of age."

"Religion? What were they? Pagans?"

"Not exactly. Not quite sure what you'd call the gods they worshipped. Their name translates as something like 'the Night Wolves.' It's like a lot of religions: starts with a period of grace, when the Night Wolves lived among us, till something happened – bit like Eve and the Apple – that meant they went away. But one day it was promised they'd return, and so they blessed the Beloved with various mystical and magical powers that could one day be used to call them home. And to enable the Beloved to grow mighty and powerful and to smite their enemies, obviously."

"Obviously."

"And from this the North Sea Culture grew, until it supposedly destroyed itself when some sort of ritual went wrong. Mind you, some of the stuff there, you could almost believe it."

"Really?" Liz looked worried.

"Almost. Anyway. I found part of a… teaching pack, I suppose you'd say. Passages in the North Sea Culture glyphs, phonetic renderings of them and English translations. It's enough to start deciphering a lot of the stuff I've found."

"That's good." Liz glanced at the blank TV screen. "Don't suppose there was a magic spell to stop idiots starting wars?"

"Not that I saw."

"If you find one," she said, "use it, will you?"

Mordake held her, very tightly. "Yes. I will."

*

Andrews' men were on parade again, backs straight, eyes unblinking. Was that sympathy on Andrews' face? Couldn't be sure. Wouldn't help Mordake anyway; Andrews was a Reaper and had his orders.

Lyson and the other technicians were huddled together under the Jennywrens' guns. The plea in Lyson's wide eyes sank quickly into despair when he saw Mordake.

The Jennywrens dragged Mordake to the Adjustment Chamber and yanked him up onto his knees directly in front of Seclusion Chamber Four. Boots crunched on the ground; Dowson marched into view, studied the seclusion for a moment, then turned to face Mordake.

"Doctor Mordake," he said at last. "You have pissed away resources, manpower, time and supplies on the biggest load of horseshit I ever heard of in my life. Commander Winterborn had faith in this project, still believed this project might contribute to the security of his Command. But his faith has its limits, which it has reached. Which is why I am out here. Which is why I have been relieved of my adjutancy. Because someone had to come out here and clean up this mess."

"You were sent to do an assessment – " A Jennywren kicked Mordake in the side.

"Which I've done."

"You haven't even heard – "

"I don't need to, Doctor. I managed to work out within two cunting minutes of touching the ground that this project is a cockeyed, ridiculous fucking waste of time and resources and has been since day one. We have men here who could have been deployed elsewhere. Technicians who could have been employed on projects that might actually fucking *work*. And you have deprived this Command of them. Not to mention the subject of Doctor Carter, who you accused of being in league with the rebels when he tried to get the project shut down, and who is now dead as a result."

"Doctor Carter never thought the project wouldn't work." Mordake flinched, but at least this time the Jennywren didn't kick him. "He just thought the risks outweighed the gain. There were those who said that about the Manhattan Project."

"Not the best example you could have picked, Doctor. Now Carter, he could actually have been *useful*. Well, the plug is pulled. Your project is finished, Doctor Mordake. Dead-and-gone. The only question now is what happens to *you*. From here I can see three options. One: I summarily execute you here and now, and believe me I am getting seriously tempted in that regard. Two: I take you back to Central Command under close arrest and make a report to Commander Winterborn on how you've fucked him over. Then *he'll* decide what happens to you, and if that happens, then quite frankly I think you'll be wishing I'd gone for option one instead. Option three: I take you back, but my report includes some extenuating circumstance that just *might*, conceivably, not get you killed. Although you'll probably be cleaning latrines with your tongue for the rest of your miserable life. To even stand a chance of me picking option three, Doctor Mordake, you are going have to work fucking hard." Dowson was breathing hard, the unscarred part of his face flushed red. "And just so I know you understand: Stone, do the honours, would you?"

Dowson nodded; one of the Jennywrens behind Mordake strode toward Seclusion Chamber Four. Like the others, he carried a rifle across his back, a sub-machine gun at his side, a pistol at his hip and a knife in his boot. Mordake opened his mouth, tried to rise; cold metal touched the back of his neck.

"God knows these fuckers you've been using as your guinea pigs would've all ended up on a clearance crew if they hadn't come here," Dowson said. "But on a clearance crew, they'd have at least done this Command some fucking good."

Stone spun the wheel on the outer door, pulled it wide, stepped through.

"Whatever they did, even I feel sorry for these poor fuckers now," said Dowson. "Which, I can assure you, takes some doing, Doctor. So I'm gonna do them a favour. Yeah. I'm gonna put them out of their misery. And you, Doctor Mordake – you are going to watch." He turned. "All right, Stone."

Stone nodded, spun the wheel on the inner door, yanked it open and drew his revolver. Mordake looked away.

"Make him watch," said Dowson.

A hand grabbed Mordake's hair and yanked his head up. He gasped and screwed his eyes shut.

"Open your eyes, Doctor, or Trooper Welles will cut your eyelids off."

Mordake opened his eyes. They streamed tears, and not only from pain.

Stone entered the seclusion chamber now and stood over Subject Four, who stared up at the ceiling from his pallet.

"Do it," Dowson said.

Stone took aim at Subject Four's head, cocked the hammer, but didn't fire.

The moment stretched out.

"Oi," said Dowson. "Stone? Get on with it. I gave you an order."

"I…" Stone stared at Dowson. "Colonel, I…"

Stone's gun hand lifted; the barrel tracked up the cell wall to point at the ceiling. Then his hand turned, bringing the gun to point at Stone's own face.

"The fuck are you doing?" demanded Dowson.

Stone grabbed his wrist with his free hand, tried to push the gun away. And then Stone started screaming. He kept on screaming, even when he forced the gun-barrel into his mouth.

"What – " began Dowson.

The gun fired; blood sprayed up the wall. Stone fell back against it and collapsed.

"Welles," shouted Dowson. The cold metal left Mordake's neck; the hand released his hair. But no gunshots came.

Mordake turned, looked up. Welles had a sub-machine gun at his shoulder, aimed into the seclusion chamber, but he didn't fire. The weapon shook and wavered. Arms shaking, face contorted, Welles lowered it to hip level, then, like Stone before him, reversed it to point at his own face.

"No," Mordake heard him snarl. "No, no, no, no, no, n– "

Mordake turned away. The sub-machine gun fired; wetness splashed his clothes and the back of his neck. When he looked up, Dowson was staring from him to the bodies of his men and back again.

Scared of a pipedream, Colonel? A shiver in the ground, a tingling in the air. *A miracle. Just in time, it's working.* The other Jennywrens had aimed their guns at the chamber, but now they, too, were bringing their weapons to bear on themselves.

"Candlemass!" Mordake shouted. "Candlemass!"

The Jennywrens froze; the tingling, the shiver, abated but didn't fade.

"Release them," said Mordake. "You won't be harmed. Right, Colonel? *Right?*"

"Right," said Dowson. "Right."

Mordake turned away to hide his smile. "Release them."

The tingle vanished from the air; the shiver left the ground. The Jennywrens stumbled, released. Mordake went forward.

"Stand down," Dowson barked. "No one do anything."

Mordake shut the Seclusion Chamber door, locked it tight. Sweat on his forehead. His legs wobbled; his kidneys throbbed.

"It works," said Dowson. "Jesus Christ, it fucking works."

*

In Mordake's office was a rare and hoarded treasure; a bottle of pre-war Scotch. Teacher's: Mordake wouldn't have given it space in his drinks cabinet before the War, but now it was nectar.

A little premature, perhaps, to break into it now before the final phase began, but justified, he decided, under the circumstances. Dowson was convinced now; Dowson had seen for himself.

Mordake splashed a generous amount into the two glasses he'd found and pushed one across the desk to Dowson, wincing slightly.

"Thanks," Dowson said.

Mordake nodded.

"I'm sorry about…"

"It's okay." And it was. Dowson had seen now. Dowson knew. That was worth a few bruises. "I'm sorry about your men."

Dowson grunted. "Are you all right?"

"I'll be fine."

Dowson nodded. A moment's silence; he took a sip of whisky. Then a larger one. He closed his eyes, took a deep breath, let it out and put the glass back down.

"All right," he said.

"So," said Mordake, "now you can see."

"See…"

"What we're doing here."

"Yes. Yes, I think so." Dowson looked at his glass, yielded and took another sip. "They're, what, telepathic?"

"And telekinetic."

"You'll have to explain that one."

"Able to manipulate matter by thought. To move it. They can pick up hostile intent, and react to it. As you've seen."

Dowson leant back, eyes narrowed.

"What?" Mordake asked.

"There's more," said Dowson. "Isn't there?"

Mordake allowed himself one more sip, then put down the glass. Got to be careful here. "How much do you know?"

"File made it sound like magic or summat. Main reason I thought it was bollocks."

Mordake chewed his lip. "Oh, it's a form of science. Just one that's been neglected for a long time. The Beloved's legends said their gods, the Night Wolves, had given them these powers. How they developed in reality, I have no idea. Your guess is as good as mine. However, the basic principle is that these abilities are latent in many, many people. In most cases they remain dormant. But using the right combination of techniques – "

"They could be activated?"

"Yes. The difficult part's been finding the right combination. Drugs, sleep deprivation, surgery and exposure to certain glyphs all play their part. Even location. Some places seemed to offer a better chance of success than others."

"How did that work?"

"Still not sure about that, but by then I had enough faith in the project to give that aspect the benefit of the doubt. Certain sites were spoken of as being important, powerful. Places where you'd have a better chance of success. The biggest one I could find in RCZ 7 – where it wasn't completely impossible to establish a facility – was a small, depopulated village called Hobsdyke. Or rather the hill above it."

"So that's why we're here?"

"It seems to have been a sacred site to the survivors of the North Sea Culture, used for a number of their rituals. Also had the advantage of being out of the city and away from prying eyes. Anyway. I'm sure I don't need to tell you the military applications of what you saw today. Imagine them affecting our enemies the same way. In the Wastelands *or* in the cities, where the rebels are hidden among the population."

"Fuck." Dowson leant back in his chair.

"Exactly."

"Just that on its own…"

"Yes."

"But there's more?"

"Possibly." Mordake sipped his Scotch. "Telekinesis, remember: the power to manipulate matter. Theoretically, at least, that happens on a very small, as well as a large scale. The molecular, atomic, even sub-atomic level."

"What would that mean?"

"As I said, this is an old science. A lot of the basis for this work came from ancient records and chronicles. They talk about these techniques being used to restore fertility to 'blighted land', increase crop yields, things like that."

"It could do that too?" Was Mordake imagining it, or did Dowson's hand shake a little, holding the glass?

"*If* we're able to operate at that level, then yes. Potentially. Of course, it can be hard to know how seriously to take some of the claims made in these old accounts," he lied. "Some of them talked about things like transmuting base metals into gold.

Even," he smiled "raising the dead. But you've seen for yourself that they can't be dismissed out of hand."

"Fuck." Dowson breathed. "And that would put our Command ahead of all the others. Militarily *and* economically."

Mordake nodded. "It's taken a great deal of time and work. And there's still work to do. But the hard part's past now."

"Is it, though?" The cold glint was back in Dowson's eye. "They just killed two of my men."

"Welles and Stone were trying to kill *them,* Colonel. What you've got is a young group consciousness that's only just become aware. They sensed a threat and reacted to it."

"What's to stop them doing that to us?"

"Post-hypnotic commands," Mordake said simply. "You saw for yourself. Implanted in every subject from day one. Whatever abilities they've developed, their individual minds – and now, therefore, this gestalt – are subject to those."

"So what happens now?"

"The final phase. A final exposure to the glyphs, tonight, and the group mind will be fully active. And as long as we're sensible, fully under our control."

"And then…?"

"And then, Colonel, the world is our oyster."

But Mordake thought: *My oyster, Colonel. Mine.*

3.

"Alannah?"

Huddled on the floor, hugging herself, she looked up at Darrow. "Where's Mike?"

"Gone to get his people."

"It's happening, then?"

"Yes. My crew, his and Mary's. I've sent word to the other crews to stand by in case we need them."

"Which way do we go?"

Darrow nodded to the ladder nearby. "Straight up, I'm afraid. Have to cut through the shantytown to get there."

"Oh god." Alannah breathed out; long, shuddering. "Oh god."

"Ready, old girl?"

"No. But give me a hand up anyway."

Alannah thought of Danny as Darrow brought her to the ladder. *Danny, Stephen; Stephen, Danny.* Daft really; she was old enough to be his mother.

"Off we go," Darrow said, smiling. She didn't want to, but she smiled back.

"It'll be all right," he said. "I'll be right with you."

"Okay," she said. "Just get on with it, you old buzzard."

Darrow nodded, started climbing. Alannah counted to five, then followed.

Still, though, she remembered the warmth of Danny's hand on hers. There was something there, even if she didn't know what.

Dream on, Alannah. Fine catch you'd be. Who could refuse? More like who couldn't? She let herself think on him though, if only to mock herself. Had to distract herself somehow if she was going to climb this fucking ladder. She gripped each rung so tight she had to peel her hands free before reaching up to the next. Bracing herself; she hadn't seen daylight in years, much less breathed clean air.

Up above, iron scraped stone. Darrow pushed the manhole cover aside; cold wind gusted down the shaft. Light stabbed at her eyes and she gasped, flinching. Her body shook, bowels cramping. Not now, not now. First day out in years, woman; don't start it off by shitting yourself.

"Alannah?" Darrow whispered.

"I'm okay." But her hands were clenched tight on the rungs, wouldn't release.

"It's all right," he soothed her. Gentling her, like a horse. She'd had one once, as a child. Before the War.

Her knuckles were white on the rungs.

"Alannah? You okay?"

Rowan, she'd been called. The skin of her neck, like velvet under the coarse fur. The sad, dark, liquid eyes. A line from the Qu'ran: *All the wisdom in the world can be found between the eyes of a horse.*

Stephen, leaning on the fence, watching her ride. Danny, smiling at her, squeezing her hand. *Where are you, Danny? Need you here.*

"I'm okay," she said, pulled a hand free and reached up. Get over yourself, girl. They're all depending on you. Darrow, Ashton and more. All the ones you haven't met yet that'll get killed if you freeze up at the wrong time.

She kept climbing, eyes averted. Darrow climbed up through the manhole; the light dimmed as he blocked it, reaching down to help her through.

The light. The searing light. Alannah couldn't keep back a cry. The flash of the bomb. She remembered that. She'd looked away in time to save her sight but she'd felt its heat on her back. Danny had been there; no, not Danny. *Stephen*. Danny was Danny; Stephen, Stephen. Stephen was then; Danny was now.

She covered her eyes. Pain. Her legs wobbled; her stomach rolled. Sick. Oh Christ, she'd fall. She gagged, spat.

After the bombs had fallen, huddled in her parents' cellar, they'd both cried, her *and* Stephen. Her parents had gone shopping in the city centre: Dad, methodical to the last, wanting supplies for the shelter. She never saw them again.

Hands clutched her wrists; she struggled. No. Don't fight. Have to do this. Have to. But the light –

Stephen was luckier in a way; his dad was long-dead, his mum in a home with Alzheimer's. Maybe there'd been a guilty relief when he'd cried, that it was over for her, the slow death replaced by a quicker, cleaner one. Didn't matter. Loss was loss and pain was still pain.

Danny. Danny. Keep going. Make him proud. He'll be back. *But what if he isn't?* He will be. He has to be.

"Alannah?"

Sharp things snatched and tore at her; things like loops of barbed wire tried to tangle her limbs. Brambles. Darrow helped her stand. The sun, the light, the background noise crashing in. The pain was like being born. The sun. The light. She tried looking at it again; it was like splintered glass in her eyes. She clung on to Darrow's arm, head down.

"I'm all right. You'll have to lead me."

They draped a poncho over her. Her head slid through the hole. Darrow tried to pull the hood up but she batted his hands away, fumbled it into place herself. She wasn't *that* bad.

"Shall we go?" Darrow asked.

"Yes," she said through her teeth. She'd given her word. It had to be kept; it was all she had. She'd given her word she wouldn't talk, and she hadn't, even after everything that bitch Jarrett did to her. Mustn't think about that.

Through the doorway, into the cold empty air; she could feel the space around her, vast and bleak after years enclosed by concrete. Shouts, screams, sobs, groans came from all around.

She'd held the line, and her reward had come. Helen had come. Got her out.

Alannah leant on Darrow's arm, looked down. A dirt path: deep puddles, fragments of loose brick. Flashes of light; the ground rippled and blurred. Head pain. Nausea. She lurched forward and vomited, splashing the poncho and the ground. But she kept going.

Helen had kept her word; Helen always did. And so would she. You are who you choose to be. You are *what* you choose. A ridiculous claim, with casual destruction so prevalent, but she had to believe it. It was the one act of resistance from which all else sprang.

Squinting against the light. Cold water seeped through her boots. Almost tipping over, over and over again, on the uneven ground. One foot in front of the other. She spat, wiped her mouth, walked on.

"Through here."

She opened her eyes; another rough, wattle-and-daub shack. A piece of sacking hung over the entrance, serving as a door. Darrow pulled it aside, and Alannah stumbled through.

Blessed darkness enclosed them. She opened her eyes, saw a cramped hovel reeking of smoke, sweat, shit and decay. Dried weeds strewed the floor. A dead, scraggy pine was propped in one corner, a couple of candles burning by it. *Christmas tree?* A crude iron-bucket stove, with a chimney of old tin cans, burned in a corner; smoke caught at the throat and eyes.

A thin woman, vast-eyed, huddled in a corner staring at them. Alannah tried a smile; the woman looked away. Daylight peeped round the sacking door's edges and through gaps in the shack walls; Alannah flinched from them, squinting.

Darrow brushed the covering of weeds from another trapdoor. "This way."

He slid the trap aside; more steel rungs lead down into the dark. Alannah took a last look at the thin, frightened woman in the corner, then started climbing down. Not much further. Danny would come soon. And then she wouldn't be alone.

*

Weedlights bloomed below her as she went. Above her, the thin woman pulled the trapdoor back into place. Alannah didn't mind; the darkness was an old friend, far as she was concerned. She knew it well.

Her feet touched solid ground; she released the rungs, stepped away. Darrow put a hand on her shoulder. "You okay?"

"Fine. Fine." She looked around. Brick walls. Earth floor. "Cellar?"

"Foundations, believe it or not. Used to be a big office complex here. Blast wave tore away everything above ground." Darrow smiled. "We just dug a bit deeper so people could stand up without braining themselves."

Alannah smiled back. "What about the others?"

"They'll be here shortly. There's other ways into this little hidey-hole. Wouldn't want to draw too much attention."

"Darrow?" someone called.

Darrow glanced into the shadows. "Come on, Ashton."

A torch flared; the big man came out of the darkness. A dozen kids followed him; the oldest was twenty, the youngest fourteen, fifteen maybe.

She turned to Darrow. "This is our army now?"

Darrow didn't answer. "So," said Ashton, "who we waiting for?"

"No one," a woman said. "We're all here now."

More torches flared, further back in the shadows. A lean woman with cropped hair and pale eyes led another gaggle of youths; beside her strode a reddish-haired girl about Danny's age – *Danny, where was he?* – who carried a sub-machine gun and stared at Alannah with hard blue eyes. "Who's that?"

"Quiet, Flaps," the tall woman said.

"Just asking."

"Mary," Darrow said.

"Roger." The tall woman studied Alannah. "I know you."

"Alannah Vale," Darrow said.

"Alannah?" Mary's eyebrows went up.

Alannah shrank back; felt like every eye was on her. "Have we met?"

Mary nodded. "Briefly. After you – "

"After the Reapers had me?"

"Yeah."

"I probably wouldn't remember then. No offence."

"No. Of course not."

"Any trouble getting here?" asked Darrow.

"Not for us. But something was kicking off out Deadsbury way."

"Deadsbury?" It came out louder than Alannah meant. Flaps gave her a look, equal parts annoyance and contempt.

"Yeah. There was shooting; a lot of it, right on the border. Lot of Reapers heading that way."

Danny. She tried to speak; couldn't.

"We had some people heading out that way," Darrow said. "Any idea exactly what happened?"

"Sorry," said Mary. "Heard there were some bodies, but don't know whose. Some Reapers copped it too, from what I heard."

Danny. Helen too, yes, but *Danny,* with her Stephen's face. *Damn you, Helen, you promised –*

The wall, hard at her back; Alannah slid slowly down. Everyone was staring. She turned away.

"Leave her," Darrow said. "She'll be all right. Now, let's get started."

*

"Reaper Station Five is the logical target," said Mary. "There's a tunnel runs under the fence, connects with the old sewer system. Bring us up right under their noses. Best of all…" she tapped the diagram. "We'll come up right next to the wires for the phone system. Cut them off straight away."

"They've still got radio," said Ashton, sat cross-legged on the floor in the flickering weedlight. The air was rank, the space crowded. Alannah forced herself to breathe slowly and deeply. And to focus on the briefing.

"We'll just have to move quickly after that."

"Phase One," Darrow said. "is taking the base. We know for a fact they're quite lightly manned at the moment. Another reason for targeting them."

"Permission to speak?" Flaps, sat with her knees pulled up to her chest, her Sterling beside her.

"Go ahead."

"So the plan is we go in at first light, cut off the comms, drop every Reaper on the ground – "

"Except – "

"Except the CO."

"Whose name is?"

"Major Bilston, who has high-level security clearance."

"Correct."

"And we do it all fast and by stealth. Then we need to hold the base against any comers so the lady here can do her thing." Flaps' eyes said *I'm risking my life for this, or you, whatever the fuck you are.*

Christ, was she *that* pathetic? Was that all she was now, a dirty old madwoman cowering in the dirt and pining for a boy less than half her age? *Fuck* that. Alannah suddenly sat up straight, got to her feet and strode over to the others. "That's right," she said, and stared at Flaps till the girl finally looked away.

Darrow cleared his throat. "Except your crew won't be in there; you'll be hidden nearby. Even if we take the base without raising the alarm, we'll be rooting around for information on one of Winterborn's pet projects. When that gets noticed – and it will – they'll send the troops in. Mine and Mike's groups will hold the base. We'll be relying on yours to hit the Reapers hard and give us a chance to get out once the mission's complete."

The fear kept trying to take over: Alannah wanted to pull back, like a snail ducking into its shell; retreat into her head, into the dark. But she didn't. Mustn't. So she focused on the map and forced herself to listen.

Darrow looked around. "Any further questions?"

"Just one." Flaps looked at Alannah. "How long're you gonna need?"

Heads turned. Eyes stared. Alannah's stomach cramped. The noise, the crowded space. The thick, reeking air. Sweat sprang out over her; she was shaking.

"Alannah?" Darrow touched her arm. Flaps looked away, shook her head.

"I'm fine," she said. But it wasn't true. Danny. She needed Danny. *God damn you, Helen, bring him back. Bring him bloody back.*

"I can't tell you that exactly," she said. "I can guess where to find the information we're looking for is, but that's all. The hard part's getting to it."

Flaps stared back at her. *She doesn't get it.* Alannah craved her little burrow in the ground, where no one even knew she existed. Too late; she'd made the big, bold gesture, climbed back up into the light. There was nothing left now but work.

"Basically," she said, "I need to get the computer in Station Five to talk to the central one in the Tower."

"Talk to?"

"Best way I can put it." *I was killing Reapers when you were a fucking baby, you snotty little cow.* "I'm risking my life too, here. I'm trusting you to know what *you're* doing."

Flaps' jaw set hard. "All right."

"It's a bit like going through a series of checkpoints. You need the right passwords to get through. I have to work out what the passwords are and use them to access the system; to get through the checkpoints and into the files we need. Now if we can take the Station CO alive, he can get us through some of those checkpoints. I won't need to work those passwords out; he'll know them."

"What happens when you get through?" asked a stocky, crop-haired girl from Ashton's crew. She had a square, blokish face and a Thompson gun – Thursday, they called her.

"I open the files, print them out and we run like hell." A few of the kids laughed. "But the files we're after will be maximum security. There'll come a point that none of the Reapers at the Station can get us past. Just depends where that point is and how many checkpoints I'll have to get through on my own, without any help."

"How do you do that?" Flaps asked. "Guess?"

"Not exactly. Let's just say it's something I'm very good at. What you want to know is how many of those checkpoints there'll be. And the answer is I don't know. If I said I did, I'd be lying." Alannah felt calm now. Her eyes didn't leave Flaps'; neither of them blinked. "I know that's not easy, but I'll be taking the same risks. And unlike you, young lady, I know *exactly* what to expect if the Reapers get hold of me." She managed a smile. "I wasn't always a wreck like this."

Flaps was silent, still; then she nodded. And, possibly, the corner of her young-old mouth might have shown the suspicion of a smile.

"No further questions?" Darrow said. "Good. Then – "

Even under the earth, they heard it; a landcruiser siren's low, droning wail. And then another, and another, closing in.

Alannah tried to breathe; it hitched in her throat.

Flaps picked up her Sterling, moved to Alannah's side. "Easy," she said. "You'll be fine."

Alannah remembered her Sten gun and took hold of it; maybe she should just put the barrel in her mouth now and –

Darrow put a finger to his lips for silence, climbed the rungs. Alannah took deep breaths. Her hand rested on the Sten's cocking handle.

Outside the Reapers were shouting; jagged, harsh voices like dogs barking. Someone screamed. Two shots rang out. More screams, more shouts. Then a burst from a sub-machine gun, a shout. Silence. Then someone speaking, but she couldn't make out the words.

This might be it, then. Funny; she felt calm. No more panic; all she could do was wait and see. And if the Reapers found them, she had the way out. She was holding it in her lap. There were thirty-two rounds in the magazine, and she only needed one. When the time came she'd be quick enough; bastards wouldn't have her again.

There was a little time before the axe fell, enough to remember something good. A heavy metal gig at the Manchester Academy; the air thick with sweat and dry ice and a thin high hum in her ears when the music died away. A thin, handsome boy with spiky hair, shouting over the dispersing crowd's babble.

Hi there.

Hey.

Cool gig, yeah?

Yeah.

Name's Stephen.

Alannah.

Nice name.

Thanks.

Want a drink?

Yeah, 'kay.

A spur of the moment decision; the best choice she'd ever made.

Darrow climbed back down, drew his Thompson gun from under his poncho, put his hand on the bolt. "They're rounding people up," he said.

Silence. Flaps' face, small and pale in the shadows. The bravado was gone; she looked very young. Funny: thinking back to that club, all those years ago, it was easy to picture Flaps there too, some pale, tiny, red-haired gamine in jeans and a black t-shirt. Maybe her mother had been there. The girl's eyes met Alannah's, narrowed in a frown. A question, maybe? Perhaps, but nothing Alannah could ever answer; nothing the poor kid would ever understand. *She should be in the moshpit, headbanging away to something fucking loud. Not pulling back the bolt on a Sterling, getting ready to go down fighting. She shouldn't know how to fire a sub-machine gun. Fucking hell, she shouldn't even know what one is.*

"What's happening?" Alannah asked. Her own calm surprised her.

"They're rounding people up. Some kind of random haul, maybe."

Alannah pulled the Sten's bolt back. From all around her, the harsh dull clicks of dozen weapons being cocked.

"Easy," said Darrow, holding her with his eyes.

Shouts, screams. Another shot fired into the air.

"Fuck," muttered Flaps. Her voice shook a little; she'd gone pale, her breathing ragged. Alannah touched her wrist. The hard blue eyes darted towards her. Alannah took a deep breath, smiled. An eyeblink later, Flaps smiled back.

She could hear a Reaper shouting, almost directly above them now. Darrow and Ashton crouched at the foot of the ladder, guns aimed up at the ceiling.

Alannah waited. The Sten's barrel would fit neatly under her chin; one shot would end it all.

The voices didn't get any closer. She could still hear screams and shouts from above, but they were receding now as the victims were dragged away. And now the hiss and clank of landcruiser engines, the wail of sirens, the bang and clatter of rattling wheels as the cruisers headed away.

After they'd died to silence, Darrow waited till a full minute had passed, then climbed the ladder and pushed back the trap door. Ashton followed, and Flaps. And then Alannah surprised herself again, after a moment's hesitation, by following them, though still she narrowed her eyes against the light.

The hut they'd entered through was empty; no sign of the thin woman anyway. At least it was still standing, though; as she stepped outside, shading her eyes, she saw dozens of the shacks and huts had been knocked down. Most were flimsily built; days or hours in the making for some desperate family, seconds in the destroying for some Reaper bastard.

A woman knelt, wailing, by her hut's ruins. All around her, though, far more ruined homes remained unmourned; the people who'd lived in them were gone.

Alannah squinted against the glare. Her head throbbed; she swayed, dizzy. Flaps put a hand on her arm, steadied her. "You okay?"

Give it time, and Alannah reckoned she could like this girl. "Yeah."

"Think they were after us?" Flaps asked.

Darrow shook his head. "Don't think they were after anyone in particular. I think they were after hostages, in which case something's definitely afoot." He caught Alannah's eye. "Perhaps to do with that business over Deadsbury way."

Alannah nodded. Danny, Helen – the Reapers didn't make that kind of fuss over dead enemies. But there was no knowing for sure; she'd have to wait.

In the meantime, she'd given her word. Others were counting on her. She had to cling to that and keep going.

"We continue as planned," said Darrow. "But we hole up somewhere else. Let's move out."

Danny, Alannah thought, *you promised.* On the heels of that: *Helen, so did you.* But she couldn't think of that now. Her hands were still shaking, but she was back in the game. She hid the Sten gun underneath her poncho, followed Darrow through the ruins.

4.

Danny jumped when the phone went; Helen, too. Old creeping death – best stop calling Shoal that, even in his head – just raised an eyebrow and glanced at the altar.

Least Danny hadn't shat himself. Though that was probably 'causethere was nowt left to come out. That fucking coffee.

The phone rang again. "You going to get that?" Helen asked Shoal.

"Still thinking about it." They were looking straight at each other, each refusing to blink or look away.

"Is it Winterborn?"

"Who else?"

The phone rang on. Each ring made Danny twitch – that fucking coffee again – and he could tell Helen hated it too, but the Grendelwolf didn't seem to mind. Then Shoal sighed and drained the last of his cup. "I expect he wants to talk to me quite urgently this time. If I ignore him, he'll probably do something even more annoying." He stood. "Let's see what he has to say."

*

The phone was picked up: a hiss of static, someone breathing. And then that voice. A rumble of thunder, dead leaves blowing through ruins. "Hello, Winterborn."

Jarrett smiled. First surprise. "Hello, Shoal."

A moment's silence. "Do I know you?"

"Is she there?"

"May I ask who I have the pleasure of – "

"Is she there?" She wasn't playing any of his games: in life you were either the hunter or hunted. She'd never been the last, never would be. She fought to win.

On the phone, silence.

"Shoal?"

A long release of breath; air escaping a tomb.

"Is she there, Shoal? Let's not play games."

"You are beginning," he said, "to irritate me immensely."

The hairs on Jarrett's arms prickled; she ignored them and carried on. "Well, that can't be helped, Shoal. Just – "

"I think you'll find it can," came the reply. "And I think it should be. I think, young lady, that you owe it to yourself to do so."

Jarrett actually laughed. "Are you threatening me?" Silence. "Shoal?"

"I don't demand a great deal," he said, very quietly. "One thing I do, however, insist on is common courtesy. If I chose to seek you out, however many Reapers you surrounded yourself with, and even if Winterborn *did* let you try to kill me, I would reach you."

Jarrett tried to speak, couldn't.

"You know what I am," said Shoal. "And you know what I'm capable of."

A statement, but she knew he required an answer. "Yes," she said. Her face burned.

"Yes," said the Grendelwolf. "So?"

"So," Jarrett swallowed; her throat felt dry. "I apologise."

"Good. Now. Shall we start again?"

"Yes. Thank you."

"You were saying?"

"Is she there?"

"She?" Bastard wasn't giving an inch. One day she'd make him pay for this.

"Helen Damnation."

"And if she is?"

"Then I'd like to speak to her."

"I'm sure you would. The question is, does *she* want to speak to *you*?"

Jarrett smiled; her pulse quickened. Now for the next surprise; this would hit Helen where it hurt. "Oh, I think she will."

*

Gevaudan turned to Helen and covered the mouthpiece with a long, pale hand. "Colonel Nicola Jarrett."

"Who?" said Danny.

"Jarrett?" Helen said. No. Couldn't be. Couldn't.

Gevaudan raised an eyebrow. "You know her?"

Helen tried to smile. "You could say that."

After a moment, he passed her the telephone. She closed her eyes, then put it to her ear. "Hello, Jarrett."

"Helen. Did I surprise you?"

"Just a little."

"Well, you don't have the monopoly on resurrections." The same voice, flat and nasal with a hint of an Essex accent.

"Can't keep a good woman down."

"Do I have your attention?"

"I'm listening."

"I'll keep this short and sweet. I've got Deadsbury surrounded. What would you say to walking out of there and surrendering before anyone else gets hurt?"

Helen gripped the handset. "What do you think?"

"I'll take that as a no, then. Which makes you responsible for what happens now. Shoal still there?"

Helen glanced sideways. Gevaudan sat beside Danny, who glanced from him to her wide-eyed. "Yes."

"Tell him to switch on his television."

"What?"

"Just do it, Helen."

She covered the mouthpiece. "She says – "

"I heard." Gevaudan waggled his ears with his fingertips and strode across the church. "One of my many talents. Now – assuming the thing still works – ah." A dull buzzing, then the flat glass television screen brightened.

"Helen?" Jarrett's voice crackled from the handset and boomed, simultaneously, from the speakers either side of the screen. "Can you see me now?"

"Yes."

A woman in a dusty grey uniform with white shoulder-flashes stood in front of an expanse of broken walls; an old factory, perhaps. Her back was straight, her hair tied back. She might have been handsome, except for her face's hardness and her eyes' empty stare. She wasn't holding a phone; it must be on speaker.

"What are you going to do?" asked Helen.

"That depends on you." Jarrett turned and called offscreen. "Bring him over."

Footsteps, muffled cries, gasps; two Reapers thrust a man into the shot, then stepped back. Jarrett drew her pistol. "Name," she said.

"Whuh?" The man had a thick beard and grey-streaked hair, but was probably no older than his late twenties.

"Your name," said Jarrett. She pointed. "Look into the camera – see? – and state. Your. Name."

The man squinted into the lens. "Yan," he said at last.

"Any surname?"

He blinked, licked his lips, didn't answer. His eyes were wet. A tear trickled down his cheek, cut a channel through crusted dirt.

"Tell us about yourself then, Yan. Have you a wife?"

"I've a woman."

"You live together? How long?"

"Dunno. Long time."

"Children?"

"Two. B-boys."

"What are their names? Your woman, your children?"

"Woman's called Cath. Kids are Jake and Pol."

"How tall are they? Your sons?"

Yan bit his lip, held a hand up around chest-height. "Pol's that tall."

"And Jake? How tall's little Jake?"

Yan lowered his hand. "About so h – "

Jarrett shot him in the face. Helen cried out; Yan fell. Jarrett aimed down, fired again, turned back to the camera and stared into it without speaking for several seconds. "Do I make a point?" she said at last.

"You murdering bitch," said Helen. She realised she was holding the handset at her side, brought it back to her ear. "You fucking murdering bitch."

"Do I. Make. A point?"

"Yes. Yes. You're a psychopath. No change there."

"Wrong answer." Jarrett nodded offscreen; a scrawny woman about Yan's age was thrust into shot. "Name?"

"Sheel."

"Hello, Sheel." Jarrett put the gun to Sheel's temple. Helen cried out, but there was nothing to do: the gun fired again and the woman fell. "Goodbye, Sheel," said Jarrett. She holstered the gun, smiled into the camera. "Have I made my point now?"

"Yes," said Helen.

"And what point's that?"

"You'll kill whoever and however many you have to to get me."

"That's right. And why's that, Helen? Think – carefully – before you answer." Jarrett waited. "Shall I help you?" Helen still didn't reply. "All right, then. Do I do it because I enjoy it? Do I, Helen?" Still Helen didn't speak; Jarrett looked offscreen and opened her mouth.

"No," said Helen.

"Then why?"

"It's your job."

Jarrett nodded. "That's right," she said softly. "My *job*. Rebuilding this country is a long and painful *job*. We do what we do because we *have* to. It's the only way what's left of this country can be rebuilt. Which I swore an oath to do."

"Finished?"

"Careful, Helen." Jarrett shook her head. "You're a child," she said at last. "A spoilt child. You want things no one can have any more. This is the world now, whether we like it or not. I accept it. You won't. And that's why we always win."

Reapers dragged Yan and Sheel's bodies away. Jarrett gestured; a third prisoner was hustled into position. A girl – twelve, maybe thirteen years old, sobbing.

"Name?" Jarrett drew the Browning, thrust it in her face. "Name!"

"Jarrett, you bitch, no!" Helen shouted.

"Shell," said the girl. "Please. M'name's Shell."

"Sheel. Shell. Very limited imaginations they have round here." Jarrett holstered the Browning, turned back to the camera. "People like this always suffer when you play your silly little games. Caught in the middle. It's too late for Yan and Sheel. But it's not too late for this one, Helen. Not yet. Not for another…" She held up an old-fashioned stopwatch. "…twenty minutes. That isn't a long time, but it might just be long enough to get out of Deadsbury and give yourself up to a Reaper patrol."

"But – " Jarrett smiled. "Don't worry too much if you can't, Helen. I've got plenty more where she came from. After Shell dies, I'll kill another one every *ten* minutes. Until you give yourself up." She clicked the stopwatch; the second hand began its first, relentless circuit. "Twenty minutes, Helen."

The phone went dead, but not the screen. Jarrett lit a cigarette, blew out a plume of smoke; beside her, the girl, sobbing and bewildered, stared out of it at Helen, a plea and an accusation all in one.

*

"You look shocked," Gevaudan said.

"Probably because I am," said Helen. She was hugging herself, like she was cold. Danny took a half-step towards her, extended a hand then let it fall. But he stood his ground.

Gevaudan glanced over at him, a faint half-smile on his lips, then back to her. "That surprises me."

Helen turned and stared at him. "What?"

"She's a Jennywren. Don't tell me you don't recognise their methods by now. If not, I'm not surprised they keep beating you."

Helen looked away.

"Oi – " Danny took a step towards the Grendelwolf. Gevaudan stood. Danny halted, but didn't look away. It was Gevaudan who dropped his gaze. "I'm sorry," he said at last. "That was cruel."

"It fucking was," said Helen. "But it wasn't that. What shocked me was seeing Jarrett alive. Christ knows I shot the bitch enough times."

Gevaudan nodded. "Of course. When she said you didn't have the monopoly on resurrections…"

"Yeah."

"Who is she?" asked Danny.

"You know who the Jennywrens are?" asked Helen.

"Course. Reapers use 'em for clearing the Wastelands. Kill mutants and ferals."

"And anyone else," said Gevaudan, "who fights the Reapers. Like the rebels, back in the Civil Emergency."

Helen sighed. "Jarrett was one of the best they had. Or the worst, depending on how you look at it. She was a Captain back then. The fight wasn't going very well for us at the time. They'd pushed us back, using the Jennywrens and – "

"The Grendelwolves." Gevaudan studied his hands. "Sorry about that."

"We needed to harry and disrupt their operations, slow the Reaper advance down so our forces could regroup and counter-attack. We called it Operation Caltrop. Small groups of us, behind Reaper lines carrying out hit and run raids. Sabotage. Assassinations. Anything we could think of. We did so well that *they* mounted Operation Predator to put us out of action."

"An ugly business," said Gevaudan. "But then war usually is."

"She got results, anyway. If they'd used her sooner, we mightn't have had time for a counter-attack. And if she'd been at Sheffield, it mightn't have gone as well as it did."

"As I recall," said Gevaudan, "it didn't go particularly well on either side."

"Jarrett might just have won it for the Reapers, if she'd been there. And if she'd commanded the attack on the Refuge – well, she'd be the one with the monopoly on resurrections."

"What's that mean, anyway? Proper mouthful."

"I'll explain later, Danny. Anyway, we lost a lot of people thanks to her. Some of them were good friends of mine. Jarrett hunted us down using small mobile units on seek and destroy missions and taking reprisals against any civilians in the area. She wasn't big on taking prisoners. When she did, it was either to make an example, or to get information." Helen nodded at the screen. "Either way, she didn't believe in quick deaths. Anyway, a few days before the battle, she pulled off something that could have got us all killed at Sheffield."

"What? Don't spin it out."

"Remember what happened to Alannah?"

"Caught her, didn't they? The Reapers. And they – " The hurt in her eyes when she'd told her story; the touch of her hand on his arm. "They tortured her. Nearly drove her mad." Drove her halfway there, maybe more. Maybe all the way, and she'd never got the whole way back.

"That's right," said Helen. "But they weren't just Reapers. They were Jennywrens."

Fucking *hell.* Of course. "Jarrett. Right?"

"Well spotted," said Gevaudan. "I got *there* five minutes ago."

"Fuck off, creeping death!" Danny took a step back, a hand to his mouth; the Grendelwolf straightened up.

"Gevaudan – " said Helen.

But he chuckled, then looked at them and sighed. "Sorry. I'm not used to company any more."

"It shows," said Helen.

Danny shook his head. Mentalists, the fucking pair of them. "So Jarrett tortured Alannah. And you were the one got her out. She said so. That when you reckoned you'd done Jarrett an' all?"

"Pretty much. I led a raid on the holding facility. The priority was to rescue Alannah, but I'd decided to kill Jarrett if I could as well."

"For what she'd done?"

"Or what she'd do. Like I said, she was the best they had. A major threat. Told myself that, anyway. Maybe I just wanted to get revenge for the people she'd killed. Anyway, we got in without raising the alarm. Once we'd got Alannah, I made a beeline for Jarrett's quarters with one of these." She tapped the Sterling. "I was nearly there when the alarm went off. She burst out of the door. And then she saw me." Helen looked at Danny. "I already had her covered. We just stood like that for a couple of seconds. Felt like longer. She knew she'd never get her gun up in time." Helen snorted, shook her head. "Still a fairer fight than she ever gave anyone. But Jesus, if looks could kill..."

"So you shot her?"

"Fired nearly a whole clip. Very bad technique. I ever catch you wasting ammo like that, I'll jam that Lanchester up your arse."

Danny had to smile.

"She'd got to me, you see. That's what Jarrett does. Probably why she's still alive, too."

"I'm not sure I understand," said Gevaudan.

"I should've dropped her with a short burst and then put one in her head. Make sure. Professional. But instead, I sprayed everything I had at her. Then half a dozen Jennywrens came running and I had to leg it. I obviously wounded her – badly enough to put her out of the game till after Sheffield, after the Refuge – but she lived. And now it looks like Winterborn's called her in specially. I'm almost flattered."

*

"You certainly cause excitement wherever you go," said Gevaudan. Like here. He'd killed Reapers, endangered his serum supply, and for what?

"So what do we do?" asked Danny.

Helen took a last look at the screen, then turned away. "I came here to do a job."

"However many innocents have to die?" asked Gevaudan.

"I'm not the one with a gun to her head."

"No. You'll just let Jarrett pull the trigger."

"You think I want this?"

"I think that you, Jarrett and Winterborn all have one thing in common."

"Oh?"

"The idea that the ends justify the means. Ultimately, it doesn't leave much to choose between either side."

"Really?" Helen jerked a thumb back at the screen. "I never pulled anything like *that*, Gevaudan. I may not have clean hands, but this? No. That's what the Reapers do. If they catch me, they'll torture me for information. Others will die."

"People who chose to fight this war. That child has had no such choice."

Helen spoke through her teeth. "I'm needed."

"Why?"

"I have the experience – "

"Of what? Losing?"

"Fuck you!"

"Helen!" Danny moved to her side as Gevaudan stood, lips compressed.

Suddenly Gevaudan wanted her gone – her self-righteous, condemning gaze, the chaos she brought – wanted to say something that would hurt. "You say you fight for her sake," he said. "But I repeat: that child and countless other hostages will die in your place, for your 'greater good'." He started to turn away, then rounded on her again. "Do you know how the War began, Helen? Because somebody decided that millions upon millions of corpses were a price worth paying for... what? Does anyone even remember, anymore?" His fists were clenched; he opened them. "Someone decided there was a 'greater good' than preventing that destruction of countless ordinary lives, homes ... families." Gevaudan breathed out. "How many corpses are too many for you, Helen?" She didn't answer; he sat back down. "*That's* why I will no longer choose a side."

That, said an inner, traitorous voice, *and you're happy where you are.*

Helen looked down. On the screen, the girl sobbed; Jarrett flicked the stub of her cigarette away, held up the stopwatch, lit another.

*

In the church, nobody spoke for some time. Danny was scared to look at the Grendelwolf. Helen kept looking down. He saw her chew her lip, then take a deep breath. Her shoulders straightened and her jaw clenched. *Shit.* He stepped back; she'd made a decision.

"Gevaudan?" Helen asked.

"Yes?"

"Can you get Danny out of here, without them picking him up?"

"Eh?" Danny blinked.

"Shut up, Danny. Gevaudan? Can you?"

"Yes," he said at last. "Yes. There's a tunnel – "

"Don't tell me." She put the Sterling down on the floor. "I don't want to betray any more secrets than I can help." She put the .38 alongside it, dropped the loose ammunition on the ground beside both. "Just get him out safe."

"Hang on." Danny caught her arm. "What about you?"

"Find Darrow. He knows everything he needs to. And he doesn't need me to get the Tindalos data out of the computer. That's Alannah's job. If it's there, she'll find it. Gevaudan, what's the quickest route from here to the perimeter?"

"Are you serious?"

"Yes."

"Turn left at the main door. Carry on up the road. You'll be there in ten minutes, if you're quick."

"I will be." She took a deep breath. "It's your job now, Danny."

"No." His voice shook; salt stung his eyes. She couldn't go. Not like this. She was a fighter. She – "You can't," was all he could say. "You *can't.*"

"I've got to," she said simply. "My love to the rest. And – "

"What?"

"Work on your burst control," she said. "Don't waste ammo."

"Helen," said Gevaudan. "If you mean what you say, you have to go now."

She nodded. "See you. Well, actually, no. I probably won't, will I?"

She didn't look back, even when Danny shouted after her. He started running when she opened the doors, but by the time he'd reached them she was running too. He yelled after her, but still she didn't turn around. He ran after her –

A hand caught his arm. "Get off, you c– " Danny fought, writhed, but then he realised he was dangling. Below him was a hole in the ground; at the bottom glittered sharp points of steel and glass.

Gevaudan hauled him back to safety. "For uninvited guests."

Danny threw his arm off and backed away, hands fisted. "Happy now?" he yelled. "You fucking happy now, creeping fucking death?"

Right then he didn't care if Shoal ripped his guts out. But the Grendelwolf just watched him. If he had any expression, it was something close to sadness. "Come on," he said. "I promised her I'd get you out."

*

Gevaudan knelt in the middle of an empty street whose terraced houses were in worse shape than the rest of Deadsbury, their windows, roofs and doors all gone. A scrape, and he pulled back the manhole cover. "Just climb down there. Go straight ahead. Shouldn't be any forks or side-tunnels."

"Shouldn't?"

"None that I recall, but it's a long time since I was last down there."

Danny looked at the pale, gaunt face, tried to read an emotion in it he could recognise, couldn't. "Right."

"It comes out into a cellar on a sidestreet off Palatine Road in Northenden. Can you find your own way from there?"

"Course."

"Good." He looked like he wanted to say something else, but he didn't. Good – Danny didn't want to hear that fucking voice ever again. He was a man now. Had a job to do. Find Alannah; find Darrow. He wouldn't think about Helen; *fuck,* he just had. Now his eyes were stinging again. Fucking Grendelwolf bastard.

He swung his legs through the manhole, hung by his fingers from the edge, then dropped down and landed in a crouch. Perfect. He looked back up; Gevaudan knelt again, reaching to slide the manhole cover back into place. "Not thinking of coming too?"

No answer. The Grendelwolf hadn't said much on the way over here.

"Nah, didn't think so. Hope you're fucking proud of yourself."

"It was her choice," said Gevaudan at last.

"Yeah, right."

"I just reminded her – "

"Yeah. People get killed in a fucking fight. Never have guessed that. Thanks a bunch. All right for you. You've got this. Rest of us have to live out there. On whatever's left when the cunting Reapers are done with it." His face burned. "Oh, fucking forget it." He dragged his sleeve across his eyes, turned away.

"Danny?"

"What?" Gevaudan tossed something to him. "Woss this?"

"Clockwork torch. It's dark down there."

A low dull metal scrape and the cover was dragged back into place. The thin winter light died away and all was black.

"Fucker's right," Danny mumbled. "It *is* bastard dark."

Something scratched and skittered in the gloom. "Fuck." Danny fumbled at the torch; a click, and yellow light shone. It glinted on damp, mossy stone, water trickling through uneven rubble on the floor, and the fur of the rats that darted away.

"Right," Danny muttered. His sub-machine gun hung on its sling. A Lanchester; she'd taught him that. He'd remember it. He started down the tunnel. *Watch your burst control,* she'd told him.

He'd remember that, too.

*

Everything seemed suddenly sharp and alive to Helen, now that it was like as not the last time she'd be seeing it. The coarse grass, the brick, glass and china fragments scattered in the thin earth leapt out at her. In the distance, the sun set; a blood and orange glow blazed through rents in the dull cloud, staining it. She had to fight the urge to stop and stare; she wanted to hold on to each moment as it passed now. Relish it. But they were fleeting, they were going. A flight of small quick birds, all hurrying past. And now they were nearly gone.

Would they shoot her on the spot? Not so likely; she knew Jarrett well enough by now. She'd want Helen alive, to finish her off herself, at least, or to interrogate for information. That'd buy time, and maybe the chance of escape. Or at least to get close enough to take Jarrett with her.

"And Winterborn," said Frank, falling into step beside her. His face was a mask of cracked white clay; his clotted eyes, sunken into it, glistened blackly. "Don't forget him."

"No. I won't."

A clatter of wings; a crow flapped by, climbing skyward. At least it wasn't sickly or deformed; at least something flourished and bred true.

"One thing we didn't fuck up," she said.

"Language," said Frank.

"Mummy," said Belinda, to her left. Small cold fingers clasped Helen's hand; she couldn't pull away, though her skin seemed to writhe at the child's touch. She didn't dare look down.

"So," said Frank, reaching out and taking her free hand in his. It felt like a dead bird's rotten claw. She thought she might vomit. "That's it, then?" asked Frank. "You're giving up?"

"I'll give you Winterborn too, if I can. Might even get to give him to you more quickly."

"Doubt they'll give you the chance," smirked Frank. "Stupid."

"They'll kill that girl."

"Like they killed ours. Like they killed me."

"Daddy," said Belinda.

"Sorry, Chicken. She's not your blood, Helen. We are."

"She's alive." She bit her lip, but too late; she'd said it.

"You promised us revenge."

"Revenge or me. Food. That's what you said."

"True." Frank sighed.

"You'll get to eat, either way."

"Mummy, Daddy, I'm hungry."

Frank smiled, the cracks in his desiccated skin widening, his bloodclot eyes never leaving Helen's. "Don't worry, Chicken. We'll eat soon."

Belinda made a sound between a hiss and a giggle. Happy, greedy. Frank's lips parted as he grinned, and Helen saw the rows of white needle teeth, built for raking flesh and stripping it from bone. She looked away and kept walking. As she went, she found she was crying.

Eventually, they let go of her hands. Up ahead, the street ended in a raised embankment taller than her head. Helen looked around; she was alone. They'd gone; off to prepare their dining table, perhaps. From beyond the embankment she heard voices. Deadsbury's edge; she wiped her eyes and walked towards it. No ghosts beside her now, no army at her back; *I walk alone.* A smile twitched her mouth at the thought.

She climbed the embankment, arms out for balance. Hopefully they wouldn't be too trigger-happy; Jarrett would want her alive. And maybe she'd proven something to the Grendelwolf; maybe this was what it took to bring him into the fight. A blood sacrifice, to appease some angry god or invoke some supernatural aid. *Still playing others, Helen?* Alannah would have said. *About to bloody die and you're still playing angles, making your little gambles. Will even death stop you doing that?*

Or maybe she was trying to impress the Grendelwolf for all the wrong reasons; those clear yellow eyes, that deep wolf's rumble of a voice. Didn't matter now. Nearly at the top of the embankment. "Hello?" she called.

"Shit!" someone yelped. A gun-bolt snapped back.

"This is Helen Damnation," she called. "I'm coming out. I'm surrendering."

She raised her hands high; best to come into view with her hands up. She reached the top of the embankment; below her, four Reapers, huddled round a landcruiser, aimed sub-machine guns at her.

"Don't move," one called.

"I won't," she said. "Now get on the blower to Jarrett."

5.

"Winterborn."

"This is Jarrett, sir."

"Yes, Colonel."

"We've got her."

"So quick? So simple?"

"Gave herself up to a foot patrol five minutes ago. They're bringing her to me now. I'm almost disappointed. I expected her to give me a harder time than that. But sometimes it's just a question of finding your enemy's weak spots."

"Ensure you watch her. She's a cunning one."

"I learned that the hard way, sir. She'll be watched closely."

Just a question of finding your enemy's weak spots, indeed. Then why hadn't he thought of it? Hadn't he once known her inside and out?

"Shall I bring her to you, Commander?"

"Business before pleasure, Colonel. Take her to the Bailey, straight away. Let's secure her under lock and key. I take it you'll want to conduct the interrogation personally?"

"If you've no objection, sir."

"I wouldn't want to deprive you of your fun, Colonel. Let me know when you're ready to begin. I may want to look in on her before you... start."

"Yes, sir."

"Good work, Colonel. Winterborn out."

Winterborn stood, went to the window, gazed out over the city. He should feel different, shouldn't he? He should feel better than this.

"Helen," he whispered. Then he shook his head and turned away.

*

ANCOATS
1541 HOURS

The landcruiser bounced over an uneven road. Helen sat in the flatbed, up against the running board; two Reapers covered her with Sterlings. Cocked sub-machine guns, nervous trigger-fingers and a bumpy road. One pothole at the wrong time and they'd probably have emptied their guns before they even knew they'd done it. Quicker and less painful than whatever Jarrett and Winterborn had planned, of course.

The cruiser pulled into a square. There was a battered TV camera, mounted on a tripod. Jarrett stood before it, Browning still aimed at the girl's head. Behind her, a dozen Reapers stood guard over a huddle of ragged figures. But no sign of Winterborn.

"Out," said a Reaper, motioning with his gun.

She obeyed, walked towards Jarrett. The two Reapers followed, spread out to catch her in a crossfire. Helen gauged the distance. Her hands were free; with a leap, she could get to Jarrett.

"I think that's close enough." Jarrett pressed the Browning to the girl's head. Helen stopped. Still too far; the Reapers would cut her in half.

*

Jarrett sighed, stomach hollow with excitement. She almost shook – euphoria. "You searched her?"

"Yes ma'am. Unarmed."

Helen stared back at her; those cool grey eyes, that white oval face, that red hair.

"Well?" said Jarrett. "Nothing to say?"

"Where's Winterborn?"

"He's shy."

"Thought he'd be here to say hello."

"The universe doesn't revolve around you, Helen. Never understood that, have you?"

"How about letting the hostages go?"

Jarrett's smile hardened. "All in good time."

"I kept my side of the bargain."

"Bargain? What bargain? You see, that's exactly what I mean, Helen. I don't bargain with scum like you. Just use whatever it takes to bring you in." Jarrett sighed. "Same old Helen. Your trouble is you think you're somebody." She clicked back the hammer. "I think you need another lesson."

She turned and shot Shell in the face. The girl fell; sprayed blood hung in the air. Helen lunged forward. Jarrett spun, gun raised; the Browning's hot, reeking muzzle was inches from Helen's eye.

"Don't shoot," Jarrett snapped at the Reapers. "That would be too quick."

She thrust her face close to Helen's. Blood speckled it. "Do you get it now, Helen?" She nodded down at Shell in her crooked broken huddle, a red-black halo coagulating around her head. "That's all you do. All you're capable of. People like this get caught up in your games, and they die. And for what? Nothing. You're a parasite, a tick."

Jarrett stepped back, breathing hard, holstered the Browning. "Take her to the Bailey. I don't want anyone screwing her, I want her alive when I get there, and leave her face alone. Otherwise, boys – have fun."

They dragged Helen off.

Jarrett looked down at Shell's body and blinked. Just for a moment, the face changed; rounder, more freckled. Amanda's face. Jarrett shook her head, and the dead face was Shell's again.

Jarrett walked back to her landcruiser, and made sure she didn't look at the bodies of Yan and Sheel, dumped nearby. She knew whose faces they would wear.

*

NEWTON HEATH
2014 HOURS

It was dark, cold; Danny was so fucked he could barely stand, and to put the tin bastard lid on it it started pissing down too. This was gonna have to be it. Last stop. He hadn't got the strength to go further and even if he had it was after curfew; bastard Reapers would get him.

Behind a row of shacks, he fell to his knees in a stretch of rubble-strewn grass and began grubbing at the earth. Anyone watching would've thought he was a nutter, or starving and hunting worms; let them. At last he found what he was after: hard wood, under the earth. He pulled at it, but it didn't budge. Locked.

They could only do that from the inside. Danny grabbed a rock and banged on the trapdoor – two short, three long.

No answer. "Come on." He banged again. "Come on, you f – "

Next he knew he was on his back with the wind knocked out of him, a hand on his mouth, a blade at his neck. Fucking Reaper–

Ashton let him go, grinned. "Still got a lot to learn, Danny," he said.

Above, Ashton slid the cover back over the entrance hole. Candles lit the cavelike space around them, reflected in wide eyes. He saw Flaps – *hullo, darling* – and Telo from Scary Mary's crew; Jake and Mackie from Ashton's, Hinge and Nikki from his own. And at the back, rising as she saw him, Alannah.

And one other, of course, pushing through the others to find him. "Danny? Where's Helen?" Darrow demanded. Danny didn't answer. Couldn't.

Alannah came to him. "Danny? Danny, what happened?"

"They got her," he said. "Helen. They got her."

"Dead?"

"Prisoner." Didn't want to say what came next. Had to. "Jarrett."

Alannah's face whitened; she swayed, sagged. Danny reached out and took her arm but she pulled away. "No," she said. "No."

Danny turned miserably to Darrow, who stared back at him; then something seemed to drain out of the older man.

"There's soup if you want it," he said, "and a blanket."

He turned and walked away through his fighters, not looking back, hands fists at his sides.

*

HOBSDYKE VILLAGE
2230 HOURS

Mordake walked down Hobsdyke High Street. He hadn't brought the torch from the landcruiser; the starlight lit the village up. Even if it hadn't, Mordake knew these uneven, overgrown streets so well he could have navigated them blindfolded.

Mordake paused outside a house, ran his fingers over the outer wall. Grey stone, then the roughness of ochre-coloured lichen.

Through the gaping doorway, he saw a wooden table and four chairs, all covered in spiderwebs. He'd almost miss this. There was something about the right kind of ruin; a pleasing, gentle melancholy. He forgot sometimes why this place was deserted –

Four people sat at the table, faces hidden by matted hair. Two adults, two children. They turned and looked up at him. Their hair fell away from their faces. Their faces were skulls.

He blinked; they were gone.

"Eddie?"

Liz leant back against the wall, wearing a padded blue gilet, a man's check shirt, jeans and brown calfskin boots, arms folded under her breasts. One leg was drawn up, foot braced against the brickwork; a pose she'd seen somewhere and struck for him when she wanted to make him laugh. Or turn him on.

"Hello again."

She didn't smile back. "Eddie, this is the last time."

"What is?" She wasn't real; he was just ghostlighting again. But if he reached out and touched her, he'd feel the smooth synthetic fabric of the gilet, the rough cotton weave of the shirt. Skin's smoothness; flesh's warm solidity.

"This," she said. "You and me."

"Oh. I see." He turned away.

"Eddie – "

"I know. Stop doing this."

"You have to."

"Can't."

"Yes, you can."

"No. I can't, Liz."

He heard her step away from the wall, her footsteps crunch in the brittle grass; she wrapped her arms around him from behind. "Because of Dowson?"

"Hm."

"I thought the project couldn't happen with you dead."

"Reapers can be very persuasive."

"I know." She stroked his chest.

"Dowson knows it's real now. He wouldn't let me stop even if I wanted to."

"And you don't."

"No."

"Why?"

"Because I can't survive without you."

"You already have, Eddie. You've survived for twenty years."

"And all that's kept me going is getting you back."

"I'm here now."

"You're not!" He tore free of her, stumbled, almost fell, then wheeled to face her. "You're not Liz. You are *not* my wife. You're... an image. A hallucination. My mind's way of helping me cope. But none of it's real. It's just ghostlight. Just the mind, playing tricks."

"And that's all I am?"

"Yes. That's all."

"Can't that be enough?"

"No. No, it's not."

"Maybe it has to be enough."

"I can't accept that."

"Eddie – "

"Liz, it's not just for you. We could wipe away *all* this. All of it. Have it back the way it was." But she was already shaking her head; he turned away again.

"Eddie."

"I can't live without you, Liz, and I can't end it all either. I've tried. What I've got is just a half life. I need you back again. *Really* back. If there's even a chance, I have to take it."

She was only a figment, he told himself, only a figment. Nothing real. For all that, Mordake didn't dare turn round for fear she'd be gone.

But instead he felt the soft, gentle pressure of her hands on his shoulders. "All right," she said. "But you won't see me again."

Her hands slid under his arms and across his chest, to meet over his heart. Despite himself, he reached up and held them. "Your fingers are cold."

"It *is* winter."

"I'd forgotten."

"Christmas soon."

"Forgotten that too."

They moved back together; she perched on the remains of the garden wall. Her breasts against his back, her cheek against his neck, her legs wrapped round him.

"So this is the last time."

"The last time," he heard himself say.

They rocked, gently, to and fro. Mordake closed his eyes, felt tears escape and trickle down his cheeks.

"Just be careful," she whispered. "The wolves are running."

"What?"

But she'd pushed him away from the wall. He stumbled, turned. She was gone.

He wiped his eyes hard, rubbed his face. An infinity of stars glimmered above, an infinity of tiny eyes. And they looked – *right,* somehow. Ready, waiting; moving into some propitious alignment.

Mordake walked back to his landcruiser, past the church, stopping briefly to look at that odd, skewed cross that was not a cross above the lintel. She was gone. No more ghostlighting. But that was necessary. No more illusions, no more hallucinations. A reality with Liz truly in it that he could at last live in, or one without her that he could finally leave with a bullet, blade or a few pills. Either way, he'd be free.

*

The armoured car rattled down the suburban street. The houses were silent and windowless; bodies lay on the pavement outside some of them, wrapped in binliners or plastic sheeting.

Mordake sat in silence. The soldiers didn't speak.

Two weeks earlier, he'd been – no other word for it – press-ganged. His name had been on a list, because of his psychiatric work. They'd reckoned

205

they needed him, so they'd sent men to grab him. Knocked him out when he'd refused to go. While Liz had been left on her own.

The armoured car pulled up; Mordake looked out of the window to see the once-familiar front of his own house. The windows were gone, and half the roof tiles.

"Ready when you are, Doctor," said the army corporal in the back with him. His tone wasn't unkind.

They climbed out, went up the drive. A woman coughed blood outside the house next door, watching them with glazed, hopeless eyes. Was it Mrs Trent, the solicitor's wife? Mordake couldn't be sure.

Liz was in the cellar. She'd tried to set up some kind of shelter there, brought tinned food and bottled water down there with her, but the fallout had crept down there too. And what was left... it wasn't Liz anymore. The worst part was that Mordake didn't weep, at least not then. He found nothing in that cellar that he hadn't expected to.

"If there's anything you want to bring away," said the corporal, "make it quick."

Mordake nodded and went upstairs. In his study he found a plastic crate. Calmly and methodically, he began packing his notes and files on the Beloved; finally, on top of them, he added half a dozen cylinders of polished greenish stone, inscribed with glyphs in an unknown tongue.

*

When he flashed the headlights outside the gates, Reapers came running; they'd been waiting. Everything waited on him tonight; just for this moment, the world revolved around him. And if things worked, maybe after it, too.

Inside the gates, Andrews ran up; beyond him, Dowson flicked aside a half-smoked cigarette and strode forward. Mordake climbed out as Andrews reached him. "Motor pool," he said.

"Yes, Doctor."

Mordake went to meet Dowson. Behind him, the landcruiser's engine coughed into life and it drove off.

"Colonel."

"Nice of you to grace us with your presence, Doctor."

"I'm sorry. I needed … a moment. Some time to myself."

"So everyone keeps saying."

"You look – "

"I look what?"

Best be careful; men like Dowson were dangerous when afraid. "Concerned," he said at last.

Dowson snorted, a sneer twisting his mouth. "That's one fucking way of putting it, pal."

"What's wrong?"

"Look," said Dowson, looking across the parade ground.

Mordake looked; Reapers stood in groups, all gazing raptly towards the Adjustment Chamber.

"Everyone's acting freaky. Expect your techies to be a weird lot, but the fucking Reapers too?"

"We *have* all worked on this project for a long time."

"And half of them thought it was a load of old shite."

"Now they know differently."

Dowson stared at him, unblinking. Was the man trying to intimidate him? Then Mordake realised he was trying to project sincerity. "I think it's more than that, Doctor."

"Such as?"

Dowson nodded across the compound towards the Adjustment Chamber. "Back in the Civil Emergency, I had to deal with a religious cult. Proper nutcases. Called 'emselves the Spared. Controlled a few towns in Cheshire, as I recall. Reckoned the war was the Last Judgement, they were the Pure, the Chosen – all that bollocks." Dowson snorted. "Cults like that were ten-a-penny back then. But most of them went under pretty fast. These, though – Jesus. Fought to the death. I mean, literally. I talked to a couple of them. We even tried to negotiate once. Didn't do any good. Couldn't bribe or threaten them. They took their orders off God. Let Him down and nothing we did could match up to what they'd suffer. We meant nothing."

"So?"

"The way this lot are acting's starting to remind me of that."

Mordake nodded. "Interesting."

"*Interesting?* That's all you've got to say?"

"Could just be that they're properly motivated now."

"Could be?"

Could this be *their* influence, too, on a gentler and subtler scale? Making sure all went as it should? Not something to suggest to Dowson; he'd start screaming about mind control. And that was silly. The test subjects were under control; if anything, they *wanted* to complete their transition. All this was – if it was anything at all – was the subtlest of influencing, a nudging. If it was even that.

If worse came to worst, there was always the big red button in the Monitoring Unit. A single spark, and all that lived therein would burn away. They could start again, pick up the threads, now that Dowson believed. Always assuming his nerve didn't fail; the man was wavering back and forth. Mordake felt the pistol's weight in his pocket.

But that wouldn't happen; this was the one. He could feel it. Excitement shivered through him; he might weep with joy. After all these years, at last – tonight, it would end. He looked at his watch. "Come on, Colonel," he said. "It's time to start."

*

NEWTON HEATH
2345 HOURS

"We can't just leave her!"

"Keep your voice down, Danny." Darrow said, teeth gritted, as they huddled round the ancient spirit stove.

"Get your heads down," Ashton called to the other fighters, hunched together at the far end of the dugout. "Big day tomorrow."

"One way of putting it. Christ, Darrow. They're just kids."

"I didn't make the world the way it is, Alannah."

"I wonder sometimes."

"Rescuing Helen, right now, would be a major operation. It would take extensive planning and…"

"And she's not worth it?"

"That is enough!" Darrow's jaw was clenched, eyes bright.

Danny looked down. "Soz."

Alannah put a hand on Danny's arm, then withdrew it. "I don't want to leave Helen in the lurch either. Especially not with Jarrett. Believe me."

"But?" Danny demanded, as Ashton sank down beside them.

"Helen came back here," said Alannah, "because she believed Project Tindalos had to be stopped, whatever it is. It came before anything else. Even revenge on Winterborn."

"And that's saying something," Darrow said.

"What did he do?" asked Danny. "Winterborn. There's more to it. I've heard how she talks about him. What'd he do?"

Silence. The three older rebels looked at each other.

"Come on," said Danny. "I'm old enough to fight for you, aren't I? Old enough to die. So I'm old enough to know."

"He's right, Roger," Alannah said.

Darrow sighed. "You know about the Refuge Massacre."

"Yeah. I *was* listening."

Darrow's mouth twitched. "Then you know a lot of good people died there. We all lost friends. Comrades. People we cared about."

"Yeah."

"Helen was married back then. She had a child."

"A kid?" Danny thought of the lean, taut figure he'd tried and failed not to notice. "No way."

"Way," said Darrow drily.

"A little girl," Alannah almost whispered. "Belinda, she was called."

Darrow actually *looked* old for once, weary and grey. "Frank – Helen's husband – and Belinda died when the Jennywrens stormed the Refuge. Helen – "

"Helen was shot," said Alannah. "Left for dead. Got out somehow, half-crazy after what had happened."

"Yeah." Danny nodded. "And what else?" Because of course there was more. He was sharp enough to know *that*.

"She was shot, Frank and Belinda and many others were killed, because of Tereus Winterborn," said Darrow.

"He was one of us," said Alannah.

"We thought so, anyway," Ashton said, and spat on the ground.

"He'd been with us for years," said Darrow. "Helen treated him like her own brother. Trusted him completely. And then he betrayed us to the Reapers. Does anybody have a cigarette?"

Ashton lit two, passed him one.

"Thank you," Darrow said. "We have a priority, which is to locate and destroy Project Tindalos. If it's important enough for Helen to give up her revenge on Winterborn, it's important enough for us to – "

"Give up Helen?"

"Do you think she'd thank us," Alannah said, "if we freed her just to be killed when Tindalos, whatever it is, gets used?"

Danny thought of the clear eyes, the lean strength, the sense of purpose, and looked down.

"If – *if* – there's a way, afterwards," said Darrow, "then we'll see. We'll do ourselves no favours leaving her with Jarrett. But until then, we have a job to do." His eyes, meeting Danny's, were sad. "This is how you fight a war. Above all, the mission. Now, unless there's anything else, let's get some sleep."

*

"In here, Colonel."

'Here' was basically a concrete shed, a few yards from the Adjustment Chamber.

"This is the Monitoring Unit," said Mordake. "If we do have to trigger the charges, the Adjustment Chamber is built to contain the blast." He opened the outer door, looked back. "We'll be perfectly safe."

Dowson felt eyes on him – Andrews, some of the other Reapers. Lyson appeared in the airlock, too, arms folded, the scraggy little smile on his weedy face saying, *Not scared, are you?* It'd be Dowson's pleasure arranging something nasty for the smug little shit, soon as he could get away with it.

Anyway, he wasn't scared. Uneasy, yes – this was beyond anything his training or experience equipped him for – but he'd dealt with worse than this.

"Right then," he said. "Just please tell me I can fucking smoke in there."

"Oh, yes," said Mordake. "I expect we'll all be lighting up. Eh, Lyson?"

The technician sniggered. Dowson gritted his teeth, stepped into the airlock. The outer door closed; the three of them were squeezed shoulder to shoulder. God, Lyson stank. Sweat, stale piss and things Dowson didn't want to think about.

Clunk; the outer lock engaged. Another *clunk;* the inner door swung open.

The inside was cramped. There were eight techies in there already, hunched over a row of control panels, above which were a row of monitor screens. There were speakers on either side of the monitors, and a microphone sticking up out of the central panel.

There was also a red button, under a plastic cover. Dowson leant forward, pointing. "What's that do?"

"Don't touch that!"

Dowson rounded on Mordake. "What's that?"

Mordake breathed out. "I'm sorry, Colonel. I'm sorry."

"What does it do?"

Mordake spoke unwillingly. "That activates the auto-purge mechanism. There are tanks full of hydrogen gas under the Unit. Push that button and they'll vent into the Adjustment and Seclusion Chambers. Then there'll be a spark. The structure will contain the explosion, of course, but anything in the chambers will be incinerated."

"Just in case?"

"Just in case, Colonel. But it won't be necessary. Anyway. Let's begin. It's standing room only, I'm afraid." Mordake smiled; his teeth were yellow, but Dowson found himself smiling back. No one else spoke or even looked up at them; they saw only their controls and readouts.

Mordake lit a cigarette. After a moment, so did Dowson.

The monitors blinked into life, showing the four surviving test subjects from multiple angles: above, from the side, individual close-ups, a shot from behind that showed the wall they faced, where a big white paper screen hung.

The subjects were strapped into a row of reclining couches; beside each was a stand with four IV drips. All were shaven-headed and wore stained, shapeless smocks. Even in close-up, Dowson couldn't tell the men from the women.

"Recording, sir."

"Will four be enough?" Dowson said.

"Should be ample," said Mordake. "Of course, I won't know what the limits of this group's abilities will be. That'll take us into a whole new regime of testing. Lyson, looks like Subject Five's nodding off. IV1, ten millies."

"IV1?"

"Amphetamine solution. Keeps them awake."

"Course. Sleep deprivation. What about the others?"

"IV2 contains adrenaline, stimulates the heart in case of arrest. IV3's a relaxant in case their vital signs skyrocket. Don't want them burning themselves out."

"And number four?"

Mordake smiled. "A little recipe from the North Sea Culture. It makes certain areas of the brain, normally dormant, receptive to certain stimuli. We call it the Tiresias solution."

"You do, do you?"

"Tiresias was a blind Greek who saw the future, aspects of existence denied to everyone else. It's as good a name as any. It sensitises the relevant parts of the brain until the subject loses consciousness. Then they have to be 'switched on' all over again. However, by preventing the subject falling asleep, we can sustain that sensitivity *and* keep ramping it up with further doses."

"And what does that do?"

"On its own, nothing. The other element is a sequence of images we have to show the subjects. In themselves they're just images, *unless* – "

Dowson finally got it. " – unless those bits of their brains are switched on."

"Exactly. It's like a binary weapon. The Tiresias solution opens the 'eye'. The visual images triggers the dormant properties in those parts."

"Telekinesis?" Dowson was proud he'd remembered the word.

"And telepathy, Colonel. Which as you can see has linked their individual minds together into a single group consciousness, acting as one. Are they all ready, Lyson?"

"Vital signs and brain activity optimal, Doctor."

"All right. PHC check."

"PHC?" asked Dowson.

"Post-hypnotic commands. Make sure we're all still on the same hymn sheet. Especially important with a group mind." Mordake switched on the mic. "Candlemass. Repeat, Candlemass. Turn your heads to the right."

A series of commands and responses followed. Finally Mordake nodded. "All right," he said, and shut off the microphone. "Let's begin. Twenty-five millilitres each from IV4."

A technician flicked a series of switches, watching the

displays, then flicked them back again. "Twenty-five millilitres administered."

"Some activity from Subject Two," Mordake said. "Looks like he's muttering to himself. Some sound on that, please."

The speakers hissed and crackled; faint, indistinct mumbling came out.

"Can we get more clarity on that?"

"'Fraid not, Doctor. Too low. Sorry."

"All right. Keeping watching their vitals. It takes a few minutes for the Tiresias treatment to kick in," Mordake explained. "Reaction times differ at first, but after a while, they start to synchronise."

"Like women when they're on the blob."

Mordake winced at the indelicacy, but nodded. "Yes, a bit. You get the best results if you wait till they're all tripping – for want of a better term – before starting Phase Three."

"Relevant brain activity in Subject Two," said Lyson.

"Good. The rest should be – "

"Subject One's started too."

"Excellent."

"And Subject Four… just waiting on Subject Five now."

"She's very much the slowcoach of the group."

"Activity from Subject Five as well now, Doctor."

"Excellent. All right, Mr Lyson. Let the show begin. Sequence One, thirty second exposures."

The screen in front of the subjects lit up, a wide square of bright light. Lyson moved a sliding switch, then pressed a button which lit up green.

Click; a symbol appeared. Dowson winced, forced himself to look. The fuck was that supposed to be? Wasn't Arab or Paki writing; wasn't Chink or Japanese either. What were those Viking ones? Runes, that was it. Didn't look like them either. Didn't quite look like anything he'd seen before. Not as far as he could tell, anyway. Hard to be sure; he couldn't quite seem to *focus* on the damn thing. Christ, it almost *hurt*. Felt like he was getting eye strain.

Click. The first symbol vanished; another replaced it. It wasn't any more familiar than the first. Or easier to look at. Dowson rubbed his eyes.

"You all right?" asked Mordake.

"Yeah, just – "

"Eye strain?"

"Yeah," said Dowson. "Or something."

"What you're feeling is the effect that makes the final phase work." Click: the symbol changed again. "They're in three sequences. We start by exposing them for thirty seconds at a time, then gradually speed it up."

Symbols clicked by. Dowson smoked another cigarette. Minutes passed.

"Increased brain activity from Subject Two," said Lyson.

"What about the others?"

"One second – yes. Subject One's begun responding too. And… yes, so's Four. Just waiting on Five now… yep, that's her too."

"All right." Mordake leant back, puffed out his cheeks, let out a long breath. "Speed up the sequence."

"Yes, Doctor."

Mordake lit a cigarette. "The speed the sequence goes by at will increase slowly. Takes time for them to acclimatise. Every twenty-nine seconds, then every twenty-eight and so on. Eventually we'll be able to run the whole sequence in less than a second."

"And that's it?"

"Not quite, Colonel. After an hour or two of that we move on to the second sequence, and then the third. Of course they'll have acclimatised by then, so we can go more or less straight into running those at full speed."

"That's a relief. What then?"

"Bit like conducting an orchestra, really. The trick's fine-tuning the brain activity. When to stimulate, when to tranquillise, so their brains don't burn out. Longer we can keep them going, the better our chances of – wait. Did you hear that?"

"Hear what?"

"Mr Lyson? The volume, please." The speakers hissed, and then Dowson heard it.

"Angana sor varalakh kai torja. Angana sor varalakh cha voran. Mantakha sa niroleph chir karagh."

Raw, gravelly voices; gears stripped bare. How many times had they said or screamed those words, till the lining ripped off their throats? Didn't matter. They deserved it. Dowson knew their kind, had signed enough movement orders for them.

"Insapa veir bereloth. Insapa. Maengrepa gir trequefa gla detiresh meirka."

That pulled him up short. Christ. What if they *knew?* Knew he was here, knew who he was? They could reach out and–

"Angana sor varalakh kai torja. Angana sor varalakh cha voran."

Mordake. Mordake was laughing.

"What?" shouted Dowson – he had to, the chanting voices was so loud now: *"Angana sor varalakh kai torja. Angana sor varalakh cha voran. Mantakha sa niroleph chir karagh. Insapa veir bereloth. Insapa. Maengrepa gir trequefa gla detiresh meirka. Angana sor varalakh kai torja. Angana sor varalakh cha voran."* Mordake didn't seem to hear him, just stared at the monitors, clasped hands at his mouth. "Mordake! What is it?"

"They're chanting."

"I bloody know that."

"Normally it takes at least a full hour to get to this point. But this time it's only taken…" he looked at the control panel "Bloody hell, five minutes! Five minutes to reach this point!"

Mordake fumbled for his cigarettes, hands a-jitter. Dowson took pity on the poor sod and offered one of his own. "So it's kicking into gear early, then?"

"Oh yes." Mordake nodded. "I think this is it, Colonel. I think this is really it."

Dowson found himself grinning back. He turned and stared into the monitor as the chanting rose, and rose, and rose.

6.

Danny woke from uneasy sleep and found fingers stroking his brow.

"Wha – ?"

Bodies shifted in the dark around him; there were grunts and mumbles.

"Sh." The fingers touched his lips. "Sorry. Didn't mean to – "

"Alannah?"

"Sh," she whispered again. "You'll wake the others."

Danny shivered under his thin blanket, even though the sleepers were packed so tight he could barely move. Christ alone knew how she'd picked her way through them to his side without waking any bugger. "What d'you want?"

She flinched, like he'd hit her.

"Shit. No. Soz. Just meant – "

"Making sure you were all right." She didn't look at him.

"I'm okay."

"Good." She fidgeted. "I'm… I'm very glad about that." Someone grunted in their sleep. "I should go."

"No." He caught her wrist. "S'okay. Can stay." He shrugged. "If you want."

She hesitated; he lifted his blanket. "Room under here if you – "

"No!" Sleepers stirred in the dark. "No. I don't know what I'm – I'd best go."

"Don't." She looked down at him. "Please," he said.

Her face softened. "All right."

Danny closed his eyes and she stroked his forehead. But sleep wouldn't come.

*

REAP HOBSDYKE
0305 HOURS

"Shit, something's caught fire."

Dowson pointed. In the Adjustment Chamber, what looked like a column of smoke hovered between the test subjects and the white, flickering screen.

"No," said Mordake.

"What you on about?"

"Look at it, Colonel."

Dowson looked. Mordake was right; the 'smoke' was thickening, but it didn't rise or spread. Like smoke, it wavered, but then writhed and twisted and seemed to *pull* itself back into shape again. "The fuck is it, then?"

"I think the closest term might be 'ectoplasm'."

"Ecto-what?"

"It's a kind of… tissue. Living tissue. They're *making* it, Colonel. The test subjects. They're creating something."

Dowson turned and stared at him. "Say that again."

"I told you, a group mind. But housed in a single body, created by them. This is what we wanted, Colonel." Mordake smiled. "Something's being born."

*

A dim flickering glow lit the church windows, so weak it wouldn't have been noticeable but for the blackness of the night; it still spat rain, and there was no other light in Deadsbury of any kind.

Not that anyone was there to see it. The only human – or once-human – eyes in Deadsbury were inside the church, trying to read with more effort than success. Gevaudan sat by the altar; the heat of a brazier's flames, a few feet away, licked at his face and warmed the bitter air a little.

"Are you going to ignore me all night?" Gevaudan stared at the page, saw nothing. Heels clicked on the church floor. "Afraid to face me now? Is that it?"

Rain rattled against the windows. "No."

"Well, then?"

Gevaudan closed the book, let it fall into the cardboard box beside his chair and turned to face her.

"Well?" she said. "Not too bad a sight, am I?"

Gevaudan smiled. "You never could be."

"Flatterer." She warmed her hands over the brazier. "Not going to offer me coffee?"

"No point."

She sighed. "You always were one for bursting people's bubbles."

"But you loved me anyway."

"God knows why, sometimes. Mind if I sit down?"

"Please do."

"Thanks." She perched on the altar steps. "Wonder what they'd say if they knew Grendelwolves ghostlight too?"

"Wouldn't change a thing. It's more convenient to all if I remain a monster."

"True."

"So, to what do I owe the honour, Jo?"

"Do I have to have an ulterior motive?"

"Yes."

"Harsh thing to say to your wife."

"I rarely ghostlight. When I do, it's only ever you, out of all the ones I've lost. And you've always got something to tell me."

Jo spread her hands. "Fair cop, guv. Can you guess what it is yet?"

"I think so."

"Well?"

"Her."

"Her?"

"Helen."

"Yes. Her. Close-run thing. You nearly actually *did* something, Gevaudan."

He sighed. "She's haunted anyway, Jo. You know that. There's a devil on her back."

"I know."

"Sooner or later, it will destroy her. It's only a matter of time."

"So, you decided to do nothing just to end her suffering."

"It's not as if I didn't take some positive action."

"Yes, all right. You killed a few Reapers and you showed the boy the way out. But that was so you could be left alone again. Curl up and go to sleep." She smiled. "I remember how you used to rant about people who did that."

"Things were different then."

"Were they? Same people giving orders. Same people suffering because of them."

"Please tell me you haven't come back just to quote old slogans at me."

"Would that get you off your arse?"

Gevaudan rolled his eyes.

"I can think of another old slogan. You used it on the other Grendelwolves at Sheffield. *Better to die free than live a slave?* Was that it?"

"Yes. And that worked very well. The Grendelwolves are all dead."

"But they died free. So what does that make you?"

"Dear God. Kill me now."

"I can't." It looked for a second as if the skin and flesh were fading from her face, leaving only bone. "You're already dead, Gevaudan. You speak and you move, but you're dead. That's one thing she never was. Helen won't be dead until they kill her."

"She's a child."

"Everyone looks like a child to you, Gevaudan. Or you pretend they do. Play the grand old man in a young body. She wants you, you know. And you want her."

"Don't be disgusting. I'm old enough to be – "

"Not physically, not any more."

"I have standards, Jo."

"She hasn't given up. Devil on her back or not, she won't have given up, not even now. That's who she is. I used to think that you were the same."

"I think it's safe to say I was quite literally a different man then." Gevaudan looked down. "And that was a long time ago."

Jo didn't answer. He looked up; she was gone.

He wished she'd said something. But, of course, silence could be far deadlier; she'd always known that.

He sat as the brazier's flames burned down, the only sound the hiss of rain.

*

"Clear," whispered Ashton.

One by one, they clambered out, shivering in the cold dark.

Danny'd managed some sleep. A bit. But his eyes still felt heavy, full of grit. Lids didn't wanna stay open.

Wouldn't last. Hoped not, anyroad; *need to stay awake now or you're dead.*

They all wore cloaks and ponchos; had to hide the guns. Underneath, they wore overalls, like the ones Helen'd worn when he'd met her at the market. Plenty of pouches and pockets to keep ammo and equipment; served as a sort of uniform, too. Danny gripped the Lanchester tight as they spread out, slipped through the shantytown's shacks and bivvies and makeshift tents. They passed through another like it, then another, before they reached a maze of terraced houses.

No roofs or windows on the house. Looked ready to fall down, most of them, but there were people there. In one, someone was crying; from another came coughing and retching. Sounded to Danny like a creeping dose at work. Poor sod, whoever it was.

"You all right?" someone whispered. He glanced over: Flaps.

"Yeah. You?"

She nodded briskly, moved on. Flaps was weird like that.

Near the edge of the terraces, they stopped and ducked into the empty shell of a burnt-out house.

"Time to part ways," said Darrow.

Scary Mary nodded, pulled her poncho off. "Ditch 'em," she said in her flat, nasal accent. She was from the Midlands, she'd said. Wherever *they* were.

Flaps and the rest of Mary's crew followed suit. Mary had a weird, tubular contraption slung across her back; an ancient, battered-looking thing called a PIAT. Anti-tank weapon, Darrow'd said. Whatever *that* was. Danny guessed it was something that'd make a big bang. Just another reminder of how big a mission this was. Biggest he'd been on yet. Except maybe meeting *her*. And that hadn't gone too well. Not for her, in the long run. If it wasn't for him ballsing up, they might never have known she was back –

Never mind that now. Just try not to fuck *this* up. Make her proud of you.

"Luck," said Darrow.

"You too," said Scary Mary. "Come on."

Mary crawled out of the house on her belly, into the thick shrubs beyond. Her crew followed. Danny caught a glimpse of Flaps' small, neat bum waving to and fro as she went. *Mind on the job, lad.* Besides, it didn't feel right, somehow. There was Helen. But there was Alannah, too. There was something there with her, even if he didn't know what to call it yet. She was old enough to be his mum. But even still.

Fucking wandering again. Mind on the cunting job, or you won't be shagging anybody. Ever.

The other kids bunched together in one corner. "Get your heads down," hissed Danny. "An' spread out 'cross the floor." Reapers caught wind of them, they'd wipe half the fighters out with one long burst.

Danny crawled to a hole in the wall, squinnied out. Beyond the terraces, a grid of bare streets; cracked, buckled tarmac, two old, wilted-looking lampposts, a few low stubs of wall. The houses were long gone, knocked or burnt down and the rubble carted off. And beyond that, the squat, square concrete box of Station Five.

Further down the same wall, Nadgers huddled, pale and shaking. Danny crawled to him. "You all right, mate?"

Nadgers looked up at him. Poor little fucker looked like he'd start skriking any minute. "Fucking brickin' it."

"You'll be all right."

"I can't do this, Danny."

"You can. You gotta. You're a medic, mate, not a fighter. Just keep your head down and fix up anyone gets hit. Yeah?"

Nadgers' lips twitched. "Just – don't wanna die without – " he glanced round, leant in close to Danny. "You know."

"What?"

"I've never had a fucking shag," Nadgers whispered. "'Kay?"

Danny thought about his one time, with Flaps, how she'd lain back and spread herself out, then snapped closed round him like a trap. Nice trap, though. "Mate, we get through this, I'll sort you out. Kay? Promise. Just keep your head together an' do your job. Got it?"

Nadgers nodded, even managed a weak grin.

"Good one." Danny clapped him on the shoulder, glanced at the others. Saw they were all looking at him the way they – and he – looked at Darrow or Ashton. He felt himself shake a little. *Fuck.*

Darrow, Alannah and Ashton crouched by another hole in the wall, peering out round the edges. Danny crawled closer to them.

"It's wide open," Alannah said. She sounded calm, certain; a long way from how Danny'd first seen her.

"That was the plan," said Darrow. "Keep the space round it clear so the likes of us couldn't sneak up. But look. What do you see?"

"Nothing. Just dust, rubble – "

"And undergrowth," said Ashton.

Alannah breathed out. "I see."

"Back when we were a threat," said Darrow, "they'd have kept it swept clear, burned anything that grew, anything that might give cover. But it's been five years since the Refuge, and as far as the Reapers are concerned, we're just a rumour. We've survived. Hung on. Waited. For something like this."

"They've let keeping it clear had become a chore," said Ashton. "Got soft. And it's just a CiviSec base; street patrols, checkpoints, basic security. Most of them won't have used a gun in ages."

"No point taking chances, though," Alannah said.

"No," agreed Darrow. "So we crawl, slowly, using the grass and bushes for cover. Get to the sewer entrance and then down we go. Up in the middle of them like a jack in the box."

"As long as they haven't blocked it up."

"Well, there's that. Cross that bridge when we come to it."

"Roger?" Alannah whispered. Thinking no one could hear. But Danny could. "What happens afterwards?"

"What do you mean?"

"They'll know. That we're still here. They'll come hunting."

"Yes, I know."

"What then?"

"To be honest, Alannah, I haven't thought that far ahead."

"Roger, for Christ's sake."

"We'll have to improvise. All right, everybody." Darrow peeled off his poncho; under it he wore overalls, pouches stuffed with ammo. A pistol on his hip, his Thompson gun in his hands. "It's time."

*

DEADSBURY
0730 HOURS

Just before dawn, the world was a dull, half-lit grey. To human eyes, the street would have looked blurred and fuzzy, half-dissolved in the fading dark. But to Gevaudan's, as he slipped out through the church's doors, it was as if the sun had already risen.

Birdsong followed him down the deserted street. Heavy trees grew either side of the road, their thick trunks bowing towards one another, branches meshing overhead. In spring, blossom would tumble, soft and pink and white; in summer, the leaves formed a thick, cool canopy of green; and in autumn, the red, gold and russet leaves would fall to fill the street with a soft patter like brittle rain. But this was winter, and the dawn, when it came, would shine through the bare branches as through a mesh of bones.

I shan't see them in the summer again. Or the autumn, or the spring.

Gevaudan emerged from the trees and turned through a set of rusted, ivy-covered gates. An asphalt path, humped and cracked by tree-roots, the cracks a-writhe with weeds and moss, led through another set of gates to the sunken garden.

The old botanical gardens were sunk on several levels. Gevaudan followed the paths winding through them as the birds twittered and the light slowly brightened, thinning the predawn haze. Here was a pond, there was the stream.

This is the last time.

When Gevaudan reached the lowest level, he stepped off the path, through a gap in the rusted railings. As he went, he stooped and picked up half a dozen pebbles. When he found the seventh – a smooth, clear piece of pale quartz – he pocketed them, stood, then slipped on through trees and bushes till he reached the willow by the brook.

Under the willow was a little cairn; a pile of rocks and pebbles like the ones in his pocket, built up year by year, visit by visit, stone by stone.

There won't be any more.

He studied the tiny stream's bright, chuckling waters for a time. He didn't speak, just stood, hands in pockets, as the morning broke. His breath plumed and hung in the bitter air.

Now and again the stream and sunken gardens disappeared, and he lived, once more, in the past. Now and again a faint smile touched his lips, then faded. But mostly, for the first time in years, he truly saw the gardens and the stream.

The first time. Because it's the last.

"If you have forever, you don't value it," he murmured. "When you only have today…" He trailed off, snorted. "And you're too old for half-baked philosophy, Shoal."

But here were the gardens, nonetheless, so clear, so present.

Because I'm leaving.

There was a lesson there, perhaps.

That which passes has value, as well as that which survives.

"You were right," he said aloud. "I am dead."

He turned from the stream and knelt by the cairn. "However, it's been a day for resurrections. Helen. Jarrett. Perhaps we should see if they come in threes."

Slowly, carefully, he dismantled the cairn, laying the pebbles out around it like stone flower's petals unfolding in the dawn. At the bottom of the pile, he found what he sought: half a dozen smooth, round pebbles, painted white; a clutch of eggs that would never hatch. The paint hadn't faded; not the white, and not the black in which he'd carefully written their names. *Jo. Michaela. Gideon.* And the others.

He took them out, laid them aside, then replaced them with six of the pebbles he'd gathered. Then, slowly, carefully he reassembled the cairn; when it was done, he placed the quartz on top. It gave him a sense of completion, real or not.

He washed the white pebbles in the waters of the stream, dried them on his coat and pocketed them.

In the trees, the birds were singing.

Gevaudan turned from the stream, the willow and the cairn for the last time, and walked back to the path.

*

NEWTON HEATH
0745 HOURS

Danny crawled through brick dust; tiny daggers of stone, metal, concrete and glass dug into him. He gritted his teeth, kept crawling.

Undergrowth helped, even if was prickly shit. Scratching at his face, going for his eyes – bony fingers, come to claw them out. He flinched. But he kept crawling. Slow going and it bloody hurt, but it beat running in like a hero and getting shot. He knew that. Been trained for it.

Hoped Alannah had. Intelligence officer, Helen said. Shouldn't think about Helen, not now. Maybe not ever again. Intelligence officers. Did they get into the thick of it, like his sort? Even if she had, she'd been stuck in a hole in the ground the last five years. Be a bit out of practice.

Enough. Mind on the job. Couldn't think like that. Not here. Not now. She was with Darrow and Ashton. They needed her for this, so they needed her safe. They'd have thought of something. Keep your mind on getting yourself through safe.

Brick dust stung his nose. Don't sneeze. Most like, nobody'd hear owt. But some fucker might. CiviSec or not, fat lazy bastards or not, they were still Reapers.

Thick bushes, standing almost half his height. Fucking hell, bastards'd got lazy. Dark bodies moved through the undergrowth. Ashton crawled past, caught Danny's eye, grinned and winked. Danny grinned back. Tried, anyroad. Fuck knew how it looked.

"Over here," Darrow whispered.

Ashton slipped a crowbar from his overalls; he and Darrow strained at the manhole cover, finally prised it free. Cold, dark air wafted out. Alannah peered down into the dark. Danny crawled alongside, let his shoulder brush hers. She smiled at him for a second.

"Torch," said Darrow. Danny handed over Gevaudan's clockwork one.

Darrow shone the torch down. A short drop; the ground below was clear. Ashton swung his legs through the hatch, lowered himself, then dropped. He landed, stepped back; Danny safetied the Lanchester and followed.

*

Gevaudan took a last look around the church, then sighed. Time to begin.

He dragged an old barrel-bag out from under the bed and started packing: ammunition and his cans of ground coffee – some luxuries, he decided, were essential – and two dozen cans of pemmican. He'd need them if he had to fight. He didn't like to contemplate the alternative; there was much he loathed about his condition, but that was probably vilest of all.

A few spare items of clothing. His supply of serum, of course. Four pistols: two Brownings in a double shoulder rig and a pair of revolvers, very like Helen's, in hip holsters.

He packed as many books as he could find room for. He hesitated over one, a book of Shakespeare's sonnets, a Christmas gift from Jo. He'd already slipped Shakespeare's Complete Works into the bag, but this…

Well, perhaps it would make a good Christmas gift to someone else. With a half-smile at his own foolishness, Gevaudan slipped it into the bag. After a moment, he crossed back to the heap of clothes and picked up an old leather belstaff jacket. Too small for him; it always had been. But it had belonged to someone else. The boy, Danny; it might fit him. He pushed that into the bag too, then went back to the books.

Once, he'd have thought it impossible to narrow his collection down to even a dozen, or twenty, but with the pressure of time he found it easy. Even though the ones he left behind might be the last copies left in the world, and Winterborn would most likely burn them out of sheer spite.

Even so, his eyes lingered on one of the guitars, and his long fingers flexed as he imagined them on the strings and frets. Again, with something about to slip from his grasp, he found he valued it intensely.

"Our revels now are ended," he murmured.

"These our actors,
As I foretold you, were all spirits, and
Are melted into air, into thin air…"

Too late now. There was no room for the big instruments; he hadn't played half of them in months anyway, or even years. He slipped a harmonica into his trouser pocket, zipped the barrel-bag up.

"And, like the baseless fabric of this vision,
The cloud-capp'd towers, the gorgeous palaces,
The solemn temples…"

Time to go, then. He'd miss the peace and the silence; re-entering the city after so long would probably be a shock to the senses, especially his. But he'd deal with that when he encountered it. If a few loud noises and foul smells shook him, he was even worse off than Jo had thought.

"…the great globe itself,
Yea, all which it inherit, shall dissolve,
And, like this insubstantial pageant faded,
Leave not a wrack behind…"

Helen's Sterling and pistol lay where she'd dropped them; he picked them up. After a moment, he slipped the magazine from the Sterling and folded the stock, then pushed it into one of his coat's deep pockets. The revolver he pushed into the other.

He kept thinking there was something he still needed to do but knew there was nothing. If Gevaudan had learnt one thing in all his years on earth, it was this: you always needed less than you imagined. Unless, he thought, glancing round the church, he hoped for a last glimpse of Jo, some blessing or benediction. But he was alone.

"…We are such stuff
As dreams are made on…" he concluded,
"…and our little life
Is rounded with a sleep."

Gevaudan hefted the bag onto his shoulder, opened the church door and stepped out into the birdsong and the morning.

7.

"Hold the torch steady."

"Keep it quiet," Darrow hissed. "They've got foot patrols up there."

"Bit more oil, Danny," Nikki whispered.

Clinging to the old iron rungs alongside her, Danny squirted more gun oil into the join. The manhole and its cover were rusted frigging solid. Should've guessed. Fuck*sake*.

"That'll do," Nikki started sawing with her file again. Rust powder fell from the join. Danny blinked hard; sweat in his eyes. "Think that's it."

"All right," said Ashton. "Everybody out of the way."

Danny stuck the oil bottle in his overalls. Scopes and Nadgers helped him to the floor. Hinge lifted Nikki down. She grinned, reached up and pinched his cheek. Funny pair they made: Hinge, big and dark-haired, Nikki, tiny and thin. Nice smile though, somehow, even when it showed off the gap where her front teeth'd been.

Ashton put both hands on the cover and shoved. It grated; Danny hissed through his teeth. Shouldn't sound so bad up top – hopefully there weren't any Reapers passing just then – but down here it was like a scream. He unslung the Lanchester, put his thumb on the safety catch.

Thin light came through the crack. Ashton squinnied out, then ducked, mouthing 'sentry'. Everyone went still, even Darrow.

Ashton's lips moved, counting. When he reached ten, he looked up again. He stared, waiting. Time ticked by; no one spoke or moved. Then Ashton ducked again. "Three minutes," he said. "That's how long he took."

Darrow nodded. "All right. Quickly."

Ashton nodded, then pushed up at the cover. Not as noisy this time; he lifted it clear, pushed it aside, scrambled out.

Darrow nodded to Danny. Alannah touched his arm lightly as he slid by her. He shinned up the rungs to the pallid daylight shining through the hole.

Ashton caught his arms, pulled him out. Danny scrambled into a crouch, eyes narrowed at the light, got the Lanchester to his shoulder.

Nobody there, just twenty yards of hard-packed ground from the station's walls to the chicken wire fence round it. Locked gates for entry and exit; a couple of landcruisers parked nearby.

Behind him, mutters and grunts as the others climbed out. A hand on Danny's shoulder: Darrow. "Over there. See that?"

A thin black cable, clinging to the wall. "Yeah?"

Darrow gave him a pair of rubber-handled cutters. "Telephone line. Cut it."

Danny crabbed sideways along the main wall, keeping low. The ground floor windows were right above; any Reaper could just look out.

He put down the Lanchester, got the cutter blades round the wire, glanced back at the rest. Alannah was out too, and all but a couple of the others. Fifteen in all. 'Bout the same in Mary's group waiting out there. And how many Reapers inside? Dozen? Twenty?

Just have to hope surprise was on their side.

Darrow caught his eye, mouthed *do it*. Danny snipped the wire and gave him the thumbs-up, then picked up his gun and ran after the others to the main entrance.

They stopped just short of it, crouched low. Darrow nodded to Ashton; the big man crept to the doors, tried the handle. Locked. He knelt, dug picks out of his pocket, set to work.

"Keep watch," Darrow said.

Danny looked from Ashton, across the forecourt to the gates, then back again, kept doing it till –

"Got it," said Ashton.

"Go," said Darrow. "Nikki, Jake, cover us."

Nikki and Jake, a gangly boy who looked a lot taller than he was, took up positions each side of the doorway. Alannah caught Danny's eye as she filed past, smiled. He followed, was in through the doors when –

"Sentry!" shouted Jake. Last thing he ever said. If he hadn't yelled, the silly sod – but he did, and he was still trying to get his gun into play when the Reaper fired. Jake dropped without a sound; Nikki was hit in the leg as she turned. She yelped and fell; her gun clattered away.

Danny ran back, aimed round the side of the porch as the sentry ran in and fired again. Bullets kicked up dust and grit near Nikki's head. She recoiled, tried to drag herself into the porch.

The sentry saw Danny, tried to bring his gun round. Too late. *Watch your burst control,* Helen said. Danny fired, trying for a three-round burst – got four or five, he reckoned. The sentry's head snapped back; his gun fell, and his legs folded up under him, dropping him to the ground.

Jake stared up, sightless, a line of holes across his chest. They'd already stopped bleeding; Nikki's leg hadn't. Danny dragged her inside; down the corridor, there were shots and screams.

Nikki knocked his hands away and grabbed her gun. She was near-white; there was blood all over the porch, spilling across the floor.

"Go on," she spat, pulling a coil of thin rope from a pouch and looping it round her leg. Her fingers were white, shaking. "Go!"

Danny ran up the stairs. Christ. They all had a job, and he might have blown his already.

Darrow would be getting Alannah to the computer room; Ashton would be hunting down Major Bilston and the others would be going room to room – canteen, incident room, controller's office, dorms – to wipe out all the Reapers they could in the first few minutes. Danny's job was the radio room on the first floor.

More shots as he pelted up the staircase. Would Darrow have sent someone else, if he'd seen Danny wasn't with them? Or would he have had time? How many seconds to kill the Reaper sentry? That'd needed doing. How many more trying to help Nikki? He shouldn't have. *Got a job to do. Above all, the mission.* Time. It was all about time.

Onto the first floor. The radio room was second on the left. He ran down the concrete corridor; two Reapers ran at him from the other end. One had a Sterling, the other a revolver. Danny threw himself sideways against the wall, fired, zig-zagging the muzzle as bullets flew past. The sub-machine gunner pitched backwards, still firing; dust showered from the ceiling. The other Reaper, hit in the arm, went sprawling. He fired as Danny ran towards him; Danny hit the floor and shot back. Bullets chipped divots in the walls, filled the air with plaster dust; the wounded Reaper scrambled through it into the radio room.

Danny got up and ran to the doorway, kept to the side. Line of fire. Keep out of the fucker's line of fire. Inside, the Reaper coughed and groaned. Static hissed and crackled. A clatter of metal.

The radio; he'll call for help –

Danny peeked round the edge of the door, ducked back as the Reaper's gun flashed and blew a chunk out of the doorframe. He poked the Lanchester round the edge, loosed off two short bursts. A yell, two shots in reply, then a dull clicking. Danny leant around the frame, aimed and fired; the Reaper flew back across a desk, slid off and was still.

He rolled into the room, scanned it. No one there. The radio hissed, crackled and squealed; Danny braced the Lanchester against his hip and shot it. A loud bang; smoke, sparks, flames. A last few noises from the radio; Danny shot it again, then went back out into the corridor as the shooting inside the station died away.

*

Alannah was already on the computer; the clock was running now. Darrow posted lookouts to watch for Reapers, sent others to drag the bodies inside; Nadgers, the medic, turned a briefing room into a make-do hospital and mortuary.

They brought Nikki and Jake upstairs, both dead. Nikki was still clutching the rope; she hadn't fastened the tourniquet in time. Blacked out and bled out. She was bone white in death; looked smaller than ever. Hinge knelt beside her, crying. He looked up at Danny once. *You killed her.* Danny turned away, went out into the corridor.

"Wasn't your fault." Ashton put a hand on his arm. "Said yourself, she told you to go on."

Danny nodded. Didn't help, though. "Danny." Ashton's grip tightened. "Look at me." Danny didn't want to, but he did. The big man's face came close to his. "Rules of the game. She knew it, same as you."

"All right." Danny pulled his arm free, or Ashton let him go.

Across the corridor, the computer room. Alannah sat at the keyboard, squinting at the flickering monitor; cold pale screenlight danced on her narrow face. She looked calm.

Behind her, Darrow stood over a dazed-looking Reaper officer with an ugly bruise on his forehead. "Password and username, please, Major Bilston."

Bilston opened his mouth; Darrow's tommy gun nudged his temple. "Let's not waste time, Major."

Bilston's head fell forward. "Username is BilstonA14. Password is rhododendron."

Danny nearly laughed. "Rhodo-what?" Bilston glared at him; so did Darrow.

Alannah was already tapping keys. "Any joy?" Darrow asked.

"Think I've ID'd the right directory, but there's one, maybe two firewalls. Knowing Winterborn, the files'll be encrypted. Probably more than once."

Danny blinked. Sounded like witchcraft.

"All right," said Darrow. Did he understand that, or was he as lost as Danny? "Fast as you can. We'll have company soon."

"Yes, I know."

"Danny. Help Mike secure the perimeter. We'll need to prepare our defences."

Danny nodded and ran.

*

Gevaudan used the same tunnel he'd sent Danny to, only without a torch; for him, the dark was light enough. At its end, he lifted the manhole cover in the road beyond, pushed it aside and clambered out into an empty street.

He straightened up, looked around, listened; from nearby came a murmur of voices.

"The fuck're we still doing here anyway?"

"Orders is orders."

Gevaudan padded to the corner. Around it stood a parked landcruiser and two Reapers, cradling automatic rifles and smoking. They had an excellent view of the earth bank forming Deadsbury's perimeter, but none at all of the street behind them, or Gevaudan himself.

"Yeah, but come on. They caught the mad bitch, so what else we supposed to do? Not like the fucking Grendelwolf's gonna come out an' give us grief, is it?"

Gevaudan raised an eyebrow.

"Ours not to reason why."

"You what?"

"Nowt. Maybe Winterborn's gonna send us in to get him."

"Don't say that!"

Gevaudan put his bag down, stepped into the street and started walking.

"Well, he did do for Kirkwood and a bunch of his lads."

"No loss. Fucking headjob, Kirky. Always was."

The younger of the two turned to flick aside his cigarette and went still, staring at Gevaudan. His face drained white. "Benny?" he croaked.

The older Reaper took one look, then dropped his cigarette and fell to one knee, rifle shouldered. The younger one fumbled his own rifle into position, the barrel wavering as he shook.

"Stay where you are!" said Benny.

Gevaudan kept walking. "And if I don't?"

"Benny, let's leg it," said the young one. "He's a fucking Grendelwolf."

"Listen to your friend," said Gevaudan.

Benny compressed his lips. He didn't lower the rifle.

"You have one chance to live," said Gevaudan. "One. Put down your guns, tell me what I want to know and go away, or – "

"Get in the landcruiser!" yelled Benny and fired.

Perhaps he'd been at Sheffield, and the sight of a Grendelwolf closing in panicked him. Gevaudan, lunging forward, would never know. A shot sang past his head; a second plucked his coat sleeve.

He could, of course, easily survive damage that would kill a human; that said, he had no intention of sustaining any if he could help it. Gevaudan sprang; two wild shots from Benny cut through the air where he'd been. Claws slid from his fingertips, as from between a cat's pads. Before Benny could fire again, Gevaudan reached him.

His left hand knocked the rifle barrel aside; the right struck, once, flinging Benny up and back. The Reaper hit the ground and lay still, blood spreading round him.

The younger Reaper scrambled behind the landcruiser's wheel; Gevaudan caught him by the scruff of the neck, flung him to the ground and kicked his rifle away.

"You still have a chance," said Gevaudan. "Take it and you'll live, waste it and you'll die in agony. Choose."

"Don't kill me. Please." The boy was Danny's age. Gevaudan pushed the thought aside. There'd be more boys like this one between him and Helen, or, for that matter, threatening Danny Morwyn's life. *Harden your heart, Gevaudan.* "Then tell me what I want to know."

"Anything."

"Helen Damnation. Is she alive?" The boy stared up at him. Why had he joined? For the Reaper Creed, for Winterborn's tinpot imperial dream? Or for three square meals a day and the hope of some kind of life? Just another young man marching off to die for a cause he didn't understand. *No time for that now.* Gevaudan leant closer. "Is. She. Alive?"

"Yes." The boy didn't blink, didn't dare.

"Where did they take her?"

The boy licked his lips. "Bailey. They took her to the Bailey."

"Where?"

"Big prison. Central one. Serious cases."

"Ah. Yes." Gevaudan's sense of the city's geography was rusty, but the details were coming back. "You're quite sure?"

"Yes. Yes."

Gevaudan held his bloodied right hand, claws still extended, till it touched the young Reaper's face. The boy's eyes rolled up and he flopped back, still.

Gevaudan flexed his fingers, retracted his claws, then knelt and rolled the boy onto his side, so he wouldn't choke.

Soft.

"I'll kill if I must," he said. "But only then."

You'll have to. And soon.

"I know."

You'll have to kill many of them.

"I *know*. But this one I'll spare."

Gevaudan tore out the cruiser's radio mic and flung it away, then wrenched out the pipes connected to its boiler and hoisted the barrel bag to his shoulder as hot steam whistled out into the air. Then he was gone, and only a dead Reaper, an unconscious one and a crippled landcruiser remained.

*

Jarrett remembered, despite the urgency, to knock first.

"Come," said Winterborn.

She walked in fast. Winterborn was in his swivel chair, his back to her.

"Commander."

He swivelled to face her, smiled. It took years off him, made him look like a boy. "Colonel."

"Sir, I thought I'd better tell you. It's REAP Station Five. Phone's dead, and we can't raise them on the radio."

The corner of his smile twitched. "Minor, Colonel. We have Helen. Take her out of the game and – "

"Project Tindalos," Jarrett said.

Winterborn went still; the smile vanished from his face. Blue, arctic eyes. "Repeat what you just said, Colonel."

"Someone in the station," she said, swallowing, "someone in the station is trying to get into a file so classified even I can't view it."

"Project Tindalos," said Winterborn, almost to himself. A muscle jumped in his cheek.

"Tindalos."

"They've accessed it?"

"Yes."

Winterborn shook his head. "I should have known. And so should you."

"Sir?"

"Helen. Sentimental enough to fall for your plan, but not enough to abandon her mission without passing the torch to someone else."

"Tindalos? That's why she's back?"

"And me too, I expect. But Tindalos will, if successful, make me very powerful indeed. That's why she's resurfaced, after all this time."

"What is it?"

"Later, Colonel. What have you done so far?"

"Sent a CiviSec squad to investigate."

"Send a CorSec squad. In fact, send two. If that doesn't work, send more. Maybe we can't stop them getting the information; their having a chance to use it's another matter. Make sure they don't get out, Colonel."

"Understood. But there's one thing I do need to know about Project Tindalos now, sir."

"Oh? And what's that?"

"Is it based outside the city?"

"Why do you ask?"

"If it is, I'd like your permission to institute total lockdown around the city limits. No one comes in, no one goes out."

"Just in case?"

"Yes, sir."

"All right, Colonel. See to it."

"Sir."

Winterborn's chair swung away from her again. Jarrett turned and went out fast.

*

Ashton poked his Sten over the windowsill and fired twice; an answering burst shattered what little windowglass remained. Danny ran sideways to the window's far end, peeped over the sill. Below stood two landcruisers, bleeding steam from punctured boilers; half a dozen Reapers lay sprawled around them. Two were still standing; Danny shot, and one of them jerked and fell. The other aimed at Danny, then slammed against the landcruiser and slid down as Ashton fired again.

Danny breathed hard. When he moved, broken glass and spent bullet cases crunched underfoot.

"Good shooting, Danny," called Ashton. "Nadgers?"

The medic stuck his head round the door. "Yeah?"

"Check on Darrow and Alannah." Ashton turned back to Danny. "How are you for ammo?"

One of the Lanchester's magazines lay empty among the glass and casings. Danny checked the one in his gun. "Half-empty. One spare."

Ashton skimmed a box of bullets across the floor. "Reload while you can."

Danny thumbed fresh bullets into the empty clip. "Reckon there'll be more?"

Ashton nodded. "'Course there will. 'Specially when they twig what we're looking for."

Danny nodded, began replenishing the half-empty magazine.

"Danny." Ashton pulled his coat back; a pistol-grip stuck out of his waist band. He pulled the weapon free; a flare pistol. "Owt happens to me, you'll need this. It's loaded. Two spares in my jacket pocket."

"To signal Mary?"

"That's the one."

"Right." Danny nodded. "Gotcha."

Nadgers came back. "Ten, fifteen minutes, Darrow reckons."

Ashton bit his lip. "Christ. All right. Pass the word along and get everyone to top their magazines up, if they've not already. We're gonna – "

Sirens wailed.

" – have company," Ashton finished. "Move it, Nadgers."

The medic bolted. Ashton pulled the Sten's bolt back. "Here the fuckers come."

Danny gave him back the box of ammo. Ashton nodded, stuck it in his backpack. If they had to break it out again in this fight, they'd be dead before they could top the clips up.

A landcruiser barreled in towards the gates. Ashton was quicker off the mark, his Sten already chattered. Danny was about to fire too; and then he saw, just before it hit the gates, that it had no driver.

Muzzle flashes flared below as black-clad Reapers pelted across the wasteground towards the fence. Smashed chips of glass, wood, brick and plaster flew from the window frames; Ashton pitched backwards.

"Shit!" He wasn't moving, but Danny didn't have time to check him. The Reapers were clambering up the wire fence; their mates below were still firing. The gates were still holding; the landcruiser's engine was dying, steam pouring from the smashed boiler. Danny aimed over the sill, fired at the climbing Reapers. He hit one as he reached the top of the fence; the Reaper flopped over it and dangled. Another fell off and hit the ground, writhing. Two others ran forward to drag him back.

Before Danny could fire again, muzzles flashed below. He threw himself prone and more bullets hammered the window. "Nadgers!" he screamed. "Nadgers!"

The medic crawled in through the doorway. "Check Mike!" Danny shouted, and poked the Lanchester over the sill. He fired three short bursts in different directions. Hopefully hit one of the fuckers. "Nadgers!"

"He's dead." Nadgers crouched, saucer-eyed, beside Ashton. The top of the big man's head was gone, blood and darker, thicker fragments strewed the floor.

"Fuck."

"He's dead, Danny."

"Yeah. Noticed. Right. Nadgers, listen up. Get Scopes up here. Tell the others to keep the front and back ways secured."

Most of the downstairs windows were barred, so the doorways would be the main worry. "But get Scopesy! Move!"

Nadgers scrambled out. Fresh gunfire rang out below. More shots whined in through the window, punched the walls and filled the air with dust; Danny crawled to Ashton, pulled out the flare pistol, fished the spares from his jacket.

He scuttled out of the room, head down, then into the one next door. This one hadn't drawn so much fire, mainly 'cause there was no one here. Some of the windows were smashed; others held.

Running footsteps in the corridor, a girl's voice shouting. "Danny?"

"In here, Scopes! Fucking head *down*."

Scopes dived and rolled in through the doorway, came to a halt beside him. "How's that?"

"Fucking show-off."

Scopes grinned back. Buck-teeth, bug eyes, greasy hair, no tits or arse to speak of, but Danny could've kissed her and given her ten years' worth of babies right then. "You wanted me?" she said. She had a bright, clear, posh-sounding voice, the three or four times a year she used it.

"They're getting covering fire from down there," Danny said. "I can't get a clear shot with this. But you could."

Scopes grinned wider and patted her Lee-Enfield rifle. She had a Sten slung across her back; not many folk got two big guns, but Scopes was special. "What's the plan?"

"I'll get back next door, draw their fire. While I'm doing that, you start picking 'em off."

"Done."

Scopes' face wiped itself clean; no smile, nothing in the world but her and her hundred-year-old rifle as she pulled back the bolt and went to the window as the guns thundered into new life below.

*

"Cov," Thursday yelled over the hammering gunfire, "go help Filly mind the back door. They'll try there. Rest of you, fucking return fire now."

"But – " Big, gangly Mackie blinked; loyal if none too bright, even he could see it was madness.

"Return fire, now." Thursday half-raised the gun. "Those bastards get in, we're done. Go. Go!"

She was already at the window – you led by example, not shouting orders from a hidey-hole at the back – but even she flinched from the bullets coming through. She poked her Thompson gun over the sill, loosed off a burst. "Come on!"

The Reapers were throwing all they had at the ground floor. She saw them moving forward; sighted, fired, knocked one over backwards.

Mackie, loyal as always, was beside her at the window; Hinge followed a moment later because he didn't give a shit any more. A machine gun traversed, firing; Mackie fell back screaming, clutching his arm. Hinge shouted, leapt up, sprayed half a clip at the Reapers. Dust exploded from the windowframe around him; he danced backwards through a haze of blood like red smoke and dropped.

"Get Nadgers!" Thursday screamed, still firing. "Nadgers! Get fucking Nadgers down here now!"

Mackie was white, clutching his arm; Hinge lay still. Christ. But she didn't dare think; there was no time. Thursday poked the gun barrel back over the windowsill, prepared to fire again.

*

Danny ran back next door; part of him hoped he'd been wrong about Ashton and that the big man'd be up and moving again. But no – still dead, brains still splattered all over the floor. Danny weaved around them. Still shooting below, but not at this window; fuckers probably thought they'd killed him too.

Peeping over the sill to check the score. Looked like a dozen dead Reapers out there. Some live ones hiding behind the trashed landcruisers; one crawled for the gates with a pair of cutters. Danny cut him in half as he reached up for the chain, then hit the ground as they opened up once more. Dust in the air, his nose, his eyes. Danny scrambled over to where Ashton lay. *Not yet, Scopes, not yet.*

And she didn't fire, though Danny knew she would soon. She'd be in the zone now, aiming, getting the range. Took her a minute to get ready, but it was worth the wait.

Danny came up and fired again. Muzzle flashes below; he dropped down and actually felt a bullet part his hair. More bullets flew overhead as he ran sideways.

Halfway between Ashton's position and his old one, he poked the barrel over and fired again. They were going all-out now, the bastards – shots were screaming through the whole window, end to end. *Don't know where I am now, do you, you fuckers?* He crawled a couple of feet back the way he came and waited. *Now, Scopesy.*

From next door, he heard it: the crack of a rifle shot. He fired over the sill again and ducked back down. They were shooting back at him, but he'd already heard Scopes get a second shot off. He ran to the far end; from below he heard ragged bursts of sub-machine gun fire, looked out of the window in time to see two Reapers who'd got over the fence go down. Behind a crippled landcruiser Danny saw three Reapers, one half-rising with a grenade in his hand. He was going to sling it at the gates, trying to blow them off their hinges. Danny fired a long burst; the Reaper fell back, his hand opening. One of the other Reapers turned to run –

Danny threw himself down as the guns opened up again, but they didn't sound as loud as before, and there didn't seem to be as many bullets coming through. A moment later, the grenade went off with a loud *crump,* and his ears sang a thin, high note, but he could still hear the rifle firing next door, each shot only seconds apart now. *Bang* and *bang* and *bang* and *bang,* fast but oh-so-fucking deliberate. He saw Scopes, working the bolt with cold, steady ease as she tracked the muzzle from one target to the next, never missing once.

Glass shattered next door. Scopes – they'd seen where the killshots were really coming from now. Danny sprayed the rest of his clip through the window, then hit the deck. A long, desperate burst raked the windows; another rifle shot rang out from the next room, and the gun stuttered into silence.

Danny changed magazines and pulled back the bolt, then peeped over the bullet-scored windowsill. Outside, the last of the Reapers were down. One crawled a few yards, then was still.

Two landcruisers had been blown apart; the flames amid the wreckage were guttering out. Black smoke streamed up into the blotched sky, and there was a reek of charred things. A smell of burnt meat made Danny's mouth water; then he spat, realising what it was.

That shrill whining in his ears. Downstairs, someone screaming for Nadgers. Danny went into the next room; Scopes sat calm against the wall, reloading. Didn't even look up at him. Plain old Scopes again, off in her own little world. Till the next time.

Which wouldn't be long; as the whining noise died, he heard sirens wail again.

"More company?" Scopes asked.

"Sounds it. Do us a favour: go see how Darrow and Alannah're getting on. Don't fancy having to do this again if I can help it."

Scopes nodded and headed out. Danny glanced out of the window at the scattered bodies and the fire, then went back into the other room, where Ashton's body lay. His eyes were already dull, the moisture dried. Danny pressed a handful of plaster dust over them to hide their stare, found the box of bullets. He did his best to reload the empty magazine, but his hands were shaking too much. Instead he scavved Ashton's gun and spare clips. If the Lanchester ran out of ammo, he'd use that.

"Danny?" Nadgers.

"What's the situation?"

"Hinge is dead."

"Fuck."

"And Mackie's hit. Got one in the arm."

"Left or right?"

"Left."

"Can still shoot, then."

"We've got to get out of here. We're fucked if they come back."

"We go when we've got what we came for. You know that."

The sirens, wailing. "We're not gonna last that long."

"Keep it together, mate. We've got to. Or they're all dead for nowt."

"Tough shit. I don't wanna fucking join them."

"I'm not planning on it either, Nads. Just hang on a bit longer."

"How bastard long?"

"Five more minutes," said Scopes. "Just five." She cocked her head, listened. "Sounds like I'll be busy."

"Yeah. Does. Get into position, Scopes. Nadgers, tell them downstairs to hang on. Five more minutes."

Nadgers opened his mouth, closed it, ran off. Scopes went next door, and Danny returned to the shattered window.

*

Gevaudan kept to the city's back ways, finding his way more by feel than anything else. A lot had changed since he'd last come this way; in other ways, of course, nothing had changed at all.

Avoiding the city centre, he found himself skirting through what had once been Collyhurst. Never the choicest of neighbourhoods from what he recalled, it was now filled with ruins no one could live in but no one had cleared, maybe because the ruins, evermore precarious with each passing year, were still tall enough to menace the unwary would-be brick thief. It hardly mattered. Around them spread crude bivouacs, tents, shacks built crudely up from loose bricks and other debris. The people they housed were the worst-off of the lot: the hopelessly disfigured, the maimed and crippled. And the addicted. Oh, there were still things to get hooked on, even now. Perhaps more now than ever, with reality grown so intolerable that no one could be blamed for wanting to escape it. Surprising what human inventiveness allied with desperation could still achieve.

Gevaudan covered his mouth against a reek of corruption; in one street, a pit had been dug and the bodies thrown in, but no one seemed to have thought to cover it over. Below the three or four comparatively fresh corpses on top were others, blackened and bloated with decay. All had been stripped to the skin first; no room for sentiment in this place. Out here, you couldn't afford to waste a scrap of food or clothing. Passing through another street, Gevaudan found the remains of a fire. Lying in it, blackened and charred, were human bones. But they weren't so badly burnt that he couldn't see the marks where they'd been gnawed.

Gevaudan kept to the shadows; he didn't speak. Those who did notice him thought better of accosting him. Perhaps they knew who he was, or perhaps they could tell from his face that he wasn't to be distracted from his purpose. Either way, they let him be.

He almost missed the woman and her child; she sat just inside the mouth of an alley, beneath the overhang of the cracked, ancient plastic crate she was huddled inside. Her eyes were vast in a face of almost translucent white; her wrists were like thin white twigs. The child across her lap, perhaps a year, two years old, looked no better; in fact, Gevaudan's first thought was that the child was dead, but then he saw the spittle bubbling at its lips with breath, the tiny pulses beating at its temples.

The mother looked up at him. There was no plea in her eyes; not for food or succour, not even for mercy. They were dull, placid, accepting. They were empty. She would do all she could to live, and the same for her child, but she'd long ago given up on any mastery of her fate. She was a plaything, a scrap of litter blown about by the wind. If he wanted to feed or kill her, she would do nothing to encourage or dissuade; it would do no good.

He'd been insulated from all this for so long. Now it was crashing in on him again, and this was the worst thing of all.

All of that passed in a second, a moment of understanding that almost made him fall to his knees. What she saw when she looked at him he had no idea.

But all the same, he bent, unzipped the barrel bag, fished out two cans of pemmican and put them down beside her. The woman looked from them back up to him, eyes empty.

Perhaps she was so far gone she couldn't even understand this any more. Gevaudan picked up one of the tins. Each was opened by turning a key; he operated it, peeling a thin strip of metal away from around the can so the top pulled clear, the handed it back to the woman. She sniffed at the dark, hard stuff inside the can, then prised a bit loose, put it in her mouth and chewed. She looked up at him again, and reached up to fumble at her rags, exposing her scrawny, pitiable breasts. Gevaudan caught her wrists, shook his head and stepped back, but now she seized his hand. And kissed it.

He pulled free, backed away. There was movement around him – he turned. And they were there. All of them. Dozens. Crawling out from under cocoons of torn rags and paper, slabs of concrete propped up a dozen inches above the ground on bricks. Even out of the earth, burrows they'd hacked there in the absence of any other shelter. Grimy and emaciated, gaunt and ragged and near-naked in the winter chill, and all with those empty eyes. And then the first of them – a man nearly bald, with terrible burn scars across his chest – extended a claw-like hand to Gevaudan. Open. The first plea, perhaps, he'd dared to make in years.

And then another did the same.

And then another, and another.

Gevaudan managed to pick up the barrel bag. He had to go. There was Helen. She waited for him. She needed him too. He had to… he had to…

The hands, around him. They were all outstretched now. It was like a forest.

They couldn't stop him, even in these numbers. He was a Grendelwolf. With his speed and strength – even if they'd been healthier, they couldn't have stopped him. But the terrible grip they exercised wasn't a matter of physical strength.

There was more pemmican in his bag – but he needed it. Needed it. Yet so did they. He dug two more tins out of the bag, then a third, then threw them randomly out and ran. Behind him, doglike snarls and screeches rose as the survivors fought over the bounty. He tried not to listen and failed; failed, too, to avoid thinking of what might now become of that woman and her child.

Helen, he thought. *Helen.*

He understood her, he thought, a little better now.

*

Outside and inside the Reaper Station, guns were firing. Alannah could hear them all: the brittle stutter of sub-machine guns, the gritty crack of rifles, and the thudding percussion of heavy machine guns. But they were distant, faint, coming in through the walls of her goldfish bowl.

Because she was only partly there. The rest of her – the best, the realest part – had returned to swim in a sea she'd long thought dried up and lost to her. It was a sea of computer code and electronic information, of defences and countermeasures, and she'd known it so well it was a joy to return.

Darrow stood nearby, keeping Bilston covered with his Thompson. The Reaper was crouching on the floor, hands over his head, and whimpering softly.

"Stay calm, Major," Darrow said, "and you might just get out of this alive."

He might, too, though Alannah doubted he'd thank Darrow. Not when Winterborn got hold of the poor bastard.

Sweat trickled down Alannah's forehead, edged towards the corner of her eye. "Wipe me," she said. "Darrow!"

"Coming. Coming." He drew the rag across her forehead. "How are we doing?"

"We?" She side-glanced at him for just a split-second. No more than that; every second was precious, could mean the life of another of the defenders. Could mean Danny's life: she redoubled her efforts on the keyboard, drummed her fingers and chewed her lip for a terrifying second as an answer eluded her. Then it came to her and she was entering another command, breaking another code.

"How are *you* doing?"

"Getting there. I'm almost through."

She was, too. At first the simplest tasks had been a struggle and there'd been the fear that all this would fail and be for nothing, that their people would die and for nothing, all because she couldn't remember any more what it was she was supposed to do. But it was just like a machine that'd grown a little rusty, newly oiled and pressed back into service; as the cogs and gears started turning, they ground and halted a little at first but were soon moving with their old speed and fluency. It was almost frightening how easily it'd all come back.

"As long as they don't cut us off."

"Can't do anything about that. Think they're more interested in stopping us getting out."

"It'll occur to Winterborn sooner or later. Or Jarrett."

"Don't –" Her hands left the keyboard. *Jarrett.* She remembered that face above her, that flat, nasal voice. *You* are *going to talk to me, Alannah. That's a given. It's an inevitability. The only question is how much suffering you're going to put yourself through first. If you're in pain, it's your own fault. You can end it at any moment.*

Blame the victim, always blame the victim – but she wasn't a victim, she *would not* be a victim–

Darrow's hand on her shoulder. "Alannah. Alannah. I'm sorry."

"Okay. Okay. Just – " She shook his hand off. She didn't want anyone touching her, not just now. Not even Danny. Not even Stephen, if he'd still been alive.

251

"Here," she said. She laughed. "Can't believe it."

"What?"

"Wait." She held up a hand. Stared at the screen for a moment. Scrolled down. "Yes. This is it." She punched buttons. "Should start printing off any mo."

There was a grinding, a whirring, a dull *thunk;* Darrow spun, fumbling at his sub-machine gun, then began to laugh as the printer in the corner began to buzz and clunk its way through the document, the first sheets of paper emerging.

"Nadgers!" yelled Darrow. "Nadgers!"

The medic stuck his head round the door.

"We have it," said Darrow. He was already picking the sheets up off the printer. "We have it. Tell the others. Tell Ashton to – "

"Ashton's dead." Nadgers was white.

Christ. Ashton, gone – but no, Alannah wasn't thinking about that now. There was still something else, something she'd promised she'd do if she had the time. And she might have now. Just.

"Right." Darrow rubbed his eyes. "Tell Danny, then. The flare. Send the signal. Right now."

"Yes, sir." Nadgers spun and ran down the corridor, shouting Danny's name.

Darrow grabbed the final sheets off the printer. "This everything?"

"Yeah. Everything on Tindalos."

"Come on then." Darrow stuffed the printouts into the inside pocket of his jacket.

"Wait."

"*Now,* Alannah – "

"One second." She opened the file she sought. "Yes. There." She stood up. "She's in the Bailey."

"What?"

"Helen." Alannah made for the door. "Come on, Darrow."

Darrow rose, and Bilston leapt for him, clutching the Thompson with both hands, fighting to wrestle it free. With a roar he drove Darrow back against the wall, forcing the sub-machine gun across his throat and bearing down on it to crush the windpipe. It didn't feel real, any of it. Felt like a dream. Including the part where Alannah walked over to them, drew the revolver she carried, put it to Bilston's temple and fired.

Darrow stumbled free, wheezing for breath. Alannah holstered the pistol; her hands shook, just slightly. "Probably a mercy," she said. "Let's go."

Darrow stopped only at the door to fire a burst from the hip, blowing apart the computer's monitor screen and shattering the base unit, which exploded into smoke and flames.

*

"Danny! Danny!"

Danny didn't hear the shouting at first. He was ducked low on the floor, the empty Lanchester slung across his back and halfway through his last clip for Ashton's Sten. Bullets were pouring through the window; massive, heavy rounds that were smashing the walls to dust. There were four landcruisers out front, all with .50 calibre Browning heavy machine guns, and they were raking the front of the building. There was one round the back too. It was only a question of which entrance would fall to them first.

"Danny!"

He heard the voice at last, through the gun-thunder and the belltone in his ears. He glanced round and there was Nadgers, huddled against the doorframe and not daring to venture into the storm of gunfire that filled the room. "They've got it!" he was screaming. "Send the signal! Send the signal!"

For a moment Danny wondered if Nadgers' nerve had snapped and he just wanted them to get out whether the mission had succeeded or not. But he'd just have to take it on trust. Besides, if they didn't get out now, they were fucked anyway.

Always assuming Mary and the others were still out there. Wouldn't they have wanted to get stuck in when they saw the pounding the station was taking? Even if Mary held it – and she *was* bloody Iron Woman – would all the others, like Flaps, have been able to hold off from attacking when it was the kids they'd grown up with getting cut to pieces in there? Chances were the Reapers had found them – CorSec weren't the same as the Jennywrens, but they were still fuckers, still all too good at what they did – and killed them all.

Fuck that. One way to find out. Danny pulled out the flare pistol and lay back on the floor, aiming up through the smashed window. He pulled the trigger. Nothing happened. Fuck fuck *fuck*. No. Wait. The trigger hadn't really pulled. The gun had to be cocked first. Single action only; he remembered that now. Single action only.

His thumb found the hammer and pulled it back. It clicked into place. Then he fired.

The gun kicked in his hand and something bright and red-glowing shot out through the window towing a banner of pale smoke. The windowsill exploded into dust a second later as at least two machine guns fired on his position, but even through the haze of powder, Danny could see the sky through the window and saw the flare explode high above the station in a shower of red sparks, a flower of white smoke.

But still the guns hammered and the sparks slowly fell and died and nothing happened. Through the gun-thunder's roar, through the shrilling in his ears and the thunder of his blood, Danny heard Nadgers let out a terrible wail. He broke open the flare gun, fumbled for a spare; he didn't know what else to do now.

And then from outside, a bright flash. Then a dull thud and the room rattling, seeping plasterdust from joists and ceiling. The gunfire was abating –

Another explosion. Then another from out back. Then gunfire. A moment later one of the .50-cals started up again, but this time no rounds were hitting the upper floor.

Danny stared at Nadgers; Nadgers stared back, with the beginnings of an unbelieving smile on his face. Danny looked out of the window.

Two of the landcruisers were on fire, blown apart. That PIAT gadget of Mary's, however weird it looked, had done the job. The other two were surrounded by the bodies of their crews; Danny recognised Flaps gripping the handles of the HMG and using it on the Reapers who'd been advancing through the shattered gates across the forecourt, another kid helping feed the ammo-belt into the gun. Another of Mary's team was scrambling on board the second.

"Tell everyone to clear out," Danny yelled at him. Nadgers nodded and bolted.

From next door, he heard Scopes' rifle go off again, and then again, and two more Reapers fell.

"Scopes," shouted Danny. "Scopes, get in here."

Feet running, and Scopes burst in, rifle in hand. "What?"

Outside, there were a last few shots, then silence.

Danny motioned to Ashton's body. "Give us a hand with him."

They dragged Ashton to the makeshift morgue, laid him alongside Nikki and Hinge and the rest. *Hope it was worth it.* "Flamers," said Danny, and each of them took a phosphorous grenade. "Rest you all," Danny said, then pulled the pin, lobbed it through the door and ran: Nadgers and Scopes, having done the same, at his heels, all of them – even Nadgers – whooping madly as they ran.

*

Again she's walking the Black Road. At least, this time, there's sound: the click-clack-click of her bootheels on the polished stone. And all around the night is everlasting.

Then something changes. The air grows cold and damp, and the sensation of empty space around her changes to a sense of being hemmed in, enclosed. A faint, silvery glow glimmers up ahead, brightens as she goes on; it flickers on tunnels of stone.

255

She keeps walking, and click-clack-click go her boots. Now there's another sound, too; a faint, low chanting, in no tongue she can understand.

"Angana sor varalakh kai torja."

A bend in the tunnel; she goes round it.

"Angana sor varalakh cha voran."

Up ahead, the silvery glow shines through a cavern entrance nine feet high and six wide. Flanking it like guards are Frank and Belinda. They smile and bow, mocking, waving her through into the cavern beyond.

"Mantakha sa niroleph chir karagh."

The silvery glow brightens; it comes from everywhere and nowhere, all at once. Things clink and crunch underfoot. She looks down; the cavern floor is carpeted with bones and skulls.

"Insapa veir bereloth. Insapa."

Up ahead, an altar; around it stands a circle of hunched figures in robes and cowls. And around *them* –

"Maengrepa gir trequefa gla detiresh meirka."

Around them, a circle of wooden stakes. And impaled on each –

– the chanting stops –

– are heads. Severed heads. And she knows them all. Ashton. Darrow. Danny. Alannah. And Gevaudan. Even Gevaudan.

A whisper: *They died for you.*

Silence. The robes of the worshippers at the altar flap and flutter in the wind. As she gets closer, she can see the robes are made of human skin.

The worshippers turn, and she can't move, can't prevent herself from seeing their faces.

Tindalos, the whisper says.

Helen rolled onto her side, opened her eyes. Frank and Belinda squatted on the cell floor a few feet away, crouched like scavenger dogs awaiting the moment of death. Their red-black eyes never blinked, and they were grinning, tongues hanging out over their sharp, thin teeth. Together, they let out long, hissing sighs of anticipation.

"Soon, Helen," whispered Frank.

She closed her eyes, opened them again; the ghosts were gone.

*

"You can't," said Alannah. "It's madness."

"I don't see any other choice, Alannah," Darrow replied. "Do you?"

Danny glanced to and fro about the coppice. It was one of the few thickets of woodland that still survived in the city. And it wasn't very big. And the two landcruisers they'd driven away from Station Five, complete with their .50 calibre machine guns and their quacking, crackling radio sets, looked pretty conspicuous. Not that there were any Reapers here to see them. Not yet. But they must have been seen driving away. The rest was just a matter of time.

"For Christ's sake, Darrow. These are all you've got to fight with, and they've just been through hell."

"Not all I have. I alerted the other cells, and they're standing by. And I think you might be surprised at what they might be able to achieve." Darrow looked around the clearing. "Am I right?"

"Just watch me," said Flaps. But she was pale, and her fingers shook.

Danny didn't know what to think. Nothing felt quite real. Suddenly he was shaking too. And he felt sick. Couldn't stand. Hands caught him, lowered him to sit on a fallen log. Alannah. "Easy," she said. "Easy." He felt his breath hitching. Christ, going like this, in front of everyone.

"It's all right," said Alannah. "It's reaction. Everyone gets it. Only natural." But then she looked up at Darrow and said: "You'll get them all killed."

"Alannah." Darrow's face was hard. "The plan – the hope – was always that we'd get another chance to damage the Commanders. Well, now we have. Besides, I know what I'm doing. You heard the orders going out on the radio. They're locking down the whole city. You know what that means."

Alannah couldn't answer. Danny closed his eyes, saw Nikki bleeding out on the floor, Ashton on his back, the top of his head bloody and gone.

"Yes," said Darrow, "we lost people – good people – back there. They were our friends. They were family. I'd known some of them since they were babies. Do you think it's easy for me, Alannah? Do you?"

"No," she said at last, looking down at the ground.

"Good. We have to get the information we have out of the city. And to be frank, Winterborn's going to come after us anyway, after the raid. A good offence is the best defence, and all that." Darrow nodded to the landcruisers. "We'll take these. The plan's simple. I left standing orders with the other cells. Unless they get the countermand, they'll start doing what we're about to as well."

"Which is?"

"Strike and vanish. We target any checkpoint or command post we can find. Any symbol of the Reapers' authority. Anything that will disrupt their operations or communications, we strike at. And wherever we can, we encourage the population to rise up against them."

"And get them killed as well?"

"You never know. We might even overthrow the buggers without any help from Helen." But Darrow's smile looked fake. Might've fooled others, but not Danny, not even in the jittery, shaky state he was in. "Afterwards, we can either try and hide in the city or head for the Wastelands. We'll see. In the meantime – Danny?"

"Yeah?"

"How you doing?"

The shakes had faded out. A bit. "Okay. I think."

"Take Nadgers, Scopes and Thursday and get Alannah out of the city, to the rendezvous with the Wastelanders Helen made contact with. You're in charge." Darrow held out the papers they'd got from Station Five at the cost of so much blood and life. "And get this information to them. Memorise it as well. It would be just Sod's Law for you to get out but lose the printouts. Everybody clear?"

There was silence. "Then let's go. Take the fight to them."

After a moment, everyone started moving. Scary Mary nodded briefly to Danny. "Luck," she said.

"Thanks."

"You did all right," she said. Then she turned and walked off. Danny's jaw hung open. From Scary Mary, *you did all right* was unprecedented.

Flaps put a grimy hand under his chin, tucked his mouth shut. "Close your gob," she said. "You'll catch flies."

"Er. Yeah."

Flaps stood looking at him for a few seconds. There was a look in her eyes it took him a sec to recognise, 'cause he'd never seen it there before: hurt. And he realised why. 'Cause Mary'd never said that to her. He wanted to say sorry but knew Flaps'd deck him if he did. "Watch yourself," she said at last.

"You too."

Flaps nodded, then turned and went after Mary.

The landcruisers started hissing and clanking into life. Flaps hopped up on one of the flatbeds, got the .50 cal by the handles, looked back at Danny and grinned.

He looked round, in his turn, at his little group. Nadgers looked pale. Poor cunt was probably wondering if he'd landed a halfway cushy job or if it was out of the frying pan into the fire. Or maybe he was still just wobbly after the fight at the station and he'd firm up again once he realised he wasn't having to go hand to hand with the Reapers. Scopes blinked at him, her rifle across her back and her Sten in her hands. As usual, she looked a bit blank and vague when she wasn't actually doing owt. Thursday spat in the dust. "We goin', then?" she said.

Christ. He was in charge now. In charge. They expected him to know what he was doing. His gut clenched.

Danny looked at Alannah. Alannah smiled at him. Warmth flooded through him, and everything felt all right.

"Yeah," he said. "Come on."

Sirens were wailing. They slipped through the trees, weaving faster. Somewhere in the distance there was a burst of gunfire; Nadgers gasped, looked back.

"Keep moving," Danny snapped. "Split up. Weave. Link up at Warwick Street. Alannah, you're with me."

They were still safer than they'd be doing like Darrow was, he reckoned. For now, anyway. What'd happen when they got where they were going, though...

Well, he'd enough to think about for now.

*

The Bailey was just over the River Irwell in what had been the City of Salford. Standing on Chapel Street, the main road to Manchester, it had been a council office of some description; a big, flat-faced, sand-coloured Victorian building, four stories high, with ornate carvings above the doors and windows. The buildings either side of it had been knocked down to leave it standing free and unmarked.

Two Reapers stood guard before heavy wooden double doors, while landcruisers and foot patrols swept up and down Chapel Street and the sidestreets around it. There were sentries posted on the Bailey's roof, but all they had to see with were old searchlights from the Second World War, whose beams roved back and forth.

The closest thing to cover near the Bailey was a shantytown on the far bank of the Irwell, a few hundred yards away. Most people stayed clear of the bank itself, venturing further upstream to draw water; after all, the Bailey was dreaded by all as a place you only went into, never out of.

That suited Gevaudan; he'd found a stub of wall to crouch behind, and no one else came near. Only a couple of people had seen him as he'd slipped silently along the shanty's pathways, and they'd ducked down and hidden at the sight. Well, he was used to that. It meant he was left alone, to watch.

Every thirty seconds or so, a searchlight swept down to street level and across the front of the shop; he ducked back out of sight with time to spare at each pass.

In the distance, he heard bursts of gunfire, a muffled explosion. A thin black plume of smoke hung against the sky. Shouts, screams.

There was a stink of urine, excrement, vomit and decay. The crusted mud at the riverbank was tangled with bones; a more recent corpse bobbed in the shallows.

"Lowry Hotel's just down there," said Jo. "See?"

She nodded down the road. Gevaudan glanced in that direction, but there were other buildings in the way that hid the ruins of what had been Salford's five-star hotel. Catching fire after the attack, it had burned itself to a gutted shell; scavengers had stripped and dismantled what was left. He'd glimpsed it earlier in passing; only blackened stubs of masonry remained, like rotten teeth still stubbornly rooted in infected gums.

"Ah, yes," Gevaudan murmured. He leant – a little gingerly – against the wall and turned his face to the nightwind blowing in across the river. It carried a little relief from the stench. "Surprised there was anything left at all."

Jo shrugged and leant on the top of the wall. She squinted as the searchlight beam swept over her and stared out across the city as if she saw the night as clearly as he. Maybe she could. If she'd been alive, it would've been too black to see anything – the only lights were the dimly-burning coals of tallow candles behind clapboard shutters or curtains of rag – but perhaps in death her sight was a match for his. "You've forgotten, haven't you?"

Gevaudan glanced at her and smiled. "That we stayed at the Lowry on our tenth anniversary?"

She smiled back, ruefully. "Should've known. An elephant never forgets."

"Watch who you're calling an elephant..." But he trailed off. They stayed looking at each other for long seconds, and the smiles faded. The old banter lost its charm when you remembered how things ended.

Gevaudan looked at the Bailey's looming frontage. "You're going in, then?" she said.

"You know I am. That's what you wanted, isn't it?"

Jo sighed and shook her head. "It was what *you* wanted, you bloody fool. Someone just had to remind you."

Silence. Wind blew; wings clattered above them as a pigeon took flight. "Will I see you again?" he asked.

"Probably not. Ghosts are unfinished business, after all. I wouldn't have thought you'd have much of that, after all this time."

"Perhaps. Perhaps not."

There was no answer; Gevaudan turned but wasn't especially surprised to discover he was now alone. "Ah, well," he murmured and waited for the searchlight to sweep past. Then he picked up his bag, took several steps back, ran forward and leapt.

The jump carried him across the river; he landed in a crouch on the opposite bank. From off in the distance – the opposite direction to before – came snarling bursts of gunfire, like metal teeth clashing.

Gevaudan dropped low and ran, darting from shadow to shadow. Across the road from the Bailey, he let the bag fall – time now for travelling light – and strode over to the main doors.

"Shit," he heard one of the sentries say. They were struggling to unsling their guns. They were boys. Neither looked much older than Danny.

Gevaudan realised he didn't want to kill them. He didn't want to kill anyone. There'd been a sick, febrile hatred in him after the encounter with the woman and her child, for the Reapers who presided over this hell – but these were the Reapers, and they were children.

But they were children with guns; their rifles were aimed straight at his head and chest now, and one of them yelled "Halt!" so he did. A heart wound wouldn't kill him, not outright; if he could keep going long enough, it'd heal itself like anything else. But a bullet through the brain was a different matter.

Above, the searchlights swept down. Inside, an alarm began to shrill.

"Good evening," he said. "You all have one chance to live. I'd advise you to take it."

8.

She didn't know how long she'd been here. The bare concrete walls and floor moved in and out of focus. The cell rocked from side to side or spun. Sometimes she felt she had to hold on to avoid flying off.

Faces, memories, crowded and jostled for attention. The living. The dead. Frank, Belinda. Danny, Alannah. Shell, Sheel, Yan. Gevaudan. Darrow.

Gevaudan, Jarrett, Shell –

Helen sat up against the wall. The cell rocked to and fro, but the bare, gritty concrete was cold and hard and real, and it brought her back to the present, just for a moment. That was good. Even though her back, ribs and stomach all ached from the kicking she'd had, though she had a fat lip where one of the Reapers had forgotten Jarrett's instruction not to mark her face. The pain throbbed in her, low dull and relentless. But she was present, she was real, and she was here. Not thinking about what had happened.

But no sooner did that occur to her than she was there again.

They'd knocked her around a little before throwing her back in the landcruiser, more for the benefit of the remaining hostages than anything else – *look, see what happens when you try and fight us, plebs* – although that had been enough to leave her woozy and dazed for most of the ride to the Bailey. Each of the three Reapers had had their fun with fist and boot. They'd contented themselves with the occasional kick to the back or thigh on the journey to the Bailey.

Once they were there –

Helen spat blood on the concrete floor. She studied it. It was a map of bare grey rock, decorated with faded continents of long-shed blood or excrement. The walls were the same. If they could talk – well, no, they probably wouldn't, she reflected. They'd scream.

Her whole body throbbed, ached. Each breath smelt of blood; each swallow tasted of it. But she was alive.

Helen crawled into a corner, at the end of the same wall as the cell door. Out of sight; at least for a time. But best to assume she was being watched, at least for now. A hidden camera, or at least a spyhole. It'd make sense. She huddled there and tried to look beaten, a bundle of brutalised pain nursing itself in a dark place and trying to make the hurt fade away. It wasn't difficult.

First, she waggled her fingers. One of the Reapers had stamped on her gun-hand during their 'fun'. It had hurt like hell; still did. But the fingers moved. No bones broken. Her toes as well; same story. Not that she used *them* to fire a gun. Be useful if she could. She stretched and flexed her body, trying to make the movements look like she was twisting and writhing in the lingering pain. That wasn't hard either.

There might be a couple of cracked ribs. Plus there were bruises flowering all over what she could see of her body, and of course she was cold. *Naked in an unheated cell, and you're cold, Helen? Get away.* Always a good tactic. Strip someone of their clothes and they're defenceless. They might have been already, of course, but naked they *feel* it. Humiliated and freezing. They expected her to spend all her time keeping warm.

Helen breathed in and out through her teeth and spat blood again.

But sod warmth. Oh, one way or another she wasn't planning on feeling the cold much longer, but that would be a by-product. Sooner or later, Jarrett would be back to see her, and what she'd already had would seem like nothing. She thought of Alannah: the bright, sassy woman she'd been and the shivering broken thing they'd got out of the detention centre. That wouldn't be her. Breakout or suicide – one way or the other, she'd escape.

And then the alarm bell started ringing.

*

Jarrett wandered up the High Street of the little Welsh town, the hoarse rasp of her breath filling the NBC suit. Looking for Tom's house, Tom's Mum's place. Tom. Mum. Dad. Amanda.

Here was the road. She turned onto it, wove down it, tired and stumbling. Through the heavy breathing she heard a voice. Cracked, croaking, choking, it sang.

"Silent night, holy night, all is calm, all is bright."

The old woman squatted outside the open door of Tom's Mum's old house.

"Round yon virgin, mother and child, holy infant, so tender and mild."

She grinned at Jarrett; bloody spittle dripped from her chin.

"Sleep in heavenly peace, sleep in heavenly…"

She choked, fell forward.

Jarrett stepped over her, into the house. She searched its rooms; each door swung open before she touched it, and she steeled herself for what they'd show. But all the rooms were empty.

She went outside. The old woman's body was gone. The other bodies, too. The street was empty. Except…

Except for a small procession heading up it, away from the house. A man and a woman, not young, holding one another; a teenage girl, a young man. Following someone. She couldn't see who. But she knew those four, knew them even from the back.

"Mum?" she shouted. She heard her own voice choke and crack. "Dad? Tom! Sis!"

And they turned. Turned and looked at her. And she wished they hadn't. The disgust on Mum's face, the contempt on Dad's. The fear on Amanda's, the hatred on Tom's. And then they turned back. Away from her. Up the road to the woman they followed.

Helen Damnation stared back at Jarrett, sub-machine gun cradled in her hands.

Jarrett cried out, fumbling for her pistol. But the NBC suit had become a vast, collapsed tent, swallowing her up; she couldn't find the gun, couldn't get to it. Any moment and Helen would fire, cut her down before the family and lover who gazed on her now with such loathing –

"Colonel? Colonel Jarrett?"

Light flared. She yelped, grabbed for the pistol on her bedside table, had it up and aiming –

"Don't shoot! Don't shoot!" A short, tubby Reaper Major shrank back against the wall, pudgy hands raised to ward off the bullets.

"The hell are you?"

"Major Thorpe, ma'am. From the Ops Room."

Jarrett lowered the gun. Bloody fool, waking her like that when she'd just come out of the field; everything was on a hair-trigger out there, had to be. "What do you think you're doing in my quarters?"

"There's – ma'am – " Thorpe licked his lips. "We've got a problem."

Jarrett's stomach tightened; she exhaled. "All right. Give me five minutes."

*

267

"Commander Winterborn. Commander. Commander."

"This is Winterborn. Why are you bothering me? I gave instructions that I wasn't to be disturbed."

"Sorry, Commander. But this is an emergency."

"Emergency?"

"Yes, sir. We've had a spate of terrorist attacks in the last half-hour. Three Reaper Stations – "

"What?"

"Yes, sir, three Reaper Stations, plus about a dozen checkpoints and landcruiser patrols – "

The room spun about him; the floor rocked and heaved.

"What are your orders, sir? Commander?"

He was shaking. And then he was hyperventilating; felt like he couldn't breathe. His hands went to his throat and clutched at it. His legs buckled. He fell to his knees.

"Commander?"

He reached for the desk's bottom drawer, dragged it open, fumbled inside. His fingers closed round cool metal. He pulled out the music box, fell forward. The carpet's weave, rough and coarse against his cheek. Popping the music box open. Play, you bastard. Play. That old tune. Soothe me. Help me breathe like you used to.

But all that sounded was a desultory *ting*. He banged the box against the floor, but it only *ting*ed again.

"Bastard!"

"Commander?" called the intercom, sounding as far above him now as his office was above the city. "Commander?"

Can't breathe. Going to die in this place, here in my office. No. Not like this. It can't end like this. It won't.

Winterborn threw the box aside, reached into the drawer again. He fumbled out a leather glove and put it to his lips. Breathe. Use the glove to regulate your breath. Yes, like that. In. Out. And in. Out.

"Commander?"

In. Out. In. He grabbed the edge of the desk, rose to his knees. Then he stood; his legs shook, but he stood. He reached for the intercom, took a last deep breath and pushed the intercom button.

"All right," he said. "This is your Commander speaking. Alert all reserves and get hold of Colonel Jarrett."

"Sir. Colonel Jarrett's already been alerted. She's in the Ops Room now."

"I'll be down shortly." Winterborn clicked the intercom off.

*

"Raise your hands and kneel down," said the Reaper to Gevaudan's left. His gunbarrel shook and wavered. "This is your first and only warning."

"And this is yours," Gevaudan told them. "Put down your guns and get out of my way."

"It's him," said the other Reaper. "The Grendelwolf."

"Shurrup," said Reaper One.

"It is. It's him. He's come here to get *her* out – "

"Listen to your friend," Gevaudan said.

"Shurrup, the fucking pair of you!"

A searchlight swept down towards the street.

"I don't want to hurt you," Gevaudan said, "but I'm coming in."

He took a step forward, and Reaper One pulled the trigger.

So be it.

Gevaudan's arms swept out, knocking the rifle barrels aside so the shots flew wild. Then the claws slid from his fingers and he struck – once, precisely, at each Reaper's throat.

He could have stunned them, perhaps. But there'd only been a brief window in which he could have shown mercy, and now it was gone. Inside the Bailey, it would be battle now, and to the death. He was fully a Grendelwolf again, a fighting Grendelwolf, and for a fighting Grendelwolf, no quarter was given or asked. Not till he had what he'd come for.

The searchlights swept in and converged on Gevaudan as he stepped back and drove a kick into the double wooden doors. They flew inward with a splintering crash, and he vaulted through even as the machine guns above opened fire, bullets drumming on the cracked tarmac. He bounded up the steps and into the lobby.

A Reaper officer, two men flanking him, was coming down the staircase above. Beyond the NCO on the desk in the lobby were eight Reapers, holding rifles and sub-machine guns. Four more ran in from side entrances. And they all had guns and they were all aiming.

They fired.

And Gevaudan summoned the Fury.

Summoning it had been a part of his training; they'd all been conditioned into it, till it was second nature. It was triggered consciously, but Gevaudan could never have explained the *how* of it as such. He did something with his brain, like flexing a muscle, and when he did –

For some reason, earlier, he'd pictured himself explaining it to Danny. Perhaps the boy reminded him a little of David, his grandson. The sad part was he couldn't be sure; it had been so long now David's face was a blur in the mists of time. *Before the War, Danny,* he might have said, *there were drugs. I tried quite a few of them in happier times. There were psychoactives – but we'll leave that for another day, I think. There were stimulants as well.*

The muzzle flashes; Gevaudan sprang sideways. The bullets flew through the air – he saw them – flying through where he'd been.

Do you remember my coffee and the effect it had? The way it made you judder with sudden energy that had nowhere to go? Well, there were other drugs – amphetamines, for example – that have a similar effect. Only far, far stronger.

Wood smashed, stone chipped. Dust and smoke in the air. The gunfire like brittle thunder.

There is an energy, a drive to do something, anything, that possesses you, so intense that it feels like rage, even if you're wanting to make love. If it has nowhere to go, it turns on itself; I remember chewing the inside of my mouth to blood more than once. Everything, mind and body, is accelerated.

The desk sergeant below him; he kicked out, his booth's steel toecap hitting the Reaper's temple. A crunch of bone. The body spun away. He landed, jumped again.

The Fury... the Fury is something like that.

The other Reapers' guns were still firing at where he'd been. One stopped, started bringing his gun about; Gevaudan leapt once more.

But the Fury is faster still, Danny. It was built into us: a way to drive our reflexes, movement, senses, thoughts – everything – to a speed so high that...

Coming down, Gevaudan kicked out with both feet; his boots caught the Reaper in the chest, smashed the ribs inward to pierce the heart.

A human body couldn't survive it. But a Grendelwolf's could. That energy, that rage – summoned in battle, it's lethal.

He landed; a punch broke a jaw and neck in one blow, the heel of a hand to the base of a nose drove splintered bone into the brain.

There are two of you. One calmly watching, planning –

Bodies falling round him. Leaping forward.

But a hundred, a thousand times faster than normal. And the other –

That Reaper was coming about, might fire a lucky shot by accident. Him next, then the three around him.

The other is the Fury.

The right hand – lunging, claws tearing through soft tissue and ripping up under the breastbone, like a dagger to the heart –

The passion and the blood.

The left hand – its edge sweeping out to crush a Reaper's throat, clawtips skimming across another's throat to lay it open to the bone.

The energy the rage and lust –

A backhanded swipe slashed a belly open.

The two working together, the one plotting moves, the other executing them –

Already he was hot. Burning up. Or he would. His heart was thundering.

– with all the precision of a killing machine.

Claws tore a Reaper's throat out.

As they designed us to be.

A clawed lunge smashed through another's chest. Twisting, tearing his hand free.

You couldn't sustain it for long, of course, Danny; only a few seconds at a time – half a minute, perhaps as much as a minute if you dared – but for you those seconds would be minutes. And for those you fought...

It was like choreography, a dance: the racing brain plotted the moves, the Fury-driven body carried them out; fluent, exact, precise. It was almost art –

– except for the bodies it left behind.

For those you fought, those seconds would be the rest of their lives.

Only the officer and his guards, halfway down the staircase, remained. The officer fumbled for his hip-holstered automatic, the guards aimed their Sterlings and –

When the Fury was on you, they had no chance.

Gevaudan bounded up the stairs as they fired. The officer had his gun free; Gevaudan's left hand caught and snapped his wrist, his right plucked the pistol from his hand. He shot one guard twice through the heart, slamming him back against the wall, then spun to shoot the other between the eyes, knocking him back over the banister.

It wasn't battle; it was slaughter.

Gevaudan grabbed a handful of the officer's tunic, turned and thrust him back so he nearly fell down the stairs. Only the grip on his tunic stopped him. Gevaudan aimed the pistol at his forehead.

And when it's over –

The walls rang with the echo of gunfire. An alarm shrilled. Up above, feet pounded the floors, voices shouted. He was shaking. Sickness. Chills. No. Not now.

– when it's over, you shake like a sickened child. Because it's a drug; withdraw from it and you suffer.

"Where is she?" he said.

The officer tried to speak, managed only a whimper.

"Where?"

"Third floor," the officer croaked. "Max security. Cell Nine. End of... corridor."

You see, they don't just shape you to slaughter, Danny —

He nodded, fired, let the body fall.

— they shape you to crave it.

Gevaudan turned and climbed the stairs, tossing the pistol behind him as he went.

*

Jarrett clasped her hands behind her back, circled the huge central table and tried to pretend no one was watching her.

Halfway up the Tower's height was the Ops Room. A scale map of the city took up Wall One; a map of the entire Command Zone, Wall Two. Wall Three was left blank. Stored in the Ops Room were maps of the Zone's various sectors, continually monitored and updated; at any moment one of these might be put up on Wall Three to help plan some new operation.

Right now, though, Jarrett's attention was on Wall One. It was currently peppered with bright red pins. There were over a dozen of them, close to twenty. And six blue ones. None of them meant anything good.

"Status report, Major Thorpe."

Thorpe snapped to attention and clicked his heels. "Yes ma'am."

Muffled sniggers.

Jarrett turned and studied him. Thorpe was a fat little man with a florid face. For the moment it wore a smirk, but it faded fast, and so did some of his colour. Soft. Doubtless he had his uses, but he was no fighter. She was still in the combat fatigues she'd come back from the Wastelands in. There were matts and burrs in her hair she hadn't had the time to clear out. It was the kind of thing that didn't seem important when you were out there. She'd probably best relearn a few social graces. But not yet.

She advanced on Thorpe slowly, not breaking eye contact. The sniggers died away.

"Even I can see," she said, "that we've had attacks on Reapers in the city, and reports of civil disturbance. That's not a laughing matter, Major."

Thorpe tried for a smile. It died. "No, ma'am."

Jarrett studied the others. "You're in a safe little bubble here, aren't you? Think nothing can touch you. Trust me, it can. People like me make sure it doesn't. Try and remember that. And if you can't, remember this: the next Reaper to snigger at me will be clearing a hot zone without a suit before the end of the day. Are we clear? Good."

"A problem, Colonel?"

Everyone snapped to attention now with no hint of mockery, Jarrett included. "No, Commander."

"Good." Winterborn strolled into the room. "Have I interrupted anything?"

"No, sir."

"Then don't let me keep you." Winterborn leant back against the central table, arms folded. "Please, continue."

Jarrett nodded, turned back to Thorpe. "Major? Your report."

Thorpe licked dry lips, bustled over to Wall One. "Following the attack on Reaper Station Five, another followed on Reaper Station Eight – here on the map. Different MO this time. They fought their way in and stole guns, grenades, a couple of old PIATs – "

"PIATs?" Winterborn cocked his head. "Remind me."

"Projector, Infantry, Anti-Tank, sir. World War Two anti-tank weapon. They're very crude."

"But in the right hands, effective," said Jarrett. "I've used them on occasion. They were used at Station Five, as well, to take out the landcruisers."

"Speaking of landcruisers," said Thorpe. "The raiders had at least two, with mounted heavy machine guns when they attacked. Of course, they may now quite possibly have more."

"Go on."

The elephant in the room was that Winterborn was down here at all. Usually he stayed in his top-floor eyrie, hatching his plans and leaving the city's running to his adjutant. But not, it seemed, today. Then again, today wasn't an ordinary day, any more than yesterday had been. And tomorrow? Tomorrow was anyone's guess.

"There've been further attacks on Reaper Stations since then by what appear to be the same terrorists. They've hit Stations Nine and Three, but again a different M.O. Raked each station's front and forecourt with gunfire, blew up or damaged a number of landcruisers with grenades – "

"Or possibly, those very crude World War Two anti-tank weapons," Jarrett said.

Thorpe flushed, licking his lips. "Yes ma'am. Basically, they did all that, then drove off fast."

"Guerilla tactics," said Jarrett. "Strike and vanish; inflict damage, get out quick. And of course, they're targeting the landcruisers above everything else."

"Why 'of course'?" Winterborn asked politely.

"Because that's what enables us to move our people around at speed. Without them, we're on foot. Maybe horseback if we've got any, but it's hard to shift heavy weapons that way. So each station, each Reaper unit, is more isolated from any support." Jarrett turned to Thorpe. "Instruct all Reaper Stations to get their landcruisers out on the streets."

"But then they'll be undermanned, defenceless – " began Thorpe.

"The terrorists are *targeting* the landcruisers, you idiot. That and the manpower. Landcruisers on the streets, nice and visible. Those blue dots mean civil unrest, correct?"

"Ma'am."

"It'll only get worse if there's no sign of any authority out there. Landcruiser patrols are to monitor radios at all times and listen out. Any station coming under attack to put out a distress call: then our landcruisers come and intercept. All they have is the element of surprise. We have numbers, and every rebel landcruiser we knock out is irreplaceable."

A Reaper trotted up to Wall One and applied two more red pins.

"Jesus," said Thorpe.

"You know, if I had to hazard a guess," said Winterborn, "I'd suspect the hand of Roger Darrow in this."

"Darrow?"

"You remember him, surely, Colonel."

"Of course. But wasn't he killed at the Refuge?"

"So was Helen Damnation, supposedly. Death isn't what it used to be. Besides, he was only *presumed* dead. They never found a body." Winterborn looked sideways at Jarrett. "Come to think of it, the skills needed to access those computer files... there aren't many people who could do that any more. The rebels never had more than half a dozen of them, and only one who was really good."

Jarrett blinked and felt her chest tighten. "Alannah Vale."

"Only conjecture, of course."

"Of course. But I'm starting to feel as if I'm ghostlighting, all of a sudden." She turned back to Wall One. "The civil unrest, Thorpe," said Jarrett. "Talk me through it."

"Mostly around the worst-off areas ma'am. The real scum-zones. The scavengers, the crippled, the useless – "

"The ones who've got nothing to lose. Always oddly easy to persuade them to give their lives to the cause."

"Some of them have guns. Probably what the raids were about."

A Reaper put two blue dots up as Jarrett watched. "It's spreading. All right, first priority: we keep the Tower secure. Double-strength guards, all CorSec."

She turned to Winterborn. "This is going to stretch our manpower quite heavily, sir."

"Your point being?"

"The increased perimeter forces – "

"They stay in place, Colonel." Winterborn glanced at Thorpe, who looked down, then motioned Jarrett to follow him across to a quiet corner of the room. "At all costs, we have to protect Project Tindalos."

"Sir, I appreciate the importance of the project," *Or might if you'd just tell me what it was,* she thought better of adding, "but the priority has to be to keep control here. Otherwise…" she took a deep breath, "otherwise, you won't have any power to increase."

Winterborn's nostrils flared. Just that. He didn't blink. Jarrett wanted to step backwards, managed not to. Finally he released his breath. "What do you suggest?" he said. "I assume you have an idea."

"We have forces in the Wastelands: I'm thinking GenRen units, in particular. They're designed for mobility, firepower and heavy combat. We can order a number of them to protect Tindalos from any terrorist attack."

"Why not just order them back to the city?"

"I intend to do that with other GenRen units – with your permission, that is. But that's not enough on its own: by the time they get here," Jarrett nodded at Wall One, where one of Thorpe's men was putting up three more blue pins, "it might be too late. The situation's accelerating fast. If we pull back the extra perimeter forces to engage the rebels, that'll buy us time for the GenRen units to relieve the situation. Meanwhile, there'll be a full GenRen contingent to defend Project Tindalos in case anyone *does* get through the weakened perimeter. We can do it, Commander. But we have to do it now."

Winterborn bared gritted teeth for a second, then hid them behind pressed-white lips. "All right," he said, "do it."

"Sir."

Jarrett spun on her heel and went to give her orders.

*

The alarm was shrilling, and there was a thunder of gunfire. There were screams.

Helen got to her feet, searched the cell for a weapon, found nothing.

Naked, unarmed –

She gathered herself into a crouch. She had her hands, of course; she'd killed with them before.

Screams, the sound of bodies falling. The chatter of sub-machine guns, the deliberate crack of pistol fire. And, one by one, the other weapons cutting out. A final volley of pistol shots, then silence.

Just the steady click of footsteps in the corridor outside. Coming closer. Might be a rescuer. Might be death.

"Helen?" A voice, calling. Deep, dark. She knew it. "Helen? Are you there?"

It was…

It couldn't be –

"Helen?"

"In here," she heard herself call.

The footsteps drew nearer. "Stand clear of the door."

"I am."

"Stand *well* clear. I'm kicking it down."

A grunt, a thud, and the door flew off its hinges, flipping and bouncing off the cell floor and thudding to a halt against the wall. Gevaudan Shoal strode in, slapping a magazine into a Browning pistol and reholstering it. "Easier than searching for the key – oh." He looked away. "My apologies. One moment."

She blinked and stared at the dust-laden shafts of light spilling through the smashed doorway as he vanished. A moment later, there was a crash and screech of tearing steel, and items came flying in through the door: a pair of heavy boots, socks, underwear, the overalls she'd been wearing.

"I'll see to it. Get dressed. We won't be staying."

She wriggled into a pair of ragged pants, strapped her breasts down with a cloth binding. "You do surprise me."

"I take it you'd appreciate a weapon?" Gevaudan called.

The alarm, still shrilling. She tried to smile. "Wouldn't mind."

"A Smith and Wesson revolver and a Sterling sub-machine gun? I recall those being your weapons of choice."

"They'll do." She zipped up the overalls, laced the boots.

Gevaudan re-entered. She saw the pistols holstered under the black coat, and a Bren light machine gun slung across his back. "Here." He produced a Sterling from one coat pocket, the .38 from the other. "Yours, I believe."

"Thank you."

"We should go." He handed her a musette bag. "There's ammunition in there, and a couple of grenades. Use them well. Come on."

She stepped out into the corridor and blinked. "Jesus Christ."

"Hardly." There were bodies scattered all down the corridor, bullet holes in the walls and ceiling. Gevaudan drew the pistols as they went, pivoted as they reached the staircase down and fired half a dozen rounds up the stairs above. Two bodies rolled down the steps towards them and a faint cry died into a death rattle. She followed him quickly down the stairs, into a lobby strewn with dead men, only three of whom had been killed by a bullet.

Gevaudan glanced at her, then looked away. "This is what you wanted me for," he said. "Remember?"

*

The city was burning.

That was how it looked when Danny glanced back from the landcruiser's flatbed. Great black plumes of smoke hung over it, and shots echoed in the bitter air.

Nadgers hunched over the wheel. Whatever he lacked in nerve, he made up for in brains and skills; he could doctor a bit, plus he could drive a landcruiser. Danny couldn't do either. And his nerves hadn't been in a much better state back at Station Five anyway. Scopes sat beside Nadgers with her rifle ready, and

Thursday clutched the handles of the .50 cal. Danny sat close by the ammo belt, ready to help feed it through.

A hand touched his, thin fingers curling round his wrist. "You okay?" asked Alannah.

He nodded.

"You were very brave back there," she said.

He shrugged, flushing. "Yeah. Well."

He didn't know where to look, so he studied the landscape around them. Here and there were ruins; now and again there'd be part of a street, and you'd see where it'd been knocked down so they could grow crops in the earth. Most of the landscape, though, it was just fields, churned and muddy. Some had bodies in them, the workers who'd keeled over hacking at the ground with hoes and never found the strength to get up again. Cold, damp mist hovering above the ground, clinging to his face like wet cobwebs.

But the monotonous landscape stretched out forever in all directions, broken only by bare black trees, hedgerows like tangles of barbed wire, and the occasional ruin. Danny was used to walls, to there not being much open space in any direction. A little woodland like the one he'd last seen Darrow and Flaps and Mary in he was used to, 'causeit was small, bordered – but this? It was fucking huge, and he was lost in it.

Alannah squeezed his hand. "Nervous?" she asked.

After a moment, he nodded. He couldn't pretend with her like he did with the others, somehow. Just couldn't. "Yeah."

"You'll get used to it," she said.

"It's not this bit I'm worried about," he said. "Been outside the city before. We're going into the Wastelands, for Christ's sake."

"I know. Hush. We've got to."

"I know that. 'S just…"

"I know."

"What's this place called again?"

"Hobsdyke."

*

Gevaudan unslung the Bren gun and went out first, carrying it as easily as Helen did her Sterling, sweeping it back and forth.

She looked up and down the street, but it was deserted. "Aren't there supposed to be landcruiser patrols?"

"There are," he murmured. "Odd..."

"Helen!"

Gevaudan spun, the Bren rising. "No," Helen said as a landcruiser sped round the corner towards them. "Darrow?" she called.

The landcruiser slewed to a halt, and the older man bailed out. "I should have known," he said. "You haven't even got the manners to wait to be rescued."

"What about Tindalos?"

Darrow's eyes followed Gevaudan as the Grendelwolf wandered across the street and over the wasteground. "We hit the Reaper station and Alannah hacked their computers. She and Danny are en route now."

Gevaudan walked back to them, hefting a barrel bag to his shoulder. "Good," Helen said. "So what are you...?"

"I didn't like to leave you in the lurch. Especially when they could interrogate you. Besides, the Reapers doubled perimeter security at the city gates, so we needed a few distractions to divert their strength. It's going rather well. You might say there's a recruiting drive."

"Oh Christ."

"Don't knock it. We might actually win here, you know." But the smile looked forced. Darrow's eyes strayed over Helen's shoulder. He and Gevaudan studied one another. "Gevaudan Shoal, I presume?"

"Yes."

"Roger Darrow."

"A pleasure, I'm sure."

Darrow turned to Helen. "We should probably clear out of here sooner rather than later. I could use your help raising havoc. Or they could use your help at Hobsdyke."

"Where?"

"Deserted village, out in Sector Twelve. Edge of the Wastelands."

"That's where Tindalos is?"

"Yes. There's a REAP base there."

"Is it just Danny and Alannah?"

"A couple of others as well."

"More kids? Christ, Darrow."

"They'll rendezvous with the Wastelanders – "

"Winterborn will order extra Reapers in to defend the base. Jennywrens, probably."

"Danny did very well on the raid…"

"They need someone experienced. Why didn't you send Ashton, or – "

"Mike didn't make it."

"Oh shit. Darrow, I'm sorry."

"Yes."

"He was with you – "

"A long time, Helen." The euphoria suddenly drained out of Darrow; he looked weary and old. She reached out and grasped his hand. He patted it and let her go.

Gunfire behind them – she spun. Gevaudan was firing the Bren upwards, raking the roof's parapet. There was a cry, then silence. He lowered the gun, turned back to them as sirens wailed in the distance. "We should go," he said.

"He's right," said Darrow.

Helen breathed out. "They're going to need me more at Hobsdyke than you will here, I think."

Darrow nodded. "All right."

Helen turned to Gevaudan, opening her mouth.

"I think," he said, "that you'll probably need me more as well."

Helen was about to argue otherwise – that they needed to put up a good fight here in the city, that the last Grendelwolf being visible and fighting with them would rally support to Darrow's banner – but she could see from the set of those wolf's eyes that he wasn't suggesting, but telling. And if she was honest, she realised, she was glad.

"Hop on," said Darrow. "Let's find you a landcruiser of your own."

They scrambled onto the flatbed. The 'cruiser pulled out. There were two kids in the back; a small red-haired girl manning the heavy machine gun and a thin black boy with a bandaged arm crouched by the folded-up ammo belt.

"You're her, aren't you?" said the girl. "Helen Damnation."

"Yeah. Yeah, that's me."

The girl tried to look unimpressed, but she didn't succeed; she squared her shoulders and straightened her back and sighted along the gun. "I'm Flaps," she said. "This is Telo."

Telo – silent, big-eyed – nodded.

"Pleased to meet you," said Helen. Gevaudan unzipped his barrel bag, pulled out a can and used the key to unscrew it. Helen caught a whiff of meat and berries. Pemmican. Gevaudan broke off hard chunks of it with his fingers, pushed them into his mouth and chewed; hard, fast, mechanical.

"Who's your mate?" asked Telo.

Gevaudan stopped chewing and looked up. Telo shrank back, but Gevaudan only smiled.

"My name is Gevaudan Shoal," he said. "I'm the last Grendelwolf." He looked from Telo to Flaps and then to Helen. "And I'm on your side."

They all stared at him. He looked down and returned to the task of stuffing the dried meat and fruit into his mouth. They drove on in silence, cutting down Oldfield Road back towards the city, while all around, and circling ever closer, the chorus of guns, grenades and sirens rose.

9.

The dying sun soaked the sky at the horizon like blood. Around it, the clouds were like the bruised discoloured skin around a wound: purple, red, orange and lemon-yellow. Inside the landcruiser, Helen's breath billowed smokily from her mouth. She glanced across at Gevaudan; his was doing the same.

It was just them inside the 'cruiser's cab – the doors and windows were closed, and there were the two of them to combine their body heat in the confined space – but the doors didn't shut properly, and the sealant holding the windows in their frames was perishing, had gone completely in places. Nonetheless, the engine worked well, and they made reasonable time across the silent farmlands.

Helen huddled in her seat, gazing out of the window. No one in sight. Here and there a searchlight's beam swept through the dusk across the fields, but they were keeping to dirt tracks and to back lanes that time had almost reclaimed completely.

Soon the last signs of the Reapers – the watchtowers rearing over compounds of prefab huts, the glittering clusters of lights, the irrigation ditches and regimented fields – had disappeared and the landscape around them was one of bleak desolation; endless expanses of empty moorland broken occasionally by a building or its remains. There could have been villages here once, devoured again by the hungry earth, collapsing under decades of relentless wind and rain, or there might never have been human habitation here.

"I met a traveller from an antique land'," Gevaudan murmured beside her,

"Who said: Two vast and trunkless legs of stone
Stand in the desert. Near them on the sand,
Half sunk, a shattered visage lies, whose frown
And wrinkled lip and sneer of cold command
Tell that its sculptor well those passions read
Which yet survive, stamped on these lifeless things,
The hand that mocked them and the heart that fed.
And on the pedestal these words appear:
My name is Ozymandias, King of Kings:
Look on my works, ye mighty, and despair!
Nothing beside remains. Round the decay
Of that colossal wreck, boundless and bare,
The lone and level sands stretch far away.'"

"Gevaudan?"

"Mm?"

"Do you ever stop talking shit?"

"Sorry. I thought you were asleep."

"If only."

"There's NBC wear in the footwell," Gevaudan said at last. "There's a Devil's Highway near here, but we might have to go off it to avoid the Reapers. You should suit up, just in case."

Danny and Alannah too would have come this way. What if they had to go off the road? Would they remember? Would there be suits to go round? She couldn't think of that now. "Oh. Okay. Right."

She bent and fumbled for it, but her fingers felt thick and clumsy. She gritted her teeth and hissed; pain shot through her from a dozen places.

"Are you all right?"

She slumped back in the seat. "No. Tired. Sore. Not everyone heals as fast as you."

A silence. Then: "Did they – "

"That's none of your business."

Another silence. "No," he said finally. "Of course not."

The road unspooled in front of them.

"Shouldn't you put the lights on?" she asked.

"They might be seen. Besides – " he tapped the corner of one eye, "I don't need them to see where we're going."

"Of course." Stupid of her.

"You should try to sleep," he said. "Get some rest." He wriggled out of his coat. "Use this."

It draped over her like a blanket. It smelt of smoke and powder residue, and of him, of course. And the fabric was rough and coarse. But she didn't mind that. Just closed her eyes and drifted off.

*

"Fuck. Grim."

Danny looked around; a narrow defile, a thin black stream winding along its floor. The landcruiser was parked under a stand of damp, heavy trees thickly patched with moss and lichen; Nadgers huddled in the driver's seat, hugging himself and shivering in the chill.

"We'll manage," said Alannah. She got out of the landcruiser and straightened up, hands on hips.

Thursday released the .50 cal's handles and sat on the 'cruiser's flatbed, legs swinging in space. "So now what?"

"We wait."

"Fuck sake. What for?"

"Wastelanders to make contact."

"How fucking long's that gonna be?"

"Long as it takes."

"Fuck sake."

"Helen said they'd be watching the place," Danny said.

"Can't see 'em."

"Be keepin' out of sight, won't they? We wait, Thursday. That's all. Oi, Scopes." Scopes had already wandered further down the defile, rifle at her shoulder, sweeping it back and forth. "Scopes!" She blinked, turned and looked back at him. "Get back here."

She shrugged, lowered the rifle, and started wandering back. "Think we're clear, anyroad."

Danny nodded. Alannah unfastened the binding on her hair; it fell around her shoulders, slimming and softening her face. She looked calmer out here, more peaceful. Almost at home. "The trees will give us some cover. It'll be a cold night, though. We've got bedding?"

"Yeah," said Nadgers.

Alannah turned to Danny. "We'll need to keep close, for warmth. And we should probably gather firewood while it's still light."

"Some fucker'll see it," said Thursday.

"The only people around here should be the ones we want to find us."

"Should," said Thursday darkly.

Alannah shrugged. Scopes, now sitting on the flatbed with her back to the cabin, smiled to herself and went back to cleaning her rifle.

"We take shifts on watch," said Danny. *You're supposed to be in charge. Act like it.* "Every two hours. Everyone except Alannah."

"I can do it."

"You don't have to."

"I want to." A half-smile hovered round her lips. "I'm not *that* bloody old."

Danny felt his face get hot. "All right then," he said. "All of us. Every two hours."

"Bagsy first watch," said Scopes and bailed out of the truck. Danny hadn't even seen her put the cleaning rags away. Alannah watched her go and smiled, shook her head.

"Right then," said Thursday. "I'm getting some kip." And she curled up in the flat bed and rolled over to wind a blanket round herself. Her hand pushed out of it a moment later, stuck her tommy-gun close by. Then she wriggled back down into her cocoon and was still, only the thicket of her bristly hair sticking out.

"You okay, Nadgers?" Bowed over the wheel, the medic nodded without looking up. "Best bed down then."

Nadgers nodded again, clambered wearily over the seats into the back of the landcruiser. Danny rubbed his eyes and stuck his hands in his pockets.

He jumped as a hand stroked his arm. "Don't worry," said Alannah.

"Whatcha mean?" He squared his shoulders. What was she trying to say?

Her smile wavered; her hand began to droop. "I just... I just meant you're doing fine. In charge, I mean."

"Oh." Fuck, he felt like a prize shit now. What did he say? He wasn't used to this. "Soz," he mumbled finally.

"It's okay." Alannah walked a couple of paces off, arms folded. Shit shit shit. Fucking bollocks. He'd fucked up. Even Danny knew that much about women.

Bollocks bollocks bollocks. He was supposed to be in charge here. Couldn't go mooning about. He stood his ground. Then stole a glance at her. She stood with her back to him, arms folded, head down.

Aw, fuck. Danny looked down again. Bit his lip. Drummed his fingers on the stock of the Lanchester. It was his gun now, that. Part of him. He was right for it, and it was right for him. But he'd sling it in a minute to make things right with Alannah. He knew that suddenly.

Fuck sake. She's old enough to be me nan.

Didn't look it though. And anyway it didn't matter. Bollocks like that didn't matter to anyone any more. You took whatever was going. Fucked whoever and whatever you wanted that wanted you back. Some didn't even care about the second part. But this wasn't the same. He felt different with her.

Danny looked back down the defile. Couldn't see Scopes. Not at first. Then he blinked and he saw she'd found a cosy little nook for herself at the base of a dead tree, huddled amid the roots and shadow. She'd be watching for danger, nowt else. He glanced at the flatbed; he could still only see Thursday's hair, but she'd be dead to the world, he knew that. Knew what she was like. Nadgers was flopped out on his back, head turned to one side, eyes weaving about under their lids, dreaming deep.

Danny looked back at Alannah again, then shuffed slowly to her side, slinging the Lanchester across his back. She didn't move or turn around as he approached. Not hearing, or ignoring him?

He touched her arm. She stiffened, nearly jumped. "Soz," he whispered.

"It's okay."

"No. Honest. Me being a dick."

He kept his hand there. After a moment, her thin fingers stole about and closed around his own.

They stood like that for a bit.

"Scopes is watchin'," Danny said. "You wanna bed down?"

She turned to face him, keeping hold of his hand. They studied each other. Her free hand reached out and ruffled his hair, those thin fingers trickling through it. Felt nice. Better than nice. He closed his eyes for a second. And then her hand went still in his hair, and the cold pressure of a blade was at his throat.

*

"Here."

Gevaudan stopped the landcruiser. The light was almost gone. The scene around them – dust, scrub, distant hills, the half-buried remains of fallen buildings – dimmed to grey. Over to their left was a stand of trees.

Helen climbed out, cocking her Sterling.

"I thought the natives were friendly?" said Gevaudan.

"Me too. But you never know." Helen rolled and flexed her shoulders.

She set off towards the trees, still stiff and limping slightly from the beating she'd had. For a moment, Gevaudan watched her go; then he glanced, briefly, into the back of the landcruiser where his Bren gun lay. After a moment's thought, he left it there. He had his pistols, and they – together with the Fury and the simple fact of what he was – ought to be enough. Enough to buy some time, anyway. He climbed out of the landcruiser and walked after Helen, quickly drawing level with her.

"You're all right?" he asked.

"I'm fine," she said through gritted teeth. "Same I was last time you asked. Okay?"

"Very well."

They entered the woods, separating as they went. Helen stepped as carefully as she knew how, but now and then a twig would snap underfoot. A soft sound, but in the still dusk it sounded like rifle fire to her. Gevaudan, on the other hand – she looked round, tried to pick him out of the thickening shadows under the trees, but saw and heard nothing. What if he'd changed his mind and slipped away? No knowing what went on in a Grendelwolf's mind.

She crouched low, the Sterling at her shoulder, and crept, cat-footed, to the edge of the defile. It was littered with leaves and twigs, mulchy underfoot where they'd clogged the source of the stream and made it overflow. She hissed through her teeth as her feet squelched in them.

She reached a sort of corner, where the rock pushed outwards. As she did, someone stepped out in front of her. She almost yelped, almost fired –

"Easy," said Gevaudan. "It's only me."

She scowled.

"Something's wrong," he whispered. "It's too quiet. No animals. But no sound of people either. Someone's waiting."

"Okay," she breathed. "With me. Watch my back."

"Of course."

Helen stepped along the defile floor, keeping low. Every twig that snapped, every film of dust that gritted underfoot, sounded appallingly loud. She couldn't hear Gevaudan. She wanted to look behind her and make sure he was still there, but didn't. She had to trust him; sooner or later, it always came down to that. You had to trust. And that could make you almost invulnerable, or it could be what destroyed you.

"There," she heard herself whisper. She moved across the defile floor, from shadow to shadow and from shrub to stump to rock, till finally she reached the landcruiser.

The cab door hung ajar; a pair of blankets lay crumpled on the flatbed.

Two soft clicks behind her. She turned – Gevaudan, pistols in his hands. His eyes flicked back and forth across the defile, upwards, towards the high ground.

"We have rather a lot of company," he said.

"Easy." She reached out and touched his arm. He glanced at her. She smiled. "I think I know who they are. Don't do anything sudden."

Gevaudan smiled. "I'll try to control my rising panic."

Helen lowered the Sterling, stood up straight, and stepped away from the landcruiser, arms upraised and spread. "Wakefield!" she called. "You there?"

Only a silence greeted her. Her skin prickled. Funny how you really could feel someone's eyes on you. Gevaudan behind her, like a rock, looming. He wouldn't fire, not yet. Not unless he had to. And if he did, he'd be fast enough. Hopefully.

"Wakefield!" She shouted it this time. Some small thing skittered away through winter-brittle undergrowth; it was so loud and sudden – the loudest thing she'd heard since creeping into the defile – that she almost grabbed for the Sterling. Stopped herself in time. Easy, Helen. Rein it in. Take it easy. "It's me," she called. "The crazy ginger." She said 'ginger' with two hard 'g's.

"Helen?" called a voice from above. It was young, thin and female.

"Yeah."

"It her?" came a voice from over to the left. Gruff, male.

"Think so." Light flared above. Movement from Gevaudan –

"Easy," Helen said again.

The light dropped lazily to earth; a bundle of dried scrub, bound and set alight. It landed a few feet from the landcruiser. Sounds of movement above them; whoever'd thrown it, she guessed, moving away.

"Step in the light," called the girl's voice.

Helen walked towards the flickering, waning fire, arms still high. Gevaudan stayed where he was.

"Both yer," came the call.

"Helen?" Gevaudan asked.

"Do it," she said, and they both stepped into the fireglow.

A long stillness; the dried weeds burning swiftly down to emberlight and nothingness. Then, from above: "Aye. Her. Bleach?"

Another call, more distant. "Is clear. Nobody else."

"All right then. Come on."

There was movement all around, and now Helen could see them too. Gevaudan, of course – he'd have been able to see them all along. They came over the lip of the defile, the bushes and scrub on the floor, from little niches and crannies in its walls. They were thin and filthy, half-naked, bound up in strips of animal skin. Many were deformed. This one had a vast club of a hand with two normal-sized fingers and a thumb; the last two fingers were tiny and wizened and useless. Another had a rudimentary second head on her shoulder; as she picked her way along the ravine floor, spear cocked back for throwing, its mouth opened and closed.

"Helen," called another voice she knew. Bushes parted and half a dozen warriors escorted Alannah out of a small, previously hidden cave, along with a scowling Danny and a couple of other kids who weren't looking particularly happy either.

"Cut 'em free," said the girl, coming into sight. Small, thin, with a sharp bird's face and narrow glinting eyes. "Meant no bad," she told Alannah and Danny. "We all right?"

"Yes," said Alannah quickly.

Danny mumbled something, looking at his boots.

"Hello, Wakefield," Helen said.

Wakefield grinned.

*

Dark of the night, and from his window Winterborn watched the city burn.

All right – not the whole city, perhaps, but there were fires enough. Some might be shanties burning – torched by Reapers or their own idiot occupants – but others might be landcruisers, or Reaper Stations, or...

Breathe in. Breathe out. Remain calm. This was just a temporary setback. Things would remain on their proper course. He had a mission, his life a purpose: a few rebels wouldn't derail that.

Through the windows came the sound of screams, the wail of sirens, the distant patter of gunfire.

This would pass. All this would pass.

A bright fat point of fire glowed in the distance. It was waning, Winterborn was sure of it. And it would pass. And things would continue back on their proper course.

Winterborn covered the distant fire with his hand, counted to ten then took his hand away. And the fire was gone; a few dying embers, perhaps, but nothing more.

And the same will happen to the others. You've only to wait and have faith.

Winterborn nodded and turned away from the window.

*

They got a fire going in the defile.

"Trex, pan," said Wakefield. One of the Foxes fetched a very big, very old, very battered metal pan. Danny reckoned they were about the same age, but Trex's hair was the colour of dirty snow. He propped it over the fire and Wakefield emptied a waterskin into it. As the water boiled, Wakefield's people dropped things into it; bits of dried meat, dried roots, dried beans and peas and stuff. *Eye of newt and toe of frog* – Danny remembered that one from somewhere. Wakefield saw the look on his face and grinned.

"Tastes good," she said. "You'll see."

Some of her people were posted on watch, but most of them were round the fire with Helen, Gevaudan, Alannah and the rest. Scopes was cradling her rifle and giving it a polish. Wakefield went to her, squatted down. "Took your weapon."

Scopes looked up; her grip on the gun tightened. Wakefield raised both hands. "Sorry I took. Can see you real fighter. You love your weapon. Part of you." She held her spear out to Scopes in both hands. "Same for me."

Scopes looked back at Wakefield for a few seconds, then took the spear, turning it over in her hands. At last she nodded and smiled, handed it back. "You good with that?" she asked.

"Drop a wild dog with it at fifty paces." Wakefield grinned. "Reaper too."

Scopes grinned back.

Well, she'd always been a nutty bitch. Danny looked away. He was sat at the edge of the firelight, far away as he could get.

Alannah kept glancing at him, patting the ground beside her. He looked away again.

Movement beside him. "Danny?"

"Look, just – " Shit. It was Helen. He looked down. "Soz."

"Not me you need to say sorry to, is it?"

"Yeah, all right, I know."

"What's the problem?"

"What?" He looked at Helen. "How can you ask that? You out of everyone?"

"What?"

"All right, I fucked up. Okay?" He hissed it out through his teeth, eyes darting left and right, daring any other bastard to look. "I didn't see them coming. Could've got us all killed. Fucked up bigstyle. Okay?" He couldn't meet her eyes after that, not once the anger had burned itself out, so he looked back down at the ground. Sullen, he knew, like a sprog having a strop, but he couldn't help it.

After a couple of seconds, Helen sighed. "That's not what I meant."

"Eh?"

"Danny, these Wastelanders wouldn't have stood a chance against you and your people in the city. You know they wouldn't."

He shrugged.

"They wouldn't. And you know why that is."

He didn't answer.

"Why is it, Danny?"

"'Cause the city's our patch," he said. "We know it all. Inside out."

"Yeah. They'd be out of their depth there. But out here is where they live. They have to know it or they die; where to get food, water, where's safe, where's not. And they spend a lot of time trying not to get killed, whether it's by other tribes or the Reapers. And not just any Reapers. You know which Reapers would be coming out here."

Danny nodded. "Jennywrens."

"That's right. And they survive. They fight the Jennywrens and they win. Enough of the time, anyway. There's no shame in being caught out by them. Don't underestimate them because of how they talk. I've been out here for a long time, and I'm still alive because they know who I am, and they know I'm not a threat. Bit of luck, you'll learn from them and me. So don't worry about that."

Danny looked up at her, trying to tell if she meant it or was just stroking him off to make him feel better. But he didn't think she was. Wasn't her style, anyway.

"What I'm worried about," she said, "is Alannah. She's upset. Thinks you're avoiding her."

"No. S'not that. It's... she could've been killed. I mean, they all could, but – "

"I understand. Alannah will as well, if you tell her. But she's not long out of the hole. And she grips onto you. You know that."

"Yeah."

"So go and tell her, Danny. While there's still time."

He looked into her eyes and nodded. "It's gonna be bad where we're going, innit?"

"Yes." She nodded. "I think it's going to be very bad."

Danny took a deep breath, held it as long as he could, let it out. "I'm scared."

"That's only normal. Don't think about it for now. Go see Alannah."

Danny got up and went to her. Helen watched him go. He sat beside Alannah. She glanced at him, then looked away. Danny's lips moved, but he spoke too softly for Helen to hear. She could guess. He reached out, took Alannah's hand. She snatched it away. Danny looked back at Helen. Helen nodded. Danny spoke again, took Alannah's hand again. This time she let him. They talked for a while; he went to sit beside her, but she patted his arm and shook her head. Danny stomped away and sat down. The grey-haired young Wastelander drifted over to him.

*

Danny looked up, saw the grey-haired boy looking down at him. The Wastelander jerked a thumb towards his chest. "Trex," he said.

"Yeah, I know. I'm Danny."

"Sit with you?"

"Yeah, go on."

The Fox sat crosslegged beside Danny. He had a spear laid down beside him, a big knife on one hip and smaller ones tucked into the wrappings on his arms. Pouches hung from his belt, along with a small stick weighted at one end.

Trex saw him looking. "Throw-stick," he said. "You lob, it spins. Hits rabbit and – thunk." He mimed falling over. "Reapers, too, if helmet's off." He grinned. His teeth were brown and several were missing, but Danny grinned back.

The stew wasn't bad either. Tasted funny – all dried stuff and weird roots like he hadn't seen before – but okay. Live with that. Danny told Trex about Station Five; Trex told him about a skirmish with a Reaper patrol; him and three other Fox warriors armed only with the simple weapons Danny saw against a fully-armed Jennywren unit on a landcruiser. Two of Trex's friends hadn't made it back, but none of the Jennywrens had.

Danny decided the Wastelanders were a bit weird, but basically okay. Bowls of some hot, steamy brew were passed around. Trex took one, Danny another. It tasted odd, but nowhere near as bad as that stuff Alannah drank. He and Trex clinked bowls together in memory of their dead friends.

After that, Trex picked up a big dogskin bag that lay beside him and pulled out what Danny recognised from old photos, with some surprise, as a guitar. Trex propped it one knee and began to beat a rhythm out on its hollow body with the flat of his hand.

"What you doing?"

Trex looked surprised. "I'm a Rhymer."

"A what?"

"You not got them?"

"No. Don't think so." Danny realised everyone was looking at them. "What's one do?"

"This."

Trex kept beating time; now and again he plucked at a string, but the important part was the rhythm. After a bit he started to sing; wasn't much of a tune to it, but it was the words that mattered.

"Six Jennywrens on backs of steel
Jennywrens with guns
Against them four with spears and shields
Fox tribe's four proud sons.

Trex and Chalk to fight the Reapers
With sling and knife honed sharp
With throwing-stick and throwing-knife
Were Wetherby and Harp.

Six Jennywrens on backs of steel
Jennywrens with guns
Fell dead that day and came no more
To the Fox tribe's four proud sons.

Call for Trex and Harp to come
Give them meat and praise
For Chalk and Wetherby, no less proud
Do honour to their graves."

For a moment, there was silence, then applause. From the rebel fighters as much as the Foxes, and from Helen and Alannah as much as the rest. Yes, and Gevaudan too. Then the Grendelwolf held out his hand.

"Your guitar," he said. "May I see?"

After a moment, Trex passed it to him. Gevaudan rested it lightly on his knee, caressed the strings with his long white fingers. "It still has all its strings," he murmured, "and they're in good condition. You've taken good care of this." Danny was surprised to see how nimble his hands suddenly were. Gevaudan adjusted the little knobs at the end of the fretboard, then strummed lightly; a rich sound filled the gully. Then he began plucking lightly at the strings, and a slow, gentle tune emerged. "I used to sing this to my daughter," he said. "And my grandchildren, too."

Grandchildren? Danny gawped but said nothing. Nor did anyone else.

"Hushabye, don't you cry, go to sleep little baby,
When you wake you shall have all the pretty little horses ..."

*

Helen, listening, felt her eyes prickle. She remembered this song, too, just about, from before the War. But a lighter, sunnier version. In Gevaudan's hands it ached with a sorrow she wouldn't have suspected him capable of; not a selfish or self-pitying one, but a lament for all that had been lost and a hymn to all you hoped, however vainly and helplessly, to protect.

"Blacks and bays, dapples and greys, all the pretty little horses..." The Grendelwolf's head was bowed.

At last he stopped. The pause was longer this time, but when the applause came, it was even louder. Gevaudan smiled and handed the guitar back to Trex. "If you like," he said, "and if we live through tomorrow, I'll teach you to play."

Trex could only nod.

"Bugger me," Alannah murmured, "the surprises just keep on coming."

If Gevaudan heard her, he gave no sign, but he caught Helen's eye and smiled.

*

299

Gevaudan glanced round abruptly. Most of the gathered rebels and Foxes were bedding down for the night, except the ones taking up first watch; them and Helen and Wakefield, who were clambering up the wall of the defile to the vantage point at the top. That was good; no one would see this. No matter how carefully and casually he took the serum, his need for it always left an obscure sense of shame.

He opened the phial and drained its vivid, almost luminous yellow-green contents. The taste was wrenchingly bitter, the aftertaste sweet and cloying. He rinsed his mouth with water, swallowed.

"One day," said Jo, "you'll be holding the last phial of Goliath serum anywhere. And what will you do then?"

"I thought I wasn't going to see you again?"

"Changed my mind. Woman's prerogative."

Gevaudan shrugged. "I've lived longer than most."

"It's a bad death, though."

Gevaudan smiled. "Maybe I'll finally find the courage to kill myself. Until then…" he held up the empty phial "I have another thirty days."

*

"So you found? Place you looked for?"

"Yes."

Wakefield clambered up the thin path along the defile wall on all fours, her thin arse waving side to side. Helen picked her awkward way up after the girl.

At the top, Wakefield turned to face her. The fire still guttered far below; up here, though, the night sky was clear, moon and starlight silvering the ground.

In the distance, foul weather; dark clouds sweeping in, forked flashes of lightning out to the west, thunder on the wind.

"Where, then?"

"Project Tindalos?" Helen took a deep breath. "Place called Hobsdyke."

"Hobsdyke?" Wakefield's face was taut, eyes narrowed even further than usual.

"Yes."

"Hobsdyke." Wakefield breathed out. "Bad place. Very bad."

Helen nodded. "Yes."

Lightning flashed, thunder rumbled.

"Wakefield? Hobsdyke? Where?"

For answer, the Wastelander girl pointed. She didn't speak. Just pointed: out to the west, where forks of lightning writhed and tangled, the white and glowing snakes of some unknown Medusa's coil.

10.

"Angana sor varalakh kai torja. Angana sor varalakh cha voran. Mantakha sa niroleph chir karagh."

Dowson kept trying to look at the screen, but his head was banging. No – worse than banging. Pain behind the eyes like drilling. Like someone'd slid in a meat skewer, one with serrated edges, and was sawing it back and forth and in and out. Felt like there was a noise in his ears, a high-pitched *eeeeeeeeeeeeeeeeeeeee* that went on and on forever –

Something on the screen. Something taking shape in the Adjustment Chamber. But when he looked at it – no, couldn't see it properly. Kept blurring. Ow. His fucking *head* –

"Insapa veir bereloth. Insapa. Maengrepa gir trequefa gla detiresh meirka. Angana sor varalakh kai torja. Angana sor varalakh cha voran."

Eeeeeeeeeeeeeeeeeeeeee –

And then the noise faded. It faded and the voices died away. New voices bubbled up over them, along with sounds he hadn't heard in years. The twitter of birds, a pop song playing on the radio a couple of gardens away.

"Tea, Rich?"

"What?"

Dowson opened his eyes. The sun was warm on his face. *All* of his face. He reached up and felt; the keloid scarring he'd carried for two decades was gone.

He was in Angela's back garden. Flowers in bloom in the borders, a bush – azaleas, hydrangeas, rhododendrons. Others as well. He wasn't good with naming flowers. That was Angela's thing.

Not was...

Had been.

"Rich?"

"Um?" He turned and looked and there she was. Twenty-three years old and lovely. Forget the other flowers; here was a proper English rose, with wavy ash-blonde hair, clear blue eyes, smooth peaches-and-cream skin.

Not anymore –

Burned to ash.

Angela rolled her eyes. "I said, do you want another cup of tea, Richard?"

"Oh. Oh, yes, please."

"Good." Angela picked up the pot, poured. She grinned over at Dowson's mother, sat in one of the deckchairs. "Away with the fairies again. God knows what the army'll do with him."

"He was always the same as a boy," said Mum. She was knitting. The needles clicked softly. "Off dreaming of who knows what. Being a famous general, I'll be bound."

"Oh, give it a rest, Mum." But Dowson was smiling as he said it. He'd missed this. He'd ghostlighted before, of course – who hadn't? – but never like this. Never this detail. Bees buzzing, the soft, honeyed scent of flowers. A distant whiff of petrol fumes from a car or mower nearby.

"Cheeky young devil. Talking to your mother like that. You're not too old to go over my knee."

Angela kissed his forehead; her soft hair brushed his face. "And I'm not too old," she whispered, "to go over yours."

Dowson laughed.

"What's that?" said his mother.

"Nothing –" he said.

"Nothing –" said Angela.

Nothing –

Nothing –

Not real –

Not real –

Eeeeeeeeeeeeeeeeeeeee –

Headache; white, searing, piercing, rising –

"Angana sor varalakh kai torja. Angana sor varalakh cha voran. Mantakha sa niroleph chir karagh. Insapa veir bereloth. Insapa."

And when he breathed in, the scent had changed: air stale with burnt tobacco, sweat, flatus, dust. Thick, foul – he almost gagged. And filling the cabin, the relentless chanting of the subjects in the Adjustment Chamber.

"Maengrepa gir trequefa gla detiresh meirka. Angana sor varalakh kai torja. Angana sor varalakh cha voran."

And keys tapping: Mordake staring up at the screens, cigarette burnt almost right the way down between his fingers, face rapt, ecstatic. And the others: Lyson, Venter, Fenner, O'Grady, Rashid –

But then his eyes, gritty from the few hours' sleep he'd managed to snatch today, between being drawn back again and again to the Unit, were straying back up to the screens again; to the blurred, crackling, grainy black-and-white images from within the Adjustment Chamber. The figures tied to their chairs, and the thing, like a thick, twisting column of pale, churning smoke, that was taking shape amongst them.

He saw it; almost saw it, anyway. Felt his mouth begin to open, to shout; felt his guts cramp and knot in fear. But then the headache came back…

And the sound –

Eeeeeeeeeeeeeeeeeeeee.

"Angana sor varalakh kai torja. Angana sor varalakh cha voran."

Jesus fucking Christ, his *head* –

"Mantakha sa niroleph chir karagh. Insapa veir bereloth. Insapa."
Eeeeeeeeeeeeeeeeeeeeee.

And then the sound, fading. The twitter of birds, the growl of the mower, the radio, instead. Angela's soft hands on his shoulders, her lips on his forehead, her hair on his face. The light, and the warmth, of the sun.

*

"Maengrepa gir trequefa gla detiresh meirka. Angana sor varalakh kai torja. Angana sor varalakh cha voran."

Mordake didn't hear or see anything anymore. Just what was on the screen.

The test subjects moved in and out of focus. Something seemed to be happening to them. They were changing. But he couldn't quite tell what, couldn't quite seem to focus. Any more than he could capture the form that was taking shape in there. Materialising. *Ectoplasm. Psychic energy.* The language of fakery, he'd have said once. Quackery. The language of mountebanks who preyed upon the desperate.

Except who wasn't desperate, now? He blinked and shook his head, and the thought was gone.

"Angana sor varalakh kai torja. Angana sor varalakh cha voran."

But now. *Now.* Ah, *now* his eyes had seen the proof. As had Dowson's. As had they all.

"Mantakha sa niroleph chir karagh. Insapa veir bereloth. Insapa."

The smoky ectoplasmic figure blurred again. He wasn't interested in it anyway. He was interested in the new occupant of the Adjustment Chamber, who stood between it and the camera. Blocking his view of the shape, but he didn't mind. Everything was going according to plan. Everything was or would be beautiful.

Liz. She'd had her doubts before – had done, when last he'd spoken to her, among the village ruins – but now they seemed to be gone. She stood there, smiling. In jeans, trainers, sweater, leather jacket. She smiled. Not just smiled; in fact, she grinned at him, then stuck her tongue out, in the old familiar way.

Mordake smiled back at her; his eyes prickled. *You understand, Liz. You understand now. At last. All shall be well, all shall be well, and all manner of things shall be well.*

He remembered his cigarette, relit it with trembling fingers. He only took his eyes off Liz for a second, but when he looked again, she seemed to flicker, to blur, and her expression seemed to change. Or be changing. Or about to change. But then she sprang back into focus, hands on her hips, head cocked askance to one side: *Well? You coming or what, Eddie?*

"Angana sor varalakh kai torja. Angana sor varalakh cha voran."

All shall be well.

"Mantakha sa niroleph chir karagh."

All shall be well.

"Insapa veir bereloth."

All manner of things shall be well.

"Insapa. Maengrepa gir trequefa gla detiresh meirka. Angana sor varalakh kai torja. Angana sor varalakh cha voran."

*

The scent of the garden, the song of the birds, the light of the sun. The click-clack of Mum's knitting needles. The taste of hot sweet tea.

"Too much sugar in his tea," said Mum. "He always did have a sweet tooth. You shouldn't indulge him."

Angela's soft fingertips stroked his chest. The caress of her soft hair against his cheek. Her own cheek, soft, against his forehead. "It'll be all right," she said. "He's got his running. And we're playing squash tomorrow, aren't we, Rich?"

"Mm? Yes." This was so easy, and desirable, to believe in.

Not real –

Not real –

Eeeeeeeeeeeeeeeeeeeee –

Dowson found himself fighting to stay in the illusion; but, shit, bollocks, he *knew* it was an illusion. How could he sustain it now? And besides, wasn't this better? The burdens and responsibilities of his role – once and maybe future adjutant, controller of Project Tindalos – all of those seemed immensely distant. Unimportant. This, though, this was what mattered. So what if it wasn't real? He could submit to it, be swallowed up. He'd never know again it was anything other than the truth. Why not?

Why not? Because duty, that's why. Because his job, that's why. Because that world was gone, always and forever. And because –

Because there was a reason for it. To make him sleep. To make him not notice…

Not real –

Not real –

Eeeeeeeeeeeeeeeeeeeee –

The headache, driving in and out of his skull, sawing at the meat of his brain; was that just some side-effect of what was happening…

(And what *was* happening? Just what *was* happening now?)

…or some sort of warning, trying to ward him off, trying to stop him seeing something?

"Rich?" asked Angela.

Not real –

"Richard?" asked Mum. The clicking of her knitting needles had stopped.

Not real –

"You're not real," he said. Mum looked shocked, hurt; Angela let go of him, backed away. She looked at him too. That same shocked, accusing stare. While under the thin light blouse he saw the soft swell of her belly, burgeoning with the child that had burned in her womb. Anger came into him from nowhere; rage, hatred that these private memories should be taken, desecrated, twisted to this end. "You're not real." He shouted it now. "You're dead. *You're fucking dead.*"

Eeeeeeeeeeeeeeeeeeeeee –

And the stale rank stench of the cabin rushed in on him again, washing away the garden and the sweetness of the past for the last time.

"Angana sor varalakh kai torja. Angana sor varalakh cha voran."

The technicians sat rooted at their posts, staring at the screens, moving only to push buttons, adjust dials as required; Mordake stood, smiling inanely at the screens. Staring at the screens; all of them, staring at the screens, as if they were hypnotised.

"Mantakha sa niroleph chir karagh."

Dowson didn't want to see it. There was nothing he wanted less. But he knew he had to. And so he turned slowly, and he saw.

"Insapa veir bereloth. Insapa."

The shape that'd been forming in the Adjustment Chamber wasn't solid yet, but it was something more than smoke now, too. It had eyes, vast pale eyes. Dowson heard someone scream as those eyes found him; a moment later, he realised it was him.

"Maengrepa gir trequefa gla detiresh meirka," the test subjects whispered in a voice that wasn't, couldn't have been theirs, with mouths that should have been beyond speech.

Dowson spun away from the sight before it could paralyse him like the rest. Tindalos was a lie, he knew in that moment; oh, Mordake's experiments had awoken something all right, but there wasn't – never had been – any prospect of controlling it. It'd been controlling them: using, manipulating, so that it could be born.

"Angana sor varalakh kai torja."

One hope, one; Dowson lunged for the red button, the scream still strangling in his throat. The only way: burn everything in the Adjustment Chamber to ashes and dust. And then he'd end it all; convince Mordake or kill him if necessary, him and every other scientist and techie here. Destroy the records, blow up the buildings blown up, plough under the earth and sow it with salt; whatever it took to extinguish Tindalos utterly, erase it from memory and existence –

"Angana sor varalakh cha voran."

His hand was almost there when something flickered at the corner of his eye – an object, close to his head. Dowson recognised it as a pistol, in the last split-second before Mordake fired.

*

Mordake had almost forgotten the experiment; instead he gazed into Liz's eyes, vast and dark and encompassing even in the small grainy TV picture, drawn in. They were all that mattered. Soon they would be real, and then…

But suddenly, her face had changed – anger, alarm – and her right hand left her cocked hip to point off-screen. Mordake turned to look, and there was Dowson, lunging across the panel, towards the button.

There was only a fraction of a second to stop him. Yet at the same time, to Mordake, everything had a stillness, a slowness and a clarity that seemed to give him all the time in the world to do what he had to do.

His hand slipped into his white coat's pocket. The pistol was still there; his fingers located it, curled easily and swiftly around it and slid it free of the pocket without a single snag or foul. He'd never fired a gun in his life, yet it almost aimed itself, with the natural ease of long practice, as he spun, levelled it, and fired.

Mordake had time to register the swift passing of a blurred memory – namely, some long-ago comment by a Reaper that a gun's trigger should be squeezed, not snapped back, to keep it steady and ensure the shot was accurate – and then to dismiss it as irrelevant in any case, as at that range even he could hardly miss, in the last moment before things snapped back into real time: the gunshot loud and sudden, Dowson's head snapping round and back, his body tumbling, arms limp and flailing, to the floor.

"Angana sor varalakh kai torja. Angana sor varalakh cha voran."

Back into real time and the test subjects' voices, their dull, relentless chanting, washing into the room over the shot that rang and echoed and faded from the concrete walls. Smoke hung in the air, acrid, sulphurous. On the floor, Dowson's body twitched and jerked twice and then was still, staring up at Mordake in mingled disbelief and reproach as blood streamed from the neat hole in his temple.

Only a small gun, but the shot had been so loud. It would have been heard. Dear God, Dowson's men were outside; Andrews, the other Reapers. He'd just killed Winterborn's adjutant. Ex-adjutant. Not that Winterborn would care about the distinction. The gun shook in his hand. "Lyson – " he began.

There was no reply.

"Lys – "

But Lyson wasn't listening; he had eyes only for the screen and the controls before him.

"Rashid: Venter; Fenner; O'Grady – "

The same story from all of them; unmoving, seeing only the screen. He grabbed O'Grady's shoulder, shook him. The technician ignored him, except to shrug his hand off so as to adjust the dial.

Christ. Dowson's men, the other Reapers. Protect Tindalos. Had to protect Tindalos. Liz.

But the technicians. Like zombies. Like automata. Tindalos had done that to them. The project. *It wants to be born.* And him? Who'd really killed Dowson? Tindalos, or him?

"Oh, I think you know the answer to that, Eddie," said Liz's voice from the screen.

He spun, stared at her. She was still smiling, arms folded, but it wasn't the same smile. It was cold, and her eyes gloated. "Don't try and palm everything off on me."

They were doing it. The test subjects. The group mind. He had to, had to...

"Candlemass," he shouted, shoving past Lyson to reach the microphone. "Candlemass!"

From the speakers came a high, hateful titter. "It doesn't doesn't work on me, Eddie. It never did. We only let you believe that so you'd do what we needed you to."

Behind her now he could see – *really* see – what was happening in the Adjustment Chamber. Hadn't before. Hadn't seen because he hadn't wanted to. It had fooled him because he'd *wanted* to be fooled. Deceived? Manipulated? Yes. But he'd allowed that to happen, and there'd been no volition other than his own on the hand that'd fired the gun.

The test subjects had to be dead. Surely they must. They were decaying even as he looked at them; rotting, crumbling away. Parts of them were already dust. And yet their mouths still worked. Or in some cases, naked jawbones. Whatever had been taken from them, the thing forming in the centre of the Adjustment Chamber was still keeping them alive, working them now like puppets to force the last dregs of whatever strength it could derive from them.

Used. I used them, but they – it – the thing that wanted to be born, that thing there, with Liz's face; all along it was using me.

Mordake stumbled towards the door.

"Eddie," said Liz, in that new, cold, gloating voice. "Where are you going? You've done well."

He twisted the handle. The door wouldn't open.

"You've called me, and I've come. And now you've shed blood in my name. I'll honour you for this. I'll set you on high."

He turned, wrenched at the handle; the door was open. Now, quickly, before –

"Eddie!"

He turned back, halfway through the door: that was Liz's old voice, the one he knew so well. He turned, and on the screen, her shape flickered and blurred and changed. She was Liz again, but the cold, gloating Liz was gone. It was the Liz he knew, and she looked afraid and agonised and desperately unhappy.

"I tried to warn you," she shouted over the rising chants. "Run, Eddie, run – "

And then she screamed, and so did Mordake as he watched her ghostly body come apart, torn asunder, and beyond it the thing in the chamber turned whatever served it for eyes upon him. They stared into him and they knew him – knew whatever little of him they already hadn't, anyway – but worse, he knew *It*. The thing in there; its name, its nature, and the fool that he'd been.

You've been had, Eddie; you've been had, you've been had…

And it was as much rage at that as any desire to retrieve his error, or stop what had been started, that sent him running back inside, eyes shut as he lunged past Lyson and the rest, the things they were becoming or had become, for the red button.

Hands seized him; he cried out in pain because their fingers now ended in talons that pierced his clothes and flesh. Mordake could still, just, recognise one of the things holding him as Lyson. The man's eyes were glazed and empty, staring through him; a dull, leaden sheen had spread over half of his face, and his mouth – the man's mouth was disappearing. The clawed hand shifted to Mordake's throat.

Gunfire exploded in the confined space; it felt as if someone had hit Mordake on each side of the head. He couldn't hear anything except the humming in his ears, but the grip on his throat slackened, and Lyson jerked and staggered, half-turned. He lurched towards the door, but the pistol fired again and again.

Lyson kept coming; beyond him, Mordake saw Andrews in the doorway, backing away and firing until the gun emptied. Lyson swayed on the threshold, teetering, then pitched forward and lay still.

"Doctor!" he heard Andrews shouting, over the hum in his ears, over the storm outside. "Doctor, come on!"

Other shapes moved towards Mordake: O'Grady, Rashid, Venter, Fenner. All barely recognisable; all changed as Lyson had been changed. He scrambled past them, over Lyson's body.

Hands grabbed him, pulled him aside. Andrews shouted an order; three Reapers armed with Sterlings ran to the doorway and opened fire. Screams from within; they didn't sound quite human.

Rain flailed at him, drops driven with a force that made them strike like pebbles, half-blinding him. He caught only glimpses of things: bright, searing flashes of light erupting above, charred marks on the ground where lightning had struck. He focused briefly to see fire erupt outside the perimeter fence as another bolt flew to earth. Thunder roared and rumbled. Then the rain was in his eyes again, slashing across them.

"Doctor," Andrews was shouting, "what the hell's going on?"

He looked up, and in the next flash of lightning he saw them, standing in ranks on the parade ground. Reapers and technical staff, Andrews' men and Dowson's: stood stiffly to attention, upright, arms at their sides, staring at Mordake, through him, into nothing. They were silent; the only sound was the wind and the rain and the chanting, from the speakers inside the Monitoring Unit; and, it seemed, coming through the Adjustment Chamber's walls, even through the concrete, even through the storm. *"Angana sor varalakh kai torja."*

So loud. Louder and louder each time.

"Angana sor varalakh cha voran."

"What the hell's going on?"

"You tell me," shouted Andrews. "They're all like this, except for us." He gestured round; Mordake saw perhaps a half a dozen Reapers with them.

"Mantakha sa niroleph chir karagh."

"The experiment's gone wrong," Mordake shouted, knowing it was a lie. The experiment was going *right;* this was what had always been intended. "We've got to shut it down!"

"Sir!" shouted one of the Reapers, and pointed. The lightning seemed to have stopped, so Mordake couldn't make out the details of the figures on the parade ground, but they looked different. Altered. And now they were moving, closing in.

"What are they?" shouted the Reaper. "Sir, what are they?"

"Quiet," snapped Andrews, shoving a fresh magazine into his pistol. "Form ranks. Any ideas, Doctor."

And Mordake realised. "The auto-purge button," he shouted. "In the Monitoring Unit."

He ran for the door, unheeding of Andrews' shout behind him. Gunfire rang out as he jumped over the technicians' bodies and lunged for the button. His hand slammed down on it –

And nothing happened. No explosion. The chanting kept coming from the screen.

He didn't look up; not even when he heard a soft, tutting voice coming from the speakers. He couldn't take his eyes from the instrument panel, where the switches and controls were now moving of their own accord.

"Eddie?" said the voice from the speakers, one that contained tiny traces of Liz's still, but which had almost entirely shed the guise now. "Now that was naughty, wasn't it, Eddie?"

From outside came gunfire and screaming, and then the screeching howl of what he'd midwifed into the world. *Carter – Carter had been right –*

"Eddie," said a voice. "Eddie, don't you want your reward?"

"Insapa veir bereloth. Insapa."

"Here, Eddie. Take it. It's yours."

"Maengrepa gir trequefa gla detiresh meirka."

"My blessing, Eddie, and my curse."

"Angana sor varalakh kai torja. Angana sor varalakh cha voran."

And then he felt it reach into him, inside him, and begin to tear him apart and unravel him at the most fundamental of levels, and Edward Mordake screamed as he had never screamed before.

PART THREE: HOBSDYKE

1.

She's on the Black Road again, and again there is no sound.

She knows, from that silence, what she's about to see. She's not wrong. Grey creeps into the black; the night sky lightens, and again she walks the plain of ash.

Someone up ahead. She thinks she knows who, almost laughs in relief. But she doesn't; on the Black Road, she knows by now, you meet nothing good.

It's Gevaudan; still, unsmiling. Something about his face: a jagged, Y-shaped scar on his left cheek.

A whisper in the hush: *He will destroy you.*

Gevaudan bares broken teeth in a snarl. His right hand rises, sprouting claws, and he strikes –

She blinks; he's gone. Only the road remains; the road, the plain of ash and the dull-grey, burnt-out sky.

Things crawling in the ash: are they struggling free of it or being formed from it? Impossible to tell. They crawl toward her despite missing limbs, lift toward her the clustered holes that form their faces; point toward her if they have hands to do so. Is she chosen or marked, exalted or accused?

As if in answer, the whisper comes again: *You're too late.*

A shadow falls across the road. Something vast, behind her.

The whisper, again: *Tindalos.*

Unable to stop herself, she turns.

It fills the sky. Its head descends. In a moment she'll see it and die.

In the second before that happens, a final whisper:

The Wolves are running.

*

A muffled cry and she was awake, scrabbling for her gun. But she could breathe now; cool clear air. And there was light, warm on her face despite the winter chill. She sat back down, breathed deep, fingers white on the Sterling.

Helen swallowed hard, studying the surroundings. Who, where, what, why? At times like this, she often didn't know the answers. Deep breaths, Helen. It came back slowly; the defile, of course, where they'd met Wakefield's people last night. She was sat against its west wall; the sun, peeping over the far edge, was in her eyes.

Someone blew a note on a whistle or pipe of some kind; it started low, rose high, fell again. Bushes rustled across the defile floor; Foxes emerged from them, shaking their heads to clear the last dregs of sleep, weapons in hand. On top of the wall opposite, a small thin figure appeared, silhouetted against the sun: Wakefield. She raised her hand in a wave, then started climbing down.

"Bad dream?"

Behind and overhead – she spun, aiming the Sterling. Gevaudan perched on a ledge about ten feet overhead, Bren gun across his knees. She breathed out. "Yes. The hell are you doing up there?"

"Keeping watch. Want to talk about it?"

"About what?"

"Your dream."

He will destroy you.

"No."

"It can help."

She stood, painfully. "What part of the word 'no' do you not understand?"

He shrugged and looked away. "As you wish."

Groans and mumbles to the south; she looked and saw Danny sitting up, rising to pick up his Lanchester, then quickly shaking and prodding his crew awake. All except Alannah. Scopes went to nudge her; Danny waved her back, a finger to his lips.

Helen stood and limped towards them. The Foxes had all grouped together, gone down on one knee. Wakefield stood before them, spear held aloft.

"Fox's Spirit, run with us.
Make us quick and cunning and brave,
Bring us victory, slay our enemies,
If we die, carry our souls."

The warriors bowed their heads, raised their spears aloft, and each let out three short, sharp barks in perfect unison; they rang and echoed in the cold clear morning air.

*

"'Lannah?"

"Mm? What? What?"

"Easy. 'Sall right. You're okay. 'S just me."

"St– "

"Danny."

Alannah breathed out. "I'm sorry."

"'S okay. Here."

"What? Oh, thanks. What is it?"

"Something Wakefield's lot knocked up. Tastes a bit like that stuff you drink."

"Thanks."

"There's some grub too. Some sort of porridge. You want some?"

She rubbed her eyes. "Probably best had, hadn't I?"

"I would. Wakefield said Hobsdyke's a good five or six miles off, and we'll need to go on foot."

"Oh, Christ."

"I'll get you the porridge."

"Thanks, love."

Danny looked down, flushing red. "No probs."

Alannah huddled back against the landcruiser and sipped her tisane, watched him go over to the fire in the middle of the gorge, where last night's stewpot now bubbled again.

"How you doing?"

She looked up. "I'm good. You?"

Helen crouched beside her. "I'm not too bad, considering. Decided to join with some of the morning exercises." She nodded across the gorge, to where the rest of Danny's crew, led by Scopes, were bending and stretching, watched by a couple of Foxes who were trying to keep their faces straight. "Helps a lot."

"Got to keep them moving if you don't want to stiffen up."

"Yeah. Thanks, by the way. Understand you made a point of finding out where I was."

Alannah shrugged. "I owed you that much. Anyway, the Grendelwolf got there first."

"Thanks anyway."

"God. Look at him." Alannah nodded over the stream in the middle of the defile, where Gevaudan was down on one knee before two of the younger Foxes. One touched his hair and let the fine black strands run through her fingers; the other stared, fascinated, at the Grendelwolf's yellow eyes. Gevaudan submitted to the examination without reaction. "What's he like?"

"Strange," said Helen finally. "But he's on our side."

"You think."

He will destroy you. "Let's hope so."

"Yes. Let's." Silence. "How are you?"

Helen breathed out. "Long as I keep doing something, I'm all right."

Alannah nodded. "Looks like I've had a bit of a lie-in."

"Danny let you sleep."

"He's a good lad." Alannah watched Danny getting a helping of porridge from the Fox tending the pot. "Don't let anything happen to him, Helen."

"I'll do my best."

"Do better than that."

Danny came back over. "Here you go."

"Thanks." Alannah ate; the porridge was simple enough – grains boiled in water till soft, flavoured with dried berries – but warm and filling.

For his own part, Danny slipped a hand in his own pocket and closed it round a little doll of twigs, wool and dried clay, bound with thin strips he'd cut from a rag of clothing. He didn't know if he meant it to be Helen, Alannah, or the mother he'd never known, the living or the dead. Didn't matter; it was something to hold on to, something to call a prayer.

Wakefield padded over. "You ready?"

Helen glanced at Alannah. "Five slings."

"How long's that?" asked Alannah.

"'Bout five minutes," Danny told her.

Wakefield pursed her lips, then nodded. "Only five. Go soon. Or not safe."

Alannah spooned up the last of the porridge, washed it down with the last of the tea. "All right," she said. "I'm ready now."

*

The upstairs room of a long-abandoned terrace in Northern Moor; all black and damp, charred and rotten, save the square of bleached greyish light that was the window Flaps crouched beside.

Five of them left, including her, and two weren't good for anything much. Telo lay in a corner moaning, a bandage across his eyes. Pipe, the youngest of them, was shaking and could barely hold his gun. He bit his lips to keep from screaming, but little whimpers occasionally got out, and his eyes always seemed to be staring off at something Flaps couldn't see. She doubted anyone but Pipe could.

That left her, Lelly and Mary, and Lelly had a bad leg wound and could hardly move. Least she could shoot though. And she'd hardly made a sound. As for Mary, she looked from one of them to the other, tight-lipped.

"What's the plan?" whispered Flaps. Mary didn't answer. "Mary – "

"I don't know," Mary said at last.

"But – "

"I don't." For the first time Flaps could remember, Mary looked lost – helpless, even. "I'm sorry, Flaps. They've been clearing out every bolthole we've got."

Outside, there was a sound. Flaps gripped her gun tighter, moved to the window, peered over the sill. "Shit."

"What?"

"Landcruisers."

There were three – no, four – of them, coming down the road. Machine guns on the backs of them. "Fuck do we do?"

The Reapers were bailing out, running towards the house; some were making for the back. "What do we do?"

"They know we're here." Lelly was dragging herself over, her pretty-pretty face white, gone taut on the bone. "We go down fighting."

"Mary?" Flaps stared at her. "Mary?"

Mary blinked. For a second her face was lost, then she grabbed Flaps' arm. "With me," she said, and dragged Flaps across the landing into the spare room.

"Here." Mary pulled up three, four floorboards. There were soft, spongy; the nails came out easily. She snatched Flaps' gun from her hands. "Get under here. Do it, now."

"Mary – "

"Do it." Flaps scrambled down into the dark. A cramped space, less than a foot between the boards and the damp, crumbling ceiling . "Hang onto the joists," said Mary. "Put your weight on them, not the ceiling. Come on, quick. Stay quiet, keep still."

Lelly's sub-machine gun started chattering, and the thunder of the .50 cals came back. Bullets smashing into bricks, stone, plasterboard. A strangled cry from Lelly, then silence. Pipe keening. Soft moans from Telo. Shouts from outside.

"Done all I can," Mary shouted. "They might find you anyway. If they don't, find Darrow. Get everyone you can to safety. You can do it. You're my best, Flaps."

Flaps stared; Mary had never said that to anyone. Highest praise she'd heard her give was yesterday, telling Danny he'd done all right. But this? Her throat threatened to close up. "Mary – "

"Quiet." Mary touched her cheek, smiled. Just for a second, the hard face softened; here was another Mary, with no point of reference to the one Flaps had always known. And there was no time to know this one now.

"Get down," said Mary, and pushed the floorboards over her as the doors crashed in below and feet thundered up the stairs. Flaps braced herself there, the stink of damp and char, smoke and blood in her nose. She heard Mary shout, heard her gun firing, heard a crash of weapons fire in response and the sound of a body falling.

Downstairs, feet stamped. Guns fired. She heard bullets punching walls. *Not the ceiling, don't shoot the ceiling.* Feet stormed up the stairs onto the landing. Doors kicked wide. Pipe screamed. A cry from Telo – then bursts of gunfire, cutting them off.

She heard the door of her room kicked down. Guns fired again. Dust seeped down into her hiding place; she wanted to choke, retch, cough, but couldn't, mustn't. *Not the floor. Please don't shoot the floor.*

Footsteps, getting closer to her. Floorboards creaking underfoot. Closer, closer. What if they reached her? The weight on her back. Even if she didn't cry out, surely it'd feel different to them. Closer. Closer.

Another burst of gunfire from another room. A loud splintering crash. Curses, laughter.

"Fuck's going on?" The voice sounded almost right above her. It was the Reaper stood a few feet from her hiding place. He was her death; waiting, close.

"Dave was up in the loft, checking. Nearly went through the ceiling feet-first. Get out of there if I were you, you'll end up in the fucking kitchen. Place is practically falling apart."

A moment that lasted forever, then "Fair enough. No fucker's in here anyway."

"Come on then. Giz a hand wi' the bodies."

Flaps hung on and waited. Even now it wasn't over; one cough, one sneeze, one whisper would kill her. She hung on, stayed silent. Something crawled over her back in the dark. Spider? No – it was warm, hairy. Fuck. A rat. If it bit her, what then? They knew, the evil little fuckers; they knew just when you were helpless.

From the next room and the landing – Mary – there was the slow scraping drag of heavy objects being pulled across the floor, then the dull thump thump thump of them bouncing down the stairs. The rat crawled down her arm.

A door thumped. The silence stretched and ached. Were they all gone now? Was the house finally fucking empty? The rat had reached her hand where it clutched on to the joist. Its whiskered nose twitched and snuffled at her whitened knuckles. Fuck, fuck, fuck. Flaps tried to remember when she'd last lit a candle at a road shrine. She wished she had. *Someone, please, fucking look after me here.*

The rat scuttled on.

Outside, the landcruisers' engines hissed and clanked into life. They rose, then receded as they drove away. Silence. The joists creaked. It occurred to her they'd hardly be very sturdy either.

Wet and rotten, they could give way any moment and pitch her through the ceiling; even if the Reapers were gone, the fall would cripple or kill her.

For all that, she hung there for some time. Finally she pushed herself upwards, feeling the rotten boards push free of the floor and fall away.

She dragged herself out of the hiding place and across the floor. Damp, slimy wood under her fingers. And no gun. Wait. Yes, she did. There was a pistol in her waistband; Mary had only taken her sub-machine gun.

Flaps climbed out and ventured onto the landing. There was blood on the pale walls, a black glisten on the rotted floor, to show where Mary had died. She only looked once in the room where the others had been. The heavy bullets from the .50 cal had almost torn the outer wall away. There were *pieces* scattered on the floor. Bits of Lelly, she guessed. Miracle Telo and Pipe had still been alive for the Reapers to finish off. Blood on the walls, holes in the walls. She looked away.

Flaps aimed the gun down the staircase and ventured downstairs. The house was empty; the Reapers had gone. She stood there, the gun in her hand at her side, and waited.

"Flaps."

She turned. Gaped. Mary stood at the foot of the stairs, arms folded.

"Darrow," Mary said. "Find Darrow."

And then she was gone.

Flaps stared at the space she'd occupied for nearly a minute. So that was ghostlighting. So that was how it was. She took a deep breath, shook her head, then thrust the revolver back out of sight under her clothes and went to the door. When she was sure the coast was clear, she went outside and started walking.

Finally, she began to run.

*

Danny's eyes ached trying to find something to look at.

He'd not seen much of the Wastelands before; by the time they'd reached them last night it'd been dark, and the gorge they'd been hiding in hadn't shown much. But now – Jesus.

Out of the gorge, there was fuck-all to see. The ground rose and fell, the way the sea had in a picture Darrow showed him once. The hills were green and brown and grey and covered in scrubby grass and mud. The ground was lumpy and slippery and a bastard to traverse. Course, bits of the city could be, too, but this was different. And everywhere the huge sky, glaring white, unbroken. No walls or tunnels, just the great, stretching landscape. White pain started nagging behind Danny's eyes. He squinted, stumbled. Christ. Keep it together. His breathing was ragged. How long'd they been going? He could hardly see – the white of the pain, plus his eyes shifting out of focus. All he could do was put one foot in front of the other.

His foot slid. He bit back the yell even as he started to fall. Rock, sticking up out of the ground, rushing up towards his face –

A hand caught his arm; an arm got him round the waist, levered him upright like he weighed nowt. "Easy, Danny," Gevaudan's voice rumbled. "Helen? Wakefield? I think we might need a brief stop."

"I'm all right."

"No, you're not. Sit down." Gevaudan pressed Danny down onto a flat rock; cold and damp began seeping through his trouser seat. "The rest of you, too. None of you are looking well." The Grendelwolf crouched before Danny, studying him.

"What is it?" Helen came up. "Not radiation – "

"Unlikely. A creeping dose wouldn't set in so fast. Besides…" Gevaudan rose and looked at the others. Alannah, Scopes, Thursday, Nadgers; all looked pale and unwell. "What's wrong?"

"Headache," said Alannah at last.

"Yeah," said Danny. "Whole place hurts me fucking eyes."

Gevaudan let out a long breath. "I think I understand." He smiled. "Simple eyestrain. And maybe a touch of agoraphobia."

The smile grew a little sad. "I'm willing to bet most of you haven't left the city in your lives."

"Not in the last five years," Alannah said.

"We have," said Danny. "Gone training in the Agri sectors."

"But still focusing on comparatively enclosed surroundings. They very rarely have to deal with anything that isn't particularly close to. That and they're not used to long marches either."

"Shit,' said Helen, 'What do we do?"

"Painkillers for the headaches, and I'm afraid we'll need regular rest stops. The rest will just be hoping they acclimatise."

Wakefield trotted up. "What wrong?"

"They're not used to things out here," said Helen. "It's making them sick. Got any willow bark?"

"Willowbark? Yes."

"If we give them some to chew, they can travel. We'll have to stop on the way, too."

Wakefield scowled. "Dangerous."

"Way we have to do it."

Wakefield scowled again, breathed out, nodded.

Danny sat, head bowed, unable to look up. Again and again, they came up wanting next to the fucking Wastelanders. Warmth at his side. A rough hand found his. He looked. Alannah.

"Don't beat yourself up," she said. "I'm struggling, too. And I've been out here before. Long time ago, but still; takes some getting used to."

"Here," said Wakefield, pushing something in his hand. Hard, brittle, brown. "Willowbark," she said. "Chew and chew. Head stop hurting."

Alannah took some too, started chewing. After a bit, Danny did the same. Bitter. He went to spit, but Alannah put a hand on his arm. "Don't spit it out. Trust me."

So he did. And within a few minutes, the white pain in his head had gone. Alannah took the chewed bark out of her mouth. He did the same, meant to throw it away, but she stopped him. "Don't do that," she said. "It shows someone's been here."

Danny looked about. The damp, drizzly air blurred the far-off hills to blackish ghosts in the greyish murk. "Just weird out here." He swallowed. There were stories about the Wastelands; there were things out here, they said. How far were they from the Tooth Hills? Wakefield's lot'd thought there was something up in those, hadn't they, up in the woods?

She squeezed his hand. "You'll get used to it."

He shook her hand off. "I'm fine."

"Okay." She got up.

"I'm sorry – " But she was already moving away. Fuck it. Danny scowled. Roll on Hobsdyke, almost. Least then whatever he had to deal with'd be easy. You either killed it or it killed you. And he'd make it, and then she'd see. She'd see he was strong, see he'd make her safe.

*

"Colonel?"

Thorpe held out a steaming mug. Jarrett nodded and took it. "What's the latest?"

Thorpe consulted his notes. "Two more landcruisers destroyed. Three more of the hidey-holes we've learned about flushed. One of them, we caught four rebels. All killed. Three of them were kids, but one was identified."

"Yes?"

"Mary Tolland. Don't know if the name rings a bell…"

"Tolland. Tolland. Oh, yes. Tolland, Mary. Junior officer in the resistance. One of the ones who survived the Refuge." Jarrett smiled. "Always good to tie up a loose end. Any further attacks?"

"No, ma'am. By our reckoning, there's only four landcruisers left unaccounted for."

"That's four too many."

"Yes, ma'am. On the other hand, those include the two that broke through the perimeter last night. That only leaves two at large in the city. I've given the designations of the missing vehicles to the perimeter guards and to four Jennywren units.

Each of those will sweep a separate city quadrant on a search and destroy basis. Pretty hard to hide a landcruiser."

"Not impossible, though. But good thinking, Thorpe. You're learning. How many rebel boltholes left to flush?"

"Half a dozen, based on the intel we have so far."

"There'll be more. Tell the Jennywrens I want prisoners. Intensive interrogation techniques. I want bases, safe-houses, and most of all I want communication methods. They work in crews, but they have to pass information back and forth somehow. I want to know how."

"Yes, ma'am. Colonel – "

"Yes?"

"Perimeter guards are on skeleton staff and half of them are nearly falling over with exhaustion. Can I – "

"Yes. Relieve the existing shift. Restore perimeter guards to full strength. Reinforce with Jennywren units, but have them stand by to deploy if we have any further emergencies in the city."

"Will do, ma'am. Just one other thing…"

"Spit it out, Thorpe."

"There were four Jennywren squads you reassigned to special duties last night. If you recall – "

"Yes, that's right. Additional security detail for REAP Hobsdyke."

"Yes."

Jarrett went still, turned to face him. "What about them?"

"We've been trying to hail them for several hours. Nothing."

"What about Hobsdyke base?"

"Nothing from them either."

Jarrett took a deep breath, then released it. A cold finger of fear. All that planning, all those precautions, and still it didn't work. Damn you, Helen. Oh, for the chance to kill her. "Right," she said. "Anything else?"

"No, ma'am."

"All right. If anything comes through, I'll be in Commander Winterborn's office."

She wondered, as she went, if she'd ever come back from it.

2.

"Jesus," said Thursday.

"Sh," Danny said.

Thursday shook her head. "Christmas trees. But big."

"Pines," said Gevaudan. Danny managed not to jump this time; the bastard had a habit of popping up at your shoulder before you knew it; cat-quiet, despite his size. "Never seen a wood before?"

"Not like this."

Gevaudan nodded. Had that sad look in his eye again, same as when Danny'd asked what coffee was. "Things are different out here."

"You're not kidding."

"Fuckin' massive," said Nadgers.

"Step quiet," Wakefield said. "Not alone in there."

"We're goin' in there?"

"Keep it down, Nadgers."

"Fuck off, Danny!"

"Oi."

"Nadgers –" began Helen, but Danny held up a hand. Shivers ran down his arms and legs; he hoped they didn't show. "I was put in charge, Nadgers. You do what I tell you."

Nadgers bristled. "Fuck d'you think you are?"

"Who put me in charge, Nads?" Nadgers glared, not speaking. "Who?"

Nadgers looked down. "Darrow."

"Right."

Thursday hid a smirk. "We goin' then, or what?" asked Scopes.

Helen nodded. "Quickest way to get to Hobsdyke. Only way we've got a chance of them not seeing us."

Wakefield nodded. "Go quiet, watch out. Gaffer's Wood. Bad place. Like Hobsdyke. All this here, bad place."

Alannah twitched a smile. "Nice to know."

Danny didn't say owt else. Nowt to say, and he had a crew to lead. Alannah to watch out for, too, even if she'd not spoke to him since the barney on the hills.

"Wakefield'll take point," said Helen. "The other Foxes'll flank us. If they tell you to do something, do it. They know these woods. We don't."

The woods were dark, the shade like wet cloth on his skin. "Watch where you're treading," said Helen. He looked down, saw dead twigs and old pine-needles like a layer of brittle rust. Tiny snaps and crackles whispered in the air.

He looked up. The Foxes were gone; Gevaudan too. Helen walked ahead. He looked behind him; Scopes, Thursday, Nadgers. Alannah –

He looked about: there she was, a few yards to the side. He caught her eye; she looked away. Danny looked down again. White gleamed among needles and black earth. Bone. A skull grinned up from the floor. He gripped the Lanchester, walked on.

Time passed; light gleamed up ahead. Thank fuck. It got stronger, brighter, coldly dappled the forest floor.

Light glinted through a gap in the trees. Thank fuck: nearly out now, nearly out. He focused on it. They were almost there when a black shape loomed in it, blocking out half the light. He bit back a yell, jerked the gun up.

"Here now," Wakefield said. "Hush."

Danny breathed out, lowered the gun.

A thin brook ran through the woods; outside them, it sank deep into a cleft in the ground. "Down here," said Wakefield; they followed in single file. Behind Danny, Thursday hissed a curse; her boots were coming to bits.

"Sh," he whispered.

She muttered something. Probably bad. He let it go.

Grass grew high on the banks. It was like a tunnel. Almost like home.

The brook whispered and chuckled. Danny found he wanted to piss. He tried not to think of it.

"Here," said Wakefield.

The grass ceiling broke; ahead was a small stone bridge. "Up the bank," hissed Wakefield. "Go quiet, keep low. Else Reapers see."

Danny clambered up the slope into more thick grass. Wakefield cat-footed to their edge. Beyond was a worn road, some weird little houses made of stone instead of brick. Wakefield licked her lips. She was scared too. That helped. She darted, cat-quick, over the road and into the shelter of the nearest house, rolled, crouched, beckoned.

Danny took a deep breath and ran after her, rolled and came up.

*

"Strange place," said Gevaudan. He ran a hand along the stone wall of the church. "It's well-preserved."

"I know." Helen wrapped her arms around herself.

"That cross there, above the door. There's something strange about it…"

331

"Bad place," Wakefield said. "Bad place."

Helen didn't speak. Shapes hovered at the edge of her sight. A man, a child: she turned away. But two others stood nearby, wavering shadows like a man and woman –

Mum? Dad?

She spun away, breathed out.

"You all right?" asked Gevaudan.

He will destroy you. She took a deep breath, nodded.

"Ghostlighting?" he mouthed. She nodded again. He nodded back. "Yes, me too."

"You – " she fell quiet as Danny looked round.

"Yes," said Gevaudan, "me too. I've that much humanity left, at least."

"Bad place," whispered Wakefield again: her free hand clutched a small token that hung at her throat on a leather cord.

"Alannah – Jesus, easy." Danny went to her; she was sliding down the wall with her hands over her face. When he tried to pull them away she cried out and fought him. "Alannah! Jesus!" He gripped her hands tight; she squeezed her eyes shut, bowed her head.

"The sooner we're out of here the better," Helen muttered.

Wakefield nodded. "Back way we came would be good."

Helen stared at her. "You gave your oath you'd help."

"This bad place. Hobsdyke. Everything of it. Bad."

"Are you afraid?"

Wakefield glared; Helen met her gaze, stared back. Finally Wakefield looked down. "We go with you."

"Good." Helen felt eyes on her; Alannah, Gevaudan too. All thinking *you play people, manipulate them.* She shut it out. This didn't matter. She was here for a short time, then gone. Until then, she had things to do.

*

332

Flaps didn't know how long she'd been there. She kept greying in and out, retreating to a numb state, like the sleepiness you got when it was really cold. She'd had that once; when she was really tiny, a littl'un, maybe ten years after the War, give or take. She'd've been what, five? About that. Not quite her first memory, but one of them.

The winters were still bastards now, they always were. But back then? Fuck. They were lethal. There'd been hardly any really ancient people left. Mary'd told her –

Mary – a sudden shock of pain and she was awake, jaw clenching, blinking the salt sting out of her eyes. Gripped the pistol with both hands, wished she had her Sterling. She wanted it back so badly. Mary had given it to her. Badge of pride, of honour, of achievement. Sterlings were about the best guns they'd had in their crew, and there weren't many to go round: most of them were making do with Stens and Lanchesters or old bolt-action rifles. But she'd been given a Sterling, 'cause she was good enough to make best use of it.

Flaps breathed in tight through her teeth and huddled back inside the car. All around, there were groans, coughs, the dull grunts and panting as a couple fucked. Someone was crying. There were muffled screams. Someone in pain. Perhaps a rape. Another time, she'd've thought of doing something about that. Mary had cured her of the habit. Keep your head down, Flaps, don't draw attention. Everyone else just looks after themselves. Start playing the hero, and you'll stand out. Or others'll expect you to ride to the rescue.

Today she didn't even have to fight the impulse; today she just curled up in a blackened car body and nursed the pain. Somewhere above her, the muffled screams went on. Flaps did her best to block them out. Just another dawn in Steel City.

Cars, they'd been called. That's what Mary'd told her. Bit like landcruisers, but faster, and they ran on something called petrol instead of steam. And every fucker had them. Flaps had trouble believing that bit. Sometimes she reckoned Mary'd just been taking the piss.

After the War, they didn't work. You couldn't get the petrol stuff any more. And 'sides, a lot of them'd been trashed in the War. Lot of the ones here were burned out. Steel City was where loads of them'd been stacked to wait to be broken up and used for something else, and it'd never come. Dirt'd built up in the cracks and crannies between them and at the bases of the piles; weeds'd sprouted, taken root. More trouble for the Reapers to knock 'em down than to leave 'em. So they were people's homes now. Two or three folk crammed into each ripped-out, gutted interior.

Mary'd somehow made sure a couple of them belonged to their crew. And now Flaps was here. In one of the top ones: good view and plenty of cars below her to try and crawl into if the bastard Reapers came. Not that owt'd stop them blasting or burning or machine-gunning all the stacks of cars to get another rebel. Maybe she'd just make a last stand instead. Or else stick the revolver in her gob and pull the trigger, so they couldn't get her and do the things they did to rebel prisoners. 'Specially the girls. Bastard Jennywrens were famous for it, and she knew that was who they'd dragged in from the Wastelands to hunt the Manchester crews down.

She was trying to stay hard and angry, but it was no good. The numbness was coming back again. It came creeping back through her like the cold had that winter. She'd wanted to sleep, felt warm; but a hand'd kept slapping her across the face – *crack*, and *crack* again – and it'd kept her going, long enough to find a fire. She'd hated the woman who kept slapping her then, but later knew Mary'd saved her life…

Mary. And she was snapped out of it again. Flaps clutched her pistol and rocked miserably to and fro.

A scratch and a scuffling sound, towards the rear of the car. She spun round crouched low, pointed the revolver at the hole above the sill, sought the hammer with her thumb.

Grey hair, a lined forehead and two blue eyes popped into view. She almost fired before she knew them; in the end it was the voice she recognised in time.

"Hello?" Darrow peered over the sill. "Flaps?"

A noise strangled and died in her throat; she lowered the gun.

Darrow clambered up on the boot of the car – she'd never understood why they called it that, it looked fuck-all like a boot – and slid feet-first through the window into the car. "Flaps? What happened?"

"What…" Her voice was gravel in her throat, bone on glass, clinker and ashes. "The fuck d'you think happened? They set the fucking Jennywrens on us and every fucker got killed. 'Cept me."

"All of them?" Darrow's face was white; she knew he was old really, but he looked *ancient* now. "All of them?"

Flaps nodded.

"Mary?"

"She hid me. Saved my arse. Told me to find you."

"But everyone else? All of them?"

"They're all fucking dead. Do you not get it?" She'd never spoken to Darrow like that before. Him, Mary, Ashton; they were fucking legends to the kids. And Darrow; everyone knew Darrow didn't like bad language. She'd only met him two, three times, but she'd had that drummed into her by Mary. 'Cause she was Mary's best and she didn't want Flaps letting her down. I didn't, Mary? Did I? I didn't let you down. Did I? Every fuck-up during training, every lapse of behaviour that'd met with Mary's disapproval, rushed back into her throat and eyes to choke and blind her. She wouldn't cry. No she fucking wouldn't. She'd got through all this, she wouldn't fucking skrike like a sprog, like a littl'un, like –

And Darrow's arms were round her as she sobbed, Darrow's voice whispered, 'Ssh, ssh," in her ear, but it wasn't enough; it wasn't Mary, and it couldn't give back what'd been taken. But she sobbed anyway because she couldn't stop it, and sooner or later she'd have to get up and follow Darrow to whatever hiding place he'd found the last of them, and best if she were spent by then. And he murmured soft words in her ear to quiet her, as outside came a soft hiss and spatter of falling rain, the sky crying too, weeping for the rebel dead, but he murmured something else too, quieter still, something he didn't mean for her to hear but which she heard nonetheless: "This had better be worth it, Helen. Whatever it is, it'd better be worth all this."

*

Winterborn heard Jarrett come in but didn't turn around. He stood with his back to her, gazing out of the window at the rain falling outside, hands clasped behind his back. He didn't turn when the door clicked shut behind her either. Or speak.

"Sir," she said.

He didn't answer. Behind his back, his hands wanted to clench into fists. He must not look at her, not yet. He might not be able to restrain the urge to kill.

"The rebel threat's pretty much neutralised, sir," she said. "Two landcruisers left unaccounted for in the city. They should be eliminated within the hour. And – "

"Sit down, Colonel," said Winterborn. Still he didn't turn around. There was only silence; he knew Jarrett hadn't moved.

"I gave you an order, Colonel," he said.

A pause. "Yes, sir." He heard her walk to his desk and sit in the same chair she'd occupied the previous day. She waited.

Rain spat and rattled like grit and gravel on the windowglass. Winterborn saw his face in it, a pale spectre. Finally he released a long breath and turned to face her. "And what," he said, "of Project Tindalos?"

Her face was calm, but he felt her fear like the heat of a fire. "No response," she said. "Not from REAP Hobsdyke, and not from the Jennywren units I sent to guard it. Nothing."

Winterborn came round behind his desk and lowered himself into his chair. Slowly, as if in pain. He wasn't, but he'd found that focusing on little physical actions helped calm him at times like this. "No," he said. "I would have been surprised if you said you had, since I've been trying to raise them on the hotline all night."

He leant back, fingers steepled on his belly. "And I believe the opposition took advantage of the weakened city perimeter last night."

"Two landcruisers got through." She was afraid, but she hid it well. "To be fair, one contained Shoal. He'd have probably broken through any perimeter."

"Nevertheless, they got through. And now we have no contact with Hobsdyke."

"Sir."

"And a project that has taken up three years and extensive resources has almost certainly been destroyed." Nothing went right. Nothing. Always something coming along. Surrounded by fools, incompetents, givers of false promises. No. Enough of that. No self-pity. But still there was the rage; it narrowed his vision to focus on Jarrett. She saw it too and was still. Then she licked her lips and spoke.

"On the other hand, sir, your Command is now secure."

"Secure," he said. "Really, Jarrett? Is that what you think?"

Her jaw tightened. "With respect, Commander, your Reapers aren't being killed, your stations attacked, your landcruisers stolen or destroyed, and there aren't any riots going on. Which was the case yesterday. In this city, which is where your Central Command is based."

*

Winterborn had gone utterly still. Jarrett took a deep breath and pressed on. She was probably dead anyway, but her one glimmer of a chance was to push this home: she wasn't ending up in the torture chamber. Central Command's interrogators were ex-Jennywrens; Jarrett knew first-hand what they were capable of. Her luck, there'd be an ex-subordinate with a grudge waiting for her down there. She'd end it herself, and if that meant dropping Winterborn before he whistled the guards up then so be it.

"As far as Project Tindalos is concerned, I agree that it doesn't look particularly good. On the other hand, the fact that we can't raise them doesn't necessarily mean that they've been hit by the rebels. There were some bad electrical storms out in that part of the Wastelands last night; several Jennywren units reported sighting it. That could have knocked out communications."

There was a slight, almost imperceptible change in Winterborn's posture. The slightest relaxation. The bastard was listening, anyway. Jarrett went on.

"The base is very well-defended. It was to begin with, because it's in an unusually remote location and it's had to function and remain secure in the middle of the Wastelands. It now has a complement of GenRen troopers installed. They should be a match for anything the rebels could send out there. Two landcruisers got through; that's maybe half a dozen people. Plus, what? Some brigands? A few half-feral tribespeople? That's exactly what the Jennywrens deal with on a daily basis."

"They also," said Winterborn, "have Gevaudan Shoal. Or had you forgotten that?"

Shit. "No sir, I hadn't. And I agree, that would give them the element of surprise. But even so; I repeat, sir, they're Jennywrens. They're trained to expect the unexpected because, quite frankly, you never know what you'll find out there in the Wastelands." She had several examples on the tip of her tongue, but decided that a selection of *I remember this one time* anecdotes weren't what Winterborn needed to hear right now. "I've ordered four new Jennywren units to investigate. They'll be there in the next couple of hours. We'll know more when they report back."

"*If* they report back, Colonel."

"*When* they report back, sir."

Winterborn smiled. "I do hope so, Colonel Jarrett."

"If worse comes to worst, sir, can the project be restarted? With respect, you still haven't told me a great deal about what Project Tindalos is or what it sets out to do."

Winterborn stared into her, that odd little smile frozen on his face, and Jarrett found herself wishing she were anywhere else. Back out in the Wastelands killing ferals, or even at REAP Hobsdyke herself. At least she'd know what the hell had happened there and wouldn't be on tenterhooks. But finally the Commander nodded.

"A fair point, Colonel. It's been remiss of me not to tell you, I suppose. All right. Drink? I have some reasonable brandy and a passable whisky."

Jarrett released a long breath. "Actually, sir, I think I will."

*

Helen slipped in through a doorway, padded up a creaking, rotten flight of stairs into the room above, wincing as pain twinged in her lower back and the muscles of her thighs. The bruises still ached, but as long as she kept moving she'd be all right.

The house was faded, withered, but otherwise intact. The curtains had lost colour and gained the texture of old paper; dust clogged the sheets on the bed and hung in the fur of the old teddy bear, but for all that they were well-preserved. God knew how; as Gevaudan had said, it was unusual. Especially out here; it was hardly dry or temperate or unexposed.

Even the brittle, crumbling wallpaper still had its floral pattern. Helen eyed the room; there were books on the shelves, so yellowed and fragile-looking she thought they might shatter into dust at a touch. She was glad the room was empty of any sign of life, at least. Most times the human bones you still found were just that – bones, waking no more emotion than a dead bird's carcass would – but settings like this room suddenly reminded you that they'd once been lives.

Helen slipped past the bed to the window, dropping low as she did, then peeped over the sill. Nice view, or it would've been once. Fields, hills. And on the hill right opposite, a squat angular shape that bristled with barbed wire.

Hobsdyke.

Helen opened a pouch on her overalls, slipped out a pair of binoculars and sighted through them. A high barbed-wire fence, three of them in rows; floodlights mounted on top, a watchtower with a searchlight. She saw landcruisers outside the gates; beyond them, prefab buildings.

Something was missing, though. Something so obvious it took her a moment to realise what it was.

You're too late. The Wolves are running.

"Anything interesting?"

"Jesus." She managed not to jump. "Will you stop doing that?"

"Sorry."

"You're bloody not."

Gevaudan smiled, stepped forward.

"Keep down."

He crawled to her side on hands and knees. "What is it?"

"You've got an experimental weapons project," she said. "You want it out of the way in case there's trouble, and a long way off in case it goes tits-up. So, you build it out in bandit country. Okay, I get that. So, you make it a well-defended military compound, and you do everything right: you put it on high ground, with a view of the area, you put up strong defences, you install an armed garrison with floodlights, automatic weapons, a watchtower, the lot. So anyone who tries to attack gets cut to pieces before they get close."

Gevaudan winced. "The last part doesn't particularly appeal, but carry on."

"You do all that," she said, "so why do you then leave the watchtower empty?"

"Can I see?"

"Didn't think you needed binoculars."

"Even I have my limits." Gevaudan squinted through the glasses. "Yes, I see. Interesting. Hullo."

"What?"

"Something else. You have to look closely because they're almost closed; probably blown shut in the storm last night. But the gates aren't locked. They're ajar."

"What?" She took back the binoculars, looked. "Jesus. You're right."

"Could be somebody's done our job for us," said Gevaudan.

"Could be. Or it could be that Project Tindalos went tits-up before we got here." Helen put the binoculars away. "Let's just hope we're not too late to stop whatever's started."

Gevaudan sighed. "Into the valley of death, rode the... how many of us are there again?"

"Gevaudan?"

"Mm?"

"Anyone ever told you you're weird?"

"More or less everyone. Shall we go?"

3.

Danny crawled up the hill, down on his belly with the Lanchester gripped tight in his hands.

Stupid really, with the grass cropped short as an army haircut and the steep slope giving anyone in the compound a cracking view of anyone coming up. Then again, even if every sign was that the place was deserted, keeping low was a good plan. Peering up the slope, he could see the two .50 cals in the watchtower. Just take one Reaper to finally show up and that'd be it.

Danny and his crew went first. Leading the way, spread out either side of the dirt track that led up the hillside. Helen and Alannah were behind them. Wakefield and her lot were coming silently up behind them, and Christ knew where Gevaudan was. He had bigger things to worry about than that anyway, like what as waiting on them when they got up top.

He wished Alannah'd stayed back in the village; he didn't like to think of her walking into this. He had a job to do, couldn't look after her. Not that she was bothered, most like, but he wanted to. 'Cept he couldn't 'cause he had his crew to mind now. Well, Alannah was a grown-up. She'd have to take her chances. That was fair enough. Didn't mean he had to like it, though.

Nearly there now. Almost at the top of the slope. Churned mud in front of the gates. Yeah, they were ajar, just as Gevaudan'd said, the chain that'd fastened them lying forgotten in the dirt. And beyond them, three landcruisers, just past the gate. Not parked up in neat rows, but abandoned at angles to each other, machine guns dipping groundwards or pointing at the sky.

Wind quickened across the hilltop. Soft creaking sounds; the gate, stirring slightly in the breeze, rocking to and fro.

Danny stole a glance up at the guard tower. It loomed silent and empty above them.

"Scopes," he hissed downslope. "Cover. Thursday, you're with me. Come on."

Scopes grinned; Thursday bared her teeth. Nadgers just looked relieved not to be going into the firing line as yet. Thursday crawled up on the opposite side of the dirt track from Danny. Scopes crawled off to his other side; with a scrape and a click, her rifle's bolt drew back.

"Ready when you are," she breathed.

"Okay." He looked across at Thursday, met her eyes, hazel in a square, blokish face. Then nodded, scrambled up and ran for the gate.

Fuck fuck fuck – sure he was going to die, that the bastard Reapers'd been playing him along, luring them into a trap – but no guns fired, the watchtower stayed silent. He skidded to his knees beside the gate, keeping low. A grunt to the side as Thursday dropped down beside him.

Deep breaths. Then Danny looked up, peering through bars and wire mesh, staring out across the Hobsdyke compound.

"Fuckin' hell," he said at last.

*

"What is it?" called Helen.

"Fucked if I know."

From her right eye-corner, Helen saw Alannah half-smile. She sighed and crawled up the slope. "Is it safe?"

"If you mean no Reapers, then yeah. Dunno 'bout anythin' else."

Helen crawled up to the top of the slope. Movement to her left; Wakefield, wriggling through the grass with gritted teeth. Scared shitless but still going on. Courage or the urge to prove something to Helen? No time to think of that now.

Helen rose, scuttled over to Danny's side, and saw.

Beyond the gates, the parade ground was empty, like the watchtower looming above. No one in sight. And only silence, but for the whistle of the wind.

"Dunno if owt's goin' on," said Danny, "but something was."

Helen found she wanted to get up, run away. Then she wanted to dash in through the gates and run toward the concrete chamber. She shook her head. No time for ghostlighting now, or whatever this was.

"Brigands, maybe?" Alannah asked. It was almost a plea.

"I don't think so," said Gevaudan. Danny jumped, muttering, "Jesus," and Helen bit back a yelp. The Grendelwolf lay prone alongside them, chin propped on folded hands, gazing through the fence. "There aren't many left for a start. And they would have burned the place down."

"Wakefield? Any other tribes near here?"

"No. No one comes near. Told you. Bad place."

"You keep saying that."

Wakefield shrugged. "Truth." She pointed down the hill, to the wood beyond the village. "Hobsdyke bad. Gaffer's Wood worse. But here? Graspen Hill is worst of all. Say the Devil makes his home here."

"Could there be an old rebel unit operating out here?" Gevaudan asked.

"Anything's possible," said Helen, "but I doubt it. I spent a year out here looking for any help I could find, remember. Be surprised if I missed something like that."

"If they weren't attacked," said Gevaudan, "then it's more likely something went wrong here."

"There's that," said Helen. She wanted to run. She wanted to run there. She wanted to run away. *The Wolves are running.* She took a deep breath, nodded. "We still need to go in."

"Afraid you'd say that." Alannah crawled to Danny's side. He blinked at her. She smiled, winked.

"All right," said Gevaudan. "How do you want to do this?"

"We go in in pairs," said Helen. She looked at Wakefield. "Me and my people first. No disrespect, but this is what we're trained for." Out of the corner of her eye, she saw Danny thrust his chest out. Man of the moment at last. But she saw Alannah's face too, the older woman biting her lip in concern. "Who are the best shots, Danny?"

"Scopes and Thursday."

"All right." Helen looked at them. "One of you, each side of the gates. You're the last through. You cover us."

Scopes grinned, patted her rifle; Thursday just nodded, face giving nothing away.

"I'll go first," said Helen. "Alannah?"

"I'll go through with you," she said, squaring her shoulders, composing her face.

"Danny and Nadgers, then you. Each pair gets to the first piece of cover in sight, secures the area and covers the next pair through. After that, the Foxes come through."

Wakefield nodded.

"And me?" asked Gevaudan.

"Depends how lucky you're feeling."

"I was thinking I can knock the gates open and just walk on in. If anyone does start shooting, I should be able to take care of myself. And we'll know if we do have any Reapers to fight."

"You *are* feeling lucky, then."

"Not particularly. I just think that when we get through that gate, the Reapers will be the least of our worries."

"Cheery sod, aren't you?" muttered Alannah.

"I do my best." Wind blew across the hillside. "Shall we, then?"

"No time like the present."

"Quite."

Gevaudan rose and strode to the gates, looking to and fro through the mesh of wire. Helen's breath caught, and she huddled down. But there was only silence.

Gevaudan shoved the gates; they swung wide. Still there was no response. After a moment, he walked through. The only sound was his boots, gritting in the dust.

Scopes and Thursday moved to their positions, guns shouldered.

Wakefield closed her eyes for a second; she clutched the little talisman round her neck and her lips moved. A tribal prayer, Helen guessed.

Helen looked at Alannah; Alannah looked back at her. "I don't like this, Helen."

"Me neither."

Alannah took a deep breath and gripped her Sten tighter. "Let's get on with it, then."

Helen rose to a crouch; Alannah did the same. They dashed through the gates towards the landcruisers, flinging themselves down low and scrambling up to sight their guns over the vehicles. Metal glittered on the ground about the abandoned cruisers; spent bullet cases. The block of prefab huts to the left of the central concrete structure had been machine-gunned; windows smashed, walls punched full of holes. A door flapped weakly in the keening wind, banging softly at the frame. And through all this Gevaudan strolled nonchalantly on, unconcerned.

"Clear," Helen shouted.

Running feet. Danny and a terrified-looking Nadgers shot by next, weaving past Gevaudan and dodging towards the central block. They dived, huddled behind the concrete shed, aimed in all directions. "Clear," Danny shouted.

The Foxes ran past next, splitting into two groups, each taking one of the prefab blocks each side of the concrete structure, which Gevaudan was by now pacing around.

"Come on," muttered Helen and jogged towards the central block, Alannah in her wake. Danny and Nadgers sprinted around the central chamber, heading for the prefab block behind it.

"Wakefield?" The Fox warrior trotted sideways to her. "Why is Hobsdyke a bad place? Come on. We need to know."

"Just *is*," Wakefield said. "All know. Some dream."

"Dream?"

"Dream. Something here. Folk hear the Sound."

"What sound?"

"*The* Sound. Some hear it. Calls them here. They go." Wakefield shook her head. "Never come back."

Helen circled the central building, aiming into each of the smaller outbuildings around it. In all cases, the story was the same. The outer door of each was open, giving a clear view of the little bare cells beyond; the inner doors stood open too, into the blackness of the central chamber they were connected to. The cell walls were padded. In one of them, part of the padding had been torn away, exposing bare concrete, splattered with long-dried blood.

Helen studied the pallets on the floor with their leather straps, thought of her cell floor at the Bailey with all its ancient stains. A shudder; she turned away.

"What the hell were they doing here?" Alannah whispered at her shoulder.

Helen didn't aswer. Something clung to the chamber's walls like a stink, like the smoke from an old fire. Fear, agony, madness, death. She'd walked through Deadsbury and countless ruined and abandoned settlements, but nowhere that evoked so profound a sense of desolation. She stumbled back and took deep breaths.

"Over here," Danny called.

Past the central chamber, the middle part of the third and final prefab block was blackened and gutted by fire and had half-collapsed. A charred door lay on the ground, in front of the yawning hole of the doorway to the worst-damaged part of the block. Danny flipped the door over to show a discoloured sign: *Project Director E Mordake.*

"Director's office," said Alannah. "Most likely place for any records to be kept."

Gevaudan peered in through the doorway. "The rain probably stopped it spreading further." He leant inside, gripped something, lifted it free.

"Anything?" asked Helen.

"Nothing of use." Gevaudan showed her a sheaf of scorched paper. What wasn't charred and blackened was sodden and illegible with water. "At a guess, someone didn't want us to know what Project Tindalos was all about." He tossed the pages back into the burnt-out office. "Or anyone, perhaps."

That was when Helen heard it. "What's that?"

"What's what?" asked Danny.

"That. Listen."

Danny did. "Can't hear owt."

"Me neither," Wakefield piped up.

"No, I can hear it," said Alannah.

"Me too," said Thursday.

"Not me," said Scopes.

"I hear it," said Trex. He looked pale.

"Well, that's interesting," Gevaudan said at last. "Because I hear nothing. And bear in mind I've probably got the keenest hearing of anyone here. What does it sound like?"

Helen listened. At first she'd thought it was a distant, muffled klaxon. But it was a low, rhythmic, pulsating throb; too melodic to be any kind of alarm. Not jarring enough. If you listened closely, its two or three notes, endlessly recycled and repeated, seemed to contain infinite nuances and variations at some subliminal level. "Bit like this," she said and hummed it.

The effect on the Foxes was nothing short of galvanic; they stepped backwards, almost as one. Wakefield raised her spear. "The Sound," she said. "That's the Sound."

"Everybody calm down," said Gevaudan quietly. "So. Some hear it, some don't. If it was an *actual* sound, I'd hear it if anyone did. But I don't hear anything. So it's an auditory hallucination, triggered by a local phenomenon."

"Eh?" said Danny.

"He means there's something here that makes some people think they can hear something," Alannah said. "Question is, does it have anything to do with Project Tindalos?"

"I wouldn't like to bet against it," said Gevaudan.

"Explain why they built a Reaper base out here," said Danny. "Out of the way's one thing, but this is fuckin' cannibal country."

"What?" Wakefield looked furious.

"Soz." Danny shrank back.

"He's right," said Alannah.

"Yes, he is," said Helen.

"Which might be an argument for reconsidering our mission," Gevaudan said, "at least until we have a better idea of what Project Tindalos is and does. If there's something here some of us are susceptible to…"

"Any other day I'd agree," said Helen, "but we haven't time to waste. Whatever Carter was trying to warn us about might have already started."

There was silence. *Everything gone. Everything. Nothing left. Nothing left.*

"What now, then?" asked Wakefield.

The Sound throbbed faintly in Helen's ears. "I think we need to check out that main chamber."

*

Weedlight torches flared into life in Wakefield's and Danny's hands, as they led the way into the central chamber.

"Jesus," Danny whispered.

The light seeped and splashed over the concrete walls and the fallen chairs. A projector lay smashed on its side; a screen hung askew on the wall. And in the centre of the floor there was a gaping hole.

There were bloodstains on the concrete around it. Buckled chairs and broken rifles lay about to show where they'd been used as clubs to try and break through the floor.

Danny knelt at the edge, extended the torch, stooped forward.

"Danny," whispered Alannah.

He glanced at her, gave a small smile. "S'okay." It split her heart, that smile; the sudden, unexpected gentleness between the hard-boy posturings, and the youth of him. A boy, a child, so vulnerable to harm. *He doesn't realise what this is,* she thought over the looping, fuddling pulse of the Sound. *He can't.*

Danny extended the torch downward. The light flickered on gouged raw earth. Below it, rock; and then a gaping split in that. Danny let the torch drop; it fell through the hole, landing on a hard stone floor maybe ten feet below the cracked rock. Its light danced on scattered rubble; they gathered to watch the torch burn out.

"Down," said Wakefield at last. "They went down."

The Sound was louder now, throbbing in Alannah's head.

"We can't be sure of that," said Helen. As she did, the torch went out, a length of grey smoke, coiling round and around like a snake climbing up a thin column of air, rising from the dark past them.

"There," said Trex, pointing.

Alannah looked. Yes it was there; faint but quite definitely real; a thin, silvery-grey glow lightly brushing the floor. If it hadn't been for the pitch dark below, it wouldn't have been noticeable. "Something's down there," she said at last. She almost couldn't hear herself saying it, because the Sound rose, for a moment, to a deafening level; she swayed, almost lost her balance. Danny's hand rested on her arm, steadying her.

"We have to go on." Helen's face was pale and serene in the flickering of Wakefield's dying torch. "We have to see what's down there."

The only response was silence. "All right," she said. "Don't, if you don't want to. I don't want to. Believe me. But I'm going. Even if it's alone."

Without another word, she produced a coil of rope and tied it round a protruding stanchion, then unrolled it and let it fall to the cave floor below.

"Helen," began Gevaudan, but she was already climbing down. The Grendelwolf watched as she dropped the last couple of feet to the floor, crouched, unslung her Sterling and glanced up, then sighed. "It is a far, far better thing…" he muttered and jumped into the hole, bending his knees on landing then straightening up.

"Show-off," murmured Helen, a faint smile on her face.

"You say the sweetest things."

Danny was next, shinning down the rope; then Alannah. Scopes and Thursday followed, followed by Wakefield and all her warriors, save Trex. Only he and Nadgers were left up top, gazing down. After a moment, Trex closed his eyes, murmured a prayer, then scrambled down the rope. And Nadgers was alone.

"Danny," Nadgers said.

"Up to you, mate," Danny said. "But we're going on."

Nadgers' lips trembled. But finally he slung his weapon across his back, grasped the rope and climbed down.

Another weedlight torch flared into life. The hole opened out into a natural cavern, high enough for Gevaudan to stand with only a slight stoop, with about half a dozen cave entrances gaping blackly in its walls like eye sockets.

"Which way?" he asked.

Alannah lowered her torch. Up ahead, she saw that faint silvery gleam issuing from one of the tunnel mouths. Even without it, though, she'd have known the way; the slightest turn of her head enabled her to position where the Sound was coming from. "There," she said and pointed.

Gevaudan sighed, unslung his Bren gun. "Helen?"

Helen looked at Alannah, then at him. "Yes," she said. "Gevaudan – "

"Yes?"

"I want you to bring up the rear. I'll feel safer knowing you're watching our backs. I'll take point."

"Is that wise?"

"It's what we're doing, Gevaudan," she said and strode into the tunnel. Gevaudan glanced at Alannah, raised an eyebrow. She almost smiled back. Almost. He was a Grendelwolf, after all.

*

The tunnel at first was painfully low and cramped, twisting this way and that. Now and then others branched off, but always that faint silvery glow crept up to show them the way. And always, of course – for Helen, at least – there was the Sound.

The tunnel sloped down; it grew colder, but at least it got wider. Not massively so; enough that you weren't permanently bent double. In places, maybe, you could have held your arms out at right angles from your body and spun a pirouette. What you gained in space, though, you lost in time. Time slipped away; underground, you lost all sense of it. All your reference points disappeared. She knew that well. But on she marched, Sterling in her hands; towards Tindalos, far below, and tried to blot yesterday's dream from recall.

They died for you.

A bend up ahead, the light spilling round it brighter than ever before. Something was waiting for them round there. The Sound throbbed louder in her ears; it was lulling, hypnotic. She heard only it, the scrape and clank of footsteps in the rubble, the rasp of her own breath –

A hand caught her arm. She jerked round, trying to bring the gun about; stopped in the nick of time when she saw it was Nadgers. "Listen," he was mouthing. "Listen."

Helen looked back along the tunnel. The others stood waiting, guns ready, Gevaudan at the back, looking right at her. He's heard something, with those Grendelwolf ears. *What's he heard?* What?

He will destroy you, whispered her dream.

But then the Sound's pulse ebbed a little, and she heard it too: coming from up ahead, around that bend.

Clinking stone; dragging footsteps; hoarse, heaving breaths. And then, painted on the wall by the silvery light, a huge, hunched shape that walked like a man but couldn't be. Couldn't. Helen's last thought, before it rounded the corner and was upon them.

4.

It rounded the bend, filled the end of the tunnel; a shape looming almost as tall as Gevaudan. A greyish material – dully metallic-looking, like lead – covered its body. Leather, or some kind of padded armour? But Helen saw no join; as she backed away from it, the thought ocurred to her it might be the thing's skin.

Its head rose, neckless, from hunched shoulders and a ridged back. The upper part of the domed head might have contained some shape resembling that of a human skull; two empty eye-sockets gaped there, the only visible apertures in that otherwise featureless head. Below the eyes – where the whole area of nose, cheeks and mouth might have been on a human head – the leathery material was sucked inward into a deep concavity as one of those hoarse, wet breaths sounded, then when the breath was released in a long hissing sigh, it regained its former shape. If there was a human skull in there, it was only the top half, and God alone knew what lay below it.

Its thick, massive arms rose. The silvery greyish leather of its hide or armour shaded into, blended with the reptilian scaling of – *hands?* – that resembled the claws of some giant bird; scaled, stubby digits, far shorter than the curved, graphite-grey talons that emerged from them, that twitched and clutched at the air.

The creature's head moved to and fro. Almost like it was sniffing, scenting prey. Those empty sockets lowered until they were gazing at Nadgers, who hadn't budged from his position. Not out of courage. The poor little sod was stood there, rooted with terror.

A word came into Helen's head from nowhere, and with it a sense of recognition, even though she knew she'd never seen a thing like this before: *Styr.*

Helen levelled the Sterling at it, finger on the trigger. "Nadgers," she said. "Move back. Slowly. Move back."

Nadgers' only response was a thin, terrified whimpering. He couldn't look away from the thing – *the Styr* – and seemed to have forgotten he even carried a gun of his own.

"Nadgers," Danny hissed. "Nadgers, mate, for fuck sake get back."

Behind that pulsing hood of leathery flesh, a low, buzzing growl began to rise. Nadgers whimpered again; there was a soft patter of liquid on the cave floor.

Helen shouldered the Sterling. "Get back from him," she said. The Styr's domed head turned towards her. She swallowed as those empty eye-holes met hers. Then it turned back to face Nadgers, and she moved forward.

The breath sucked in again. A hole appeared in the skin over the lower part of its non-face and widened. Beneath was what looked like a raw, red, crater of a wound; in its centre was a hole sucking air, surrounded by rings of stubby, serrated teeth. The Styr's indrawn breath became a brief wind, blowing down the tunnel towards it. Then the suction hole flared, and it screeched; a high, hissing, grating noise that hurt the ears and for a moment even overwhelmed the Sound that was rising around her.

Nadgers screamed. Helen fired, ducking as bullets ricocheted from the walls. Some missed, but just as many hit. And they changed nothing. The Styr didn't even seem to notice as it lunged forward, seized Nadgers and clamped that wet, rasping crater over on his face. Nadgers' screams were muffled, but climbed upwards into new and grating registers of agony. His body bucked and convulsed in the Styr's grip and then went limp. It flung him aside and screeched again.

Helen stepped back and put another burst into its chest, a long one that drove it back. She doubted a single bullet missed its mark. It slammed back against the wall. Then its head swung towards her. The hole in its face shrank and sealed shut. She could almost have imagined the mouth, she thought, but in the corner of her eye she could see Nadgers' body and what was left of his face. And the blood over the thing's chest.

It pushed itself away from the wall; its chest was pocked, but the hide was unbroken. Its talons flexed. And the Sound rose. Helen's vision blurred as it stood and came on.

"Back!" she shouted, retreating.

"Move," she heard Wakefield yell. Helen glanced down the corridor and saw her, and one of the other Fox warriors, trying to drag Trex back. The boy's eyes were unfocused; he stood swaying on his feet, as if in a trance or seizure.

Someone ran past her; Danny. He threw the Lanchester to his shoulder and fired a burst, hitting the Styr in the chest. It stumbled back, then recovered and advanced.

"Danny, get back," shouted Helen over the echoes.

"Get her out of here," he yelled back, and fired again.

Helen turned. A few yards behind Danny, Alannah, like Trex, stood swaying in the middle of the tunnel, eyes unfocused. Further behind her, Thursday, also blankly staring, had sagged against the tunnel wall, gun slipping from her hands. The Sound rose louder, throbbed in Helen's ears. For a moment, the tunnel faded, and in its place was the plain of ashes, and a huge, silhouetted shape lying down, slowly rising and turning gigantic eyes that shone with a pale, lambent glow towards her–

Helen closed her eyes, growled in her throat to drown out the Sound, grabbed Alannah's arm and pulled; the older woman staggered, stared at her. "Move. Come on. Danny – "

She dragged Alannah back down the tunnel. Thursday. She had to help Thursday too. Danny fired again. A neat three-round burst, Helen noted: he was learning well. Then the hissing screech sounded again, muffled by the thick hide. Helen turned in time to see the Styr lash out with a taloned hand. The sweeping blow knocked Danny sideways into the wall. He dropped, lay still.

Alannah cried out, fought towards him; Helen fought to drag her back. The Styr leant over Danny, talons flexing, the hide over its mouth sucking in once more.

She could shoot at it, risk it turning on her, but buy Danny a chance of survival. Or shoot the boy instead; a mercy shot, to save him from what Nadgers got. Alannah would never forgive her, but –

Something swept past her, something huge and fast and black. What looked like wings flapped behind it; it took her a moment to realise it was a coat. And then Gevaudan flung himself at the Styr. They grappled for a moment, and then he flung the Styr back down the corridor. It crashed to the ground and lay still.

For a moment she thought he'd killed it, but then it moved, sat up. The empty eye-sockets focused on Gevaudan. It stood and moved into a fighting crouch, talons hooked and raised.

Gevaudan, stood over Danny, snarled. For a moment, his face was wholly feral, and Helen remembered what she'd almost forgotten: what the Grendelwolves were, and what they'd been built to do. *He will destroy you.* And yet he was doing this for her and hers. Everything she had said *trust him;* everything she had said *don't.* What help was she to anyone, then?

The Styr stepped forward; Gevaudan advanced to meet it. Alannah ran forward, falling to her knees by Danny.

The Sound rose higher, higher, ever higher, throbbing in Helen's ears. The Styr – how did she know that name, how *could* she? – flung itself at Gevaudan; they grappled again, and suddenly were crashing from wall to wall of the tunnel in a blur, snarling; but it was all silent, because there was only the Sound. And then, beyond them, in the faint silver light at the tunnel's end, she saw three, four hulking figures emerge and advance on them. More Styr, all closing in.

Thursday; Helen grabbed her, shoved her, stumbling, down the corridor, shouted *run*. But she couldn't even hear her own scream over the Sound.

Wakefield charged past, shouting to her people. Something whipped past Helen; one of the Styr flinched, no more than that, as it walked, an arrow sticking out of its chest. Missiles flew past from slings, hitting with deadly accuracy, but the things just came steadily, relentlessly on.

And the Sound. The Sound.

Helen raised the Sterling and fired again, but on the Styr came. Careful. Had to be careful so as not to hit Alannah. Alannah was still kneeling over Danny. Except that now she wasn't. Now she was getting slowly to her feet, letting Danny slip to the floor. He reached for her as she moved away, but she ignored him. Ignored him and walked towards the Styr.

The Sound was deafening; the Sound was the whole world. And it was rich and varied, despite those few, repetitive notes. It was drawing Helen in. She was swaying, like she was drunk, could barely remember that she was holding the Sterling, let alone that she was supposed to be firing it. But still she tried to shout a warning to Alannah.

Except that none was needed. The Styr simply stepped aside to let her pass. Then a moment later they did it again, as Thursday walked past first Helen and then Danny, down the corridor, towards the silvery light. Then another figure – one of the Foxes, the one Wakefield had called Trex. Again, the Styr let them past, then came on, heedless of the bullets and arrows.

I should stop them, Helen thought thickly. *I shouldn't let them go.* But she couldn't seem to move, couldn't seem to think. She wasn't even sure if she was still holding her gun, useless though it was against these things. There was only the Sound. There was only the Sound. Only, only, only the Sound. And it was great and rich and beautiful, and the louder it was in your ears the more you heard – the more levels and layers and nuances and aspects and wonders. And the closer you were to it, the louder it got. And so Helen did the only thing she could, the only thing that still mattered; she followed Thursday, Trex and Alannah. Toward the source of the silvery light, toward the source of the Sound.

*

One thing about being a Grendelwolf was that it made some things almost too easy. Hand to hand, except against another Grendelwolf – which wasn't likely nowadays – Gevaudan had little or no chance of losing. He'd been all too aware of that since the fight in the lobby of the Bailey, the first time he'd really fought – as the beast, the warrior, the monster that the Reapers had sought to make him – in years. Even with their guns, the Reapers had hardly stood a chance. A part of him had almost wished that it could be different; wished for a fight he could actually lose.

Be careful what you wish for, an old saying went. That was the main thing on Gevaudan's mind at that moment; that, and trying to survive.

His claws had failed to penetrate the thing's armoured hide; some had actually splintered on it. Not that they wouldn't heal, but he'd actually have to live long enough to do so. Not only that, but even blunt-force trauma wasn't doing any good against the thing, whatever the hell it was; some bastard offspring of Project Tindalos, Gevaudan would have guessed, which at least made the dire warnings Helen had relayed make a little more sense. Something that seemed to want only to kill, which couldn't be killed itself? No, there was no potential for disaster there; none at all.

Gevaudan could die, however; it was difficult, but not impossible. And there was a good chance that the beast might manage it. After he'd flung it for no more than the third time, with an impact that would have shattered a human's bones beyond all hope of repair, it'd sprung to its feet and returned the favour in kind. The worst damage Gevaudan thought he'd sustained from that had been a few cracked ribs, but then it'd hurled itself on him and wrapped its taloned hands around his throat.

He was trying to reach its eyes – the one spot that he could see on it that looked even remotely vulnerable – but its arms were long, and it had them fully extended. All it needed to do was to keep its weight bearing down on the talons at his throat, and gravity would do the rest. Gevaudan could feel the hot blood trickling down his neck from where the thing's claws were cutting into the flesh. It was just a toss-up whether he died first of a crushed airway or from the talons slicing an artery.

Someone walked past; not one of the things, but a human. Alannah. Gevaudan managed a gargled cry for help, but she just walked past him, receding down the darkened tunnel. Thursday followed a moment later, then Trex, the Wastelander. And then Helen.

Helen –

The thing's empty sockets stared into him. Gevaudan struck weakly at its face, but his broken claws barely skipped along the leathery surface.

A heaving breath sucked in the hide over the lower part of the thing's face, which began descending towards his. Gevaudan remembered what had happened to Nadgers and fought harder, striking at it, trying to force it back.

A hole opened in the thing's face. The raw, red, toothed sucker descended. It stank of blood and decay.

And that was when it came to Gevaudan. It might work, it might not. But it was worth the attempt, because otherwise…

He balled a fist and punched upwards, aiming not at the eyes but at the mouth – at the sucking hole in its centre, to be precise. The sucker curled inwards, clamped around his hand and arm. The teeth rasped at his flesh. Pain erupted; Gevaudan bellowed. The worst pain seared his hand; some sort of digestive acid or enzyme, he guessed. The thing howled muffledly around his arm. Gevaudan opened his fist; the acid seared his palm and fingers. He extended his claws and began to reach and grasp and tear, till his fingers closed around something solid that resisted movement. It was like holding fire or heated steel, but he tightened his grip and tore, twisted, wrenched. The howling became a high grating screech; the thing jerked and thrashed, talons gouging at his neck, but its grip was weakening. He held on, kept twisting and wrenching. Something gave and tore; the thing's screech gargled and choked, its grip slackened and it began to convulse. With a final, violent motion Gevaudan tore his hand free. The thing reared back and fell off him, thrashing on the floor with a reddish froth boiling up out of its mouth. A last choking noise, and it was still.

Gevaudan stumbled to his feet, barely daring to look at his hand. The sleeves of his coat and sweater hung in black tatters below the elbow. What he could see was a livid weeping red, the white of bone showing through in places. Yet already the pain was fading as his body reacted to it.

Helen. He remembered Helen. And so he stumbled down the corridor, towards the silvery light.

*

Alannah had gone. Off down the corridor, where those things'd come from. And so'd Thursday, Trex; Christ, even *Helen* had gone with them. Danny needed to get up and get after them. Only, something was looming over him. Looming over him and reaching down. Oh fuck. One of those fucking mutos that'd taken Nadgers' face off.

The hide over the muto's mouth caved inwards; Danny heard the hoarse, sucking breath and knew what that meant. He scrambled backwards till his back hit the cavern wall, and the muto came out him, crouching, claws raised; but most of all, with its face coming in.

What happened next took a second, and he never worked out if there'd been any thought or logic behind it. But suddenly the revolver was in his hand and his hand punched out with it, and the gunbarrel went into the empty socket of the muto's left eye. The barrel hit what felt like bone. And Danny pulled the trigger.

The hammer rose and fell. A muffled explosion; a warm wet spray in his face, and the muto pitched backwards with a hissing screech, thrashing briefly on the floor – Danny scrambled aside from its windmilling arms and legs – and then lay still.

Blood on the barrel, blood on his face. Alannah. He got up, staggered down the tunnel, the way she'd gone.

*

The tunnel wound downwards, into silvery-tinged darkness. Gevaudan followed it, risked a glance at his hand. It was healing; red in patches, but no longer raw, and muscle tissue had already knitted back into place over the exposed bone.

Dark, but he could see. Grendelwolf healing, Grendelwolf eyes; he had no need of the others' torches to find his way, wouldn't have even had there been no light at all. And swimming up through the murk, dim figures, plodding dully, hypnotised, ever downwards into the dark. The silvery light was no stronger than it had been before. It occurred to Gevaudan it might only brighten when its purposes were suited, to lure the unwary down.

They were plodding in single file, and the one he wanted most of all was at the rear. He wanted them all back, of course. Whatever he'd become, he wouldn't leave anyone to the attentions of those things. But Helen; Helen was the one he must not, above all others, fail.

He gained on her, seized her arm. She fought against him, face blank, eyes staring. Even he was having trouble pulling her back;

didn't help, of course, that he didn't want to actually harm her. He'd been shaped for killing and maiming, not peaceful restraint. But he was more than what they'd made him; he had to cling to that hope. He was much more.

"Helen. Helen." He shook her. She blinked. The blankness ebbed from her face. But already the others had gone on ahead, passed from sight. And now other shapes came round the tunnel's bend; hulking, hunchbacked figures with no necks.

They advanced: Gevaudan drew a pistol, pushing Helen behind him as he backed away, less to protect her from the things than from any urge she might again experience to follow the Sound.

Feet clattered behind him. "Shit!" It was Danny. He had the Lanchester at his shoulder. "Go for the fuckers' eyes," he shouted. "That kills 'em."

"The mouth works too," Gevaudan said. "Of course, they do have to be virtually eating you at the time."

"Where's Alannah?" Danny asked.

"Went ahead, with the others."

"Shit."

Danny levelled the Lanchester at the nearest thing's face. Gevaudan took aim with his Browning. There was a soft click as Helen drew, cocked and pointed her revolver, moving to his side.

There was a still moment, facing the creatures. Then suddenly they moved, ducking backwards into the shadows as the guns fired so that the bullets cut empty air. Gevaudan glimpsed one of them leaping, hands clawing at the ceiling, finding something, wrenching downwards. And then there was a hissing of dust, a rattle and rumble of rock, and the three of them went stumbling backwards as the tunnel roof crashed in and down, dust boiling through the air, dry and scratching the lungs, like smoke.

5.

"Alannah," shouted Danny. "Alannah!"

He ran forward to tear at the heap of rubble blocking the tunnel mouth. Gevaudan caught his arm. "Save your strength. We'll never get through that."

"You could."

"Perhaps. Given a couple of days. But there must be another way down. They wouldn't seal themselves in without a chance of escape. We need to find a different route. Quickly, now."

Danny found himself obeying. Gevaudan turned, led the way. Helen lit another weedlight torch and followed. Danny walked alongside her; the tunnel was wide enough to permit that. The flames played across her pale, tight-lipped face. She glanced sideways at him; he couldn't look away in time.

"We'll find her," she said quietly.

Lights flickered up ahead. "Who's there?" Wakefield's voice called.

"Just us," said Gevaudan.

Wakefield came forward to meet them, followed by Scopes. "Where's the rest?"

"Followed the Sound," said Helen. "It almost got me, too."

Wakefield nodded. Helen held up her torch and looked around. Nadgers, poor bastard, had been dragged away from the corpses of the two dead creatures and laid out with his hands folded over his chest, but they hadn't found anything to cover what was left of his face. It was virtually all gone; all that remained was a mix of red pulp and scored, fused white bone. *Poor little bastard; I made him come here.*

Danny heard a sigh; Gevaudan was looking down at Nadgers too. He looked – sad. "Another young man marching," he whispered.

"You what?"

Gevaudan shook his head, looked away. "Nothing. What are those things?"

Danny stared down at the two dead things. The one he'd killed still had a featureless dome for a head; the one Gevaudan had finished had its gaping toothed sucker, whatever the hell it was. "Some sort of muto."

"They're called the Styr," said Helen. Everyone looked at her.

"How you know?" asked Wakefield.

Helen looked up blinked, shook her head. "I just… do. Came into my head before. When I heard the Sound." She frowned, knelt. "And they're not mutants either."

Scopes looked down at Nadgers' corpse. "That come into your head as well?"

"Scopes," snapped Danny. Helen was in charge, whether she liked it or not.

"It's okay, Danny. And no, it's nothing like that. Look at this."

She held up the arm of one of the dead Styr. It took Danny a moment to register what she was showing them, but then he saw. Its pattern and colours were faded and broken up by the scaling on what had been its right hand, but he could still make it out: a skull, a black cloak and a scythe with a cross behind it, and an inscription he couldn't understand below.

"What's it say?"

"*Spiritum Meum Pro Patria,*" said Helen. "It's Latin. *My Soul For My Nation.*" She looked up. "It's the official motto of the Jennywrens. Only a Jennywren would wear it." She let the thing's hand fall. "And they're not big on mutants in their ranks. This thing used to be a human being."

She straightened up.

"What about Alannah?" asked Danny. He slipped his hand into his pocket, felt for the effigy; he found dust and pieces of half-dried mud, broken twigs, loose wool.

"We've got a job to do, Danny."

"What about Alannah?"

"I was going to say, if we can find her and the others, we'll probably find the heart of what's going on here. Which I expect will be something to do with Project Tindalos." Helen nudged one of the dead Styr. "Maybe they're breeding these things. Last thing we'd want is a plague of them spreading across the countryside."

"I could take 'em," said Scopes.

"Let's hope you don't have to," said Helen. "So we go around. We find wherever they've taken Alannah and the others. We get them and we destroy the Styr. Or whatever controls or creates them. Sound about right?"

Throughout, Danny had been thumbing bullets into the Lanchester's half-empty magazine. "Fine by me. Now can we go?"

"Wakefield?" asked Helen.

The Fox warrior tilted her chin up. "We fear nothing. And better we fight now. Better now than later. When there are more."

"Just one thing," said Gevaudan. "We need to watch you, Helen."

"What?"

"You nearly followed Alannah and the others. You're susceptible to whatever influence this has. We need to make sure it doesn't get you too."

"I'll have to rely on you guys to watch my back," she said. "I can do that, can't I?"

"You know you can," Gevaudan said.

"Yeah," said Helen after a moment. "Now, let's finish this."

*

They backtracked along the tunnel. They passed other entrances as they went but these were all dark. No silvery light. No trail to lead them. Danny gripped the Lanchester tighter. Fucksake, they'd be back in the big cavern under Hobsdyke at this rate. And what if the light was gone and they couldn't find a way down from there? Fuck. The Styr might've turned it off so no one could find their way down. And then they'd just have to crawl up through the tunnels to look for the intruders. And all the while Alannah – yeah, and Thursday, and Trex – were wandering about below.

Trex. Danny'd been sat next to the bloke last night when they were eating and they'd talked a bit. He'd been okay. And course, he'd known Thursday for years. But Alannah; he'd known her two days, three, but she mattered most to him. That didn't bother him. He was used to going day to day; things changed fast. New things came in. Old things went out. That was how it was. But Alannah mattered. And he knew that if he could only get one of them out, it'd be her.

Gevaudan was leading the way; torches burned behind him. They needed them; the Grendelwolf didn't. Useful fucker to have around. Actually more than just that. He'd jumped in, stood over Danny, fought the Styr back. Danny'd remember that. A debt was a debt. And he'd killed one of those things by shoving a hand down its throat: the coat was wrecked from the elbow down, but the skin was unbroken; a bit of a bright pink instead of the normal white, with a couple of red spots, but otherwise unharmed.

"Helen?" Gevaudan whispered. "Can you still hear the Sound? At all?"

367

Danny looked at her, but she was already shaking her head. "Sorry," she said. "Nothing. It stopped after you snapped me out of it."

"Just wondered."

"Yeah, that could work. Put me on a lead and use me like a sniffer dog. Thanks a bunch."

Nervous laughter rippled through the group. But on and up they went, the upward climb making every step a fight. And Danny's palms were slippery on the Lanchester. Time was ticking away. Alannah, wandering in the dark below.

And then Gevaudan stopped. "What?" whispered Helen.

Gevaudan held a hand up. "Do you hear that?"

At first Danny didn't; he heard nothing. But then it seeped in, through the whispers of wind and the drip of water. It was the sound of someone sobbing. He thought he heard a voice, mumbling. Maybe two. One might have been a woman's. Alannah? Had she got clear when the Sound stopped, run up? Christ, what state would she be in now?

"Where's it coming from?" Helen asked.

"There, I think." Gevaudan pointed to a tunnel to their left. He moved to the entrance, peered into the dark. "Can't see anything. There's a bend." He drew his pistols and ventured forward.

"I'm going with you," muttered Danny. "Might be Alannah."

Gevaudan looked back at him, opened his mouth, then closed it again and nodded. "I suggest the rest of you wait here. Just in case."

"All right," said Helen. "Scopes, can you cover the way we've come?"

"Course." Happily, Scopes unslung her rifle and got into position. Never happier than when there was a chance of using the damn thing. Sometimes Danny envied her.

He took a weedlight torch from Wakefield, lit it and followed Gevaudan down the tunnel. The weeping got louder, and the voices. There were two. One male, one female. But the female one wasn't Alannah. Please, God, it wasn't her.

"…enough of your moaning, pathetic worm. What you seek you'll have. But first you serve us."

"No," said the man's voice. "No."

"Yes. Yesss." No, it wasn't Alannah. It was a younger woman's voice, a girl's. Cruel and gloating in a way Danny doubted Alannah's'd ever be, not even if she had that bitch Jarrett strapped down and at her mercy.

"No. You're a liar. All liars. Tricked me. Not this. Didn't want this."

"Ah diddums. Poor baby. You'll have what you want. Maybe not as you expected, but you'll have it. But you will serve."

"No! No – "

The man's voice broke off as Danny and Gevaudan rounded a bend in the tunnel. There was a gasp, a scuffling movement; Danny glimpsed a huddled shape in a stained white coat trying to crawl away.

"It's all right," called Gevaudan. "It's all right. We don't mean you any harm."

The man sagged, groaning faintly. The woman giggled. Where the hell was she? Maybe she was just in his head. Maybe he was mental. Danny'd heard of that happening, sometimes, something beyond ghostlighting: the people you'd lost came and lived in your head, shared your body with you. Christ, the thought of that.

They closed in on the man. He was in his forties, with black, tangled hair, an unshaved face and broken, tape-mended glasses. There was an ancient plastic bag beside him, stuffed full of paper files; he grabbed at it as they approached, hugging it to his side.

"We don't mean you any harm," Gevaudan repeated. Danny was surprised how soothing the Grendelwolf's voice sounded. "We want to help you."

The woman's voice cackled again. "Too late. They can't help you now. No one can. All you can do is serve. Obey us." Danny noticed the man's mouth didn't move.

"Shut up," the man said. "Shut up. *Shut up.*" He slammed his head backwards, into the tunnel wall. Hard. There was a crunch.

"Jesus – " said Danny.

The man moaned in pain, but the woman's voice rang out over it, something between a screech and a snarl, followed by a voice that sounded muffled, even half-choked. "Fucking scumbag cocksucking shitlicking cunting bastard cumsock. Your mother sucks cocks in – "

The man slammed his head back again. The female voice snarled again, died to a groan.

Gevaudan crouched by the man. "Calm down. You'll hurt yourself."

The man focused teary eyes on him. "Had to make it stop. Had to."

"Make what – "

"You can't," screeched the female voice. "You can't. You'll never be rid of me."

A sick lurch in Danny's stomach as he realised where the voice was coming from, in the moment before the man's head snapped forward and he twisted it round, so the back of his head faced them.

All the man's thick black hair had fallen out of the back of his head. For a merciful moment, Danny thought *a creeping dose, he's dying of radiation poisoning,* but the white flesh underneath wasn't the bare, porous grain of the scalp. It was smooth, impossibly so; it bulged outwards more than the back of a head should. And it had features.

Eyes, nose, lips, forehead, even a small neat chin. It was the face of a woman or a young girl. There was blood on it, issuing from the mouth and nose. The eyes were closed, but then they snapped open. Behind the lids, there was only smooth, glistening blackness, like dark polished stone. No whites, iris or pupil; only blackness. The lips peeled back from white perfect teeth, currently etched red with blood.

"Fuck off, you cunts," said a woman's voice, high and clear and lovely, almost musical. "You can't have him. You can't do anything for Mordake now. He belongs to me."

6.

The man snapped his head back again twice, smashing the second face into the wall. The cold voice yowled, moaned and fell silent. The man slumped, blood trickling to drip on the shoulders of his white coat. His eyes rolled white for a moment, then blinked, then opened.

"You're here to help?" he asked. "Then kill me. Please just kill me before she wakes up again. I've tried to kill myself but I can't. Even when she's not awake I can't. Please. They lied to me. Tricked me. I can't go on like this, and I can't go back. Please just fucking kill me."

"If that's what you want," said Gevaudan. "Unless there's another way – "

"There isn't."

"If there's no other way, we'll kill you. But first, we need your help. We need to know what happened here."

"Why?"

"So we can stop it."

"You can't. It's too late."

"Was it to do with Project Tindalos?"

The man nodded.

"You know what it is?"

"Oh yes. Oh yes. God help me, I do. My name's Mordake. Dr Edward Mordake. I created it."

"You…" whispered Wakefield, reaching for her knife.

"No." Helen held a hand out. "No. We need to know. And besides, he wants to die. Let's not give him that. Not until he's earned it."

Mordake's eyes shone with tears. "It wasn't meant to be like this." The face in the back of his head still seemed to be quiescent, at least for now. Propped up in the larger tunnel they'd come to him from, with what remained of Helen's team around him, he drank water, but refused the offer of a piece of dried meat. "It doesn't matter now," he said.

"All right. We're not judging you here." At least not aloud. "Just tell us."

"I wanted to bring things back," he said. "Bring them back the way they were, I mean. I lost… my wife was killed in the War. She was the only thing that mattered to me. When she died, nothing mattered. Nothing mattered at all."

Helen wondered if she'd ever felt that way about Frank, even Belinda. Flickerings in the corner of her eyes, things that might have been glimpses of them. She blinked them away; what mattered right now was this.

"When that happens," said Mordake, "you'll do anything – anything at all – that promises even a chance of getting it back. It doesn't matter how ridiculous it sounds, how absurd, how stupid, how dangerous. Ultimately, you're willing to try anything that might work. And that's why we're here. And that's why…" his face crumpled. "Carter was right. This is worse. This will be a million times worse than the War. There'll be nothing left. Nothing. Nothing and nobody."

"Fuck sake," said Danny. "Get to the point."

"Danny," said Helen.

Mordake looked at Danny. Danny held his gaze. "There's someone who matters to me," he said. "And she's gone wandering off down there. Only chance of getting her out alive is finding out where she'll be and what the fuck's goin' on. So – with all respect and everything – it'd be nice if you could get to the bastard point some time soon."

Helen sucked an indrawn breath through her teeth. Gevaudan, much to her annoyance, was trying not to chuckle. Whoever's side he was on, however reliable or otherwise her judgement might be, he was still an annoying git sometimes. But Mordake just nodded. "No," he said, "I understand that. In fact, that's how all this came about. Everyone else accepted the old world was gone. That we had to live in what was left. I refused to. Not without Liz."

Danny nodded, crouching in front of him. "Go on." Mordake looked at him. "Please," said Danny, almost gently.

Mordake fumbled a packet of Monarchs from a pocket. "Does anybody have a light?"

Danny lit the cigarette with his torch. "Thank you," Mordake said, and began.

*

"What went wrong?" asked Danny, when Mordake fell silent.

Mordake laughed. The laugh made Helen's fingers twitch; she wanted to take her gun and shoot him for making that sound. "Nothing went wrong. That's just it. It went *right*. It went exactly how it was intended to. Just not as *we* intended."

"What do you mean?" Helen asked.

Mordake laughed again. "That's the worst. That's the worst. There's potential all right, waiting to be woken in almost all of us. Except most of the tribespeople out there. Those with any potential were drawn to places like this long ago, and it didn't end well for them. The ones that are left have no potential we can

373

use." He glanced at Wakefield, then back to Helen, half-smiled. "We've tried."

Wakefield's face tightened; her hand slid once more to the knife at her belt. Helen motioned her back.

"There's something dormant in most of us," Mordake said, "something that waits to be woken. But it isn't human."

"What do you mean?"

"I'm assuming you've already met the Styr?" Mordake said.

Helen's stomach tightened. How did he know? She felt the others' eyes on her. "Yes," she said.

"You know their name, don't you? Heard it in your head, when you met them? Then be careful. It means you're touched by the Night Wolves. There's some trace of them in you. That makes you susceptible to their influence. Like me."

Christ, she'd die before she became like this –

"Night Wolves?" said Danny.

"The Night Wolves," said Mordake. "The gods of the North Sea Culture. But they're not legends. They are very, very real."

"One thing at a time," said Helen. "What the hell are those... Styr?"

"They were once human. They were members of the facility's staff, or the Reapers who provided security, or the Jennywrens later sent to guard Hobsdyke – from yourselves, I presume." Mordake looked at Helen, smiled. "I take it I have the honour of addressing Helen Damnation?"

"That's right."

"I thought so. Commander Winterborn redoubled his demands for results when he heard you'd appeared. He really is afraid of you, isn't he?"

"He has cause."

"Mm. I'm sure he does. But we were talking about the Styr. Which brings us to the Night Wolves."

"What are they?"

"They're not wolves, of course. Not *real* wolves. Or any kind of animal, as you or I would understand. But once, this was their world, not ours. They had the power to shape reality, to change physical reality. But, something changed."

Mordake's cigarette was almost out; he lit another from it, tossed the stub aside. "Exactly what changed, I'm not sure; probably something we wouldn't even be aware of. Their nature, their powers, the way they understood reality; all of that was beyond anything we're capable of. The price they paid were weak spots, vulnerability to things we wouldn't even notice. Whatever had changed, even they could neither prevent nor escape it. They were doomed to extinction."

Mordake drew the smoke deep into his lungs, held it for a moment and then released it. "However, they also knew that one day things would change and they'd be able to survive here again."

"That doesn't help if you're already extinct," Gevaudan observed.

"True, but as I said, they didn't reckon time or reality the same way as you or I. Their bodies wouldn't survive what was coming, but other forms of life on Earth wouldn't even notice it. And so they put, you might say, a little of themselves into us, to wait for the time when they could return."

"What exactly does that mean?"

"Do you know what DNA is?"

"Yes," said Helen.

"No," said Danny.

"Your body's made up of cells," said Mordake. "Each of those contains a substance called DNA, which is basically the instructions for who and what you are: a man instead of a woman, a human instead of a frog. The Night Wolves didn't have DNA, but they had something else – something better – that would let them be reborn full-grown, with all their memories, as if they'd never died. They pooled their... substance, which was then scattered far and wide and found its way into the bodies of primitive humans. Not all of us, but many. Enough. It would remain within these people. Become a part of them. They would pass it on to their children. At first it would do nothing. Nothing at all. Just lie dormant, and be passed down and down through the generations until thousands, millions, even billions of us carried within them the substance of the Night Wolves. Long after the event had passed, waiting for the time, waiting for things to be right again."

"What's that mean?" demanded Danny, who was clearly struggling to keep up. Not that Helen couldn't sympathise there.

"Some of those who carried the… seed were drawn to one another, had children. In each generation, the power of the Night Wolves grew stronger. Stronger. And the higher the potential, the more chance that a child would grow up with some of the Night Wolves' powers or knowledge. They'd be known as magicians, sorcerors, saints, demons. Some of them would start cults or religions. The North Sea Culture, I believe, grew from such people, and might have grown to the point that the Night Wolves could be brought back. They tried to bring them back; all of them, at once, in a vast ritual of a scale and complexity you can't imagine. But something went wrong, and the entire North Sea Culture was destroyed, leaving only scattered survivors trying to keep the remnants of beliefs alive as they migrated south through Scotland and Northern England. And the window closed. And we were all safe, just for a little while. But enough fragments survived that I was able to piece things together. And I think those fragments were left for me or someone like me to find. They promised power and… not this." Mordake lit another cigarette; there was only one more left, Helen saw. "Another window is now open. When the experiment succeeded, the potential of four test subjects was awakened in full. And then they reached out to the others in the base."

"And created the Styr?"

"Yes. All those possessing any potential were… transformed. The test subjects, and others, were physically transformed into creatures you won't have seen yet. Drones, for want of a better term."

"Drones?"

"In an insect colony, you have the workers, who gather food and build the hive, and you have the drones, who exist only to breed. They'll be far below, in the caves. The Night Wolves' substance within them is becoming active. It's absorbing their human tissues, and merging with that of the others to form a new physical shape. When the last of the drone's substance is exhausted, it dies, and another emerges to take its place. And every so often, they make the Sound. Anyone with the potential can hear it and gets drawn in, to be used."

"Alannah – " said Danny.

Helen quieted him with a hand on his arm. "What do you mean by forming a shape?"

"One of the Night Wolves, of course," said Mordake. "That's what's being born down below. The others, the creatures you've encountered – the worker Styr, if you will – their task is to defend the hive until the Night Wolf has been born. When they were… becoming… the drones, the test subjects, could defend themselves psychically. Make anyone trying to attack them turn their weapons on themselves. But they can't do that now. They have to focus everything they've got on creating – re-creating – the Night Wolf. So they need the worker Styr."

"But not everyone's got this… potential," said Danny. "So where's everyone else?"

Mordake smiled weakly. "The Styr are born hungry."

Helen thought of Nadgers' face. "That's nice to know. So how do we stop it?"

"You don't," said a gloating female voice. Mordake's face contorted in agony; he twisted round to show the back of his head, the white, smiling face there. "You just die. All of you. Our time has come. The time of the Night Wolf – "

Mordake roared and smashed his head, the face, backward into the tunnel wall. The female voice screeched. He did it again, and the voice fell silent. Mordake slumped against the wall, gasping.

"What the hell is that?" asked Helen.

"It changed me too," said Mordake. "But not into a drone or a worker. I'm to be its priest. It couldn't change me like it changed the others; I'd be a mindless thing like the Styr. That thing on the back of my head… my devil twin… would eventually take control. And… powers… would awaken in me. I was to go.

When that's done, I was to go out into the world and change more people. Create new hives. That's why you've got to kill me." He shook his head. "It'll only delay the inevitable, of course. When the Night Wolf is ready, it'll come, and it'll create new hives, new priests to spread its word."

"There must be a way to stop it," said Helen. "There must be."

Mordake gulped air, nodded. "Maybe. Maybe just one." He fumbled through the bagful of papers and cassettes. "I kept these. I burned the office up top. You saw?"

"So that was you. Yes."

"Yeah. So that nobody could pick up where I left off. But I kept the important stuff. Like tapes. There's a videotape in there, shows what happened. Because I know Winterborn. Whatever happens here today, he will try and restart this project. And that can't happen. It mustn't. So this is evidence, for him. But this; this was all I could think of that might help." Mordake dug out a crumpled page, thrust it at them. "There, see? That symbol?"

"A crucifix?"

"No! It's not a crucifix. Looks like one at first, but you have to look closer. The upright isn't quite straight; the arms ... see?"

"Yes, okay."

"I've seen this before," said Gevaudan. "In the village. The lintel above the church door."

"That's right. It's called the Hobsdyke Cross. Pretty much peculiar to this village and the immediate area before the War. You'd see it in stonework, decorations. And in the church. But it's not a religious symbol; not a Christian one, anyway. It's a symbol from the North Sea Culture, adopted as a ward against evil."

"So?"

"Remember what I told you? Despite their power, the Night Wolves were vulnerable to things we wouldn't even notice. Such as certain symbols. Like this one. There was always the chance a ritual might go wrong and the... result... might have to be destroyed. That's what this glyph's for. It has to be... you need a weapon of iron. I don't know how well-up you are on folklore, but there's an old tradition that unnatural creatures fear cold iron. This is why."

"Why believe him?" snapped Bleach. "He is Reaper. Say anything to trick us."

"Because I was lied to," said Mordake, glaring straight at her, "and cozened, and manipulated, and betrayed. Oh yes, call me a monster if you want, but I did what I did to – "

" – to get your wife back," said Helen. "Let's not dress it up as anything noble. And you got shafted on the deal, and now you want revenge."

Mordake laughed, a high hysterical noise. "And what about your motives, Helen? Do they really bear close scrutiny either?"

"We're not talking about me."

"We don't have time for this," said Danny.

"Danny's right," said Gevaudan. "And at the end of the day, low motives have a habit of being far more reliable than high ones."

Mordake smiled up at him. "Good point, Grendelwolf."

"Thank you."

Mordake pointed. "Carve that symbol on an iron weapon, and if you can get close enough to the Night Wolf, and strike at the heart of it, you can destroy it before it's born. But if you fail, God help you." He started laughing, crying too. "Except of course that there *is* no god. There's none. There can't be."

The laughter rattled on inside him; finally he slumped back against the wall, spent, and said, simply: "Now kill me. You promised me. Kill me. Now."

7.

Helen knew there was a lot that could be said against her. She'd been guilty of foolishness in the past, of neglecting those she loved – to say nothing of one occasion she wished above all others she could wipe from her memory – and there were those who'd say, not without justification, that she was ruthless when it came to manipulating others to get her own way.

And to all those things she might plead guilty. But no one had ever said she wasn't a woman of her word. She'd made a promise to Mordake, and now she reached for her pistol to keep that promise.

But then–

"Company!" shouted Scopes, and her rifle barked, the shot echoing in the tunnel. A moment later, familiar hissing screeches rang out.

"Styr – " Mordake scrambled up. "They'll take me... they'll – "

"Mordake, wait." She understood terror like that; whatever he'd done, she'd promised to spare him. But before she could fire he'd flung himself into the tunnel where they'd found him and was running. Helen shouted after him, but he was gone.

"A little help here," Scopes yelled, firing again.

Helen holstered her pistol and shouldered the Sterling, flicking it to single shot. Two Styr were already dead – she'd heard of Scopes' skill with a rifle before but now she saw the proof – but other shapes were moving in the dimness.

"Stand your ground!" she barked. "They must have cleared a way through to us. We'll use it to get to the Night Wolf once we're past them."

"Oh, that's all we've got to do, is it?" Danny was down on one knee, aiming the Lanchester. "How many of the fuckers are there?"

"Watch out," said Gevaudan, a revolver pointed into the black and a long-bladed knife in his free hand. "They're about to – "

The Styr charged; there were a full dozen of them. Scopes' rifle fired again, but this time none fell; they were running head down, shielding their eyes and mouths.

Helen sighted, fired, aiming at the eye-holes of one of the creatures, but couldn't get a hit. She flicked the Sterling's fire-selector to fully automatic; perhaps that would help. Scopes bolted past Helen, a few feet from an incoming Styr.

She really needed to fire the Sterling again, but everything was swimming. A throbbing in the air. The Sound; she could hear the Sound again.

A whistle in the air and the Styr chasing Scopes fell screeching, a Fox's arrow in its left eye. Wakefield nocked a fresh one to her bow.

Gevaudan stepped forward, pistol firing. A Styr screeched, its facial hide dilating to show that horrible lamprey mouth: Gevaudan fired into it, and the creature fell. He rammed the knife through the eyehole of another of the things, then closed and grappled with another, drove his pistol into its eye to fire at point-blank range.

Screams; a Styr seized one of the remaining Foxes, its claws ripping and tearing at him. His shrieks died fast. The Styr's face rose; red, dripping. Shoot it. Shoot you stupid cow –

But the Sound. Everywhere, the Sound.

A Styr, in front of her, claws raised. Its empty sockets gazed into her; its lamprey mouth gaped and pulsated. But it didn't attack. No; of course it wouldn't. She had potential. The blood of the Night Wolf. No, that couldn't be real. Mordake couldn't have been telling the truth. Wasn't possible…

And yet, there was the hideous fact of the Styr themselves. The Jennywren tattoo on the wrist of something more mutated than any of the mutants GenRen swore to kill. There was the face on the back of Mordake's head, his devil twin: he was too old for the War to have made that of him, even if it could have, and nothing like that could have existed before the War. Could it?

Hands grabbed her, pulled her back; a small, leathery hand cracked across her face. "Fucksake!" Wakefield shouted. "You want die?"

Helen stared about her. She was about ten yards down the tunnel from their last position. The Styr lay dead, many with Fox arrows or knives in their eyes or lamprey mouths. The remaining kills, she guessed, were probably down to either Scopes or Gevaudan. Gevaudan himself stared at her, blood running dark down his face from his slashed cheek; Scopes, crouched on the ground, glanced briefly and indifferently up from reloading her rifle.

Danny kicked at one of the dead Styr, Lanchester hanging at his side. A Fox warrior – Bleach, that was her name, a wide-shouldered, barrel-bodied woman looking close to Helen's age – tightened a bandage on her arm with her teeth. And that was it, Helen realised; of the Fox warriors who'd come to Hobsdyke – the bulk of their small fighting force – only Wakefield and Bleach were left. One of their number lay with his face still engulfed by a Styr's sucker mouth; a second lay like a doll, neck snapped by a single blow. Another still was a smashed mangled heap, barely recognisable; of the last Fox warrior there wasn't even a whole corpse, just a scattering of body parts.

And through all that she'd just been strolling, sleepwalking through the tunnels. While these died for her.

Tears stung her eyes; she turned away.

And all along, in the distance, the Sound continued to throb.

*

Thursday barely noticed the others with her, any more than Trex and Alannah took stock of her. She barely even registered the tunnel or the silvery glow that lit it. All she saw was Lelly.

Lelly from Mary's crew; Lelly of the heart-shaped face and violet eyes and the body that curved like the guitar Trex had played last night. (*Who was Trex? Last night? Why did that seem so important? Where was she now?* The questions multiplied, but they were distracting, so she ignored them and they trailed off.) Lelly, who, unknown to Thursday, was already dead, cut to pieces by Reaper machine gun in a ruined house in Northern Moor. Lelly, who Thursday had kissed and licked, Lelly who'd pushed finger after finger inside her till finally her whole hand had slipped inside, filling her up and driving her to realms of joy she'd never known or even thought possible; Lelly walked ahead of her naked, the round curve of her bottom swaying, tick-tock, from side to side, pausing occasionally to look back over her shoulder and smile back at Thursday with eyes that promised everything.

That was what drew Thursday on: different versions, different visions, would be reeling the others steadily in.

And so she, and they, walked on, through the tunnels under Hobsdyke, drawn down towards that silvery light.

*

"It wasn't your fault," said Gevaudan. "You're the only one of us left who's susceptible to the Sound."

"Yeah." She knew he was right; still she didn't believe him. Gevaudan studied her for a moment, then vanished up the tunnel, heading back the way they'd come right at the start.

Danny was pacing furiously up and down, chewing his thumb. "Where's he going?"

"To get something we're going to need," Gevaudan's voice echoed back down the tunnel.

"Fuck *sake*," said Danny.

Helen sighed.

"We need to get a fucking skate on," Danny said to her. Scopes glanced up from cleaning her rifle, studied him for a second, then glanced down. "That's Alannah down there, and Thursday, and your fucking pal Trex too."

Wakefield, crouched over the bodies of the dead – or more exactly gathering the illegible charnel that had been one of her warriors into some semblance of order beside the other corpses – shot him an angry glare. Bleach glared too, but went further; she straightened, stepped towards Danny. Danny squared up to her.

"Danny," snapped Helen. "That's enough."

Bleach, not taking her eyes off Danny, spat on the floor.

"Bleach," said Wakefield, bending back to her task. "Back here. Styr have his woman. His warrior too. Make him brain-funny. Help here." She looked up. "Bleach, *now.*"

Bleach breathed out, wiped her mouth, turned back.

"They've got their way," said Helen. "It matters to them. Let them do it, and then we'll go."

His face was suddenly raw and young and naked, a world of pain in his eyes. "I promised her, Helen."

"I know."

"I promised I'd keep her safe. And Thursday's me mate. But… I promised Alannah. And that fuckin' matters to *me*."

"I know, Danny. She's my friend too."

He looked at her but didn't speak; she thought she knew what was on his mind, though. *Yeah, but you'd put your mates in the firing*

384

line without a second thought to get what you want. Sacrifice them in a heartbeat. Then something else occurred to him. "And what about this Night Wolf thing?"

"Yeah. I know. We've got to do this right."

"And how do we do that?"

"Like this," said Gevaudan, coming back down the tunnel, carrying what looked like a huge spear, or a harpoon.

"The fuck's that?"

"It was," said Gevaudan, "an iron reinforcing rod for the concrete chamber's floor. It's now sharpened to a point and…" he held it up, "engraved, as you can see."

In the torchlight, Helen could see that the cross-like symbol Mordake had shown them had been engraved on the makeshift spear over and over again.

"We're ready," said Wakefield. She and Bleach stood, ready and impassive.

And the low throbbing noise, shifting between two or three notes, began again. Helen swayed.

Gevaudan steadied her, a hand on her arm. "Helen?"

"It's the Sound," she said.

"Shit," said Danny.

"No. Wait. It's what we need." She blinked, shook her head. Had to keep it clear just a few seconds longer. "It'll draw me down. I'll follow it. And you follow me. It'll take us right to the Night Wolf. We can kill it, save Alannah and the rest." *If they're still alive.* "And everyone's a winner. Just remember to snap me out of it once we're there."

*

Once she got going, the only trouble Danny had was keeping up; lucky old creeping death thought to tie a coil of rope round her waist and hang onto the other end. Like a dog on a lead. All they needed to do then was keep a few weedlight torches burning to light the way, and keep their guns handy for when and if they ran into any of those fucking Styr.

They didn't, though. Must be a game the fuckers played. Weighing up the risk of a fight against the need for more 'potential'. But fuck, if they needed more, what did that mean for Alannah and the rest? Or were they just doing it to build up more stock, ready to go?

Christ's sake, what was waiting for them down there?

Faster they raced, down through the tunnels. The weedlight snatched images from the darkness; glyphs were etched on the walls, like the mad ones on Mordake's pages. His bag was back in the big chamber, with the bodies of the dead; Nadgers, the Foxes. They'd grab it when they got out. *If* they got out.

And there was a sound in the air. Fuck, was it *the* Sound? Couldn't be. Danny didn't have the 'potential' Mordake'd gone on about. Or what if he did, though – just like a tiny, tiny little bit out of it that didn't pick owt up till you were right on top of the source – the Night Wolf? Fuck, what was that gonna be like?

But no; he'd heard them describe the Sound, and it was nowt like this. This was voices, words, and it was a chant. No music in it, just noise. A mumbly sound, you couldn't quite make the words out, but everytime you nearly heard them it felt weird, almost painful. Same way those weird fucking letters and symbols had.

"Up ahead," called Gevaudan and, true enough, Danny could see the silvery light up ahead of them. It was bright now. Might be too bright to look at when he finally got through. He hung onto the Lanchester, wondered what chance he was gonna have when they ran into –

Shadows flickered in amongst the light; big, man-shaped shadows with massive humped shoulders and heads without necks. Styr, the fucking Styr. They dodged around Helen, leapt at Gevaudan. Gevaudan staggered, the rope fell, and Helen was gone, plunging past them into the light beyond.

A Styr's clawed hands reached for Danny. Something flew over his shoulder – a Fox's throwing-knife, taking it cleanly through the eye. He spun, shouted, aimed the Lanchester as his rescuer ducked aside, fired a short burst into the lamprey maw of a Styr that'd been about to grab her from behind.

Bleach looked down at the fallen Styr, then back to him; nodded. Then they were turning back to the fight as Wakefield leapt past, dropping one Styr with a flung knife and another with a spear lunge. And Gevaudan –

Gevaudan, roaring, rose from the floor, flung a Styr bodily away, snatched up his iron spear and used it as a quarterstaff, knocking two of the fuckers to the floor and then finishing them with precise stabs from it. But there were another dozen Styr, coming at them.

Gevaudan thrust the spear into Danny's hands, drew his pistols. "I'll deal with them," he said. "Get through. Save her."

Her. Danny guessed he didn't mean Alannah. All the same, looked like him and old creeping death had something in common after all. *You too, you poor bastard. Christ, we should form a club or something.*

Gevaudan leapt forward, firing, hurling himself into the Styr, driving the mass of them back. Just for a moment, there was a gap at the tunnel's end and the light blazed through it, a big enough gap to run through. "Come on," Danny shouted and ran, Wakefield and Scopes and Bleach following; behind him, the Styr screeched and howled and Gevaudan's pistols thundered, punctuating Danny's battle-cry as he ran on, into the light.

8.

Danny'd seen inside a building once, middle of Manchester. A big fuck-off church. Only it wasn't called a church. When a church got that big they called it something else. Cathedral – that was the word. And that's what this cave was. Its ceiling, hung with stalactites to match the stalagmites jutting up from the floor, looked easily a hundred feet above them; maybe it formed the floor of the chamber under Hobsdyke. A fucking black cathedral, to the worship of the Night Wolves.

The pale silver light flickered across the floor and lit up bones. Gnawed and broken bones – the skulls'd been split wide open – and bits of torn, bloodstained cloth and leather. Reaper uniforms and bits of white coats. *The Styr are born hungry,* Mordake'd said. He hadn't been kidding; the proof was here. Danny'd never thought he'd pity a Reaper, but he did now.

The glow seemed to emanate from the centre of the chamber. Around it stood tiny figures Danny couldn't quite make out. In the heart of the glow was… something. Something vast. And whatever it was, it moved. It lived. It was being born.

This was the Night Wolf, then. The thing Mordake'd called the Night Wolf. *It's the closest thing they've got to a name. They're not wolves, of course, not real wolves... Or any kind of animal, as you or I would understand.*

Danny understood that part of it now. Whatever it was, the light was only enough to show it as a silhouette, which struck him as a bloody good job.

Because he could see Helen. Not running anymore, walking slowly and placidly towards it. Danny went after her. Scopes was next to him, squinting against the glow; Wakefield and Bleach spread out to flank him.

The iron spear weighed heavy in his grip. The Foxes'd know how to use the damn thing; he hadn't got a clue. Yeah, but Gevaudan had given it to him. That didn't mean much, of course; he'd been the closest to hand. Should give it Bleach or Wakefield. And he would. Just in a mo. Once he found Alannah.

Helen neared the glow surrounding the beast, then stopped. Something moved forward to meet her. A worker Styr. There were still some here in the cathedral; Gevaudan wasn't fighting them all. It didn't attack her, but it didn't ignore her either; instead it pointed with a bird-claw hand, and Helen turned, went off to the side, and knelt beside three other figures; Alannah, Trex and Thursday.

"Bleach," he said. She turned towards him. He held out the iron spear. She took it, nodded once. Then, for an instant, she smiled. Danny grinned back, then cradled the Lanchester in his hands. This was his gun. This felt right.

Then, as he watched, Thursday rose, blank-faced, and walked towards the light.

Stood around the glow in the cave's centre – one, Danny guessed, to each point of the compass – were four shapes that'd been human once. They weren't any more, but they weren't Styr either.

From round their waists, four black, spiny legs, like a spider's or cockroach's, had sprouted. Their sharp points rested on the floor, suspending the body they were attached to so that its toes swung above the stone surface. From their mouths jutted thick, black, elongated probosces, and to the ends of these were attached long, white tendrils that snaked down from the shape at its centre.

As Danny watched, one of them wavered on its legs, tottered and fell. The white tendril snapped free of the proboscis rose, waving to and fro in the air. The body suspended by those legs was withered, barely a skeleton; it broke apart when it hit the floor, half-dessicated and half-rotted. Now he could see other remains like it, scattered all around. And now Thursday stood up.

*

Thursday had been sat, happily watching, as Lelly danced for her. Slow and gentle, tender and sexual, a promise and a gift. Thursday knew she could have Lelly again, could have her any time she wanted, but till now she'd been content to watch, to let her desire stir and rise and mount. But now Lelly walked away, turning back to beckon and smile, and Thursday knew that it was time.

She stood and walked towards Lelly as her girl backed into the silvery light and stood there waiting. She went to her, went to her Lelly, and reached out to fold her arms about her.

Except that they closed around nothing; just as she expected the thrill of the girl's naked skin on her fingertips, her hands passed inwards through where Lelly had been, and her arms embraced empty air.

Thursday spun about, dazed, confused. This place – what was it, where was she? There were bones on the floor, there were other creatures about her, grotesque things that nonetheless might once have been human. And looming over them all was something – something that stared down at her with pallidly glowing eyes and –

And then the silver glow blazed about her, and the pain began. It ripped through her belly, her chest, along her limbs. It was like movement, like things waking and stirring inside her, like chitinous limbs moving – reaching, clawing, tearing. And she was screaming, but she couldn't move. Not even when the flesh at her waist and flanks tore and the four huge, spidery legs unfolded. Her own legs collapsed, and she fell, but she never hit the floor; the spider-legs flew outwards as if on springs, the claws at the tips slamming into the ground and boosting Thursday's body clear of the floor, hoisting her aloft. And still she screamed.

She kept on screaming till she began to choke. Something was rising in her throat, like an arm pushing up through her gullet, impossibly, from inside her, forcing itself up through her mouth. She felt her throat, her neck, thicken and swell; felt things break and tear. Her jaws were stretched wide: bone cracked and she would have shrieked, but her screams were muted, reduced to a faint, agonised mewling. As she watched, a long, thick proboscis slid into view, and she realised it was coming out of her mouth; from above, a thin white tendril like a pale root snaked down, attached itself to the proboscis' tip, and she felt it begin to suck.

The agony was worse than ever now; the feeling of insect legs unfolding within her grew and multiplied, but it didn't feel as if they were just extending and flexing. They weren't just waking up any more; they were scrabbling furiously, and she realised they were ripping and tearing, with a frenetic and ruthless efficiency, at her flesh and organs, stripping and devouring them to convert into food for the white tendril to suck out of her.

I want to die. I want to die. Thursday's body began to convulse; tears trickled from her eye corners. *Lelly. Lelly? It wasn't really you was it? Tell me it was a trick.* She knew, could feel, the skin of her face and limbs and torn, desecrated torso withering, growing yellowed and brittle and dry like old paper. *If you're alive, I'll wait for you. If you're dead then wait for me. I'll be along soon. Please God let this end soon. Let me die. Please let me die.* And still the thing within her tore and rooted, mining her to fuel the beast whose vast bulk grew above. *Lelly. Lelly. Oh my God. Lelly.*

*

And finally Danny was close enough to see it, or as much of it as a mind could take: the Night Wolf.

Wolf? Mordake had been right: it wasn't any fucking wolf. It didn't look like anything he'd seen. But at first glance, you could see where it got its name; its long body was stretched out, limbs folded, long head raised aloft – even with what looked like ears pricked up. Yes, at a glance it looked, for all the world, like a huge dog, lying down but alert. A dog nearly a hundred feet long. The light even gleamed on what looked like fur.

But then it rose, head sweeping up to point skyward, then down to stare at him, and everything changed.

An elongated, segmented body balanced on four long, thin legs. They looked a little like a spider's or insect's – hard and jointed – and somehow a little like a horse's too: thin, delicate, poised. The body was segmented too; thick plates of some greenish stuff that looked hard and spongy-soft at the same time. And the fur wasn't fur; it was a swarming forest of grub-white rootlets, tendrils like the ones that sucked the life from the drones below.

And then there was the head, long, narrow and tapering. The jaws seemed to be in four parts, instead of the two you'd expect a wolf to have. They opened and closed; above them were two round, cold, vast eyes like searchlights. They swept across him as the thing turned their way; it was like the blast of a wind or a surging flood of ice water. It drove into him, through him, left him feeling scoured to the bone.

Danny recoiled from them, turned away – and that snapped him out of paralysis. "Bleach!" he yelled. "The spear! Throw it!" And then he was firing, a long burst, at Thursday, who'd been his friend, bullets stitching across her torso, blood spraying, the last few rounds smashing into her head, making sure her agony was ending, the spider-legs of the thing she'd become collapsing, her body dropping to the ground.

"Scopes, get the other drones. Wakefield, with me!"

"Gotcha," he heard Scopes call, then the bark of her rifle. And from above, as they ran, a howling screech that seemed as much in his head as anywhere else; a bit like the sound the Styr made but a thousand, a million times worse. The Night Wolf, in its rage.

"Get Helen," he told Wakefield, and grabbed Alannah's shoulders to shake her. She blinked, eyes clearing, and Danny dragged her to her feet.

"Shite – " he heard Wakefield call as she dragged Helen up, and he looked to see Scopes falling back towards them, four or five Styr in pursuit. Beyond them, Bleach drew her arm back and threw the spear, and it flew towards the Night Wolf. *That's you done for, you fucker, that's you finished –*

But one of the Styr was already leaping into the spear's path. It caught the weapon in both hands and held it aloft. Its arms flexed; the spear bent, buckled, snapped. The Styr flung the two halves aside. Before Bleach could even move, three Styr hurtled towards her. She reached for her own spear, but one caught her in a tackle and brought her down. The others fell upon her. She screamed once, and then blood sprayed across the cavern floor and she was silent.

Scopes reached him and Wakefield, then spun round and aimed her rifle. She didn't even look bothered about the Styr swarming in behind them. She fired, and one fell, head snapping back. She worked the bolt and fired again, dropping another. She worked the bolt, fired again –

…and the rifle clicked.

"Fuck," said Scopes and reached for more ammunition. But the Styr were closing; she'd never make it. Helen, Trex and Alannah were still groggy and dazed – no help from them, not yet, not here; not with the Sound still roaring through their heads.

Wakefield flung a knife; it glanced off a Styr's armoured head. She reached for another as Danny aimed the Lanchester, knowing even as he did that he wouldn't stand a chance unless the bastard's mouth was exposed. Three Styr, closing in; they didn't stand a chance.

Gunfire, the chatter of a machine gun. Bullets slammed into the Styr; they were driven back, staggering, but didn't fall.

"To me," a voice bellowed. "To me."

Gevaudan; Danny looked and there he was all right, firing the Bren gun from the hip like it was a Sterling, raking the Styr with it. "To me, now," he shouted.

"Come on, move – " yelled Danny, and he was running, hanging onto Alannah and dragging her after him even as she wove and stumbled.

"Move," shouted Gevaudan. And so Danny ran, with Alannah, Wakefield dragging Helen after him, Scopes hauling Trex. He looked back just once, in time to see Gevaudan snatch the Bren's magazine out and slam in another, sweeping the gun back and forth across the Styr – the ones that'd been attacking them and the ones rising from Bleach's butchered corpse – to drive them back before turning to run. Revealing, as he did, a final vision of the Night Wolf, the bodies of its drones scattered around it, howling in its rage.

9.

In the tunnels' darkness, Mordake ran.

Blind in the dark – the silvery light from below suddenly denied him – he cannoned into walls, even with hands held out ahead. He slipped and tripped and stumbled on the wet, uneven floor.

In the tunnels' darkness, Mordake ran.

Light glimmered up ahead; he dashed toward it. A silver glow. He emerged at an intersection of tunnels. He saw dead Styr; he saw human corpses. He knew this place. He knew –

A thin, cold voice laughed in his ears. "You can run," it said, "but you can't hide. You can't leave. You're ours now. Ours."

"Shut up," he said, then screamed it. "Shut up." And then he was sprinting up the main tunnel; toward the light, the true light, not this glamour of the Night Wolves, up towards the light of a real sun and clear winter air, his devil twin's laughter, unceasing, in his ears.

In the tunnels' darkness, Mordake ran.

There was no time for talking at first, scrambling up through the tunnels. No time at all till the Night Wolf's howling had faded enough that Helen could even hear herself think; up till then, it was just about running and increasing the distance between her and it.

She felt weak, shaken, as much by the knowledge of how close she'd come to giving up as anything else. She'd have fallen if not for Wakefield supporting her. God, she'd fall... any moment now, she'd fall.

The tunnel opened out into a small chamber and he turned. "Wait," called a deep voice, one she knew. The others up ahead stopped running; so did Wakefield, and so Helen did too. She turned: Gevaudan glanced back down the tunnel, then stepped into the chamber. "Rest," he said. "We have a moment."

They sank gratefully down. Alannah and Helen blinked, rubbed their eyes. Danny knelt beside Alannah. Scopes sat back against the wall and slid down into a sitting position, shaking; Wakefield went over and sat beside her. They exchanged dazed, silent glances, then slumped, heads back, breathing heavily. After a moment, Trex slumped down beside them too.

"How are you?" Helen looked up, saw Gevaudan. That white, sombre face, concerned. *Fake. He will destroy you.* But he'd just saved her from... *that.* Saved her from what had happened to Thursday and the others.

"I've been better," she said, and buried her face in her hands.

"Me too," said Alannah, forcing a smile, but she squeezed Danny's hands, shaking, where they gripped her own.

Helen looked around the cavern. This was all that remained, all that was left. The rest, taken by the Styr or the Night Wolf. A parade of the dead, multiplying, all calling her name.

"Helen," a voice whispered. She looked. Frank and Belinda crouched in the shadowed mouth of the tunnel they'd emerged from, faces white blurs in the dark.

"Your fault," Frank whispered. "All your fault." He stretched out his arms: they were so long and thin and white it was hard to believe they could be more than bone. "Come on, Helen. Come to us. End it now."

"What about Winterborn?" she whispered.

"Hungry," Belinda whispered back. "Hungreeeeeeeeeeeeee."

"We don't care," said Frank, "we just want to eat. Nothing else matters."

And it didn't. Nothing they said meant anything more than that; how hungry were they, moment to moment? It had its peaks and troughs: given a trough, it was weak enough that they'd defer it, the better to savour a finer feast later on; but at a peak, they'd return, inconstant and rapacious, to demand her flesh and blood.

"Does it matter?" he whispered. "Look at all these dead." They'd shrunk back into the tunnel; their faces had sunk as if beneath dark water, and only the moist, spilt-blood glitter of their eyes remained. The light in them was silvery. "Stay alive and there'll be more dead. Winterborn will still be alive too, and we'll still be hungry, and you'll still be haunted. Come to us, and it all ends."

A line, she knew it was a line; self-serving and with no purpose other than to claim her. But even so, her strength had ebbed; she hadn't the energy to fight any further. She glanced round the chamber; Scopes and Trex were slumped in exhaustion, Danny busy tending to Alannah, who seemed equal parts annoyed by the fuss and charmed by the attention, Gevaudan and Wakefield deep in conversation. She was, for the moment, forgotten.

That seemed best.

Helen stood and moved quickly, silently into the tunnel.

*

"The spear," said Gevaudan. "What happened to it?"

"Bleach had," said Wakefield. "Styr kill her."

"She lobbed it at the fucker," Danny said, "but one of the Styr jumped in the way and grabbed it. Snapped it in half."

Gevaudan breathed out. "But the other drones are dead."

"Yes. Scopes' work."

"Wasn't anything," Scopes said.

"At least the Night Wolf can't grow any stronger," Gevaudan said. "And it can't be *that* strong, yet. Otherwise it would have attacked us directly. It still needs the Styr to guard it. If we can come back with reinforcements, maybe a few more of those iron weapons, we might still have to stop it. If someone stays here to keep watch; how does that sound, Hel– "

Gevaudan broke off. He blinked. Where Helen had been sitting, literally seconds before, was empty.

Wakefield gawped. "Where did she – "

"The Sound," said Alannah. She was pale and swaying, clinging on to Danny. "It's calling. It's almost whole. It wants to be whole."

Danny's presence must have helped her keep it together, stopped the spell reasserting itself, at least for now. *I should have done the same. But of course I can never tell. It would be grotesque to her. Monstrous.* Gevaudan stood. "All right. The rest of you get out of here. Get back to the Fox tribe. Take Mordake's notes to warn them with."

"Gevaudan – " Danny half-rose.

"Danny," said Alannah, gripping on to him.

"Do it, Danny. I'm the one with the best chance here." The boy looked back at him – less a boy, now, than a man – and nodded. Gevaudan nodded back. A good lad. But another soldier, another young man marching. Ready to die for a cause, a flag; for something, anything, rather than just live. But relieved, too, for now, and no wonder; his grip on Alannah's hands showed where he had to be now; she needed him again, after fighting to shake him off for so long. *Am I that obvious, too? Am I ridiculous to her?* "Take care," said Gevaudan.

"You too, creeping death."

Gevaudan had to smile. He gave a last nod and was gone.

*

It hadn't taken long at all, to retrace the steps of her journey. The Sound was clear in her head, and the silvery glow of the Night Wolf shone ever brighter as she went down to it.

A woman walked ahead of her – in her forties, with red hair and tie-dyed clothes – turning to smile at her with bright green eyes and beckon her on, beckon her home. *Come to Mummy, darling.*

It wasn't new, of course; Helen had seen it before, last time she'd followed the Night Wolf's call. She knew this time it wasn't real, but she didn't care. She might have resisted, could have tried, but why should she? Everything passed easy and painless, as in a dream, or one of the films she'd seen as a child.

No. You should fight. You'll die. You'll die in pain. You're needed. There are things you promised to do.

For a moment she slowed; almost turned, even. But then she relaxed again, and was walking forward.

Yes, it'd hurt soon enough. She wasn't under any illusions about that. There was agony ahead, and then death. But the agony, with any luck, wouldn't last too long; death, and oblivion, would be forever.

The cathedral's entrance was ahead. It was filled with clear, dazzling, terrible light. No Styr barred the way; why should they, after all?

Helen went through. The Night Wolf was poised above it all, silent. Waiting. Her gun bumped against her side, but even if it hadn't been useless, the thought of reaching for it never occurred to her.

All around was the charnel – the bodies, the remains. The gnawed remnants of the unchosen; the Styr fallen in defence of their master, the drones cut down before they could fulfil the destiny forced upon them.

Four Styr were left, standing guard. They advanced, stepping aside to let her pass, then closed ranks again, against anyone who might come through to save her.

Nobody come. Nobody try. It's not worth it. I'm not. It's better this way.
The Night Wolf settled slowly, laying itself down on the cavern floor. It didn't need to go anywhere; she was coming to it.

Shapes flickered in the Night Wolf's glow. A man and a child. Belinda and Frank. If they spoke she couldn't hear them, of course; the Sound drowned them out. And they were in silhouette against the glow, so she couldn't see their faces; couldn't tell if they stood in warning or welcome.

It didn't matter now; none of it did. She'd done all she could; others would have to carry on now. Now that all control was surrendered, the path to an ending set, all she could feel, at the last, was relief.

*

Gevaudan didn't have the Sound to guide him, but he had his sight – even in the dark – and his memory of the route they'd taken, and soon he was running; it didn't take him long to find the glow seeping up from the cathedral chamber. As he ran towards it, shapes appeared to blot the light out.

Styr. Still, silent, their gunmetal bodies glinting dully with the light from the chamber, eyeholes staring at him.

Even a Grendelwolf would struggle against these, so Gevaudan kept running; in fact he speeded up, flinging himself headlong at the Styr from a few feet away. They crashed to the ground and him along with them. He rolled clear, across the rubble-littered floor, stood and ran. Up ahead, a tiny figure was nearing the vast, luminous shape above. Howls rang out at his back as the Styr pursued him, but that was of no importance, not now. All that mattered was preventing Helen from suffering the same fate as Thursday, as so many countless others.

He told himself it was only because she was a comrade, that he'd fight the same for her as for any of the others, that he felt no especial tenderness or affection towards her. And unwelcome though the knowledge was, he knew each claim to be a lie.

The bodies of the Styr the others had killed lay before him. And somewhere on the floor, the broken spear. One end of which would have a sharp point, and that all-important glyph. Gevaudan ran in, looking about, saw something that might have been –

A screeching howl behind him: Gevaudan whirled as the last four Styr ran in. They spread out around him in a rough semicircle, continued to spread apart, working to encircle him entirely. One by one, he saw holes appear in those faces that weren't faces, widening relentlessly to expose the lamprey sucker that itself resembled a ravening and endless scream.

Their posture shifted; almost in unison, they were starting to crouch. They'd leap together. Even he couldn't take them all at once, and once those rasping suckers where clamped to his skin it would only take one of them to eat their way through to something vital.

The Styr leapt.

And Gevaudan summoned the Fury. He drew his pistol, fired into a gaping mouth; the first of them fell. He tried to spin aside, out of their path, but one of them slammed into him, bringing him down in a tackle. His pistol flew away from him; it pinned him down, brought that sucker towards his face. He twisted, flung it aside, scrambled out from under and rolled as the other two shot towards him.

The Fury granted only seconds. No time to waste them reaching for a gun. The three Styr rushed him. Gevaudan sprang his claws and struck at an eye socket, driving two fingers in. An explosion of pain, but a screech and the Styr fell, dragging him. The others – he tore free, caught one by the arm as it slashed at him, then spun, flinging it headlong at the cavern wall twenty feet away. It hit with a brutal crunch and dropped like a sack of stones.

And then the last one landed on him.

It was on his back; his neck burned as acidic drool fell from that gaping, sucking crater of a mouth. *Get it off, get it off* –

Gevaudan realised he was roaring, maybe even screaming. Heaving, thrashing, trying to throw it loose. But it clung on fast, and there were only seconds of the Fury left.

Something glinted in the dirt, and Gevaudan remembered what he'd seen. He grabbed it, turned it so its sharpened point jutted upwards from his clenched fist, then struck backwards, hard, over his shoulder. There was a screech, a choking sound, and the weight fell off his back.

Gevaudan grabbed the haft of the broken spear and wrenched it from the Styr's throat. The acid in the thing's mouth... but no, it wiped off readily enough, and the spear point was intact. More importantly, so was the Hobsdyke Cross.

Yes. He had what he needed and turned towards the Night Wolf as the small figure up ahead fell to its knees before it.

And then he began to run.

The Fury surged through him now, stretching this last moment out and out as far as it would go. To run in as close as he could, to fling the weapon with all the strength and accuracy in him –

He leapt, landing in front of Helen. The Night Wolf writhed and shifted above him, with searchlight eyes blazing down at this odd new thing neither fully human nor Styr. Gevaudan drew back an arm to throw.

The Night Wolf's head swept down; those jaws gaped and those vast pale eyes filled the world. Gevaudan stumbled, dazed, and something seized him. A moment later, he was hurtling upwards.

The eyes. The Night Wolf's eyes were below him now. Something was wrapped around his waist; it felt like a cable but had the thickness of his arm. Looking down, he only caught the vaguest impression of its head. That was all he wanted. The jaws splitting into four parts, the eyes, the pricked ears – or were they horns? – and, writhing around the jaws like an animate beard, tentacles like those wrapped around him and drawing him down.

He wasn't afraid. That wasn't the right word. There wasn't a name for this. He was nothing to this thing; an insect, a food animal. Slightly bigger, perhaps; slightly stronger. Nothing more. Just food. Fear might be a part of it, perhaps, or terror, but there was a kind of awe, too. And beyond that, there was despair.

No. It could die; he still had the spear point clutched in one fist. But when he drew it back, another tentacle flew up and wrapped itself around his arm. The grip tightened; Gevaudan cried out and the spear point fell, tumbling down to the cavern floor.

He was shaking in its grip; the Fury had left him and what was left now felt all too human. Normally he'd be glad of that, some recapturing of his lost state, but not now.

A brittle chattering noise from below: the Night Wolf's vast shape twitched, and then the grip slackened. The head turned and Gevaudan saw; down below, Helen had struggled up onto her knees, her Sterling cradled in her arms, and was emptying the full magazine, screaming with rage, into the Night Wolf's side.

A pinprick, an insect bite; the head shifted, turning, the eyes returning to him. The tentacles' grip tightened, and they drew him down; the Night Wolf's jaws gaped open to receive him.

*

The Sterling was empty. Helen fumbled for a spare magazine, then stopped.

There'd been a noise a second ago. Metal hitting stone. Something had fallen, landed on the cavern floor. She looked, blinking in the silver glow.

And there it was: the spear point. She ran, seized it. The Sound swelled around her, beckoning her to listen, but she shook her head hard. Surrender would have been easy a minute ago, but not any more.

Up above, she heard Gevaudan cry out in agony.

The spear point was tiny measured against the Night Wolf's bulk. A needle, a pin: less threat even than her bullets. But Mordake had said it would be enough.

If he hadn't been lying; if he was right.

Nothing to lose: Helen ran forward, arms aloft, and struck downward, aiming at the join of two leathery plates of hide.

She missed and a struck a segment full-on, but the spear point punched through.

The Night Wolf roared, and she reeled from the force of it, falling. But already a stain grew from where the spear point had struck. It was the grey of brittle ash, and the Night Wolf's substance crumbled as it spread.

*

The Night Wolf's howling filled the chamber; the tentacles holding Gevaudan writhed and tightened. Ribs cracked. *So; this was it.* But then the tentacles opened, and he was falling.

The ground rushed up: he flailed, ran at the air, and then hit the cavern floor; he flipped, rolled. His head –

A blurred, dazed, moment, and then he was staring at the cavern. The silvery light was flickering, jagged and wild; in it, he caught glimpses of the Night Wolf's huge shape, whipping from side to side. Its body was sinking downwards. No, not sinking – *collapsing.* The ground thrummed, began to shake. Vibration, like a tuning fork.

It was howling; a million voices screeching, hissing, howling. Helen was screaming, her hands to her ears. His head throbbed, ached, swam. He managed to get up, swayed, would have fallen if Helen hadn't caught his arm. But nothing, bar some ribs, seemed broken.

Above, there was a sound like cracking ice. Splitting rock. Dust rained down, billowed up from the floor in choking clouds.

"We have to go," he shouted.

"No," she shouted. "Really?"

He hobbled for the exit; she propped him up, stayed with him. Behind them, the Night Wolf, howling.

Almost at the exit and a dark shape rose, staggering towards them; the Styr he'd flung into the cavern wall, not killed even by that, it seemed. But it was swaying, tottering; its lamprey mouth flared wide, blasting out a last screech, followed by a foam of blood and liquefying tissues that came bubbling out of its eye sockets too, before it stumbled sideways and then crashed to the floor.

"Come on, Gevaudan, for Christ's sake."

And then they were stumbling on, as close to running as he could get in his state, and he was smiling as they went despite himself, despite it all.

*

Mordake howled as he burst from the tunnel, yet again, into another false dawn of silvery light that returned him exactly to his starting point. The devil twin howled and cackled. It hadn't stopped; it would never stop. *Kill me. Kill me. Somebody. Please.*

He spun and ran back the way he came. There had to be a way. Had to be. Break the spell somehow. Had to –

A rumble, a groan, a shiver in the earth.

Dust pattered on his face, his hair. Mordake looked up and saw the stone ceiling above him crack and split.

Mordake hurled himself back towards the exit, trying to get clear, but the rocks were already falling, smashing down on him like the fury of a jealous god.

*

The first explosion rang out when they were about halfway back to the surface, or so Helen guessed. The tunnel shook, the floor jerking out from under her like a pulled rug: she almost fell, steadied herself against the wall. Streams of dust hissed from the ceiling; tiny torrents of pebbles fell and rattled down.

She'd nearly given in; nearly given in, and what would have happened then? But worst of all, she'd wanted to.

"Helen?"

A hand on her arm; she shook it off. She spun, expecting to see Frank and Belinda, but it was Gevaudan. He swayed, steadied himself against the cavern wall. Frank and Belinda were gone. For good, maybe? "I'm fine. Let's go."

"Please!" The cry came from a tunnel to the side. She turned, looked, and there he was: Mordake, the poor, monstrous bastard, legs crushed and trapped under the rubble of a fallen roof, an imploring hand stretched out towards her. "Please. You promised. Kill me."

A promise was a promise. And this would only take a second. Helen drew the gun, aimed it, cocked the hammer, but her finger was still closing round the trigger when another muffled explosion made the tunnels lurch, and as she fired the side-tunnel's roof collapsed completely. She thought she might have heard a scream from Mordake, but she couldn't be sure, and she'd never know, she realised, if her bullet had hit home.

"We have to go," Gevaudan was shouting in her ear.

"All right," she yelled, and they ran on.

*

She shinned up the rope still hanging from the hole in the concrete chamber's floor; Gevaudan, more stiffly, clambered out after her. A third muffled detonation sounded below and the floor split wider, cracks racing up the walls. They ran through the doorway into one of the seclusion chambers, and then out onto the parade ground, where the others were waiting.

"Helen!" Alannah, stepping forward, her arms round Danny, his round her.

And then came the final explosion: a brutal, percussive thud from deep underground. A gale of dust and a final dreadful, cheated, inhuman scream erupted from the pit below, blasting out through the Adjustment Chamber's doors and walls. With an ice-like cracking and splitting of stone and a squealing of tortured metal, the whole structure caved in and collapsed, falling back into the interior of the hill. The ground around it split, cracks racing outward; one of the sets of prefab blocks sagged alarmingly sideways. The hill shuddered. Then slowly the shudders died away, and it was still. And there was only the keen and whistle of the wind, and a thin high belltone in Helen's ears.

They exchanged glances as they sank down among the ruins; whatever danger came now, they needed, and had earned, a moment's rest. "Thanks," wheezed Helen. She coughed and spat dust; she could hardly hear herself.

"You're welcome," Gevaudan mouthed.

"I knew you'd come," she half-heard herself say, and was surprised to realise she meant it.

"Danny," she heard Alannah say, and turned to see the boy standing at the edge of the hole where the Adjustment Chamber had been. He looked back, smiled. "It's okay," he said, dug something out of his pocket and tossed it into the hole. To Helen it looked like dust and broken twigs, a couple of strips of rag, but it must have been more than that, surely?

Wakefield reached out, ruffled Scopes' hair; Scopes grinned back, ruffled Wakefield's. Trex slumped down and sat alone, gazing out into the pale afternoon. Danny went back to Alannah, knelt beside her, took her hands.

Gevaudan looked at Helen, and she looked back at him. Then he closed his eyes and sank back; Helen sat there and listened to the howl of the wind and crackle of flames as the belltone faded, amid the compound's wreckage and the reek of smoke and dust and of some other, unrecognised substance that had, like so much else, burned away.

10.

Her footsteps click on polished cobbles; edged in bone, the Black Road leads on and on into the endless night. And somewhere in the distance, the City is waiting.

The black stays black; no plain of ash swallows the Road, and she takes that for now as a good sign. But in the distance, there's something, drawing closer; a tiny white blur, growing steadily larger and more distinct.

At length, she's able to see what it is, or rather who; it's not one figure but a pair, one much smaller than the other, and of course she knews then who it is, who it has to be. She stops walking and folds her arms and waits; after a while, she sits. The Road is cold beneath her.

"Get up," said Frank at last, when they reach her.

"No," she says.

"Get up, Mummy," says Belinda.

Helen shakes her head.

"Then we'll take you," says Frank, and reaches out bird-claw hands.

She raises the gun and they stop.

"Put it down and come with us," Frank says.

"No."

"Mum-*mee*."

"No. I'm staying. I didn't kill you. Winterborn did."

"And how did that happen, Helen?"

A tear runs down her cheek, but she holds the gun steady. "I'm not coming with you, Frank. I'm sorry that you're dead, but…" at last she says the words "…I have a right to live."

"How can you say that? How can you?"

She doesn't answer. Frank and Belinda look at one another, then back at her. "You can't stay strong forever," Belinda says. "We'll come back."

Helen shrugs.

"All right," says Frank. "You remember our bargain. It's you or Winterborn."

"I'll bring you Winterborn. But I need time."

Frank's nostrils flare. "We grant you a season," he says. "We return in the spring."

Helen doesn't answer.

"Accept it, Mummy," Belinda says. "It's the most we'll grant you."

"All right," she says at last. "The spring."

Frank nods. Then he and Belinda turn and, hand in hand, disappear down the Black Road.

*

"Mum. Dad. Tom. Mandy."

Jarrett couldn't shout it any more. She was too out of breath. Couldn't see. Couldn't see in the NBC suit. Couldn't run either. She was drowning and floundering in it. Her hands rose and tore at the suit; she ripped the mask from her face, struggling free of it like a shed skin, kicked it loose and ran. Ahead, the High Street seemed to stretch on endlessly; rows of stone houses, bodies on the pavement, bodies in the road, wrapped and unwrapped. And in the distance she saw their retreating backs. Mum and Dad, holding hands, Tom, now carrying Amanda, and that lone, hated figure, a drab Pied Piper with a Sterling instead of a flute, leading them on... to drown in a river, or into some magic land inside a mountain?

She'd die, of course; she knew she'd die, exposed to the fallout like this. But her family – her family hadn't been dead when she'd seen them, or looked sick. Neither had Helen. Perhaps they'd stayed safe somewhere; perhaps the danger was past. Even if it wasn't, better death than living with her family's hate. If she could reach them she could talk to them, beg their forgiveness, try to explain. *I thought I was saving you. I did my duty. Did what I had to do. What had to be done. The greater good. I –*

And then the ground ahead of her was gone, and she was falling, flailing, a scream in her throat. A pit, she had time to realise, before she hit the ground. Bones cracked. She rolled over, crying out, screaming for help, but no one came.

The pit was wide and deep. How could she have missed it? Too busy gazing up the road, at what she'd been trying to reach. And now, here she was, on a bed of rubble and stone, in a pit of steep sheer rock, and –

Silhouettes appeared around the edge of the pit. Jarrett squinted. There was Mum. There was Dad. Tom. Mandy. She shouted up to them, held out her hands, but their faces were blank and expressionless. And then Mum bent down and picked something up; a shovel. She thrust it down and Jarrett heard it crunch into the earth. Then Mum raised it and flung earth and grit down on her.

Jarrett screamed. From all around came the crunch and bite of shovels in the earth; dirt and stones and worms rained down on her. She flailed to ward it off, saw Amanda picking up rocks to throw down on her. One hit her leg, another her face. She screamed again, helpless.

More rocks hit her; she fell back dazed. Earth and more earth fell on her, in impossible quantities and at impossible speed.

When she looked up again, she saw more figures around the crater. Mutants and rebels; Yan, Sheel, Shell. All shovelling dirt and hurling rocks. Her legs and lower body were already buried; one arm wasn't obeying her either, but she couldn't tell if that was because it was buried or broken. And still the earth and rocks rained down.

And above, at the edge of the grave, arms folded, looking down, a bitter smile on her face, she saw Helen.

Jarrett jerked awake with a muffled cry, biting at her wrist. Breathe. Breathe. Deep breaths in. Deep breaths out. Calm. Calm. And she lay there in the cold dark of midnight, alone and afraid and hating; hating above all.

*

The little cottage stood on the hillside, only a few hundred yards from the mill. It wasn't a great distance, but it was enough.

The windows were long gone; Gevaudan had tacked pieces of sacking over the holes. A fire burned in the grate; it kept out the worst of the winter chill. He'd cleared out the place and little by little it was becoming some sort of home. Enough, at least, for this.

Come the spring, he'd attend to the garden properly; grow some food, perhaps, or a few flowers. For now, there wasn't much to do. Except for this.

The sky was white, but the snow had stopped, just for now; a few flakes still clung to his long black hair and thick sweater as he knelt and swept the hard ground clear. When he'd done so, he laid half a dozen smooth pebbles, painted white, on the ground. Then he began stacking other rocks and pebbles atop them, from the pile beside them, till they were covered over and kept safe.

As he worked, Gevaudan heard soft footsteps inside the cottage; he didn't turn around. They stopped at the back door, which opened out into the garden. He felt her eyes on his back, but she didn't speak. Only when he'd laid the last pebble in place, completing the cairn, did he say "Hello, Helen."

A sigh. "I'll never be able to sneak up on you, will I?"

"Unlikely." He rose, brushing snow from his hands.

She leant against the doorframe, arms folded. "Aren't you cold?"

"Not unbearably. Even so…" he smiled. "So much for the predicted mild winter, eh?"

"Never believed them to begin with. Got something for you."

"Oh?"

"Inside."

He followed her in, wondering. She gestured to the kitchen table; on it was a wooden crate and his coat. "Alannah said the coat's her Christmas present to you. She put a lot of time in getting it fixed."

"So I see." Gevaudan picked the coat up; you could barely see the repairs. "That was good of her," he said at last.

"You saved Danny's life back at Hobsdyke. Helped save hers too, of course. Think that meant something to her."

Gevaudan hung the coat on a wall hook. "It's almost a shame to wear it," he said. "It hasn't looked this clean in a long time. And this?" The crate.

"That's from me."

The lid was loose; Gevaudan lifted it back. Inside were dozens of vials packed in straw. He lifted one out; the liquid inside was an almost luminescent green. "The Goliath serum?"

"I keep my promises," she said, not meeting his eyes.

"Yes." Foolish to think it'd be anything else from her. Even so, it was never pleasant to be reminded that your life was effectively in another's gift. Especially someone who'd do whatever she had to for her cause. "Which reminds me, I have Christmas gifts of my own to give out."

From under the table he took a sack. "This is for Danny. It belonged to my daughter's husband"

Helen touched the leather belstaff jacket. "Gevaudan, that's beautiful. Are you sure – "

413

"I've spent too long hoarding things and trying to cling on to the dead past. I'd rather someone put this stuff to good use."

"Okay."

"I haven't much to offer you or Alannah. But I expect you both read from time to time. So. For Alannah, a copy of *Great Expectations* – I seem to remember her saying she enjoyed Dickens – and this is for you."

He studied her face closely as she turned over the leather-bound hardback edition of Shakespeare's sonnets and ruffled through the yellowed pages. Did she see the inscription on the title page: *To Gevaudan. Happy Xmas, Love, Jo?* He couldn't read her expression. "Thanks," she said at last. She looked around. "You've settled in okay, then?"

"Yes. I think it's better that I'm here."

"Can't say I particularly like the mill either." She put the book down, rubbed her hands together for warmth. Gevaudan blinked; for a moment, he thought he glimpsed two blurred shadows standing behind her. A man and a child. Then they were gone. From nowhere, his own words came back to him: *There's a devil on her back.*

"I know. But it's probably just as well for everybody else's peace of mind that I'm not there."

"Gevaudan, don't be silly. You're our ally." But even she sounded as if she was trying to convince herself.

"But I'm still a Grendelwolf."

She looked down. "Yes." There was silence. "I'd better get back," she said. "Lots to do."

"Yes."

"Don't forget, you've – "

"Got a meeting to go to later. Yes. I hadn't forgotten, Helen. You can rely on me."

"Yes." She looked up at him, half-smiled. "Of course."

But she didn't sound sure.

*

Helen trudged back along the hill, slowing as she neared the mill's looming bulk. As she'd said to Gevaudan, she didn't like the place. Perched on a hillside above a wide valley with a view that stretched out for miles, it felt too visible. Exposed.

Then again, the Refuge had been below ground, and that hadn't saved them. Maybe, after so many years in constant motion, it was the very idea of a fixed base that the Reapers could find and destroy. But it and the surrounding buildings served, at least for now, as a rallying point, and it was easy to defend – not that a Jennywren attack out here was considered likely, but with the Jennywrens you played safe.

Light machine guns pointed out of the windows. Some of the gunners were Foxes, newly trained; others were from groups of ex-rebels who'd been living in the Wastelands. Whether any of Darrow's rebels had escaped the carnage in the city, there was still no word.

"Hoy! Crazy ginger!"

Helen had to grin. "Hello, Wakefield."

The lithe little Fox warrior strode up. She carried her spear over one shoulder; two ducks hung down from it, tied by the feet. Helen nodded. "Been out hunting?"

"Few of us. We have enough for the feast now."

"That's good." There was silence. "And you?" asked Helen. "You're well?"

"Yes."

"I'm sorry about – "

"What?"

"Bleach. Your friends."

Wakefield shrugged. "Warriors. All warriors know must die one day, might die any day."

"You don't... blame me?"

"Why? We chose. And you right; Reapers come, Jennywrens come. For us, no choice. Fight them or we die. No other way."

"No." Not the same as those others who could at least choose slavery and survival. One less load of guilt to bear, though what she had was enough.

"Saw travellers on road."

"Travellers?"

"In landcruiser."

Helen went still. "Reapers?"

Wakefield shook her head. "One was old, old man. Thin. Grey hair, like winter sky before a storm."

"Darrow."

"Who?"

"Sounds like a friend of mine."

"Good news then," said Wakefield.

"Yes." Helen forced a smile. "Yes."

She looked out across the snow, remembering *we grant you a season* and wondering when the wintry white would melt away to reveal the Black Road again.

*

"All right. Ready. Take aim. Wait. Hold it… hold it… All right. Fire."

A brief, spattering storm of shots in the cold winter air. The row of lined-up targets twitched; snow spurted from the ground where stray rounds hit.

"Cease fire," Danny shouted. "All right. Make safe. Make your weapons safe, then put them down."

Scopes moved along the line of prone figures, checking the weapons as Danny went forward to inspect the targets. Most of them, spread out on sacking mats in the snow, were Wastelanders more used to hunting with spear, knife or throwing stick than firearm. Some of those weapons would come in handy for stealth work – Wakefield had promised to teach Danny and the others their use – but in direct battle with the Reapers, the tribesfolk would need guns to stand even a chance.

"Fucksake, Trex," Danny called. "Time you can hit owt you're firing at, we'll have no fuckin' ammo left." Trex scowled. "You're pulling up and to the left: watch for that, all right? Pin!" A small, nut-brown Crow tribeswoman looked up. "You must've have blown off ten, twelve rounds there. Start workin' on your burst control." Pin nodded. "Good shootin', though." Pin smiled.

Danny moved on to the next target. As he did, he saw another line of figures in the snow beyond. He knew them all: Nadgers, Ashton, Nikki, Hinge, Thursday. Nadgers was crying. Danny closed his eyes, reopened them; they were gone.

So: that was ghostlighting. That's what it was to become a man.

"Danny?" he turned. Helen stood alongside the firing range. "Got a second?"

"Sure." He crunched through the snow towards her. "Scopes, take over here."

"Will do."

*

In the lee of the hill, out of the wind, on an upper slope free of snow, Alannah ran.

Breath went in and out. Sweat trickled down her face; a cloth band tied round her forehead kept it out of her eyes. A holstered pistol beat time against her hip; it wasn't wise to venture out unarmed. Danny'd never let her hear the end of it. *Danny – no, best not thinking of him now. Just run. Focus on the run.* Her feet hit the packed earth and hard rock, didn't slide; she kept her balance, ran on.

This was still Wastelander territory; the desire-lines carved onto the hillside by generations of walkers hadn't fallen into disuse or become overgrown. On this section of slope you could go from one to another and circle round and round. Every day for the past fortnight, Alannah had been doing that. She stumbled, steadied herself with a clutched handful of coarse grass, ran on.

At times the aches and pains in her legs faded away and it almost felt like she was flying; a gull or a crow, circling round and round the hill. She'd be sore afterwards, but that'd pass.

She was still building the number of laps up; later she'd try and find a way of timing them. As the winter got worse, she'd probably have to exercise inside the mill, but when she did it would be in a room with a window, facing the sun.

The sky was white; she forced herself to look at it. Looking up the hill, she saw a silhouette. Danny. He started down towards her. She gritted her teeth, kept going.

What do you want, Danny? I don't need a crutch to lean on any more. Don't need anyone but myself, or soon I won't. I'll walk in the light like anyone else, and protect myself as needs be.

Harsh, she knew; his puppy-dog eyes with their echoes of Stephen, not understanding things had changed – *she'd* changed – made her harsher still. He'd stopped, a couple of yards above the path; she ran past him twice, even though the first should have been the end of her final lap for the day, just to show him.

Finally she went past him a third time, but by then she was slowing, letting herself come to a halt. She bent, hands on knees, breathing deep. The grass rustled with his footsteps as he came towards her. *Don't touch me, Danny. Don't put a hand on me, please. I don't need to be cuddled or comforted, not anymore.*

"Alannah?"

"What?" It came out as a gasp. She took deep breaths. "What do you want, Danny?"

A moment's silence. She wouldn't look at him, the uncomprehending boyish hurt she knew his face would show. "Helen sent us."

"What?" She looked across at him now. She'd seen him training the new recruits, looking straight and steady and a man; now he had his hands in his pockets and was fidgeting foot to foot, a boy again. "What for?"

"Looks like Darrow's here."

Alannah went still, then straightened up.

"You want your towel?"

"Yeah. And my jacket."

He handed the first over. She rubbed herself dry, then took the jacket and pulled it on. "Let's go, then."

*

All around the village at the foot of the hill, there was a double wall; a palisade of cut-down trees, and a stone wall built from packed and bound rubble. There was a single gate through each, and the battered landcruiser stopped at first one, and then the other. By the time it rolled to a halt in the middle of the mill's forecourt, with a final hiss of steam like some wounded, wearied beast about to give up the ghost, Helen, Danny, Alannah and Gevaudan were all ready and waiting.

Danny adjusted the jacket the Grendelwolf had given him, zipped it up. It felt nice. Comfy. Kept out the cold. Hadn't known what to say when Helen'd given it to him. Still didn't know what to say to Gevaudan, not that he'd really had a chance yet.

The 'cruiser's frame seemed to creak under its load; it was heavily laden, with about a dozen kids ram-jammed into the back. They started hopping down. Danny only recognised two of his crew; Mackie, his arm still in a sling, and Cov, plus Filly from Ashton's. They were thin and pale and dirty; looked tired and sick, with long-range stares in their eyes.

Darrow got out from behind the wheel. Flaps climbed out of the passenger seat and looked around at them, a Sterling cradled in her hands. She wasn't marked, but she had the same stare as the rest; cut right through Danny and anything else she looked at.

"Roger." Alannah went to Darrow and threw her arms around him. He hugged her back, but it was a weak, tired thing, without strength. He patted her back and let her go. He looked tired, thought Danny; he looked old. "Hello, Alannah. You're looking well."

She tried to smile. Her eyes were bright. Danny wanted to take her hands like he'd used to, but she didn't let him do that any more, didn't like it. "Feeling a lot better."

"That's good. Helen."

"Darrow." She took a step towards him, faltered; he didn't move towards her. "Darrow, is this… I mean, are these – "

"They're all that's left, Helen." Darrow's eyes were dead. "This is it."

"I'm sorry."

"Was it worth it?"

"We destroyed Tindalos."

"Was it worth it?"

"I don't know," she said at last.

He nodded tiredly. "We never do. Hello, Danny."

"Darrow." He stepped forward, stopped in front of the man, didn't know what to do. "You all right?"

"Not particularly. Is there anywhere… anywhere these can go?"

"Course there is. There's – " But Danny couldn't think of anywhere.

"I'll take them," said Gevaudan. He nodded. "Darrow."

Darrow nodded back. "Shoal."

"This way," Gevaudan said. None of the kids moved. They all looked to Flaps, and she didn't move, just stared at the Grendelwolf.

"You're safe," he told her. "I won't harm any of you. I'm on your side."

Flaps pursed her lips, looked sideways at Darrow.

"Go with him," he said at last.

Flaps looked back at Gevaudan, then the other kids, and nodded. "Come on," she said at last; her voice was hoarse and gravelly, as if she'd spent a long time screaming. Gevaudan turned and led off; she followed, and the rest of the weary, ragged band of kids trailed, stumbling, after her.

Helen went to Darrow; after a moment, she put a hand on his arm. He looked down at it, then up at her. For a moment, he looked as if he'd pull away, but then he forced an empty smile and patted her hand. "Merry Christmas, Helen."

"I'm sorry," she said.

"I know."

"Let's get you fixed up," she said. Alannah took Darrow's other arm, and they walked him towards the mill. Danny stood and watched them go, not sure what to say or do, as the first white feathers of snow began falling from the bleak, dirty sky.

*

At Central Command, Winterborn leant back in his chair and watched the snow drift by his office window. It calmed him, a little; bought him a little distance from the rage and panic that boiled up in him and threatened to overwhelm all judgement.

"Nothing," he said at last.

"I'm afraid not, sir," Jarrett said. "The rebels were very thorough. Practically the whole base is gone: there's just a big bloody hole in the hilltop where it used to be."

Winterborn pinched the bridge of his nose, released a long breath.

"Is there no way we can salvage any of it, sir?" Jarrett asked.

"Not without Mordake's notes. And he was the only one who understood it all, anyway."

Jarrett bit her lip. "On the bright side, sir, the rebel problem in the city is broken. It took them years to build up any kind of network to pose a credible threat, and it wasn't enough. We've smashed it, and the reprisal killings are working. None of the population are going to support the rebels now."

"Unless the rebels do something to make them believe they could win." Winterborn watched the falling snow. "And the real threat's not here, Colonel; it's out there in the Wastelands. In the places we don't control."

"Then that's where I'll turn my attention next, sir. With your permission, of course."

"Of course."

"It's something of a speciality of mine."

"I know," smiled Winterborn. "I was going to say, after all, that the responsibility for clearing the Wastelands once and for all lies with you," the smile faded, "since Project Tindalos can no longer offer us that."

"Give me the resources I need to do the job, sir," said Jarrett, "and I'll clear them, all right. Call it my Christmas present to you. Although it may be a bit belated."

"Oh?"

"I don't want to leave anything to chance this time, sir." No, no more chances. Helen had to die; till that happened, nothing else mattered. "For now, we'll continue normal clearance operations as planned, step up defences around reclaimed sectors, prevent the rebels from causing more damage."

"How will that stop them?"

"That won't. But it will buy us time, and it'll let them think they're gaining ground. Meanwhile we build up information on how they're organising and operating, so we can devise a single counterstrike to finish them off."

Winterborn smiled. "I think I may have chosen well with you after all, Jarrett."

"Thank you, sir."

"Thank me when you've won, Colonel, not before."

"Yes, sir."

"Don't you have an appointment to go to?"

"Oh, yes, sir. I hadn't forgotten."

"Well, you'd best set off now. It's a long way. And it gets dark early this time of year."

*

Gevaudan inched back the sacking over the window and peered out. Behind the blanketing cloud and the flurrying snow, the sun was the vaguest of blurs, but he could just make it out, starting to sink. It was maybe an hour or so after the noon. Soon it'd be time to leave.

He was about to let go of the sacking when he saw a small, huddled figure, dark against the hillcrest's white. It rocked to and fro, and when he listened, a faint sobbing was carried to him on the wind.

He released the sacking; the shadows inside the cottage folded round him. Better, most likely, to pretend he hadn't seen it. Everyone out here had something to grieve; the little shape on the hilltop, he suspected, more than many others. Best to leave it.

Outside, the wind gave a bitter howl. He sighed, pulled the coat on and went out into the snow.

The little redheaded fighter who'd come in with Darrow huddled against the stub of a tree. Snow clung to her jacket and hair. Her face trembled; her lips had a bluish tinge.

"Are you all right?"

"Piss off," she muttered. Her teeth were chattering.

"Sorry." He crouched. "Can't do that."

"Why not?"

"It's rather cold out here. You may have noticed."

She gave him a look, then went to gazing back across the snow-blanketed hills.

"I'll put it another way; what is it they call you again?"

"Flaps."

"Dare I ask why?" She didn't answer. "Flaps, if you stay out here you'll die."

"Good. 'S what I want."

"How can you say that?"

"How can I – " Her voice choked and she turned to face him. "They're all dead, you fucking freak. Everyone. Mary. Rest of me crew. They're all. Fucking. Dead. And I fucking see 'em. They're fucking everywhere." She shook her head. "I've done me bit. Got the others somewhere safe. Now I just wanna stop seeing 'em."

"I understand."

"Fuck off."

"I do. Your crew were like your family, yes?" Flaps nodded. "The ones who raised you, who you grew up with. Well… I lost *my* family." Flaps opened her mouth. "And before you say it, I was human once. Just like you. It was before I became what I am. I lost my wife, my daughter, and my grandchildren."

"Grandchildren? Fuck *off*."

"You really need to broaden your vocabulary, young lady."

"You what?"

"I rest my case. But yes, I'm older than I look. I wasn't particularly young when the War began. It's one of the things about being a Grendelwolf. You don't age. But you do ghostlight. Which I'm guessing you've started to do. Yes?"

The anger went out of Flaps' face; she nodded, lips trembling, weeping. Her voice was strangled. "How? How do you keep going? It fuckin' hurts. It hurts so fuckin' much."

"I know."

"How? How do you…?"

"It's like an illness, I suppose. You have to let it run its course. But there are ways of easing the pain, a little."

"Like?"

"Well, there's one that worked for me. If you want to come back to the cottage I'll show you."

Flaps scowled. "Try owt dodgy, and I'll cut your rogers off, pal."

Gevaudan had to smile. "I can promise you that your virtue will be safe with me."

"I'm not worried 'bout that, I'm worried 'bout you tryin' to get up me chuff."

Now Gevaudan laughed. "And I promise I won't do that either. Well? Or are you determined to freeze to death out here?"

She was too cold and stiff to get up normally; she caught his hand and he pulled her upright.

"I'm going to have to trust you," he said as they went. "I'll have to leave shortly, but you can stay, if you think it'll help. I think I can even offer you a cup of coffee."

"What's that?"

Gevaudan smiled sadly down at her. "You'll see."

*

Later, in the former church hall that served as a canteen, volunteers from the kitchens moved from table to table, collecting the empty dishes. Helen and Alannah pushed their plates away, leant back and looked at one another.

"What do you think?" asked Helen.

"I think we're probably best not knowing whatever kind of bird we were actually eating there," Alannah said.

"Might be swan."

"God. Used to be illegal to eat that."

"Really?"

"Yeah. You don't remember that?"

"No."

"Times change. Happy Christmas, by the way."

"Thanks. You too."

"As to what I think," Alannah said. "I think you've done a pretty good job of getting everyone together here. *Keeping* them together will be the tough part. As for how they'll do against the Reapers, we'll just have to see."

"Pretty much what I thought. Come on."

They got up; the tables were pushed back.

"Now what?"

"Dancing's about to start."

"Oh god."

"Get into the festive spirit, girl."

"Watch who you're calling girl." Across the hall, an old – *very* old, Alannah thought – record player crackled, and music started playing. "Bloody hell. I know this one. My *mum* used to listen to it."

"Bloody hell."

"Could do with some live music."

"It's not big among the tribes; they've been a bit busy staying alive. And it wasn't high on Darrow's list of priorities either."

Alannah glanced across the hall; Darrow was slumped in his chair, against the wall, gazing at the floor. "Shouldn't joke about that," she said.

"No."

"Where's Gevaudan, then? Wouldn't have thought he'd miss dinner. Or a chance to play a few tunes."

"He's making a small delivery for me."

"On Christmas Eve? Bloody slavedriver."

Mackie moved onto the dancefloor, shuffled his feet about and looked around, grinning stupidly at the others. A couple more of Darrow's survivors followed him, then half a dozen Wastelanders, including Wakefield and Trex. The music played on; some of the dancers paired up and danced together.

"Heads up," Helen murmured, smiling, then moved away.

Alannah looked up. Danny shuffled over. He looked like a boy again.

"Hiya," he said.

"Hi, Danny."

He held out a hand. "D'you wanna dance?"

"No. I don't think that would be a good idea."

"Aw, come on. Just give it a go. We could – "

Anger flared. "*No*, Danny."

He dropped his gaze, stepped back, lowered his hand and walked away, head down.

"What did you do that for?" Helen had come back over.

"I've been using him as a crutch, Helen. I'm not going to be dependent on anyone else, again."

"You don't have to be. Don't think that's what he was after."

"Yeah, well, that's not on the cards either. I'm old enough to be his mother."

"Wouldn't stop most people these days."

"I'm not most people."

"True. You've been a bit hard on him, though."

"It's for the best, Helen," said Alannah, thinking *Stephen*, thinking of spiky hair and puppy-dog eyes, of warm hands holding hers.

"If you say so."

Alannah ignored her, got up and crossed the floor towards Darrow. She'd dance with him; just a dance and nothing more, to take his mind off his own pain. After all he'd done for her, it was the least she owed him.

*

On the hill, it was twilight, slipping slowly into dusk. The snowfall had slackened off; a few flakes still drifted down, but Flaps didn't notice.

She could write; it wasn't her strongest skill, but Mary – *Mary* – had taught her. So it was her name she wrote last.

The pebbles lay by the fire, round and white like eggs. The white enamel paint had dried quickly in the heat; now, with a thin little brush, she drew the last name, then put the pebble down to dry.

She cleaned the brushes and put away the pots the way the Grendelwolf had shown her, washed her hands in a bowl of freezing water. Then she gathered up the pebbles and went outside.

A couple of yards from the cairn he'd built, she scraped away the snow and neatly, carefully arranged the names of her dead. Mary, Lelly, Pipe, Tello and all the rest. The other stones were already gathered to hand; she stacked them up till the white stones were hidden.

There was something the Grendelwolf had muttered before; a line from a poem, he'd said. She murmured it now: "Upon a little grave, under a white hill, throw a rock and bow your heads." It sounded right.

She put the last rock in place and sat back on her heels. There. That was all. She cast about for something else to do, but there was nothing. It was done.

She stood and went back through the cottage, let herself out and locked the door behind her, hiding the key where Gevaudan had shown her, then walked back along the hillside, toward the mill.

She felt – she wasn't sure – not *better* exactly, but as if she'd done something. Gevaudan said he'd find a stone to add to the cairn whenever the sadness came, so she hadn't made the pile too high; she reckoned she'd be back a lot in the days to come.

As she descended towards the church hall, she saw someone stomping out of there, head down. Something about him – the spiky hair, the high-collared leather jacket – was familiar, and then it clicked. "Danny."

He turned, faced. "Oh. Heya, Flaps."

Silence. Snow ticked down between them.

"How you doing?" he asked.

She sniffed, shrugged.

"Yeah," he said.

Inside the hall was warm light, music, laughter. Flaps half-yearned towards it and half-wanted to flee it. Danny took a step toward her. "You wanna have a dance?"

"No," she said. "Don't fancy that."

"Kay." He looked away.

"I can think of something better we could do."

He looked up, smiled. She smiled back. "Know anywhere we can go?"

"I reckon," he said.

She took his hand and led him away. It was Christmas; she didn't want to be cold and alone. Warmth and wild fucking; between that and the pebbles, she'd keep the pain away for a little while.

*

Around the same time, two Jennywren landcruisers pulled into a defile at the edge of the Wasteland, a few short miles from where REAP Hobsdyke had stood. The heavy .50 cals sniffed the air; the Jennywrens bailed out, rifles aiming.

Jarrett stepped clear, hand on the pistol at her hip. The sky was the same thick dull grey, bordering on black. The snowstorm had passed over here, for the most part; the odd last, stray flake still drifted down.

"Anything?" she said.

"Nothing, ma'am."

She nodded.

"Colonel Jarrett," said a voice.

She spun; Gevaudan Shoal stood not six feet away. Guns swung towards him; he eyed the Jennywrens contemptuously, then returned his attention to her. "What part of 'one-on-one meeting' was unclear?" he asked.

"Did you seriously expect me to come out here on my own?"

Gevaudan shrugged. "Here," he said. "This is for your Commander." He set an ancient carrier bag down. "Salvaged from the cameras at Hobsdyke. Video footage of what happened when Project Tindalos achieved some measure of success."

"And what's that meant to achieve?"

"We're at war, Colonel Jarrett. Make no mistake about that. However, there are some weapons that shouldn't be used, even in a battle to the death. This is one of them."

"Sounds like you're afraid of it, Shoal."

"Which should tell you something, Colonel. Project Tindalos wasn't just a threat to your enemies. It can't be controlled. It's an enemy to anything remotely human." Gevaudan allowed himself a wintry smile. "Even me."

"So you've thrown your lot in with her."

"Let's just say that I became more choosy about the company I kept."

"I'd watch yourself with her, Gevaudan," Jarrett said. "She's out for revenge, nothing more. She'll do whatever she has to to get it. And if you think that doesn't include shafting you, you're a fool."

"You, of course, are very different."

Jarrett flinched. "Yes. Yes. I have duty." And nightmares that would plague her unto death while Helen lived.

"Which covers a multitude of sins in its own right."

"She'll say anything, do anything to get you on her side. The ends justify the means for her."

"Careful, Jarrett. The pot calling the kettle black is always amusing. I may rupture something."

"What's she going to build, Shoal? What can she build? Hm? This is all we have left. Think she's got any real plan? What? A vision? Some mad utopia? Those kill more people than any Jennywrens could."

"In your pursuit of a genetic utopia, you mean?" Gevaudan sighed. "I've done what I came to do, Jarrett. You've been warned. There've been enough resurrections this winter: let Project Tindalos stay dead."

The Grendelwolf turned, and began clambering back up the defile wall towards the top. The wind blew; snow or sleet stung Jarrett's eyes. She flinched, blinked, wiped them; when she looked again, the slope was empty.

"Where – " she turned to the nearest Jennywren. "Where did he go? Where the hell did he go?"

"I don't… I didn't – " the man blinked. "He just… vanished."

"Just vanished," spat Jarrett. "Useless bloody idiot. Didn't anybody *see?*"

But nobody had.

"Useless." She shook her head, then looked up, scanned the slopes of the gorge. Nothing. There was nothing.

"She's using you!" Jarrett shouted. One last throw of the dice; he must see that. All people were rotten to the core when you came down to it; the only variation was in the flavour of their corruption. "Shoal? She's using you!"

There was no answer; there was only the wind. The gorge, in the twilight, suddenly seemed very cold and alone, its dark, empty slopes filled with the menace of a myriad unseen, watching eyes. Jarrett swallowed hard; fear was an unfamiliar emotion to her, and she hated it. Almost as much as she hated Helen.

"We're done here," she said. "Let's go."

They clambered back into the landcruisers. The engines hissed and clanked into life; Jarrett kept her hand on her gun long after the vehicles had pulled clear of the gorge.

And in the gorge, the minutes passed. Flurries of snow returned; the twilight deepened. Finally, one shadow stirred amongst the others that lengthened among the boulders, bushes and scree.

Gevaudan stood on the slope and watched the landcruisers recede, vanishing into the distance. He was still; only his long black coat and long black hair, flapping about him in the wind, moved. His long, sombre face remained impassive, the yellow wolf's eyes hooded; what went on behind them, no one else, even if there'd been another present, could have told.

The wind howled, and the night came on.

And Gevaudan Shoal turned away and walked into the deepening night, where Helen Damnation, and the devil on her back, awaited him.

THE END

ACKNOWLEDGEMENTS

This story's been twenty years in the telling, and in that time it's been a screenplay, an unfinished novel, a radio drama and now, finally, the first in a four-book sequence. It, and I, have had a lot of help along the way.

The first and biggest thanks of all goes to Anna Torborg, Emma Barnes and Rob Jones at Snowbooks for agreeing to put this monster out there.

As if writing a book isn't enough fun, the joys of trying to find it a home can feel like banging your head against a brick wall, and it's driven better writers than me to despair. At times like that, a good review or even a kind word can mean everything. Any reader, writer, reviewer or blogger who's chipped in in that regard – Raven Dane, James Everington, Jim McLeod, Ross Warren, Graeme Flory, Andy Angel, Paul Campbell and Adam Nevill among others – has my heartfelt gratitude.

Sarah Pinborough and Paul Finch offered good, hard-headed advice about the publishing and agenting sides of the business, and a host of commissioning editors and agents offered words of encouragement – thank you Lee Harris, Jon Oliver, Jenni Hill,

Gillian Redfearn and Piers Blofeld. Thanks, too, to Fox Spirit's Adele Wearing (I owe you one, Miss Honeybadger) and to Graeme Reynolds at Horrific Tales – (likewise, mucker.) Sharon Ring proofed and edited the MS to clean up the worst of my punctuation blunders (I'm a semicolon addict, I admit it here and now.)

Simon Coxon-Jones read over the manuscript, particularly the battle scenes, and assured me I hadn't screwed anything up – not too badly, anyway.

The music of Ladytron, Apocalyptica and (as always) Dark Sanctuary kept me going.

Mark West, beta reader supreme, read and critiqued the MS before I started inflicting it on agents and publishers.

Indirect thanks are also owed to the following actors, who shaped the development of the characters when I was drafting the unproduced radio script: Bronwyn Ebdon, without whom Helen wouldn't have been Helen, Lynn Roden (Alannah), and Andy Conroy (Danny).

Cate Gardner has been an unfailing source of love, faith and support over the past three years, in what were often trying times for us both. As well as also reading the book before it went out in search of a home. Thank you, my love. Even if you did threaten to elope with Gevaudan.

Cate's Mum Pauline read the novel's manuscript as well; a hard woman to impress, she liked it a lot. I'm just sorry she didn't get to see *Hell's Ditch* in print. She'll be sorely missed.

A SNEAK PEEK FROM

THE DEVIL'S HIGHWAY

BOOK TWO OF THE BLACK ROAD

COMING SOON FROM SNOWBOOKS

PROLOGUE

The heart of winter, and all the world was snow.

In the howling force-ten gale, it piled inch-thick on the landcruiser's plating; the wipers fought in vain to clear the windscreen, and the headlights' glow, alone in the night, showed only a whirling white vortex up ahead.

"Christ," moaned Walters. It was pretty enough to watch; that was what made it dangerous. The swirling patterns hypnotised you, your mind wandered – and out here, that was enough. Their fuel was dwindling, and if the 'cruiser's boiler went cold, so would they. "The hell did this come from?"

Patel scowled, shook his head. "Fucking MetSec. Couldn't

predict steam rising off me piss."

"Fuck-all chance of *that* right now. Where *are* we?"

Patel adjusted the radio. "Sunray from Delta Oscar Four, do you copy? Over."

Static was their only answer. Somewhere in it, Walters thought he heard voices, but he couldn't make out any words.

He glowered at Patel. "Join the Jennywrens, you said. Better pay, you said. Thanks a fucking bunch for that one."

"There," said Patel. "There's a road, going up."

"So?"

"High ground. We make for it, try for a signal. It's our best chance."

"Not much of one." Even so, Walters steered the 'cruiser up the worn track.

*

"This is Delta Oscar Four. Any REAP Command personnel receiving, please respond."

The static squealed and hissed. Patel scowled and threw down the mic.

Outside was only darkness, half-hidden by flurrying white; no light but their own. And any other lights would probably be those of tribesfolk or rebels: as lethal as the cold, but more painful.

Snow thickened on the windscreen; the boiler's pressure gauge sank another notch. Walters' teeth chattered. He huddled in his seat for warmth. Tired.

Patel's head was nodding, his eyelids drooping shut. Walters closed his eyes.

"Delta Oscar Four, do you receive? Acknowledge. Over."

Walters grunted, blinking. Patel sat up straight, rubbing his eyes.

"I say again. Delta Oscar Four, do you receive? Acknowledge. Over."

An ugly voice. Grating, harsh, almost metallic. But a voice all the same. "Get it for Christ's sake," said Walters.

Patel grabbed the radio mic. "Delta Oscar Four here. Over."

"What's your status?"

Patel glanced at Walters. "We're a GenRen patrol – out on recon when this storm blew up. Unable to establish contact with unit, and our location is unknown."

"Is your compass functional?"

On the dashboard, the compass needle swung and spun. "Not very."

"All right. Stay on the line. We're triangulating your signal now."

"Understood." Patel licked his lips. "Who am I talking to?"

"A friend," said the voice. "That's all I'll say for now. Never know who's listening. Now: hit your transmit button every ten seconds till told otherwise. Copy?"

"Understood." Patel looked at Walters. He counted to ten, pressed *transmit*, held it down, released it. "What d'you reck?"

"Long-range fieldbase." Walters fumbled out a pack of Monarchs, took one, offered another to Patel. "Somewhere out in bandit country. Not gonna risk giving owt about *that* away to the rebels, are they?"

Cigarette smoke filled the cabin. Patel pressed *transmit* again. "Wouldn't break radio silence for two stragglers, though, would they?"

"Maybe not ordinary Reapers, but GenRen, like us? Base like that'd have to be a GenRen op too."

"Even so."

"Is that ten?"

"Dunno." Patel pressed *transmit* again.

"Delta Oscar Four?" said the voice.

"We're here."

"We've triangulated your signal and have your position."

"Where are we?"

"Can't tell you, I'm afraid. Because then if I guide you here, and the wrong people are listening, they'll find us. For the same reason, I can't give you my ident."

"Secret base," said Walters. "Told you."

"What I *can* do is direct you to us from where you are now. In the meantime, just call me Ned."

Patel looked at Walters. "No call sign, no details, and we're driving blind. Could be a trap."

Walters' teeth chattered. "Got a better plan?"

Patel picked up the mic. "Okay, Ned," he said. "Standing by."

*

An hour later, Walters thought Patel could be right. Fuel was running low, and the 'cruiser's boiler pressure starting to inexorably dip. And all either of them had seen, so far, beyond the white and whirling snow, were odd glimpses of ruins and twisted woodland.

But then the wind dropped, and the buildings loomed out of the night. Little stone cottages, shops, a church. A village of some kind – empty, abandoned, by the look of it. What got him most about it was how well-preserved it all was: most still had their roofs, even glass in their windows. Walters had only the haziest memories of the world before the War, but he remembered places like this, just about.

As they passed the church, a light flashed – high above them, on a hill.

"Delta Oscar Four, I can see your lights," said Ned. "You should have us in visual range by now."

"That's affirmative," Patel said. "Can see a light shining on higher ground."

"That's us. Carry on out of the village, and you'll find the road to the base."

"Understood."

The village's buildings fell away from them, and the full fury of the snowstorm blew across the exposed ground to buffet the landcruiser.

"We're nearly out," said Walters. The boiler pressure was almost at the red line as he forced the 'cruiser up the hill. The headlights were dimming too; the battery was failing. He focused on the light above them: the beam shone out over the hill's brow.

"Just a little further," said the voice. "You're nearly there, Delta Oscar Four. Nearly there."

And in that moment, the light went out.

"Ned?" Patel said. "Ned, you still there? Ned!"

But the only sound was static.

"The fuck just happened?" Patel asked.

"Maybe the generator blew a gasket or something. Long as they've got walls, heat and shelter, I couldn't give two shits."

The landcruiser's innards groaned and clanked. "Come on," snarled Walters. "Come fucking *on*."

"There," said Patel.

A pair of gates stood open in a chain-link fence, but no one came to close them when Walters steered the landcruiser through. Patel climbed out and blundered through the snow to drag them shut; Walters spat curses as the cold air rushed into the cabin and the engine sputtered.

He peered out through the windscreen. Everything was dark. There were cracks in the ground. A watchtower loomed above them nearby. The light that guided them in must have come from there, but now it was dark and looked empty. There were buildings nearby, blurred silhouettes in the snow; Walters shone a torch at the nearest. A prefab hut, used to build barracks in a hundred compounds like this one, but lightless, with soot smudged round the empty holes that had been windows and doors.

Patel climbed back in, yanked the door shut. "Seen the state of the place?" said Walters.

"Looks a bit fucked."

"It's burnt out. A fucking ruin."

"Maybe something deep cover? Secret base, you said it yourself."

"Yeah, or maybe something else."

"Like what?"

"I dunno."

Rebels. Tribesfolk. Ferals. Or worse. They both knew that out in the Wastelands, whatever pockets of life clung on to existence usually had to find harsh and often twisted ways to do it.

"There," said Patel. Walters looked and saw another light, shining through the billows of snow.

"Not much choice, is there?" he said.

"Not really."

"On guard, then."

Both men reached under the dashboard and unclipped the Sterling submachine guns secured there. Jennywrens always went heavily armed; as well their revolvers and the Sterlings, there were two automatic rifles in the back of the cruiser's cabin.

Walters cocked the Sterling. Then, with the last of the boiler's steam, he steered the landcruiser towards the light.

The ground tilted underneath them, sloping down towards somewhere in what Walters guessed was the middle of the compound. But they were heading away from that: the light was coming from a small hut on the compound's edge, near the fence. It still had windows and a door, and the glow that shone from it promised comfort, shelter and warmth. A stubby metal chimney jutted from the hut roof, leaking pale smoke.

"Let's go," said Walters. He shouldered his rifle and swept it to and fro across the compound, backing up steadily after Patel as they neared the hut. Patel's rifle was slung across his back, the submachine gun ready for close combat. The air smelt of woodsmoke.

Walters flung the door wide; Patel dived through, rolled and came up on one knee, the SMG at his shoulder. "Clear. Get in and shut the door."

Walters slammed the door and bolted it. The hut's warmth was sweltering after the cold outside. Lanterns hung from the ceiling, emitting the glow they'd seen. There was a double bunk against one wall and a couple of chairs against the other. Walters slumped gratefully into one. "Proper little home from home. Where the bloody hell is he?"

Patel propped his rifle against the wall and went to the far end. There was a pot-bellied iron stove, neatly-chopped wood piled up beside it, and a table bearing a heavy radio set with earphones and a small metal box. "Dunno. But he didn't call from here."

"Eh?"

Patel motioned to the radio set; now Walters saw the bullet holes in the casing. "This hasn't worked in weeks, or months," Patel said.

"Well, *that* has." Walters nodded at the stove, then the lanterns. "Them, too."

"Yeah. I know." Patel studied the metal box. "Bloody hell."

"What?"

"Have a look."

The box was a plain thing of dull grey metal, tightly sealed. Resting on top of it was a clean white paper envelope, which read, in neat but spidery block caps: FOR THE PERSONAL ATTENTION OF COMMANDER TEREUS WINTERBORN.

"What is it? A bomb?"

"Doubt it." Patel prodded the box. Walters yelped. "Whatever it is, think we're best off letting them find out back at the Tower."

The wind howled outside. "The fuck's going on, Saeed?" Walters asked.

"Pete?"

"Yeah?"

"Reck we should sleep in shifts."

"With you on that."

And so their watch began.

*

The Black Road winds on, endless, through ruins and dust, although the dust is one with the night. All that separates road from wilderness are the cobbles of white bone that mark its edges. Above, below, before, behind, there's only the dark. And no hope of any end to it; nothing to do except go on.

So on she walks, tattered coat flapping round her, gun weighing heavy in her hand.

Cold light flickers in the distance, limning the City's broken towers.

This isn't fair, isn't right. *We give you a season,* Frank had said. *We return in the spring.* But it's still winter: months to go till she walks the Black Road again or meets the ghosts it hides.

And as if the thought had summoned them, they appear. Two figures, one tall, one tiny. Pale blurs in the darkness up ahead. Frank. Belinda. The husband and child she lost. Lost because –

She doesn't want to think of how they died or why. What she wants is to stop walking: to turn and run. Her ghosts are hungry and wait to feed. But on the Black Road, there is only one way to go.

The pale shapes turn away, dissolve back into the eternal night. It isn't time yet. This is just a reminder. But it means something, even if she doesn't know what: on the Black Road, signs are hard to read.

She looks ahead, to the City. And beyond it something rises, dark and hunched, like a huge dog climbing to its feet. A dog, or perhaps a wolf. A long head turns towards her, and two vast pale eyes, like lamps in the night, pin her in their glare.

*

Helen woke, gasping. The room's dark was thick around her: she struggled upright and fumbled for her bedside lantern. Light spread and filled the room. Shadows danced on the walls.

Steady breaths, in and out, till her heart slowed.

Outside the room there were sounds: muffled conversation, footsteps, laughter and a distant song. Even in the dead of night, the Fort was never wholly still. It had been strange, at first, after so long alone. Now it was a comfort.

She went to the window. Wind howled; a thin sharp draught sliced in through a crack in the glass. Helen lifted the curtain, peered outside.

Waves of snow washed across the landscape, shining in the light from the Fort. The world beyond was hidden. She kept watching, though, and remembered other dreams – if dreams *were* only dreams on the Black Road.

Tindalos, she thought. *The wolves are running.*

Only a dream. She told herself that: only a dream.

But still she was glad of the snow. If it hadn't been there, she'd have seen a long way. Maybe all the way to that huge shaggy head, and the glow of its lamplike eyes.

*

"Wakey-wakey, you cunt." Patel shook Walters awake. "Anyone told you you snore like a fucked pig?"

"Lots of times." Walters yawned and sat up. "How would you know, anyway?"

"Thought it was your mother at the time."

"Fuck off." Thin chill light shone through the window, bright enough to make Walters wince. "Time is it?"

"0800. Getting light out, and the storm's dropped. Reck we should get moving."

"No-one came to look in on us, then?"

"Nobody," said Patel. He had the gunmetal box and the envelope in one hand, his Sterling in the other. "And you know what? I don't mind that at all."

"Me neither." Walters picked up his rifle, creaked open the hut door.

Everything was white, except the remaining huts, which were charred and blackened. Walters went across the compound. The cracks in the floor grew wider and more jagged, and he saw they radiated from a gaping hole in the compound's centre. The ground underfoot suddenly felt fragile and unsteady; Walters backed away towards the landcruiser.

"Come on, you lazy sod, give us a hand with this." Patel re-emerged from the hut with an armful of wood, dumping it in the 'cruiser's flatbed.

They stocked up on fuel and set the furnace going, eyeing the white stillness around them until the boiler pressure rose high enough for them to drive. Walters stopped at the main gates, ran out and pulled them wide. That was when he saw the sign.

"Fuck me," he said, and ran back to the 'cruiser.

"Let's go," he said, "and I mean fucking *now.*"

"Shouldn't we try and work our position out?"

"I just have." Walters pointed.

Patel looked, then went still. "You're bloody joking."

"Some fucker might be, but I'm not. Now *come on.*"

The radio crackled. "Delta Oscar Four," said the voice they'd called Ned. "Are you sure you've got to go so soon?" Its metallic, grating quality increased: at the same time, it started laughing. It hurt to hear it. "Wouldn't you rather stay for breakfast?"

"Drive," Patel shouted.

As they rolled out through the gates, the voice sounded again. "Fly back to your nest in the Tower, little Jennywrens," it said. "While you still can. Fly away. Fly away."

The landcruiser hurtled down the hill. Patel was staring back at the base, but Walters kept his eyes on the road. It was a long and dangerous way home, and anyway he never wanted to see that place again. Not the hut or the burned-out barracks, not the watchtower or the fence, and not the gates with the rusted plaque that read *HOBSDYKE.*